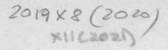

PENGUIN BOOKS

A Cornish Summer

A Cornish Summer

CATHERINE ALLIOTT

PENGUIN BOOKS

PENGUIN BOOKS

UK | USA | Canada | Ireland | Australia
India | New Zealand | South Africa

Penguin Books is part of the Penguin Random House group of companies
whose addresses can be found at global.penguinrandomhouse.com

Penguin
Random House
UK

First published by Michael Joseph, 2019
This edition published by Penguin Books, 2019
001

Set in 12.5/14.75 pt Garamond MT Std
Typeset by Jouve (UK), Milton Keynes
Printed and bound in Great Britain by Clays Ltd, Elcograf S.p.A.

A CIP catalogue record for this book is available from the British Library

PAPERBACK ISBN: 978–1–405–94071–9

www.greenpenguin.co.uk

MIX
Paper from
responsible sources
FSC® C018179

Penguin Random House is committed to a
sustainable future for our business, our readers
and our planet. This book is made from Forest
Stewardship Council® certified paper.

For my god-daughter, Jemima.

I

Celia peered nervously through the rain-spattered wind-screen at the towering hedges lining the narrow lane we were snaking along. Sodden trees formed a dark canopy overhead. She wrapped her vintage silk shawl more tightly around her bony shoulders and gave a mock shiver. 'Remind me again why I'm coming with you?'

I gave a small smile. 'You know very well. To paint the swirling seas and the billowing blue skies – your words, I believe, to persuade *me* to let you come in the first place.'

'I had an idea it would all be bathed in golden hues and honey-coloured light, that's all,' she said petulantly, gazing out into the gloom.

'It is, for about ten days a year,' I told her cheerfully. 'If we're lucky we'll catch one of them.' I gave her a bolshie grin and her eyes widened in genuine alarm. 'And – for moral support,' I reminded her. 'Your words again. For which I'm super grateful. And don't worry, the weather will perk up. It's always a bit mercurial down here.'

'Yes, well,' she rearranged her shawl and slid her bottom forwards in the passenger seat beside me, setting her faded orange espadrilles on the dashboard. She lit a cigarette. 'Can't have you entering the lion's den on your own, can we? Might never see you again. And anyway, I've heard too much about this famous family to pass up the chance.' She dragged on her cigarette, narrowing her eyes contemplatively. 'Actually, I might paint the old girl, Belinda, while you do Roger the Dodger. They won't know I only do landscapes, will they? I could do a Francis Bacon on her,' she said suddenly, sitting up delighted. 'All naked and bloody and flagellated – the final reveal coming to light in a dramatic spin of the easel! Can't you just see her face?'

'She'd faint clean away,' I told her as I hit the brakes. A speed camera heralded yet another grey, damp little village with opposing rows of blank-faced stone cottages, punctuated by the ubiquitous green Spar at the end. 'Roger, on the other hand, might like it.'

'Oh? Is he into bondage?' She glanced at me, encouraged. 'Bit of a Max Mosley? The gentry often are.'

'I've no idea what his sexual predilections are, but he's certainly not the crusty old buffer you're imagining. He's quite open-minded.'

'Oh good. I'll twinkle at him.' She grinned. 'See if I get a response.'

'Do not,' I said nervously, knowing Celia's charms of old. Twinkling was mild within her repertoire.

She chuckled darkly, flicking ash out of the window. 'Don't worry, I'll be demure and saintly. I'm on my best behaviour, remember? Your ex-father-in-law is safe with me.'

'Is he an ex?' I wondered aloud. 'I mean, Hugo's my ex, sure, but Roger is still Peter's grandfather, and I haven't remarried, so technically . . .'

'Yes, but Peter's his blood, you're not.'

'True. Ridiculously, I still think of them as my in-laws. Isn't that weird?'

'Beyond bonkers,' said Celia cheerfully. 'But then I think you prolong the whole relationship just to get up Christina's nose.'

'Absolutely not,' I replied vehemently. 'And anyway, nothing could get up Christina's nose,' I added, somewhat ruefully.

Christina, my ex-husband's second wife, a lovely, gracious creature, the soul of kindness, actually, had been nothing but tremendous to me and Peter: so inclusive and generous and uncomplicated, never questioning that I might want Hugo to go to every single rugby match at Peter's school, every parents' evening, every house play – with me beside him, of course – even *persuading* him to pitch up, and not to worry if it clashed with their own children's events, she'd go on her own; they were too young to mind. I told Celia so now.

'Making sure he's perceived as the model divorced father,' she said caustically. 'Just as Belinda and Roger are keen to be perceived by one and all as the model ex-in-laws and grandparents. They're a calculating lot, those Bellingdons.'

'And you, Celia Lonsdale, have got a nasty mind. They were all totally beside themselves at how it turned out, as well you know.'

'Guilt,' she said primly, flicking ash out of the window again which promptly blew straight back in. 'They all know they behaved badly and are praying you'll find a new man and be happy. Belinda is on her knees most nights.

The deliciousness is that you categorically *won't*, so they can't all relax, dust off their hands and say, "There. How splendid. Flora's found someone *at last*." '

'Only because they want me to be happy,' I replied uncertainly.

'Bollocks.' She snorted. 'As if they care.' But this last was said softly and I ignored it. I was well ahead of her, anyway.

'She will ask, you know. Belinda. About my love life.'

'Oh, I don't doubt it. And you'll say it's all going swimmingly, when in fact we both know it's Tim when you're really bored, and Rupert when you're feeling up to the banter.'

I took a hand off the wheel and bit the skin around my thumb. 'Thing is, Cele, I don't really fancy either of them. Wouldn't actually care if I never saw either of them again.'

'I know,' she said quietly.

It was all there, in those two little words: and I'd thought it such a state secret. Such a revelation. I was pretty sure I talked the talk about them both when I came back from dates, said what a marvellous time I'd had. Clearly I wasn't going to win a BAFTA. Celia stared diplomatically out of the window, knowing, occasionally, when to stop. Knowing not to say, get *on* with your life, Flora Bellingdon, fifteen years – yes, *fifteen* – after your husband has left you. Hanker no more for a man who's happily remarried with two children. I also knew the real reason Celia was coming with me. To stop me making a monumental fool of myself in the bosom of my ex-in-laws, which, trust me, I would only do if I was catastrophically drunk, and

4

those days were over. Sort of. As we rose to the top of a hill and the countryside opened up tantalizingly around us before disappearing as we plunged once more into a valley, I recalled Celia's eyes, some weeks ago, huge and horrified in the studio we shared, when I'd told her where I was going this summer. She'd lowered her brush. Turned slowly from her easel to face me.

'Sorry . . . *sorry*, Flora. Run that by me again? You're going to paint Hugo's father, in Hugo's family pile, to add to the groaning collection of oils in the ancestral hall, when we all know—' She broke off, stunned. 'Why in God's name did they ask?'

'Because I'm the natural choice, surely?' I'd said defiantly. 'They want to commission a portrait and – well, I'm a penniless portrait artist. I'm also Peter's mother. Of course it should be me. Imagine if they *hadn't* asked me, you'd be up in arms about that,' I finished triumphantly, which was true. Celia would certainly have had something to say. Then again, she had something to say about most things.

'Yes, but they expected you to turn it down, don't you see?' she'd implored. 'They expected you to say – I'm incredibly touched, Belinda, but I've got masses of commissions this summer, why don't you try so-and-so, I hear he's terrific. I mean, sure, if you were neatly remarried, or at least attached . . . but this is supremely insensitive under the circumstances.'

'Oh, they won't know that, will they?' I'd muttered. 'They don't know how I feel about Hugo.'

'Belinda does, you've seen to that.'

Belinda, like Christina, had been on the receiving end

of one or two of my more shameful, demented phone calls. But not for a good few years, as I'd told Celia.

'I know,' she'd said quickly. 'I just think they could quietly get someone local and you'd never know. Or even someone super famous like Nicky Philipps – they've got the dosh, and you wouldn't question that. You'd just think, ah yes, well, of course.'

'Well they haven't, have they?' I'd said shortly. 'They've asked me. And anyway, it's only the two of them rattling around on their own down there. Hugo and Christina are sailing round the Greek islands or something.'

'Great. While the ex-wife works her butt off for his parents.'

I hadn't responded. And I was quiet now as I navigated the lanes, remembering the two spots of colour which had risen in anger in her cheeks, her sharp eyes fierce as she'd resumed work on her canvas. We drove on in silence. At length the rain abated. The sky began to clear and, as we reached the top of another hill, the sun finally came out. In a blaze of glory, the beauty of the Cornish countryside suddenly unfolded dramatically around us: a panoramic sweep of granite walls, sheep-dotted fields flowing over lush green hills and flooding into valleys: countryside I knew so well, having grown up here. Not in one of the pretty, low-lying farms, or in a grand house overlooking the sea like the one to which we were headed, but a stone cottage on the outskirts of a closed-looking village, similar to the ones we'd already passed through.

My mother no longer lived here, having darted instinctively to London to be near me when Hugo had left me and Peter was small: she knew viscerally I needed her, even though I had funds enough for all the help in the world. There she still was, round the corner from me, this born-and-bred countrywoman, in a one-bedroomed flat off the Wandsworth Bridge Road, a good twenty minutes' walk from a decent patch of green, traffic roaring past her window every day. Our old home, or indeed, just Home, was coming up in moments but I wouldn't tell Celia. She'd be far too fascinated and want to stop and peer, but I'd have to do it with several boulders in my throat. Instead we cruised on past the plain granite house, set back from the road, with its four sash windows and garden at the back, plus a small paddock for the pony which was all I'd ever wanted in life.

The field and the pony had been rented and bought for a song respectively by Mum when my father had died, in some vain attempt to plug an enormous gap, which, to our intense mutual surprise, it did. Mum was so like that, I thought, as the house disappeared in my rear-view mirror: making impulsive decisions which confounded all expectations and turned out to be dynamite. I certainly couldn't do without her in London, but I knew she missed her friends, her own life, her little decorating business, which had worked so well down here, but was harder to set up in town with all the competition.

'Oh nonsense, I've got heaps of friends and loads of clients,' she'd say, if I even vaguely suggested her returning to Cornwall.

I knew she had friends – Mum made friends wherever she went – but on the client front there was Mrs Farr downstairs who she did curtains for, Charlie and Anna who adored her and I suspect invented work for her, and

Odd Brian who liked to change his walls as regularly as his boyfriends and got Mum in to supervise. But choosing paint colours doesn't pay the bills, and what little money she did earn was mostly from tutoring History of Art, which, years ago, she'd taught. Sometimes she'd pass a few students on to me, particularly if they were rich Russians, claiming she had far too many, but really I knew she worried I didn't make enough from my portrait commissions, about which she was not wrong.

Fortunately, that only affected my own finances. Peter was superbly looked after by Hugo, whose career, after he'd taken over from his father as head of the family water company, had soared to stratospheric heights. I never had to worry about school fees or his holidays, which were coming up, now that school had ended. Hugo was supremely generous – too generous, I sometimes thought. Belinda and Roger, too, showered him with birthday money: a car, I knew, was coming for his eighteenth. None of them could have been kinder, I thought with strange mixed feelings as I gripped the wheel. We plunged down yet another steeply banked lane, one which I knew led eventually to the sea. And as Peter had got older – well, he'd appreciated the finer things in life. Of course he had. His expensive boarding school, and Hugo's alma mater, had seen to that. So if his friends took him scuba diving in the Caribbean, leaping from their fathers' boats, well, it was only natural he'd repay their hospitality at either his grandparents', or his father's, in Hampstead. I mean, naturally they came to me, too, had always come when he was younger: Jamie, Sam, Freddie – all the gang. But Freddie's parents lived down the road from Hugo, and Sam's

just across the Heath, which made it far more convenient to be at his father's when he only had a weekend from
school before heading back on a Sunday night. He'd felt
uncomfortable, though: and when it had been two weekends at Hugo's on the trot, and then potentially half-term,
I remembered him ringing from school.

'The thing is, Mum, Sam's asked me sailing in Nor-
folk for a few days, and I'd really like to go. And then
Phoebe and Minty have both got parties near Dad's, so I
thought—'

'Yes, of *course* stay with Dad, makes *complete* sense,' I'd
said quickly, never wanting him to feel awkward, ever,
about a situation that was not remotely of his making. I'd
vowed long ago never to play the guilt card.

'But I thought maybe I could pop over on the Sunday,
before I go back?' he'd said, nevertheless feeling that guilt.

'Oh, that's mad, Peter – it's no "pop", as we know. Tell
you what,' I'd said, making it up on the spot, 'I need to
go to Green and Stone for paint that week, why don't we
meet halfway and have lunch in the King's Road?'

He'd agreed happily, relieved. And I'd taken him to the
Bluebird. Even though Peter went carefully for pasta and
not a steak, and I even more carefully went for a salad,
what with a glass of wine each and then two tubes of
oils in the ruinously expensive paint shop opposite – he
insisted on coming with me so I'd had to buy something –
I'd had to ring Mum on the bus on the way home and grab
a Russian, pronto, to pay.

It had been lovely to see him, though; we hadn't drawn
breath. Luckily, Peter wasn't of the grunting, laconic
school of teenage boy. He was open and chatty about

school, work, mates, sailing, which he loved – girls, even – and I'd drunk in his floppy blond fringe, huge smile and creasing blue eyes over lunch. So like his father. And I'd almost fainted with pleasure when he'd asked me to look around Oxford with him.

'But don't you want Dad to do that? He'll know far more than me about colleges.'

'Exactly, and I know he'll push Brasenose – and why not, I might well apply – but I kind of wanted to look with my own eyes. And actually, I thought you might like to.'

'I'd adore to,' I'd beamed. Of course I'd adore to. The culmination of all my motherly pride and his hard work – the final hurdle. I couldn't stop smiling, actually, and had recklessly ordered us another glass of wine on the strength of it.

'What are you looking so happy about?' Celia cut into my reverie as I wound down a now extremely familiar lane, brimming with red campion and orange *crocosmia*, to the coast.

'What? Oh, I was just thinking about Peter and me looking round Oxford.'

'Oh, right. I thought you'd already done that?'

'We have. I was just remembering us creeping round Christ Church. We weren't supposed to go in but a door was open and we got lost and giggly up a staircase. Some crusty don threw open his door and barked so ferociously we nearly fell down the stairs.'

She smiled. 'You've done a good job there,' she said candidly, which was high praise from Celia, who mostly said I obsessed about Peter. 'Or the school has. But at that price they bloody well should. Is that the sea or the sky?'

'The sea,' I said happily, my heart rising inexorably at the sight of it, and also, at getting Celia off the thorny topic of the iniquities of a private education, despite the fact she'd had one and I hadn't. 'It'll flit in and out from now on, but keep your eyes on that gap in the hills.'

She did, and buzzed down her window too, sticking her sharp little elfin face out to feel the air, which, now that the rain had cleared, was fresh and soft, full of that just laundered smell of soaking wet grass upon which the sun has settled to steam dry. You could practically see it growing by the roadside from that heady combination.

'So we must be nearly there, then,' she said, bringing her head back in and taking her feet off the dashboard, edging to the front of her seat like a child. 'Didn't you say they lived near – oh, hello.' She lurched towards me in surprise.

I'd taken a sharp left turn through a gap in the hedge into seemingly open country and was driving my poor ancient car at some speed down a red clay track with grass growing down the middle, bumping her up and down along the ruts. Celia clutched her seat and looked alarmed. But I was determined not to ease her in gently. She was such an urbane fount of knowledge in London where she'd grown up; such a sage generally about life, the mind, the heart, despite – or perhaps because of – her own disastrous love affairs. Sometimes I wanted to shake her out of her cool, implacable composure. I knew I had the upper hand in the country, and I wanted her to get a sudden eyeful of Trewarren, with no warning. The back drive, coming as it did across the home farm, afforded that better than the front. I wasn't immune to the grand old estate's charms either and, as we drove under the tall avenue of chestnut trees, the lush green pastures stretching away in an erratic jigsaw of low stone walls, it cast its shimmering, ambiguous spell upon my heart.

I had to slow down, though, when a heifer blocked our way.

'How many bulls *are* there in this field?' Celia asked nervously, closing her window. 'Surely they fight?'

'Cows,' I told her. 'Highland ones, hence the horns. Roger's into rare breeds.'

'Like his wife, by all accounts.'

I shot her a reproving look. The shaggy blonde moved slowly away, looking unnervingly, as Celia observed, like Boris Johnson, and sent us a baleful stare. We rumbled over the cattle grid to where gravel replaced clay. Past the agricultural barn we went, with hay bales stored one side and loose boxes the other, the latter these days housing classic cars rather than horses, and on towards the arch of the coach house and stable yard where the real equines lived. We purred through the yard, slowing down for the cobbles, and anything that might be tied to a ring and ready to swerve its backside nervously into my path. All the gorgeous creatures my hungry eyes sought, though, were sensibly in the shade, at the back of their stables: only a noble iron-grey had his Roman nose over a door and regarded us with mild interest as we rolled on through and under a corresponding arch. As we emerged, Celia was treated, not only to the best view of the house with its famous John Soane façade creeping with pale pink roses, but crucially, to a panoramic view of the sea, which we drove towards, and which faced the front.

'Oh!' She sat up, duly impressed. Speechless, actually.

The large, rambling old manor sat serene and comfortable, its windows glinting in the sunlight, presiding over a shimmering sweep of pure blue. Out of sight, at the foot of a cliff, which wasn't as steep as it looked and which I knew every inch of how to clamber, lay a pale sandy beach. In a far corner was a small wooden boathouse, inside which Hugo and I had spent many happy hours. All we could see from here, though, was the edge of the garden, which stopped abruptly at the cliff, and was a riot of daisies and cowslips. A more manicured lawn and a formal gravel sweep led to a curving flight of shallow stone steps, worn thin by centuries of feet – not to mention bottoms, for this spot afforded the best view – then double front doors, invitingly open under a splendid fanlight. So many laughs on those steps: so many friends gathered, so many flirtations, so many intense, moonlit conversations. If only they could talk.

'Did you fall in love with the house or with the man?'

I hesitated, remembering the first time I'd come here, on a very different sort of day. It had been the dead of winter, with a frost so hard it made everything sparkle, the windows glittering even more brightly than they did today.

Celia saw my hesitation and laughed. 'Oh, don't worry, Lizzy Bennett gets off on Pemberley, which all the feminist literature professors determinedly overlook. Bugger the wet-shirted Darcy, it's his gaff that clinches it for her.' She gazed out speculatively. 'This is certainly working for me. I say, who's this bucolic character straight out of central casting?'

Celia was prone to saying things like 'I say' which unwittingly betrayed her cultivated right-on persona. I turned. Small, slim and crumpled looking, with a hobbling gait, wearing old-fashioned breeches tied up with binder twine, trying to keep from smiling because she didn't do that sort of thing as a rule, and who, on approach, was actually prettier than you'd think, came the only person I was truly looking forward to seeing. Someone who you'd better think twice about before purring through her stable yard and getting away with it.

'This,' I told her happily, 'is Iris. One of my most favourite people in the world.' I jumped from the car and ran to meet her.

2

Iris didn't really entertain hugging – she was not of that generation or persuasion – but she nonetheless submitted woodenly to the one I forced upon her.

'Sorry,' I told her, grinning as I released her, returning her to her solitary status. 'Couldn't resist. It's *so* good to see you, Iris.'

'Yes, well, it's been a while,' she admitted stiffly, but her mouth was twitching and her piercing blue eyes gleamed. 'I was expecting you, though. I gather you're painting his highness, not that anyone bothered to tell me. Letty Parker in the pub got wind.'

'Yes, well, they offered me a socking great fee so I couldn't really resist,' I admitted, looking apologetically at my shoes.

'Couldn't resist coming back here, you mean. I think you're barking, incidentally. Who's this?'

Celia had approached with her most dazzling smile, hand outstretched. 'Celia Lonsdale,' she told her. 'And I think she's barking, too. I'm the bodyguard.'

'Ignore Celia,' I told Iris hastily. 'She's a painter, too, but she used to be an actress so she overdramatizes. For some reason she's become a great friend and she's also Peter's godmother.'

Iris scrutinized Celia carefully. 'The christening was here. In the village. I don't remember you?'

'I'm an honorary one,' Celia told her. 'Peter asked me about four years ago. Said he only had one godmother, and both his godfathers were friends of his father's, not Flora's.'

'That's true,' said Iris slowly. 'Shona, obviously. And cousin Ben. And the other one's that American fellow he met at school.' She turned to me. 'Who's here, by the way.'

'Tommy Rochester?' I gasped, horrified. 'Here? He's not. Why?'

Iris shrugged her shoulders. She took the butt of a cigar out of her pocket and lit it. 'No idea. Holiday, I imagine. He says he's between jobs.'

Celia's eyes grew round as Iris puffed away. She hastily lit a cigarette even though she'd just put one out, a companion in this archaic ritual, rare these days. Especially one who went for the big guns.

'Bugger,' I seethed. 'That wretched man. He's like a bloody boomerang, always hurtling back. Peter says he's always coming to London.' I was furious. Tommy Rochester was the last person I wanted to see, particularly down here. He really would wonder why I'd come, and suggest the unthinkable with his knowing looks and mocking smile. A supposedly self-made man – albeit with wealthy Connecticut parents who no doubt still lobbed him a trust fund – he didn't have a creative bone in his body and ran something odious like a hedge fund, or a management consultancy in New York. Something hard-nosed and financial, anyway. I have no doubt he looked entirely the part too, all slicked-back hair and snappy braces. He was also the worst sort of Lothario with a penchant for married women. It was said that Tommy had been in and under some of the smartest beds in Manhattan – and out of their windows. Nothing was lost in the telling, of course, and I have no doubt he delighted in these scurrilous tales of modern piracy, pillage on Wall Street by day and seduction on the Upper East Side by night. Doubtless he added his own, apocryphal embellishments. Temperamentally he was anathema to me, he pressed all my buttons, not least because I still blamed him, in some part, for Hugo and me breaking up.

'Oh, this is too exciting,' Celia breathed huskily, sucking hard on her Marlboro Light. 'The famous Tommy Rochester. I've heard about him. Is he attached?' Out of the corner of my eye I saw the front door opening slightly, although no one actually appeared. Most country houses used the back, but not Trewarren: traffic resolutely went up and down those steps, mostly because the mistress's study was at the front, and thus a vigilant eye was kept.

'Seems to be. He's brought someone with him, at any rate,' said Iris. 'Nice girl. Good little jockey.'

I was surprised. Not that Tommy had brought someone with him, that was par for the course, but Iris had an acerbic word for most people. She was certainly still eyeing Celia suspiciously, having not made up her mind. Being a good jockey helped, of course. Anyone who rode well started a few rungs up Iris's ladder.

'A tart, naturally.' She sniffed. 'But I don't hold that against her. Anyway, I'd better bugger off,' she said, glancing at the front door.

Sure enough, Belinda was sailing down the steps.

Dressed in a voluminous blue and white floral frock, a welcoming smile on her round face, she was very definitely making her entrance. Still undoubtedly pretty in a plump, peaches and cream, English rose sort of way, her blonde-grey curls swept back from her forehead and tucked behind pearl-studded ears, she radiated lady of the manor.

'Flora! You're here. My dear, how lovely.' Her plummy tones floated tunefully on the breeze. 'I was hoping you'd make it in time for lunch. Was the traffic ghastly?'

'Not too bad,' I told her as she drifted across like a stately galleon and enveloped me in her soft, velvety arms, very much a hugger. She smelled wonderful, as always. I'd once asked Hugo what scent she wore, out of interest, but disconcertingly he'd looked thrilled and given me a bottle of Arpège for Christmas. I'd conveniently lost it, not entirely sure I wanted to smell like his mother. Her beady gaze had fallen on Celia, now.

'And who is this?'

'My friend Celia, remember? I said in my email . . .' I reminded her, colouring up. Iris took the opportunity to hobble away. 'When you offered the cottage. I said I'd love to bring her, because she paints seascapes and—'

'Oh yes, yes, I remember,' Belinda cut me off in midstream. She flapped her hand dismissively. 'But so much is going on here I clean forgot. I'll have Yvonne make another bed up down there.'

'Oh, well, no, I can do that,' said Celia. 'There's no need to trouble Yv—'

'No trouble,' Belinda interrupted. Her face was all glittery smiles as she extended her hand. 'Belinda Bellingdon,' she purred.

'Celia Lonsdale. And it's lovely to meet you. I've heard so much about you.'

Luckily Belinda was far too imbued with her own self-worth to spot any irony, and she smiled graciously, taking the compliment at face value. Celia was looking for somewhere to put out her cigarette, not so confident now her partner in crime had gone.

'Oh, just squish it on the gravel. I'm sure they biodegrade,' Belinda told her airily.

Celia, who knew they didn't, looked dubious. But she did as she was told.

'And you've seen Iris, who's no doubt already told you we've got a houseful. Come in, my dears, let's not stand around out here.'

'A . . . a houseful?' I faltered.

'Yes, so actually it's splendid you've brought Celia. The more the merrier. And thank goodness the weather's changed – it's set fair for weeks now, apparently.' We were moving towards the house, but Belinda went back and stooped to pick up the cigarette stub, pocketing it. Celia reddened. 'Hopefully we can have all our meals outside,' she went on, as if nothing had happened.

'Oh – n-no, Belinda,' I stammered. 'Remember I said we'd fend for ourselves? At the cottage? Which was why I invited Celia . . .' I felt a familiar prickly heat and a general confusion to do with history always being rewritten by Belinda, who was not as sweetly vague as she seemed, and would never have forgotten I was bringing a friend and wouldn't want meals at the house.

Belinda contrived to look astonished and hurt. 'Oh well. As you wish, my dear. But don't forget, you're family, and you must help yourself to anything. Don't ask. I was just saying to Tommy and his girl, for heaven's sake, don't stand on cerem—'

'Why is Tommy here?' I asked abruptly.

Belinda turned to look at me in surprise. 'Why, because Hugo and Christina asked him, of course. He was in London anyway, and—'

'Hugo and Christina?' I stopped, halfway up the flight of stone steps. Celia almost cannoned into the back of me, but her eyes, when I glanced round, were huge too. 'I thought they were abroad for the summer?'

'Well, darling, *they* thought so, too. But it turned out there was some fuss at the works. Something to do with a pipeline, urgent maintenance or something. They had to cancel. Honestly, that wretched business! It was the same in Roger's day. Couldn't seem to do without him for five minutes! Naturally they're disappointed, but there we are. These things happen. I thought Peter would have told you?'

'No . . . no. He – he must have forgotten to mention it.'

She led us inside. 'Well, it's a blessing, too, of course, because it means they're here for the summer, which is lovely for us. And they're *so* dying to see you. Oh Lord, is that a mouse she's got? Truffle, come here!' She bustled after their ancient black Labrador who'd appeared with a welcoming present, wagging her tail. Seeing it was not appreciated she fled with her prize to the kitchen. Belinda gave chase.

'I'd never have come,' I muttered, horrified. 'If I'd known . . .'

'Don't panic,' Celia murmured, 'we'll handle it.'

'We'll find an excuse. Mum's broken her leg, or – or a fire in the studio. Yes, a fire—'

'It'll be fine,' Celia soothed as Belinda returned, bearing the dead mouse triumphantly by the tail. 'At least it's not a rat!' she cried. 'She's done that before.' She leaned past us and chucked it through the door into the flower bed. 'Wretched dog, she *collects* them, would you believe. I found *three* in her basket the other day, and let me tell you, they reek. Now, in you come. I think everyone's on the terrace. Lunch won't be long – we waited, which means they're probably well oiled by now.'

Dumb and speechless with fear – me, not Celia, who looked horribly enthralled – we had no choice but to follow Belinda's swaying floral behind through the drawing room and towards the open French windows, which gave on to the terrace and a sweeping lawn. A huge cedar tree spread its branches centrally over it, like wings, and another beautiful sea view unfolded beyond. It was years since I'd walked through these rooms: years since I'd been here with my baby in my arms – I'd breastfed him over there, by the fire, when I'd brought him here for the first time from London, on that sofa. He'd taken his very first steps out there, on the terrace we were making for now, cheered on by his father and grandfather, who'd applauded as if Peter were winning the Grand National. Roger had taken his finger and walked slowly with him down the lawn whilst Peter, unsteady and wobbly on chubby legs, had beamed toothlessly, as I'd taken pictures.

Roger was rising from his chair at the head of the table. He was a tall, statuesque man, with a shock of white hair, a little stiffer perhaps these days, but still handsome. He was smiling broadly and his face looked even more brick-red than I remembered, but perhaps the hair was whiter. He held out his arms and came towards me, beaming.

'Flora! My dear. How *lovely* to see you.' He embraced me warmly and then stepped back. He struck a classical pose, hand on hip, chin in the air, a finger poised beneath it. 'Will I do?'

I laughed, despite myself. 'Of course you will, Roger. Very Gainsborough.'

'Only I'm sure you're used to nubile young chaps with chiselled chins and lean thighs, eh?' He lurched towards me, twinkling. 'Possibly in the buff these days, too. What with all those life classes. Well, you'll be delighted to hear I'm clinging to the garments. Belinda wants me in the High Sheriff garb, but I thought like this? Trousers and a jersey? More relaxed?'

'Definitely. Although we could always try you in your hunting pink?' I said mischievously.

His eyes popped with pleasure as I knew they would. 'I say, why not! Terrific idea! Bit of a clash with the old complexion, though?'

'Definitely,' Belinda said briskly. 'And there are more than enough hunting portraits in this family. Now, don't monopolize the poor girl, Roger, these two are dying to see her.'

I was entirely happy with the genial Roger though, and would cheerfully have never left him, but Belinda had her hand under my elbow and was steering me lightly but firmly on. To be fair, I think she was lending me her strength. She might guess this was an ordeal.

I'm not entirely sure how I got through it. My heart was

leaping in my ribcage, but I greeted my ex-husband and his wife as if I did this every day. Not just a few times a term at school events, totally psyched up beforehand and with a couple of glasses of white wine under my belt. And the thing was, I had divorced friends who did this regularly. Josie even went on holiday with her ex and his new wife, and she didn't have a partner either, so I knew it was me. But it still hurt so much. Those Wendy Cope lines: '*And yet I cannot cure myself of love, For what I thought you were before I knew you*,' sprang perpetually to mind. Not that he was horrid now, or mean; he hadn't changed, however much I sometimes tried to persuade myself he had. He just didn't love me. And since no one had ever come close since he'd left, how on earth was I supposed to get over him, as everyone said I should, and as I knew I should, too? Not by smiling into his blue eyes which matched the sea beyond as he hugged me warmly, that's for sure. His face was wreathed in genuine pleasure, clearly hoping my presence here marked something of a watershed. The beginning of a new chapter, Flora? A much less emotional chapter. Emotional was a word that was used a lot. As if I was neurotic. Unhinged.

Well, true, some of my behaviour had been less than hinged, I supposed, as I looked into the equally hopeful eyes of his tall, blonde, attractive wife. The one with the wide smile and the longest legs – about twice the length of mine. The one I'd sobbed down the telephone to in the small hours and who was giving me the warmest of greetings as she told me, confidentially, that she was *so* pleased I'd come. *I hadn't known you'd be here!* I wanted to screech back as she stood, holding both my hands in hers to get a proper look at me.

'It's lovely to see you too,' I told her, hyperventilating.

Apart from anything else, I'd barely brushed my teeth this morning. Certainly not my hair, and I didn't have a scrap of make-up on. Had literally just fallen out of bed at sparrow's fart, piled up the car with easels, canvases, paints, a battered suitcase, popped a key under a pot for the Airbnb girl and beetled over to Celia's, where she'd done the same. I hadn't even glanced in the rear-view mirror, damn it.

'And Tommy, of course, you know,' Belinda was saying, sweeping me on to where the permanently amused Tommy, looking even more of a rake than usual, his auburn hair swept back off his forehead, greying somewhat at the temples now, was getting languidly to his feet. His face was thinner than I remembered, and as I determinedly kissed the air to either side of it without touching, it was all he could do to keep from laughing.

'Flora, what a surprise,' he drawled.

'Oh no, it's all mine, Tommy. I had literally no idea any of you were going to be here. I imagined I was just coming down to paint Roger, but instead I find a cast of thousands. This is my friend Celia, by the way.' Celia was already leaning in, hand extended with a beaming smile. She was loving this. A rangy, attractive-looking blonde woman with a lot of lipstick got up from the chair beside Tommy.

'Janey Karachin,' she said in dry, East Coast tones one felt Nora Ephron might well have employed. 'Along for the ride. I'm what you might call a freeloader.' She winked. 'Luckily the Bellingdons haven't sussed me yet and turned me out.'

'Oh, me too,' agreed Celia, shaking the bejewelled hand she was offered. 'I'm firmly in the waif and stray camp. But I'm afraid a summer in Cornwall was too good to pass up.'

'I couldn't agree more. And isn't it heavenly? We were out on the ocean this morning in the most adorable little boat, darting up creeks and gullies – I felt like I was in a Du Maurier novel. "Where's the Frenchman," I asked Tommy, "in his tight breeches?"' She leaned in confidentially. 'Frankly, that's all I require, and then I'm never going home.'

'And where's that?' asked Celia.

'New York City. Hot as hell and twice as dirty at this time of year. Mostly I love it, but not in July. As a matter of fact, I feel like I've died and gone to heaven. Hello there,' she said to me, together with a wide smile. 'I gather from Iris you're the rider.'

I took her hand. 'Actually she said the same about you.'

'Iris is obviously on uncharacteristically flattering form,' observed Belinda caustically. 'Now, lunch everyone. Come along, sit down.'

'Quite!' boomed Roger, rubbing his hands. 'Enough chat, I'm starving. Children, sit yourselves down.'

'We *were* sitting, Grandpa, but nothing happened.'

'Yes, well it will happen now, you'll see. Ibby, here. Theo, over there,' he pointed.

Hugo's twins – 'IVF, I bet,' Celia would always say darkly – clearly bored with waiting, had got down to play with Truffle and Flurry the Border terrier, but now dutifully returned to the table. I went round to say hello and shake their ten-year-old hands. Their eyes were wide at this rare sighting of their adored elder brother's mother. The bad one. Peter had once laughingly told me that when they were younger, he'd read them *Snow White*, and Ibby had pointed at the Wicked Queen and asked if it was me.

'You see!' I'd gasped in horror. 'That's what they tell them!'

'No, Mum, it's not,' he'd insisted. 'It's because you won't ever let them be around.'

'Be around? What d'you mean – be around?'

'Well, they're my brother and sister. They'd like to see my school, where I live, that sort of thing.'

I'd had to clutch the furniture and breathe.

Obviously it was me. Obviously. Clearly I should be able to play happy, disparate families: have them all to lunch, go to Christmas parties with them, and perhaps, it occurred to me now, as I felt their fascinated blue gazes, so like Hugo's, rest upon me, perhaps Peter had even engineered this? Or, at least, been sparing with the truth. Not informing me of the sudden change in his father's plans. Of the revised guest list for my summer. I wanted to be furious with him, to ring him right now, protest in the strongest possible terms, but I knew the fault lay with me. Instead, I sat dumbly between Roger and Janey and opposite Hugo and prepared to behave. Hugo leaned across to chat and I even managed to commiserate with him over his cancelled trip: listened, as he told me that of course, if they'd booked a house in France, say, or Italy, it would have been fine, but sailing around the Ionian did not guarantee good Wi-Fi, or indeed any Wi-Fi at all. He knew it would be a stressful trip, trying to respond to emails and phone calls.

'You shouldn't be so indispensable,' I told him with a smile.

'Oh, I don't know about that. I think it's more about being around for moral support for the managers. It doesn't look great to say, "Sorry, folks, can't talk, I'm on a yacht for the summer." And anyway, I never spend enough time down here.'

'And don't you dare add with the aged P's! Who aren't getting any younger!' interjected Roger.

'Wouldn't dream of it, Pa. And anyway, you're a million miles from being decrepit. I saw you leaning out on your boat this morning. Very agile.' Hugo smiled, his eyes disappearing like Peter's. I had to look away.

Poached salmon arrived, with warm new potatoes in chives, and a delicious tomato salad of all shapes and colours – from the greenhouse, we were told by our hostess. I ate in a trance, my tummy clenching with every mouthful. It was followed by a pear sorbet of such sophisticated taste and style it took a while for anyone to determine its flavour.

'That's it! Sweet William, from the south wall,' cried Belinda happily, when Christina finally identified it.

Everything was from the kitchen garden, of course. And the salmon was farmed locally. It was all desperately ethical, and I felt grubby, full of London grime. I curled my ancient trainers under the table and wished I wasn't in short dungarees. I did manage to answer all the polite questions about my practice, though, ran through my commissions, and even tried to look thrilled when Christina told me she was sure their neighbours would adore to have their children painted, although she tactfully didn't go so far as to suggest her own, for which I was grateful.

Because there was no bloody way I was staring at Hugo's offspring for hours. Everyone persisted in taking an interest until I felt so like the poor relation everyone was being kind to I wanted to scream – *Actually, I'm doing the Queen and Prince Philip next! And I'm getting a knighthood!*

'Damehood,' Celia corrected me later, as I seethed to her in the car, finally on our way to the cottage.

'Did you not feel their pity? Their charity?' I spat. 'Or is it me?'

She hesitated. 'Yes, it is you. I mean, I did feel it, a bit, but I think you're overdoing it. So what if they're being kind? I'm inclined to lap up kindness these days. Take a bit more, if necessary. I thought they were sweet, actually.'

I gripped the steering wheel as we bounced down the track, my knuckles white. 'It's different for you,' I muttered eventually. 'You don't have the baggage.'

'Of course it's different. All I'm saying is, now that we're here – and I hate to say it but I did warn you – but now that we *are* here, be smart. Play along. Don't dig your heels in, because actually, this arrangement, this inclusiveness, will help you to move on. If you get used to it here, it'll be much more natural to carry on at home. I thought Tommy and his bird were nice,' she said quickly, changing the subject as my face turned to stone.

Carry on at home? I took my time to reply. 'She was,' I managed to agree, at length. 'In an upfront, no-nonsense sort of way.'

'Quite. I like that.'

'But he's devious. A snake,' I hissed. Celia blinked. She looked alarmed. 'And a smart alec. Quieter than usual, today, I admit. Usually he likes the sound of his own voice.'

Celia was silent. She knew I was angry and probably guessed, as I did, that I'd been outmanoeuvred by Peter, and didn't necessarily disagree with him. I'd felt Tommy's eyes on me at lunch, watching in a how-the-mighty-have-fallen sort of way. Look what you're reduced to. Working for your ex. Admittedly he'd been more serious than usual, chatting to Roger about sailing, in an effort, I felt, to impress Janey, who was wiser than him, a commissioning editor at a famous publishing house. A cool job, surely? Although she'd assured me darkly it had its moments.

'Now and again you get an author who's written precisely one novel and thinks he's the next John Grisham. It's my job to gently inform him every thriller writer thinks that. A friend of Tommy's was one, it won't surprise you to know,' she said wickedly. 'That's how we met. This guy was doing a reading down at Barnes and Noble, and to my horror, he didn't just stop at one page as agreed, he went on and on like he was going to finish the book. I tried to interrupt but he wouldn't shut up. Eventually Tommy started clapping loudly at the back, and everyone joined in, which finally stopped him in his tracks. When I thanked Tommy afterwards, he told me the warm white wine I was serving was undrinkable and we should repair to the Monkey Bar forthwith. Naturally he worked his magic.' Her hazel eyes had sparkled at me.

'Naturally. And what a suitable-sounding venue.'

'Wasn't it just?'

I glanced at Tommy who was obviously listening and loving every minute of this. More tales of derring-do. More rake's progress. An involuntary mouth twitch gave him away as he purported to listen to Roger, and Janey winked at him, letting him know she'd seen. I could tell she had his measure. I was just surprised he had hers. I also had a sudden feeling they'd just had sex. They had that recently showered, bedroom-eyed look about them.

'Hey, is this it?' Celia broke into my reverie as I stopped the car. 'This isn't too shabby, is it?'

I came to. She was gazing delightedly at the cottage I'd parked in front of. Belinda had wanted to drive us down here, but I knew exactly which cottage she had in mind. It was right at the bottom of the track, before the lane plunged into the sea: squat, white, small and comforting, the very last house before the dunes. No rambling rose or clematis snaked up these white walls; the stiff sea breeze saw to that. Instead, flaming banks of *crocosmia* and tough sea grasses blew defiantly about it. The front of the house gave on to the lane, but the back, aside from a few rocks, almost merged with the beach, just a little picket fence dividing it. Even in my deranged mental state I could see it was idyllic.

Celia was open-mouthed with wonder. Even more so than she'd been up at the house.

'Oh Flora, this is *fab*,' she breathed. 'I'll be as happy as a sand girl down here with my easel. Is that seriously the beach? Shit. Look at the *dunes*. Aren't we getting out? Don't tell me this is some kind of tease?'

I roused myself wearily, knowing I was being the worst possible version of myself. Knowing we were bloody lucky to be here, away from London. Away, too, from Trewarren. And in a cottage they usually rented out to holidaymakers, so super kind. I detected Roger's hand in this. Yet still I felt sick to my stomach. I was sure I'd made the most catastrophic mistake. Why hadn't I listened to Celia in London? Why had I ever embarked on this?

'Who's that?' asked Celia, as I finally got out of the car and went round to join her by the boot. As we hauled our luggage out, I turned and followed her gaze. A slight, solitary figure in a royal-blue swimming costume was sitting on a rock, at the edge of the beach, but also, in our back garden. Her skinny brown back was to us, and her fair curls blew in the wind. I felt my heart rise and settle into its more natural position. My stomach unclenched and relaxed slightly. Suddenly I felt better than I had done all day.

'Oh, she's lovely,' I said happily. 'That's Babs Trewellyn. She's Roger's mistress.'

3

'His *mistress*? You mean *Roger* Roger?'

'The very same. Rogering Roger, in fact.' I giggled. First laugh of the day, it seemed to me.

Babs had turned at the sound of our voices. She got to her feet and waved extravagantly, both arms windmilling about as if she were bringing in a light aircraft. 'Helloo! Darl-ing!' she cried.

'Babs!' I shouted back, waving.

Grinning broadly, I nipped through the front garden, around to the back, and down the rocks to greet her, still as nimble as ever on this slippery, hazardous terrain, I was pleased to see. 'Did you know we were coming?' I called as I approached.

'Of course I did, I know everything. And I was reasonably sure you'd want to tootle down here on your own, so I thought I'd be your welcoming committee.' She was slipping a short white towelling poncho over her swimsuit which I remembered from years ago, when she'd gone through a phase of making and selling them to loyal friends, complete with matching towelling turbans.

'Mum's still got one of those,' I told her as we kissed,

and as her little Yorkshire terrier, Piggy, climbed up my leg, wagging. I picked her up and petted her.

'I know, we modelled them on the beach the last time she was here, a couple of old bags still trying to drum up business. How is she?'

'She's well.' I put Piggy down. 'And she sends her love, although you've probably spoken to her even more recently than I have.' Mum and Babs were constantly on the phone.

'Oh, you know.' She gave a secret smile and looked beyond me to Celia, who was picking her way much more cautiously across the rocks, arms outstretched for balance. Babs' green, cat-like eyes were alive with interest.

'So this is Celia, who your mother tells me is rather out of my mould.'

'Lordy, did she?'

Babs gave her famous gin-and-fags cackle then coughed violently. 'You mean you don't entirely approve of the comparison? Hello there.' She extended a slim brown hand adorned with unusual chunky rings and red nails as Celia approached. 'I'm Babs. I expect you've heard the most terrible things about me.'

'Do you know, I haven't,' said Celia, clearly most put out. 'I'm rather disgruntled. We've had five hours in the car and billions of years in the studio – wouldn't you think?'

'Ah, but our Flora's discreet. Still harbours secret hopes in a certain person's direction, you see. Doesn't want to be the one dishing the dirt on his parents in case she's accused of saying anything that can later be used in evidence against her. She protects herself. No disloyalty to "The Family".' She made quotation marks with her fingers in the air.

'Ignore Babs,' I told Celia. 'She makes mischief.'

'What else is there to do down here, darling?' enquired Babs, lighting a cigarette.

'Bloody hell, does *everyone* here smoke?' Celia boggled.

'Like I say, what else is there,' said Babs. 'Apart from sex, of course, there's masses of that. Do you want to see the house?'

'Yes, dying to,' I said, although I could see Celia was riveted by Babs, with her wicked green eyes and fabulous indiscretion, and could cheerfully have stayed out here for hours. She was certainly very beautiful and in her day had constantly been snapped getting on and off planes by the local papers, national ones too: model Babs Trewellyn, back from Paris, dressed in Dior – although it never was, she told me confidentially; always a copy, they never checked. An It Girl, I suppose, of her day. The camera loved those startling high cheekbones, slanting eyes and long blonde hair, streaked with grey now, but still with a good bust and skinny figure. Not that she cared. Babs didn't seem to give two hoots what she looked like. Oh, it was fun dressing up, and there were lots of shots of her and Mum posing in their youth, drinks in hands, arms around their boyfriends, always in pursuit of fun – but she didn't work at it. It was a lark. Iris was in the pictures too sometimes, but Iris would be smiling more sardonically in the background, even then a sphinx-like creature with a grip on reality. Someone had to have one, Mum would remark; left to her and Babs it was a shrieking melee of beach parties, camp fires, dancing by moonlight and – well. Not my mother, so much. She'd got her own grip when she met Dad. But Babs had been unlucky.

'I saw Iris,' I told her as we went up the garden towards the cottage. 'On splendid, caustic form as usual, but she didn't come in for lunch.'

'She rarely does these days, and I can't say I blame her.'

'Why would she come for lunch?' Celia asked, surprised, as we ducked under the low oak beam above the front porch.

'She's Roger's sister,' I said, turning to her. 'Didn't I say?'

'Roger's *sister.*' She stopped, flabbergasted. 'I thought she worked in the stables!'

Babs and I laughed.

'Well, she does,' I told her. 'Although she doesn't get paid – or perhaps she does these days. But you're right, that's her life, always has been. She lives above them in the coach house.'

'Right.' Celia was trying to absorb this. 'So – you, and Iris, and Flora's mum, Maggie—'

'Were all at school together,' Babs said simply. 'Boarding, in Dorset, at the convent. There's nothing round here so they sent us all away. The boys too, of course. The Scarlet Virgins, they called us, bright red uniforms.'

'And Belinda?'

'Oh God, no.' Babs took a drag of her cigarette and turned to her, eyes dancing, in the doorway. 'She's frightfully common. Local comp, I expect.'

'Like me,' I told her cheerfully.

'Oh yes, why not? Nothing wrong with it. Just don't pretend you're Lady Muck, which you certainly don't.' She turned back to the house. 'Got terrible taste, hasn't she?'

We walked through the long, low living room. Two smaller rooms had been knocked together to make a sitting area at one end and a kitchen at the other with French doors to the garden, which were extravagantly swagged and draped.

'Look at those,' Babs waved her hand at them. 'Wouldn't look out of place in Blenheim Palace, and that sofa.' A very formal, high-backed pink damask affair with gold fringing stood in front of the wood-burning stove. 'And a fire in a box.' She sniffed. 'Is there anything uglier?'

'They throw out a lot of heat and they're frightfully economical,' I said in some display of loyalty.

'That's what they say about sensible shoes, they're frightfully comfortable and go on forever, but nothing beats a blazing log fire. Oh well, you'll muddle through, I suppose.'

'I think it's amazing,' Celia enthused, eyes shining. She went off to poke around in the little wooden kitchen at the end. 'And the floor's gorgeous,' she said, gazing down at the traditional dark Cornish slate.

'Yes, well, you can't ruin that. And upstairs is better. She kept it simple, thank God.'

We went up the stairs that led directly from the sitting room to where a bathroom and two double bedrooms, each decorated with plain white bedspreads, wooden chests of drawers, mirrors, and blue cotton rugs on the floor, were indeed simple. Celia went straight to the window, flung it open to the beach below, and leaned out. The sand was pale gold and seemed to stretch for miles beyond the dunes until it reached the sea. The blue-green water was calm and limpid as it lapped the shore. A few children paddled and a man walked his dog.

'Look at that.' She breathed in deeply, shutting her eyes.

Babs smiled and came to suck her ciggie beside her. 'Heaven, isn't it? You can never tire of that. But if you're thinking of painting on the beach down there, it gets a bit windy, and obviously it's quite accessible since it's only a hop and a skip over the dunes, so you might get a degree of interest. You'd be better off going down the coast path a bit to the one around the corner, down the cliff. It's more sheltered and private. Anyway, you'll work it out.' She turned and headed back towards the stairs. 'Drink? I took the precaution of bringing a bottle. I bet it flowed like glue at lunch.'

'Actually, it was OK,' Celia told her, following her down. 'Although I could have done with a top-up. Flora was better placed, next to Roger, but Belinda seemed to be on water so I didn't want to lunge across her for the bottle and look like a dipso.'

'Oh, you poor love. Here.' Babs was already bustling across to the kitchen, where, handily placed in the fridge, was a bottle of wine, which she opened. She reached in the cupboard for glasses. 'Although don't fall for that water-glass trick of Belinda's. If you tried it, you'd find it was neat gin.'

'No!' Celia was entranced. Babs raised arched eyebrows meaningfully and nodded.

'Don't believe a thing Babs says,' I told her hastily. 'She's full of stories about Belinda.'

'And you grew up with her?' Celia asked, ignoring me and encouraging the storyteller. She sat on a stool at the breakfast bar and took the glass that was offered, supping thirstily.

'Well, she grew up in Truro, on a modern estate. The

38

rest of us were round here – Iris *right* here, of course. The worst sort of snobs are very often those who aren't born to it, I'm afraid. That's one of the reasons she was against Flora marrying Hugo, because there was no money in her family.'

'Oh Babs, *stop* it!' I squealed. 'Stop feeding Celia all these terrible lies. She'll lap it all up and enjoy it *far* too much – she's just like you!'

'Except it's not all fiction, as you know,' Babs grinned. 'And anyway, why tell the boring truth when you can tell a good lie? The other half?' she asked Celia, wine bottle poised above her glass, which, curiously, appeared to be almost empty.

'Why not,' Celia agreed.

'Anyway,' she went on, pouring away, 'I thwarted her by getting you to paint Roger. He's thrilled. He can't imagine why he didn't think of it before.'

'Oh, it was you. Hang on – and Belinda's *not* thrilled?' I said, horrified. A terrible thought struck me. 'Did she even *know*?' Babs' face was horribly mischievous.

'Oh, in the end she did,' she said airily, stubbing her cigarette out in a rather hideous little cactus plant on the counter. 'But by then it was all a bit of a fait accompli. You'd emailed Roger back saying you'd be delighted—'

'I emailed *Belinda* back,' I corrected her.

'Oh well, he may have been using her email – they have kind of a family one – and then your mum said you'd rented your flat out with Airbnb, so there was no going back, and it all sort of fell into place.'

'Mum told you that?' I was surprised.

'Well, you know. Something along those lines.'

'Oh, you're wicked, Babs!' I breathed. 'I only found a tenant – finally – on Tuesday!'

Babs suppressed a smile, but not terribly efficiently.

'Is she really dreadful? Belinda? Do you hate her that much?' Celia clearly thought she'd found a new best friend and needed to forget incidentals and cut to the chase.

Babs gave her glorious throaty chuckle. 'No, I don't hate her. I don't feel that strongly about her – what a terrible waste of energy that would be. But I do so love to tease. And it's so much fun, you see, because she bobs so magnificently.' Her green eyes gleamed. 'And isn't that what life is all about? Having fun?' She drained her glass and picked up her beach bag. 'And now I must leave you girls. You'll want to unpack and set your easels up – I can't wait to see what you're doing, by the way – and I'm going to walk back along the beach while the tide's out. It'll be turning soon. Toodle pip!' She gave us an enormous wink and slid her bony bottom off the bar stool, elegant in her poncho and espadrilles. Swinging her basket, her little dog trotting after her, she departed. She gave us a last dinky wave.

'I like her,' Celia said, moving to the open French windows to watch her go down the garden and across the dunes. 'She's got style.'

'I knew you would,' I said, sipping my drink. 'She's another reprobate.'

'And does Belinda know?' she said, still watching her.

'She must do. Mum says she must do, everyone else does. But it's never talked about. It's been going on for years. I mean, donkey's years.'

'Really?' Celia turned back to me. 'So why doesn't he leave her and shack up with Babs, then?'

'Mum says neither of them wants that. Once, perhaps, Babs might have done, but Mum thinks increasingly not, these days. Thing is, Celia, Roger is a genuinely nice man. He doesn't want to split up the family and desert his wife, and Belinda is a thoroughly determined woman. This is all she ever wanted, being Lady Many-Acres, and she's quite tough. Admirably tough, if you ask me. My feeling is, she knows – she's not a bloody idiot – but she thinks, I'll live with it. A lot of women do, you know. Some men, too, look at Lloyd George in *The Crown*. It's sort of stiff upper lip and old-fashioned. And actually, for all her teasing and taunting, Babs is quite happy with the arrangement. She has a gorgeous house along the coast – you'll see – her own life, loads of friends, Roger now and then, and countless admirers, mostly quite young, who are just that, I think: admirers. But Babs likes nothing more than sitting in the local with her colourful coterie getting thoroughly pissed and staggering home without having to cook supper for someone. She only once cooked for Roger and she was cleaning her tropical fish out at the same time. Roger pulled two fish skeletons from his beef stew, apparently. They couldn't stop laughing.'

'I love her.'

'And she doesn't want Belinda's life, that's for sure. Doesn't want a huge house full of chintz and brown furniture. Bridge parties, local fêtes in the garden, the flower rota at church, pillar of the local community. The only local establishment Babs props up is the pub. They'd be lost without her.'

'But did she never marry? Never have children?'

'She did marry, very young, same as Mum, at twenty-one,

and apparently he was gorgeous. Italian, ten years older, from a very wealthy family and absolute heaven, Mum said. The kindest man. And adored Babs, who in those days was still pretty wild, but not such a loose cannon. With no one holding the reins she's more out of control, and Filippo had those reins, albeit with a very light touch. They lived in fabulous splendour, mostly in Rome, but there was a family palazzo in Venice too, on the Grand Canal. But no children. Although, Mum says she did get pregnant once, but then got German measles, so – you know. She never talks about it and I've never asked.'

'And Filippo?'

'Died of cancer when she was thirty-two. Terribly young. So Babs was a very young, very beautiful widow. Loaded, too. A house in Rome, but also something here, always, where her roots were. Filippo was like that. Knew she needed it.'

'God, how sad. How *tragic*. Was she devastated?'

'Obviously. But she doesn't talk about it.'

'You mean you've never asked her.'

'No, she doesn't talk about it. I can sense that. She's from a different generation. You didn't blab everything to friends and therapists like we do now, you kept a lid on it, and I respect that. I'd rather you didn't, Cele.'

I could well imagine Celia, spotting Babs sunbathing on the rocks, nipping down and wanting to get to the bottom of it, and of course I couldn't stop her.

'And then along came Roger?'

'Not for some time, but yes, along came Roger. They'd all grown up with her, you see. She was the pin-up girl of their generation, way out of their league in terms of beauty, style, fun – really great fun – and she'd gone for a glamorous Italian count, who luckily had also been Steady Eddy. But, suddenly, she was back. Roger was married by then, but he couldn't resist her.'

'I bet. Quite a contrast to Belinda.'

'Belinda had her moments. Have a look at the wedding photo in the drawing room, she looks lovely.'

'Yes, but I can imagine what sort of lovely. An icy satin gown and demure little cape over her shoulders. A ring of white flowers on her ash-blonde, tightly piled up hair . . .' She trailed off, having almost perfectly described Belinda's wedding attire, which Belinda would have scoured the social pages of *Tatler* for, to get it just right.

'Whereas Babs . . . ?'

'Very pale blush pink, quite short, with the family tiara at a jaunty angle. There's a photo of her coming out of the family chapel in Venice with Filippo, both roaring with laughter.'

Celia gazed at me, rapt. 'I've got the most terrific crush.'

I smiled. 'I know.'

I turned to wash the glasses at the sink. I knew, too, that Babs sort of vindicated Celia's rather rootless, nomadic existence: her refusal to find Mr Right. Her attraction to Mr Wrong, to married men, actually, or to introspective loners like the current one, Edward. But I also knew that pitching it low as Celia did, never pitching it too high, stemmed more from a fear of being hurt. And Babs wasn't like that. She wasn't afraid of anyone.

'Come on, let's get the stuff in from the car, then we can go for a swim.'

Celia watched as I went outside, still deep in some

romantic reverie of a few decades ago. I went back and forth to the car, but when I was halfway up the stairs, she was behind me suddenly and helped me with a heavy case to the landing.

'But do you not look at her sometimes, Flora, and think, for heaven's sake?'

I knew where she was going with this. I turned.

'You mean, for heaven's sake, why am I still metaphorically walking across a desert with a burning cross in my hands? When there are other ways of being, of living, which don't involve a husband and children and all that I envy, aspire to, and once had?'

'Well, I wasn't going to be quite so—'

'Brutal. Yes, I get all that, Celia. And funnily enough, although we're very different people, Babs is an inspiration to me. She's strong, she's brave and I have to force myself to be those things.' I paused. Narrowed my eyes contemplatively beyond her. 'But she's also a minx. And I have a nasty feeling I've been set up here.'

'What d'you mean?'

'I don't know yet. But trust me, I can smell that particular Scarlet Virgin –' I sniffed the air theatrically – 'a mile off.'

I smiled and sailed back downstairs, past her, through the sitting room and out to the car, for more luggage.

4

Hugo and I first met when we were about seventeen, at Pat Hendrick's farm. Oh, I knew about him and had seen him around before that, everyone had, but it was the first time we actually made contact. Previously it had been rare sightings in church, on Christmas or Easter mornings, or at the Cheshires' annual drinks party where children came, too. As far as Belinda was concerned, of course, we were obviously in the wrong camp since Mum was Babs' best friend, so we were never invited to the Boxing Day shindig at their house, or to summer parties in the grounds. My dad shot with Roger occasionally, though, and they had mutual friends in the army and liked each other, so there wasn't much Belinda could do about that. Belinda was actually always terribly friendly towards us on those few churchy mornings: she'd make a point of coming across and chatting to my parents, greeting me warmly, asking me what I was up to. She had her own style, whatever Babs said. And who knew if her heart was breaking inside? The older I've got the more I've sympathized with Belinda – for obvious reasons – and admired her courage. It can't have been easy to have the whole neighbourhood know about your husband's philandering, whispering about you in public, although Babs would say Belinda was not the victim.

My mother wouldn't discuss it, and whenever I brought it up in a cosy moment and asked her what Babs meant by that, she'd sigh and say it was all terribly difficult, but really there were only three people who knew the true story and she *did* wish Babs wouldn't feed me snippets of gossip. To be fair this had only happened once, when I'd pumped her for information at the Cheshires' party, one of the few occasions Babs and Belinda were in the same room.

Hugo had been at the party as well, with his elder sister Etta, looking bored, as we all were. Awkward, too, in that in-between-age sort of way: we knew each other well enough to recognize, but not to go and talk to, being at different schools. Anyway, I'd see him there every year, tall, blond and a bit gangly, looking up from under his long fringe which he'd sweep impatiently to one side, with his father's blue eyes, muttering to Etta occasionally, but we never actually met. Also, to be fair, we both knew a few people there of our own age, girls from the Pony Club for me, and local boys who sailed for him. So we chatted to our own set and circled each other warily at these events, only our heights and our hairstyles and our terrible complexions varying. Two young people, without dislike or suspicion, just an awful lot of issues and hang-ups and insecurities of their own.

For my part my father had died three years earlier, when I was fourteen, and I was still emerging from that dark tunnel. He'd been in Bosnia, and although I was vaguely aware of the danger he encountered there on a daily basis, nothing could prepare me for the shock of it actually happening. There were moments when I thought I'd never survive. The initial shock, the impact, took weeks to bed in, for Mum too. It was as if we'd both been blasted into the sky by the mine ourselves, and the pain didn't show any sign of abating.

We'd clutched each other for days, and then un-clutched and avoided each other, before clutching back again, like magnets. We literally didn't know what to do with ourselves. If we were together, we needed to be apart. If we were apart, a walk along the cliffs alone, we needed to fly back to each other's side. I remember running over two miles once, through Hogan's meadows, down the Bolithos' track, hands trembling to open the back garden gate and race down the lawn. I remember going upstairs, weeks after, into my bedroom. Then Mum's. Then down again to the kitchen. Then outside. Then shrieking up at the sky. 'I don't even know where to be!' I'd raged. 'I don't know *how* to be!' Mum had run out and held me and we'd sobbed and held on tight. But tears like that were rare. Mostly we were numb. I hesitate to say this, but a terrible lingering disease at least gives some warning. This was a whole chapter, the best chapter, ripped violently from a book.

And we were such a happy band of brothers, we three. Mum hadn't been able to have any more after me, and though they'd briefly thought about adopting, they later told me they realized they were actually terribly happy, and lucky, so they didn't. I think because they were so in love, one was enough.

'We're a tripod,' Dad would say, when I was little. Or, 'a three-legged stool', or 'a three-legged race'.

'That's two people,' I'd point out.

'So it is. Well, you're the funny leg in the middle,' he'd say, making me squeal with indignation.

When I was even younger, he'd read me Aesop's Fables at bedtime. Our favourite was the one about the bitchy vixen mother with all her fox cubs, who taunts the lioness, who's only got one. Together, Dad and I would widen our eyes and chant the last line: *'Yes, but mine is a lion!'* We'd roar and flex our claws. As he snapped the book shut and got up to go, I'd employ delaying tactics:

'Ess! I'm a lioness!'

'Of course you are.' He'd smile from the doorway. 'And, as we know, those are far more dangerous.'

I'd giggle under the bedclothes, because we both knew there was nothing dangerous about me. I was shy, skinny and slightly built. Dad wasn't tall, he was certainly an inch or two off six foot, but his shoulders were broad and I'd look at him and think, he *is* a lion. He commands a battalion. He did, too: he was a colonel. At a very young age. And I knew that gave us kudos in some quarters. Roger, for instance, always made a beeline for my father at parties, sounding him out on the current state of play in Afghanistan, the Middle East. People liked to have a genuine point of contact, a thoroughly reliable source, our man in the conflict zone, so they could later say: 'Well, of course, Bill Penhallow says . . .'

Mum and I were incredibly proud of him. And he wasn't a typical soldier, either. He painted, when he was home. Outside, with the easel and palette I still use and treasure more than my life. Because of his rank, we no longer had to live on the base in Falmouth as we did when I was tiny, and Dad, who like Mum was from around here, bought our cottage, primarily because although you couldn't see the sea – those houses were way out of our league – the garden faced the right direction so you could smell it and imagine it. And if you walked fast, in a straight line, for half an hour, with your rucksack of paints and sandwiches on your back and your portable easel, you could reach it. Dad did, and I went with him, with my own rucksack of watercolours, rather than oils. The deal was I could stay as long as I painted. He didn't mind if I chatted, that was allowed, although he'd often only murmur back, but handstands and wandering off and bringing the dog were not. I loved to go. I didn't see enough of my father – he was away so much – and this was our special time. And I got quite good. I'm not sure if I'm a talented painter, although others like my work and it sells and I see it on people's walls, but I certainly started young, and practised a lot, which is not so different to a four-year-old learning the violin and getting results. Most children like to mess around with paints, but how many do it all day, as I did?

The other thing we did together was ride, with Mum, who was better than both of us. This was a source of huge amusement because Dad was in the cavalry, but of course that mostly meant tanks, apart from ceremonial stuff. We didn't have horses of our own, there wasn't the money, but Iris, Mum's great buddy, was always grateful to us for exercising hers. She competed in those days, three-day eventing at quite a high level, and she needed them ridden daily. Most were home-bred and she was always bring-ing on a youngster, although they were precious, and not everyone was granted this honour, but my mother had the best seat in the county and the lightest hands so Iris trusted her with her babies, as she called them. Dad was also considered up to scratch for an older horse and I often got one of the children's ponies to exercise, because, Iris said, they couldn't be bothered, which struck me as extraordinary.

I didn't actually fancy Hugo, as I recall, but he was good-looking and frankly, being at an all-girls school, one of the few boys I knew. I had two cousins in Devon and there were a few boys in the Pony Club who were sweet, but Hugo was the pin-up boy for the area: rich, remote, a bit shy which sort of helped, and away at school, so slightly mysterious. The whole package, if you were a bit shallow like me, and a bit of a sheep – ditto – was super glamorous. I often thought, as I rode Hugo's new Cleveland Bay, I'm sitting in your saddle, mate. My bum's where your bum's been. Childish.

When Dad died, though, I put away childish things. The punch and the guts went out of me for anything friv-olous, and with it went the posters on my bedroom wall of the young Prince William, who so closely resembled Hugo, and I put up prints by Monet, Constable and Henry Moore instead, all great favourites of Dad's. That was the furrow I ploughed: the one into my father's world, getting inside his head, spending hours painting the same views he'd painted, in oils now, but still in the fields because I liked the elements. And when the weather was fine, and not windy, I'd paint his face. I'd prop up a photo of him on my old child's easel and paint it time and again, wanting to get it exactly right. I think Mum worried a bit at this stage and would come and find me, knowing exactly where I'd be, halfway down the cliff, just inside a little cave Dad and I had found, which at least afforded some protection from the wind. She'd pop her head round and usually I wouldn't have heard her.

'Coming back soon, darling? It's nearly supper time.' I'd meet her anxious eyes and I knew she was reading mine, too.

Luckily we'd never gone through the backing away and closing down stage some mothers and daughters do, and after a moment's internal dialogue and resentment at being disturbed, I'd nod and agree to pack up my things and come with her. Making my dear mother anxious in order to deal with my own grief was not something I was going to do. I worried about her far too much for that. She was still young and very pretty, with a heart-shaped face, auburn curls, dancing hazel eyes and fabulous legs, and many men in the county, or even outside the county, would be thinking – golly, Maggie Penhallow. Give her a couple of years to – you know – then I'd definitely have a crack. But I knew it wasn't like that. It wouldn't be a couple of years, or indeed ever, to my relief in the early days, and to my sorrow now.

Mum and Dad had something infinitely special. They completed each other. They were outrageously silly together, they laughed until tears rolled down Mum's face, and although of course they bickered, I never heard a flaming row. Not like my friend Shona's parents, who I'd heard more than once when I'd stayed the night. It seems to me a good marriage is one where the whole becomes more than the sum of its two parts, and that was my parents. An average marriage is when two parts operate competently, but separately. A disastrous one is when the two parts are actually reduced by the whole, and that is what happened with me and Hugo. Mum and Dad galloped along joyously together, just as they hunted, side by side, popping over life's obstacles, with me in their wake. And of course, it might have helped that he was away a lot. She missed him, so why waste precious time arguing when he was at home?

I sometimes wonder if that's how Mum got through it: she was used to his absences, and this was just a much longer one. Indeed, when we were riding along the beach one day, her on one of the youngsters, and me on my now three-year-old that Mum had bought from Iris as a yearling, she admitted, with a smile, that a lot of the time she lived purely in her head and pretended he was away on exercise.

'So do I.' I'd turned to her wide-eyed, as if surprised that was allowed.

She'd shrugged. 'In the immortal words of John Lennon, whatever gets you through the night.'

We'd cantered on, at the edge of the surf.

That three-year-old, Farthing, had already got me through many days and nights and I really hadn't wanted her, which was why Mum didn't ask. She just rented the back paddock from Reg Francis next door, bought the yearling no doubt ridiculously cheaply from Iris, and borrowed a Shetland of Reg's for company. To my complete surprise, Farthing was there, in the field, skinny, skittish and nervous, when I got home from school.

'I was going to give up riding,' I said, aghast, when Mum led me through the garden to meet her. Head and tail held high, she was cantering in an abandoned manner about her new territory, skidding to a halt in front of us, red velvet nostrils flaring. She gave a rolling snort.

'So you said, too frivolous, but you don't have to ride her, just bring her on. Iris says you can return her when it's time to back her, in a couple of years. And you'll make a profit.'

'Oh.'

This did appeal. For complicated reasons still to do with Dad, money was part of my crazy, half-formed plan for life. Lots of it. Back then, I associated it with success. Although, of course, this didn't come to anything with Farthing. Anyone who's brought on a young horse, overcome its manifold fears and suspicions, fed and watered it, brought it in when it's wet, pulled its cold ears in the stable till they're warm, murmured to it, rubbed a handful of straw on its back to dry it, kept the flies off it when it's hot, soothed and stroked its terrified neck all night in the stable on Bonfire Night, will know. Anyone, who then, a couple of years later, has gently, gradually introduced, not just a head collar, but a bridle, rested a saddle, too, lunged it on the end of a long rein, head on one side – me, that is – watched every tiny movement, every flicker of the eye, always on the lookout for fear, admired the flowing, fluid movement Mum was so clever to find, knows there's only one person who's eventually going to lie gently across that back, and finally sit upright. Who would I trust to do otherwise? Farthing stayed, and although hunting wasn't something I did regularly, I knew it would be good for her and, since the Cornish, like the Irish, bring horses on quickly, I took her out when she was four, with my mother, Iris and Babs beside me.

The first season was terrifying but thrilling: two emotions which my canny mother knew could have a bloody good stab at trumping grief. Another was worry for my precious Farthing – was this all going to be too much for her? It was like her first day at school, and again, shrewd on my mother's part: I was caring for someone other than myself.

And Penhallows were skilled in the field. Dad's job was too peripatetic for him to be offered the Mastership, but he would have been perfect, and Mum even more so: it was offered, actually, but she turned it down with a laugh, knowing she was not temperamentally suited. She was too polite, too much of a follower herself, like me, and all Masters had their egos and their fiefdoms.

It was Sean Coats's turn to flex his Master's muscles today. Otherwise known as Saintly Sean, he was a lay preacher in his quieter hours. Old, venerable and well liked, he knew every inch of his country, but you certainly wouldn't want to get on his wrong side, or any of the hunt staff's for that matter. Particularly the grim-faced whippers-in, intent on controlling their hounds, who were spilling down the ramp of the lorry even now, in a black, brown and white flood, baying and calling, making a hell of a racket, as Farthing stiffened beneath me and pricked her ears.

As I sat, at this, the opening meet, on my coiled spring of a young chestnut, I knew I had to be quiet and still and just let her bed in a bit. We'd managed it during the short autumn hunting season of the previous two months, but those few successful outings were only dress rehearsals and didn't prevent me from feeling nervous today.

The first meet of the season proper was quite different. This was the real deal. Always on a Saturday, it attracted a scrum of gung-ho, testosterone-fuelled alpha males, keen to let off steam after a week in the office or on the farm, and lots of over-excited teenagers. It wasn't the midweek event with the careful band of mothers, retired gentle-folk and occasional children like me – with yet another orthodontist appointment, and a huge wink from Mum, who thought coping on the hunting field a different sort of education. I was always made aware of the argument on both sides, though, and we had heated debates with my cousins in Devon who were anti, and sometimes came to wave their banners and follow on foot, before – no doubt bizarrely to some – coming back to our house for a rau-cous, riotous tea.

No antis today, I thought as I surveyed the scene with my best friend Shona beside me. Across the teeming mass of beautifully turned-out horses and riders, the former plaited and clipped, the latter snug in black coats and snowy white stocks, I saw Hugo with a couple of boys I didn't recog-nize. They were already being pretty loud, yelling at each other and roaring with laughter. Saintly Sean had them in his sights, however. He'd turned in his saddle and was nar-rowing his eyes as if he might ride across for a quiet chat.

'I'd be surprised if any of them have ever done this before,' remarked Shona, on a piebald pony.

'Hugo has,' I said loyally.

'Once, last season, we saw him,' she said with a sniff. 'But look at his hooray friends.'

There was a great deal of larking and whooping and swigging from hip flasks going on, even though there was plenty of port on offer, which they were also helping themselves to, as it came round on trays.

'Oh, you'll probably find they were born in the saddle. That one on the roan can certainly ride.'

'The one on the grey I was on can't.'

I frowned. 'What d'you . . . ?'

But Iris was already between us, asking the same question, on her sensible Irish gelding, a frown on her face. 'Shona, I thought I gave you the grey mare to ride this morning?'

'I know you did, Miss Bellingdon, but that friend of Hugo's asked me to swap.'

'Oh, did he now? Well, we'll soon see about that.' She began to turn about.

'Oh no – please don't, honestly, I don't mind at all. I love Barney.'

'Yes, but in the first place it's bloody rude, and in the second place, is he up to the mare?'

'I think he thought I'd have a better day on this one.'

'Nonsense,' Iris snorted derisively. 'He wasn't thinking of you at all! He just didn't want to be on a pony when his friends were on much bigger mounts.' She rode away towards them.

'Oh God . . .' Shona said faintly. 'Please don't let her make him swap back. He'll think it's me . . .'

I silently implored along with her. The local state-school girls making a fuss, when of course all the horses actually belonged to Hugo's father. We held our breath, eyes glued, as she talked to the red-headed boy on the iron-grey, who was now the epitome of good manners and charm, even at this distance. Iris listened and nodded.

The moment she'd turned and was riding back towards us, out of earshot, a remark was passed and one of them stifled a laugh. Not Hugo, though. After a moment, he rode across, threading his way competently through the field on his nonetheless prancing bay, his eyes on my friend.

'Thanks, Shona. Iris says you asked not to swap back.'

'Oh . . . that's OK.'

It was all Shona could manage, so flabbergasted were we to be spoken to.

'Still, it was decent of you. Barney's a good ride, but he's a bit where's-the-cart.' He grinned.

Shona and I laughed, knowing exactly what he meant. Barney could jump anything he came across, but looks-wise he could also be pulling a gypsy caravan, with his thick, shaggy mane and flowing fetlocks.

'Nervous?' he asked, ice broken.

'*God*, yes,' we chorused.

'It's the bloody opening meet. Aren't you?' Shona asked.

'Terrified,' he admitted. 'I haven't ridden for six months, and this one's properly revved up.' As if to demonstrate, his horse snatched irritably at his rather serious-looking bit, mouth frothing already. 'And there are a load of idiots out today, as ever. Cut you up at the first fence if you're not careful.'

'Always are at the opening meet,' agreed Shona, totally at ease now, whilst I was still getting used to him being there. 'So it's either right at the front, or right at the back to give them room, don't you think?'

'Front,' said Hugo firmly. 'Up with people like Babs, Iris and your mum,' he nodded at me. Ridiculously, I flushed. 'Just don't go anywhere near my dad; he's over-horsed himself as usual. He'll be off at the first if he's not careful, causing a pile-up. Iris wanted him to ride his old faithful, but he's on that mad Piper.'

'He's not!' Shona exclaimed. Piper was a notorious bucker, and we could see Roger even now, in his red coat, on a bunched-up black horse who had his head between his knees and was reversing at speed as Roger swore loudly at him.

'And Mona Hartley is to be given *acres* of space.'

'Oh, we've already spotted her,' I told him, finally managing to find my voice. The local hotty – all red lips and peroxide curls just about contained in a hairnet, her vast bosom straining at her skin-tight black coat, buttons fit to ping off, and looking equally likely to be pinged off her enormous dapple grey herself – was beside us.

'Just take him away,' murmured Shona, watching. 'Walk him quietly about.'

'She can't, she wants to stick like glue to Neville the Devil,' Hugo told us. We all giggled as, right on cue, the devastatingly handsome local farrier who, with his black curls, hooded eyes and wicked, flashing smile had more than a touch of the dark side about him, rode past on a flashy thoroughbred type, all jingling bit and glistening spurs. He swept his hat off in a debonair gesture as he greeted Mona and murmured something as he passed.

'What did I tell you? It's back to the forge for her later.'

'Over the anvil,' agreed Shona.

As we snorted, both secretly delighted to be talked to like this, I spotted Hugo's two friends, watching and wondering who he was speaking to. Debating, perhaps, whether to come across. Just then, Saintly Sean cleared his throat. He stood up in his stirrups and beamed around at everyone.

'Could I have your attention, please?' he called.

Silence reigned. Total, respectful silence, actually. Any child still chattering was glared at hotly as Sean removed his ancient Patey hat. In his lilting Cornish accent, he spelled out what he expected from his flock today, in terms of respecting farmers' property, keeping off the crops and shutting gates. Then, when he'd thanked the Hendricks, whose farm we were meeting on, he broke into a benevolent smile and wished us all a happy day. One almost felt he might be tempted to make the sign of the cross over us. Mike Harris sounded his horn, and together with Malcolm, who was Second Whip, they gathered up the hounds and trotted smartly off towards the first cover, which was a good couple of miles away, with plenty of open countryside to gallop across first. There were some very solid stone walls too, which required serious jumping, being high, wide and, unlike hedges, very unforgiving if you dropped a hoof. Plenty had ditches in front, and at least one had barbed wire on top, whilst another had a hideous drop into a lower field on the other side. To accommodate the drop you had to let out the reins, lean back, shut your eyes and pray. I obviously hadn't had breakfast, never could when I hunted, like many disciples of this terrifying, glorious sport, and I felt my heart change places with my stomach as we gathered up our reins. We set off in the jostling scrum, and my eyes darted about as I tried to locate Mum. She, Babs and Iris were all in a row, looking incredibly slim and glamorous in their white breeches and navy fitted coats, and with many eyes upon them. Mum's pretty Arab mare tossed its head. They were well ahead of us, right behind Sean, in fact, who led the field in his red coat.

'Come on,' said Hugo, spotting them, too. He gave his two mates a jerk of the head to follow him up to the front, neither looking quite as confident as they did a few minutes ago. 'Chop-chop, we need to get up there. We certainly need to avoid this idiot.'

One of the fishermen from Port Tavern, on what looked like a very green youngster, was taking great leaps and advancing precariously on his quarry, Tanya Roland, who put it about a bit locally. As we passed we heard Tanya say: 'Don't waste your time, Bobby Summer. I'm not a novice ride.' She cantered towards Charlie Pascoe, a rich divorcee, whose land we were heading towards.

'Her eyes are on a much bigger prize,' confided Hugo, and I laughed.

It seemed he'd rather fallen in beside me, and the field had turned hard left down a muddy, wooded path, with room enough for only two abreast. We were cantering beside each other now, and Shona, when I glanced behind, was with Hugo's red-headed friend on the grey.

'I didn't see you at the Cheshires this year,' Hugo called, and I felt myself blushing as I ducked a branch. He'd noticed.

'No, Mum and I decided to give it a miss.'

'Fair enough.'

'Not – you know – for any particular reason. We just thought . . .'

'Usual crowd? Same old same old?'

'Exactly.'

I felt hot. That had come out wrong. As if the people there bored me. Before I could think how to remedy it, though, he was speaking.

'Um, Flora, I've never said it, and I've wanted to, and it's probably too late, but I wanted to say how sorry I was about your dad.'

I looked at him, surprised. His cheeks were pink and his eyes half shut with embarrassment, just a sliver of blue. I shored up the most tremendous smile which came right from my rapidly reverberating heart.

'It's never too late,' I told him gratefully.

At that moment, the track opened up, and glorious green, open country appeared before us. Hounds fled eagerly across it and horses spread out behind them. Across the wide pasture and beyond, the panorama of the undulating North Cornish countryside in all its hilly, patchwork glory revealed itself for miles around. For the first time that season the horses felt the intoxicating thrill of springy grass beneath their hooves and pulled hard. We stood up in our stirrups, kept our reins short and tight, and galloped, hearts pumping, every man for himself, towards our first jump.

5

There it was, down at the bottom of a sloping valley, one of the famous five Pascoe walls. The farmer, Charlie, one of the few wealthy landowners round here courtesy of a wind farm he'd somehow been allowed to throw up while no one was looking, was forever having another layer of drystone slapped on his walls. Up ahead the hounds were already flowing over it like a river, whippers-in on either side. Then Saintly Sean gave us a master class in how to do it, taking hold a few strides out so as not to come in too fast, sitting up, and letting the horse do the rest. Harder, obviously, that restraining hold, for the rest of the field, not in splendid isolation like Sean's mare with her considered thoughts, but instead, racing as a herd, and Hugo and I had left it late to get to the front.

I saw Mum, Iris and Babs soar across it as one, and then, where we should have been, Mona, making a meal of it as she got too close and her horse cat-leaped, allowing us to see daylight between Mona's ample behind and the saddle, almost unsettling her. It was too much for Bobby Summer's youngster, who wrenched the reins from his rider's hands and leaped it much too fast, causing him to peck badly on landing and Bobby to fall down the neck, hat over eyes, just managing to stay put. His horse, however, out of control, staggered about and cut up the next horse who had to swerve violently to avoid him.

'Over here!' called Hugo, but I'd already seen it. A stretch of wall which, although it was higher, hence everyone avoiding it, nevertheless didn't have half the field causing chaos in front of it. Cold, grey, solid and uninviting, I felt Farthing consider it, taking in its height and girth, plus, courtesy of the slope, the rapidly disappearing ground before her. She cocked her ears intelligently, got the stride exactly right, and flew over. Beside me Hugo's sensible gelding, a very old hand, did exactly the same as he sat still and tight. We beamed in pleasure at one another as we landed safely and galloped on, so pleased to have got that out of the way, and a glance behind told us Shona and the boys were over too, albeit in the middle of the jostling muddle that we'd avoided.

On we flew; across three more fields, these with open gates, which many sensible people took and who can blame them, but some braving the walls like Sean, who was still making them look easy. Mum and her crew followed suit, a couple of young farmers who were not to be budged, and then Hugo and me. It occurred to me that I was obviously going to be jumping everything today, which I hadn't planned to do on a young horse in her first season, but it couldn't be helped. Where Hugo went, I would go too. I had a quiet word with Farthing and she got the picture. Shona was in the same boat behind me. No way would she be taking the open gates with these two boys beside her, but she was on the safest of mounts, which I suspect she was rather glad about now, as the ginger-haired boy suddenly shot past us on the grey she should have been riding, thoroughly out of control, the mare's head high, mouth well above the bit.

'Turn a circle, Tommy!' Hugo roared.

Happily Tommy heard and managed to yank with all his strength on his left rein and bring her up beside us.

'Tuck in behind us!' Hugo yelled as we pounded across the ground together. Tommy, to his credit, just about managed to do that, and Hugo, Shona, the other boy and I formed something of a wall for him to shelter behind as we galloped along.

'Barney won't kick, you can get right up my arse!' Shona shouted, which under different circumstances would have had the boy shrieking banter back, but all we heard was a breathless:

'OK.'

He didn't have too long to hold on: just one more wall, which, unfortunately, he was committed to if he came with us and, as the four of us sailed over in unison, glancing quickly over our shoulders on landing, we saw Tommy's grey, knowing full well she was on her own without a competent rider, rise up like a stag. Tommy's legs were horizontal in mid-air – no reins, hands clutching plaits – but fortunately he landed in the saddle, though with a hell of a bump, so that the mare bucked angrily. Heaven knows how he stayed on.

'Jesus,' muttered Hugo, as thankfully his other friend, Lucas, who'd grown up hunting in Leicestershire, was safely over and 'having a brilliant time, thanks' when asked, his face a picture. Not so Tommy, who was positively green at the gills, but, recognizing immediately he was the underdog here, was buggered if he was going to let it show.

We were almost at the first cover now, slowing down as we approached, and I saw Shona hang back to talk to the boy alone, ask him something. I knew what, because we would be standing here a while whilst hounds drew, but it didn't go well.

After a moment, she rode back to me. 'Charming,' she muttered, her face taut.

'Doesn't want to,' I said quietly.

'Couldn't have been more emphatic.'

'Still, at least you've offered.'

Hugo had also clocked the kindness and sensed, too, this wasn't the moment to offer his mate any advice. He came to a halt beside us with Lucas, giving Tommy no choice but to join us. Our horses, sweating and breathing heavily, snorted and tossed their heads, steam rising from their backs in the cold air. Everyone who'd made it this far – and there were one or two who hadn't – chatted and laughed and retold the walls; exhilarated, relieved, and high on the adrenalin of still being alive. All around, hip flasks were opened and offered and swigged on hard.

Tommy offered me his flask and I took a grateful slug. Then my face contorted.

'God, it's strong!'

'Bourbon,' he laughed. 'Not your tipple?'

'Not sure I've ever had it. You're American?'

'Ten out of ten for observation.'

I blushed, and then in my confusion said without thinking: 'So have you done this before?'

His face darkened, male pride pricked. 'Just because I'm

American doesn't mean I can't ride. Funnily enough we have something of a tradition in the Wild West, which is clearly where you think I'm from.'

'Oh – no, it's not that. It's just – well, this is so English, I imagine.'

'Hunting? Pretty universal, I think you'll find. Hugo, your Cornish girlfriends are giving me a master class in international diplomacy, I must take notes.'

We all laughed, but Shona and I were embarrassed. And the Cornish bit. As if we'd never been out of the county.

Mum rode up to see how we were getting on.

'Farthing OK?' she asked.

'Amazing.' I beamed. 'Loving every minute of it.'

'Well, Sean wants us to spread out.' She smiled around at everyone. 'So if you wouldn't mind awfully . . .'

As she rode away to inform the next group, I thought how good she was at this. Some hunts yelled orders, but Mum would help Sean out in the nicest possible manner, not barking commands as the neighbouring Devon lot would. Tommy's eyes narrowed into the distance.

'I could be her toy boy.'

I suddenly realized what he meant.

'She's Flora's mum,' said Hugo quickly.

Tommy blinked. 'Oh. OK. Sorry.' He didn't look too embarrassed, though, and a slow smile spread across his face, so it wasn't really enough. The apology. It was gauche at best. 'I see where you get it from,' he drawled. What was I supposed to say to that? *Gee, thanks*? Flutter my eyelids?

'Good to see your small talk is as good as your riding,' remarked Shona, and the other two boys roared and slapped their saddles. Tommy had no choice but to grin sheepishly. Why hadn't I said that? Why?

'Spread OUT!' yelled Reg Francis, who was my next-door neighbour, a thickset, burly plumber. He was bearing down on us at a rapid trot on Phantom, his huge, eighteen-hand black bruiser, his face furious. 'This isn't a fucking drinks party.'

We scattered like marbles, standing about twenty yards apart around the cover, slapping our legs and calling 'hi-hi, Charlie', which Shona and I could never do without laughing, while Charlie, aka the fox, now safely in the next county having cunningly giving us the slip hours ago when he'd heard us at the meet, no doubt laughed too. It was a rare hunt to outsmart him. When Reg was safely round the corner, Hugo rode up beside me.

'Sorry about Tommy. He can be a bit of a dick.'

'Yeah, I spotted that.'

'Actually, he's OK, he's just a bit out of his depth today. Brings out the worst in people.'

'That's true.'

I regarded his narrow, intelligent face, adding 'sensitive' to my list. This boy was not at all as I'd imagined. The athletic blond jock was disappearing rapidly.

'It's not just being out of your depth, though,' I reflected. 'Hunting shows people's true colours. Because it's . . .' I felt my own colour rise as I tried to explain. 'So raw? So . . . I don't know . . .'

'Primeval?'

'Yes, that's it. It strips you bare, somehow. Leaves you nothing to hide behind.'

'That's because there's authentic danger, which is rare

in our lives these days. And it also channels some ancient romance of the soul, I think. It's weird . . .' His turn to look a bit embarrassed. He went on more pragmatically: 'On a practical level it should be available on the National Health. Hunting three times a week would sort out a lot of people's mental-health issues, plus the obesity crisis – there, I've halved the budget in one go.'

'Except Sally Chambers hunts three days a week,' I reminded him, as a huge, scary blonde on an equally enormous Irish roan cantered bossily past as if she was part of the management. 'And she's foul to that poor tiny husband of hers.'

I was keen to keep the banter light, but also thrillingly aware he'd said romance. Oh, it was said in a different context, but still, he was lyrical. I added that to my list.

Suddenly the rest of the field were cantering up behind us and we were off again, but it was with an even greater sense of excitement that I gathered my reins and cantered amongst them.

We were going across to Larks Ridge now, further inland. Here there were fewer wealthy wind-farm owners, and more tenant farmers trying to keep body, soul and smallholding together. These walls were not remotely manicured: they were crumbling and patched, some with rusty corrugated iron, and I'd even seen an old radiator filling the gap in one. Local knowledge was key. Unexpected bogs, ditches and sudden drops were not uncommon, and if you didn't follow Sean closely and went blithely off piste, eagerly jumping a nicely collapsed low wall, you could easily hit the deck with your horse on top of you, courtesy of a pile of fallen stone on the other side.

Hounds were speaking now and streaking away from us in the distance as the land rose steeply towards the horizon. The wide, grassy hill was one I knew of old and always greeted with relief, as the horses invariably lost a bit of steam, but what goes up must surely come down and you had to really take a hold down the other side, particularly with the wide gaping ditch at the bottom. A couple of small stone walls were also thrown into the equation before the ditch for good measure, which, if you were in control, had the advantage of steadying you for it, but if you weren't, being small and easily leaped, could have you flying even faster for the water.

Farthing came back to me immediately as we cantered down, all my thoughts concentrated now on my own survival without consideration for anyone else. Hugo's bay with its long, easy stride was just ahead of me and I managed to keep a careful distance as we popped over one wall, then down to the other in the valley, clearing it, then checking immediately on landing and not letting her roll on as I cantered towards the ditch. It was more of a stream, actually: wide in places and occasionally deep. You could either kick on and hope for a good stride, or let the horse pause, consider, then give a massive leap which had the danger of unsettling you in mid-air.

Ahead of me, Mum and Iris were sitting straight and tight and putting their legs on as they approached, and I saw them jump long, flat and beautifully. The young farmers flew across, and then Hugo, with perhaps a little less style, but nevertheless, he was over. My turn. I asked Farthing the question a few strides out and the reply could not have been more unequivocal. Her stride lengthened immediately and she soared across the muddy water which glistened darkly beneath us, landing with feet to spare on the other side. Lucas was quickly over too, and then Shona – quite a leap for a small pony and I saw her delighted face – but when I glanced back, I was in time to see Tommy's horse in the water, struggling up the bank. Tommy was clinging to the plaits for dear life as somehow the grey scrambled out, wet and filthy.

We swung back, eyes front, knowing he wouldn't be thrilled to have an audience, and galloped on. The walls came thick and fast now including the next, the biggest and scariest of the day. It was locally known as 'Oh God' because Roger's aunt, on encountering it for the first time, had uttered these immortal words, to which Babs had remarked dryly, 'Lucky it wasn't my aunt or it would be called Holy Shit.' As the four of us checked quite far back, letting the horses have a good look at it, Tommy's grey suddenly tore straight through the middle, banging mine and Shona's legs. Thoroughly out of control, it charged straight past my burly neighbour Reg, past Mum and Babs, and seemed intent on committing the cardinal sin of overtaking Sean, galloping fast.

'Jesus!' I heard Hugo yell beside me. All we could do was watch in horror as we saw Tommy's mare clock the height and girth of the wall too late. With no one aboard telling her she needed to slow down and collect herself, telling her anything at all, in fact, the mare lost her confidence and ducked out at the last minute, swerving violently. As the horse went one way, Tommy went the other, flying out of what is colloquially known as the side door. He'd comprehensively cut up the rest of the field, but Mum and Babs, who were committed, somehow managed to avoid him, the young farmers swore violently and got over too, and the rest of us held hard since jumping on top of someone is not actually in the rule book.

As the rest of the field, with much cursing, fled down the hill to jump the wall elsewhere, Lucas disappeared after Tommy's horse. That left the three of us, who straggled to a halt around Tommy, who was still on the ground. Hugo leaped off and I held his horse as he ran up. Shona threw me her reins, jumped down and ran too. Badly winded, Tommy struggled to his feet.

'I'm *fine*, fucking *fine*. Fucking bastard horse refused – where is she?'

'Lucas has gone after her,' Hugo told him as, away in the distance, we could actually see someone else had caught the grey and was handing her to Lucas to ride back with, the saddle pretty much slipped right over to one side. A couple of people who usually rode at the back anyway had ridden across to help. Lovely Liz Price, who was a nurse at the same hospital as Shona's mum, so that was always a bonus, and her sister Kim who ran the local kennels.

'Everything all right?' Liz asked, eyeing Tommy's very white face as he staggered a bit.

'Everything is fine and if everyone would stop fussing I'll just get back on my horse! *Fucking* animal.'

Lucas was amongst us, handing him the reins.

'I'm not sure that's a good idea,' said Liz with a frown, as the grey, thoroughly overwrought, circled manically around Tommy, tossing her head. Froth was pouring from her mouth as he tried to keep her still. 'You look a bit concussed to me. I should hop back on but ride quietly home.'

'I'll take him,' Hugo told her.

'I don't need any fucking nursemaid – we're riding on!'

He shoved the saddle back into its rightful position without undoing the girth, which frightened the horse. She was going up now, lifting her front hooves off the ground, preparing to rear, eyes rolling with fear and anxiety, her sides sodden, steam pouring off her, pink nostrils flaring.

Shona was still on the ground.

'If you're determined to carry on you really need to ride Barney,' she told him earnestly, helping him hold the mare down, grabbing the reins on the other side.

'And you need to get back where you fucking well belong!' he roared.

There was a stunned silence. We all froze.

'Well, that will be Truro, then,' said Shona lightly, but her face was frigid. 'Or did you mean halfway up a gum tree on some Caribbean island?'

Tommy stared, stupefied. 'God, no, I sure as hell didn't mean that. Jesus – you surely don't think . . .' He glanced around, aghast.

Liz and Kim didn't speak, but I could tell they were thinking, *unforgivable*. Hugo's face was puce with embarrassment, but he was calmly telling everyone what to do next, and we all listened, relieved to have the distraction, the field away in the distance now.

'Right. Tommy, get on Barney right now. Shona—'

'Actually, I'll ride the grey,' I said, leaping down and handing Shona my reins. 'I've ridden her before and Shona hasn't.'

This much was true, although this was a very different

beast to the one I'd calmly trotted along the beach with Iris when we'd brought her on a couple of summers ago. This was a nervy, frightened animal, but Shona and I both knew I was the one to get her confidence back, being more experienced, and she'd ridden Farthing loads of times and would be light and considerate. No more argument was brooked and Tommy did indeed look thoroughly ashamed as we were helped back on our respective mounts by a tight-lipped Liz, who'd dismounted. Kim then rode down along the wall, leaned over and expertly opened a gate with her whip, which, when Liz was back on, we all filed through.

We could see the rest of the field in the distance, gathered by Larks Ridge, and we cantered silently to join them. The grey sprang ridiculously beneath me, not taking a great deal of notice of my hands and legs, but it was early days, I told myself nervously: a stop at this cover, a bit of rest and recuperation, and hopefully she'd calm down and get her confidence back. As we joined the group, some people turned enquiringly. We nodded wordlessly back. And actually, there were quite a few muddy backs; a number of people had come undone at that wall, and some possibly had mild concussion, too – it wasn't of any great consequence.

What happened next, though, we were later to learn, hadn't happened in our particular hunt for many years: fifteen, I'm told. I saw Liz ride across to talk to Sean. I couldn't see Sean's face from where I was sitting, Lucas was in the way, but I did see it when he rode across to where Hugo, Lucas and Tommy were standing, Tommy looking much more settled on Barney and, although pale, less green. I watched as Sean spoke to them. I saw Tommy's face go from white to bright red. The boys nodded. Then Hugo turned his bay around and came across to me and Shona, his eyes lowered.

'We're going,' he told us. 'Master's orders. Tommy has been sent home.'

6

Tommy's disgrace was essentially my gain, as it turned out. Roger was horrified when he heard, and insisted Tommy apologize properly to Shona, in person, the following day. Mum later heard from the Bellingdons' daily that Tommy already had his coat on and was sitting hunched on the front steps waiting for Hugo to drive him across when Roger found him, but I can't see it myself. Irrespective of how it happened, however, on Sunday morning, there they were: Tommy and Hugo, at the front door of our cottage where Shona was staying the night, Truro not being hugely convenient for hunting.

It was still relatively early for two teenage girls – ten-ish – and Mum had to come up and wake us.

I sat bolt upright in bed. 'What? They're here?'

'In the kitchen. I'll go down and make them some tea.'

'Did you have to let them in?' muttered Shona, from under the duvet.

'Certainly I did. He looks wretched, actually. Now get dressed and go down.'

'I just want the whole thing to go away; this is beyond embarrassing. Such a stupid misunderstanding,' Shona said faintly.

Down we went, though, dressing quickly and brushing our hair and definitely our teeth but no time for make-up. And there the two of them were, looking sheepish and drinking tea at our little kitchen table, Mum, diplomatically, having made herself scarce.

They both rose from the table when they saw us. Tommy went very red and came forward.

'Shona, I'm so sorry. I know what it sounded like, but swear to God I didn't mean that. I just meant get lost, small-town girl, which shows what an ignorant, preppy jerk I am. I'm sorry for how it sounded, though. Like, the worst thing ever.'

'Don't be silly, I got that as soon as I saw your face. And I'm gutted you were sent home.'

She had been: had said, with tears in her eyes, that it had made it much worse, but Mum, whose judgement I trusted, said Sean had been right. Older, more sophisticated children might now have debated this, leaning on the Aga with their tea; might have wondered whether Shona's feelings had been taken into account, but we were gauche and young and Tommy had done what he'd come to do, looking her in the eye, cheeks the colour of his hair, and that was the end of it. Personally, I thought he could have been a bit more charming afterwards, but he wasn't. He stared at the floor and let Hugo carry the show for the next half an hour, as he asked us about school, our plans when we left, which was next year, and as we compared subjects and groaned about Maths – Hugo and Shona – and History – Hugo and me. It was run-of-the-mill stuff. After a bit they got up to go. On the way to the door, Hugo asked me if I was going to the carols at the Fothergills' in a few weeks' time, which I wasn't, but I said I was. We called cheery goodbyes as they went down the front path, then shut the door. My heart was pounding.

'Phew. That wasn't so terrible,' I told Shona.

'Total result for you. He likes you.'

'You think?'

'Oh, come on. You've got a date at the carols.'

I pulled a face. 'Bit weird? Crooning away beside him?'

'Mulled wine afterwards, a snog in the moonlight? What's not to like?'

'Let's not get ahead of ourselves.' But I couldn't disguise my excitement. 'As for Tommy . . .' I rolled my eyes, feeling this was too much about me.

'Oh, he was all right,' she said, 'for an over-privileged knobhead.'

'You think? All that small-town crap!'

She shrugged. 'Honest.'

'And then he hardly said a word!'

'Oh, I don't hold that against him. I'd have thought less of him if he'd turned on the charm. He looked like he couldn't speak. Like he couldn't just carry on with idle chit-chat after what he'd said – or hadn't said. Trouble is,' she said ruefully, 'I'm so used to the real thing.'

We wandered back to the kitchen. 'Weird thing is . . .' I hesitated, because it was weird, in that it was the first time we'd ever talked about it, 'and I say this with huge guilt, Shona . . . I've never noticed.'

'I know,' she told me. 'And shall I tell you my much bigger, guiltier secret? When your dad died – and I adored your father, as you know – a bit of me was pleased.'

I froze. My hand was on the kettle, about to make more tea. I turned to look at her, horrified. Her eyes were full.

'You were going to boarding school on that army bursary, but instead, you stayed here with your mum. You're the only person I've ever met who's genuinely never noticed.'

My eyes filled, too, but we didn't fly across the kitchen and hug each other: we nodded tersely, and I made the tea and she busied herself with our terrible old CD player on the shelf by the cookery books. Fleetwood Mac filtered through and we hummed along.

Hugo didn't mention it again either, at the carols at the Fothergills' house, which I'd never been to before principally because I'd never been invited, but I was buggered if I was going to let a tiny detail like that stop me. I rang Babs, who I knew went every year, and asked if I could go with her.

'Of course, darling!' I could hear ice tinkling in her glass as she knocked back her six o'clock tipple. 'Is it Sabrina's solo rendition of "Silent Night" that attracts you? Or have you got the hots for Hugo Bellingdon?'

'Sabrina's solo,' I told her sternly. She roared, and I knew she absolutely couldn't be trusted not to make trouble, but she was all I'd got.

Babs was not a natural carol-concert-goer either, but aside from the Cheshires, this was the only event at which Belinda had to be in the same room as her, and Babs enjoyed it enormously. Sabrina Fothergill was Belinda's best friend, but she was also Babs' sister, and much as Sabrina regarded her as a bad influence and rarely had her in the house – which actually hurt Babs, Mum said, more than Sabrina could know – at Christmas she could not in all conscience exclude her.

There we all were, gathered around the huge twinkling tree in the Fothergills' splendid oak-panelled hall, various select families from the county (of which we were not one), everyone looking shiny and bright-eyed. Well, the parents anyway, thrilled to have their offspring around them for a change, and the offspring, mostly teenagers, were not that dismayed either, if truth be told, to put the alcohol and the cigarettes and the relentless competitive partying aside for a few days, with the biggest excuse in the world to be children for a brief spell. The excuse Himself was before us in the crib, at the centre of the charming nativity scene of naive wooden figures that Sabrina had arranged at the foot of the tree.

'It's mine, actually,' Babs told me when I admired it. 'Belonged to our paternal Danish grandmother. But Sabrina claimed it on the grounds that I don't have children to enjoy it. Hold on, here we go.'

A hushed silence had fallen, and Sabrina was opening her mouth to sing her legendary solo, eyeing her murmuring sister furiously. It wasn't that she couldn't sing, but *why* was she singing on her own? If a solo was called for, why not a child? And her voice had that terrible shaky vibrato so that 'Heavenly peaaace . . .' seemed to go on forever. Babs lit a cigarette, which struck me as unbearably funny, and every time she exhaled, it was with a bored, exhausted breath. I stared at the Persian carpet, knowing my only hope was to think hard about global warming or the economic deficit, but my shoulders were beginning to shake. Every time Sabrina hit a high note, Babs exhaled more wearily, and when she'd finally finished I had tears streaming down my face. I wiped them carefully with one finger before I looked up, but when I did, it was straight into Hugo's highly amused eyes on the other side of the tree. He was grinning with delight at my predicament, absolutely beaming, and refusing to look away, even when I pretended to study my hymn sheet for the next carol. When I looked up, there he was again.

'You were in serious trouble,' he told me later, when we were indeed supping mulled wine and having a cheeky fag on a freezing little bench on the terrace outside.

'I'm afraid Babs has that effect on me. She's just the naughtiest girl in the school.'

He didn't say anything and I realized what an incredibly crass thing I'd said.

'It's OK,' he said, seeing me suddenly confused and tongue-tied. 'I'm totally used to it. And actually, it's a relief to talk about it. Etta doesn't feel that way, but I do. I'd rather it was out there. Can't bear everyone privately thinking, I wonder how those kids feel about it.'

I glanced up at him, my face asking the question.

'I don't,' he said truthfully. 'I mean – really think about it. And it would be cruel to say Mum brought it on herself, but Dad had a chat with me when he realized I knew. Apparently Mum shut up shop almost immediately after I was born.'

Half of me couldn't believe I was having such a grown-up conversation, the sort you might have after a year of going out with someone, and half of me was riveted.

'But why? Isn't that just asking for trouble?'

'Exactly. What was Dad supposed to do?'

'Of course, you've only got his word for that,' I reminded him.

'Except they have separate bedrooms. Have done ever since I can remember.'

'Oh.' I thought back to my own parents, with their tiny double bed, the laughter reaching right to my room down the hall.

'Mum has insomnia, apparently, and Dad snores and likes a really hard mattress – that's the party line. But still.'

I nodded and we both dragged thoughtfully and frightfully maturely on our cigarettes. Golly, I *was* in the know. And I wouldn't tell a soul. Not even Shona. That lasted until Tuesday.

Suddenly Belinda put her head around the French windows. 'Oh, there you are, Hugo. The Maxwell-Clarks are going, would you come and say goodbye?'

Hugo muttered something as he stubbed his cigarette out on the York stone, but he dutifully got to his feet and went in. As he passed his mother, who was holding the door open for him, she gave me a thin, frosty smile. I knew exactly what it meant. *Don't even think about it.* The door shut firmly after her. I finished my cigarette and, after a bit, went inside too.

Obviously, the subterfuge appealed to both of us. Hugo got the vibe, too. We'd yet to kiss, but we managed that at the end of the Christmas holidays, at some terrible Pony Club dance at which neither of us would normally be seen dead. Then we managed much more at my house, when Mum went to visit her sister in Devon.

The logistics of a long-distance relationship also appealed: perhaps there was a mutual desire to tick that box without too much pressure. He was away at school and could claim a girlfriend, as I could claim a boyfriend at my all-girls high school in Truro. We telephoned regularly and chatted for hours, but exams were upon us and we rarely met. He went somewhere worthy for the first part of his gap year, six months in India building an orphanage – which he told me he was convinced was knocked down when he left for the next batch of wealthy gappies to rebuild – and after I'd worked in a local restaurant, I went Interrailing with Shona, then helped at my old school in the art department. By now Hugo was training to be a ski instructor in Verbier with all the right sort of girls. Oh, Belinda was on it. Somehow, though, we both kept the faith, and I have to say, I never really doubted him. This was in the pre-Facebook days, before I could torment myself with shots of him being drunk and outrageous and draped in silky blondes but, if anything, he was more territorial than me, and would ring to see how Mr Parker was shaping up.

Mr Parker was thirty-ish, single, had damp hands, and palpitated with nerves behind his glasses whenever he spoke to me. He lived with his mother and was the art teacher. Nevertheless, at an all-girls school, where even the Very Average Gardener became The Fit Gardener, collective breath steaming up windows as he pruned the roses, and then, in a leap of hormones, The *Really* Fit Gardener, Mr Parker was often up for discussion. Not just amongst the girls, either, but also in the predominantly female staff room where the only other male teachers were over fifty. I'd play to the gallery on the phone to Hugo.

'He let me wash his brushes yesterday. And tomorrow

we're getting messy with clay. But there's only one wheel, so I'm thinking Patrick Swayze and Demi Moore?'

'Definitely. And you should sleep with him afterwards. Demi would.'

'I should, shouldn't I? Can't think why I haven't already. Got your grouse moor sorted yet?'

'Coming along nicely, thanks. Bubbles seems to have one in Scotland and Millie's family have one in Yorkshire. Both eminently marriageable. I'm wracked with indecision.'

'Yorkshire's a bit gritty,' I told him. 'I'm not sure I can see you there with all that muck and brass. You're a bit too sensitive.'

'You're right. And I've always rather hankered for a kilt. As you know, I've got great legs. Bubbles it is.'

I'd spend the rest of the day in a flushed, smiley, post-flirtatious haze after our chats, and even though our university choices were equally insane, geographically speaking, his being Oxford and mine the School of Art in Glasgow, we stayed the course.

He loved coming up to Glasgow – he flew, of course, having more of an allowance than I did – and I could tell that, despite already being well travelled, something about the muscular architecture, the tough, seemingly terrifying and incomprehensible but hilarious locals, the poverty, but also the hard graft, spoke to him in a way that the deliberately sheltered part of India he'd been exposed to, the luxury of the mountains and the gentle, rural nature of our joint childhoods, hadn't. He liked nothing more than drinking in the pub above which I lived with three other students, and where the tough Glaswegians finishing their shifts at the dock would sink pints amongst the outrageously flamboyant art students. It was an eclectic mix and even Shona, who was pretty unshakeable, found it eye-poppingly odd when she came to stay one weekend.

'OK, don't look now,' she murmured into her lager. 'But that one at the bar with the eye make-up is so obviously gay, but he's kissing a girl. Hugo, I said don't look.'

Hugo's glance came back. 'Colin's straight, actually,' he told her. 'But he's an installation man, so he's always a piece of art himself. Last time I was here we had a long conversation about how for his final piece – one third of his degree, by the way – he intends to walk naked into his tutor's office and discuss Picasso's early cubism, thereby recreating the scale of shock it engendered on society at the time.'

'Excellent,' she breathed. 'Might try that in my Geography practical.'

Whilst I took personal pride in Hugo's delight in my new city, I, on the other hand, found Oxford rather intimidating. Obviously, it was stunningly beautiful and I joined the goggle-eyed tourists marvelling at what we'd previously only seen on *Morse* – the honey-coloured architecture, the flashes of emerald green quad through doorways – but the people were so flipping clever. An idle conversation in a pub could turn on a sixpence, so that I was out of my depth within moments. And they weren't showing off, either. It was just the way they could go seamlessly from the delights of cheesy chips from Ivan's van to the complexities of Occam's razor in seconds flat. Oh, and posh – Hugo and Tommy's crowd, anyway. Oh yes, Tommy was there. Being loud and outrageous as usual, and, if I was feeling mean, very much a conscious card, as my father would say. Bright-eyed and flushed with drink, he'd invariably be the one standing on a barstool, conducting some pissed rowers in a rowdy boating song, until the landlord chucked him out.

'Sent home *again*,' he'd muttered to me in mock horror on that occasion as he passed me en route to the door. It was pretty much the first thing he'd said to me all evening.

'Must be a conspiracy.'

'Which always seems to happen when you're around. Funny, that.' He gave me a twisted little smile before exiting, pissed and angry, banging the door behind him. I watched through the window as he swayed down the wide pavement of St Giles.

Post-university he was equally ubiquitous. I'd walk into a bar in London to meet Hugo after work, and there Tommy would be, together with all their mutual friends, all confident, beautiful and clever. His eyes would mock me as I went to greet my boyfriend, whose eyes were never like that, never snide, always open and friendly. Tommy, though, I knew, saw into my very soul. He saw all its insecurities, its lack of expensive education and brain cells, its reliance upon painting – which no one could argue with, but was I any good? – as my only calling card. He'd watch as, joining the table, I'd deliberately sit next to Vicky, the only other non-Oxbridge graduate, who could be relied upon not to ask me my thoughts on the political issues of the day as we happily compared suntan marks under our watches.

If I'm honest, I only said I'd go to Wales for that long weekend because I knew Vicky was going. Otherwise I think I'd have turned it down. Let Hugo go alone with his hooray crowd. Obviously now, in retrospect, I wish I had. Flick, real name Felicity, who'd read Classics at Merton which apparently made her off-the-scale bright, had a cottage down there. Or at least her parents did. Most of them had one hidden away somewhere. Down we went, one windy, autumnal Friday, to a glorious secluded spot in the Teme Valley, where, tucked in a vivid green pocket, sat an ancient yellow-brick house beside a stream. There was only one girl coming we didn't know, a new girlfriend of Sam's, and, as we arrived, pretty much simultaneously, I spotted her getting out of Sam's tastefully distressed Land Rover Defender. Hugo and I drew up beside them in his MG and as the Land Rover door opened a girl jumped out. She was wearing run-of-the-mill trainers, tight blue jeans and a crisp white shirt, and she was called Christina.

It didn't happen in a lightning flash, in fact I'd say I noticed her before Hugo did, but it certainly happened pretty damned quickly over the course of that weekend. As she shut the car door and came confidently across to say hello, she could have been Hugo's sister. Other people have commented on it since. She was tall and slim and athletic-looking; not sexy, but fit, in the old-fashioned sense, as if she'd just come off the lacrosse field. Her short blonde hair was shiny with a floppy fringe and she had friendly blue eyes and a wide, gleaming white smile.

The two of us smiled and said hi, and then we chatted whilst Hugo was still getting our luggage. He was a bit preoccupied, and no glances were even exchanged, so why was my heart already sinking a bit? I couldn't take my eyes off her, if I'm honest. And for the rest of the weekend, after that initial distraction, neither could Hugo. She was fun, she was amusing, she was friendly. She was a trainee PE teacher at a London school, so not scary on that front, but she had the confidence to laugh off her terrible mistakes in Trivial Pursuit that evening, her wild guesses, which I didn't, so that everyone laughed with her, not at her. As the games got more cerebral and she became more hopeless, she got even more amusing. I could see Hugo's eyes on her all of Friday night.

Flick had organized team games and obstacle races for the following day, and we all gamely joined in, getting pissed on terrible cider. The sports descended into idiotic wheelbarrow and egg-and-spoon races, and although she couldn't have taken it less seriously, shrieking as she continually dropped her egg, running out of control in her sack and falling over, Christina looked fab. Despite being a rider I'm not remotely sporty, and in the final race of the day, I dropped the baton in the relay race to the groans of my team. Luckily, Christina was our final runner, and amazingly, she made up the ground to win by a short head, urged on by the crowd, no one roaring more loudly than Hugo. Tommy's eyes came round to meet mine in delight. Oh yes, he was there. And he was having the best time.

It wasn't just me and Tommy who noticed Hugo's distraction, either. Vicky shot me a pitying look before supper when Christina came down from her bath wearing simple white jeans with a blue shirt and espadrilles, glowing with health and vitality, whereas my forte, being small and dark, is pale and interesting with quite a lot of eye make-up. Oh, and heels are a must, which isn't really the form for a country house weekend. And the thing is, because I was feeling insecure and jealous, I didn't rise to the occasion. I didn't behave very well. I'd smile thinly at Hugo, letting him know I knew. I chatted most of the evening to Vicky, even when he tried to include me after supper when we'd left the table for coffee. And we didn't make love that night, which was rare for a precious week-end away. Interestingly, Christina's boyfriend seemed oblivious to it all. Sam looked rather chuffed, actually, revelling in the reflected glow of his new girlfriend, who, he confided to Vicky, he'd thought pretty enough, but no great shakes. She wasn't, if I'm honest. But she definitely had something.

The following week was Hugo's birthday and I bought him a very expensive pen which I couldn't afford. We were in his car when I gave it to him, in Parson's Green, outside the pub. I saw his face go a bit pale when he opened it.

'It's great,' he said, taking it out of its case. 'Wow. A Mont Blanc. That's hugely expensive, Floss.'

I shrugged. 'I wanted to give you something special.'

Odd, how, when you're in the grip of love and panic and total horror at the ground slipping away beneath you, you'll grasp at anything: do everything wrong. He shut the case and swallowed.

And it got worse. Or I got worse. But not deliberately so, I swear. The catalyst for the horror that unfolded occurred before we'd even met Christina, about a month before. I'd had a terrible bout of food poisoning, courtesy of some dodgy prawns in our local Tandoori, and Hugo had held my hair as I'd lost the contents of my stomach down the loo at his flat. It meant, I was later to learn, that the Pill lost some of its efficacy, something I'd genuinely been ignorant of at the time.

I was so shocked, so horrified, as I watched the stick turn blue in the loo at my communal studio in Clapham some weeks later, that I ran, still in my overalls, still with oil paint all over my hands, to the phone box down the road to avoid using the one in the office. Hugo was at his desk in the City. My voice, when it came, was strained, my breathing shallow.

'Oh my God, Hugo, I'm so sorry. I've totally fucked up. I'm a couple of weeks late and I've just done a test. But don't worry, don't worry, I'm going to sort it out.'

I heard him gasp at the other end of the line. Then there was a certain amount of crackling and confusion as he clearly tried to take his phone elsewhere.

'Are you sure?' he whispered eventually.

'Positive. I've done it twice and it's as clear as anything. But I'm not panicking because Lily, who paints next to me, literally had one a month ago, and it was fine. I mean – not fine, but – you know. There's a place in Soho in Whitfield Street, the Marie Stopes clinic. I'll book it this lunchtime, promise.'

There was a long pause. 'I'll meet you this lunchtime. That bar in Maiden Lane. Don't do anything yet.'

'OK.' I put the phone down. Panic briefly subsided and I felt love and relief flood through me that he wasn't cross and would, I was sure, come with me. That I wouldn't have to do this alone.

When I met him at lunchtime, his face was pale but set. He took my hand and we went to sit at a private table in the corner of the dark cellar bar. He couldn't bear the thought of me getting rid of it, he said. Could I? I hadn't really thought. I'd just panicked. I thought now. He made me, as we sat, holding hands across the gingham table-cloth, him in his suit, me in my paint-spattered jeans. No, I agreed slowly, after a long pause. It wasn't good. Wasn't a nice feeling. We'd been together so long. *Think about it*, he urged me. *Just think about it. We've got a bit of time.* But I had thought about it. If he'd thought about it and was happy – well, resigned – I jolly well was too. If he could put another girl who he'd literally just met, to the back of his mind, so could I. Heavens, it would be odd *not* to have the occasional attraction, wouldn't it? It meant nothing. Hugo and I were as strong as ever. And a baby would strengthen that bond, naturally it would. In reality, of course, I wasn't thinking straight at all. Not properly. Just reacting to my emotions, which were tidal. I remember nodding in agreement at the Toulouse-Lautrec poster on the brick wall behind him, but being unable to look at him: wondering if he even knew himself.

We had to tell certain people quite quickly, obviously. Mum was good and supportive although she did ask me a few searching questions, and Belinda, dreadful. I don't know exactly how dreadful, but Hugo, white-faced and shaken when he came off the phone, said she'd said some terrible things. I could imagine. But he didn't change his mind; if anything he became more resolute. I wondered later, if, in some complicated way, it was precisely because of her reaction that he didn't budge. That she'd unwittingly backed him into a corner. In some other bizarre way I began to feel like a spectator at my own execution.

We got married quickly and without fuss at the registry

office in Marylebone, because actually, since I was small and skinny, I showed quite soon. Mum came, rather quiet, and Roger, but not Belinda, who was ill, apparently. Roger beamed and was sweet and said how delighted he was. Etta was her usual silent, enigmatic self, but Shona was all I needed on the girlfriend front, and she was there. Tommy, too. And just before the service, as we waited for the registrar to arrive, I walked in on the two of them in the little back office behind the room where the ceremony was to take place, Hugo and Tommy. They were sitting at the registrar's desk, talking in hushed, urgent tones. Tommy's face was the most serious I'd ever seen it, his eyes fierce and intent on Hugo's face, which had gone white. I stopped in the doorway. Tommy stared at me. Then he got up so abruptly his chair fell over. As he brushed roughly past me in the doorway he said bitterly: 'So you got him in the end.'

Roger set us up in a little flat in Fulham, near the river, and Peter was born that summer. And, actually, because the weather was so beautiful and Hugo was so busy and London so hot, I popped down to Cornwall quite a lot. Hardly a pop, admittedly, but I managed it. In fact, we managed everything quite well for the next couple of years. We were happy if not ecstatic. But then coping with a small baby and scraping a living together in London is not always blissful, is it? Vicky, who also had a baby by now, would tell me it was the happiest she'd ever been.

I think it took every ounce of courage for Hugo to tell me the truth about that which I already knew. That he didn't love me. Not like that, anyway. Hadn't for some time. That he was incredibly fond of me, but felt about me as he would a sister. No real surprises there – after all, we hadn't slept together for months and certainly we'd waited ages after Peter was born. But that's not unusual following a reasonably tricky birth, although again, Vicky would disagree. She said Martin, her husband, could barely make it to the six-week check-up.

When Hugo said he was leaving me I was completely and utterly devastated. I have been ever since, but equally, I put up no resistance. I didn't feel I could. My heart was breaking, but deep down, I felt responsible. I should have made him examine his feelings more. I felt huge guilt and shame. And when he married Christina two summers later, at St Mary Abbots Church in Kensington, in a riot of orange blossom and confetti, and with a champagne reception afterwards at her parents' house in Holland Park, I was not in the least bit surprised.

7

Roger's study, where I would be painting him, was darker than one would have wished for. Really rather gloomy, in fact. It was part of the original fabric of the house, which, together with the sitting room, was possibly the only remaining section of the sixteenth-century core, despite Belinda rhapsodizing about the whole place being Jacobean. It was just as well it wasn't, actually, because the rest of the house and the majority of the rooms benefited from later additions, like huge Georgian sash windows. There was only one window in the study, however, and it was small with leaded lights and faced east, which was not ideal. Roger had arranged himself facing it in his red leather chair behind his red leather-topped desk, dressed in his best bib and tucker, which consisted of a dark flannel suit no doubt hauled out of mothballs for the occasion, a white shirt and a scarlet tie. He was beaming broadly over the top of the desk, face florid, arms folded in front of him. What with the desk, the chair, the tie and the face there was an awful lot of red going on.

'*Comme ça?*' He beamed at me, like a benign bank manager.

I hovered doubtfully in front of him. 'Right . . . um . . .

weren't we going to go for a more casual look? Jumper and trousers?'

'Ah, no. Belinda vetoed that. Wants me in a suit, in here.'

'OK . . .' I backed away towards the window, trying different angles. But the room was too small.

'Um . . . this isn't really working, Roger. Maybe not behind the desk?'

'Oh – gotcha. Further back.' He pushed his chair right back to the wall on its casters. 'Legs crossed, perhaps?' He flipped one over the other. 'They're not bad, actually – yes, the desk rather cuts me in half, doesn't it?'

'It does rather.' I moved around the room, pretending to consider from the doorway, but it was hopeless.

'It really is so dark. I'm wondering, what about the gunroom? Isn't that where you normally sit and read the paper? And it's got those great tall windows.'

He looked alarmed. 'Lord. Not sure Belinda would like that, she says I spend far too much time in there as it is.'

'Well, because you love it, and you could even clean your guns and stuff, while you sit for me.'

His face lit up like a firework. 'Naughty girl! What an absolutely terrific idea. Come on, let's do it while the old girl's at her parish meeting. I say, won't the dark suit look a bit odd? Got my tweed one – won't take a mo. Nip up and change?'

'Yes, I agree, not the suit. But what would you normally wear in there of an average morning? Not a tweed one either, surely?'

Conspiracy shone in his eyes. 'Well, if I did happen to pop in there and polish the Purdey while I was supposed

96

to be gardening, I'd be wearing my usual kit. Old cords and a jersey.'

'Exactly. That's what I'd like to have you in, Roger, if you don't mind. So you're relaxed and happy.'

'Splendid.' He beamed. 'Won't be a tick. You potter down and I'll see you there in a bit.'

Relieved, I collected my easel, my bag of oils and my palette and went down the hall. I was sounding far more confident than I felt, if truth be told, but if I was to spend the next few weeks painting Roger in a dark little hole as he sat miserably and uncomfortably before me, trussed up in a suit probably last seen at Peter's confirmation, this would surely end in tears.

When he came down and met me in the gunroom where I was already flinging open tall shutters to the vivid green garden beyond, he was wearing a cornflower-blue jumper which matched his eyes under which a pink shirt peeked cheekily, plus baggy fawn cords and suede shoes. I knew we were in business. He rubbed his hands in delight.

'Excellent! Where d'you reckon – over by the window?' He scuttled across and draped himself theatrically on the sill of the sash window. He cocked his head dreamily towards the garden, chin raised.

'It's moody,' I agreed, suppressing a smile; one could never quite tell if Roger was for real or hamming it up. 'But you might get rather uncomfortable holding that pose. How about in that chair?' I nodded across to where I was pretty sure he habitually sat, nursing his arsenal, and possibly a whisky, in an ancient, faded, exploding, pre-war armchair.

Roger looked genuinely scared. 'She'll freak,' he said weakly.

'Oh, I'll tart it up a bit, don't worry. Won't show the stuffing. And if your arms are over the bad bits, we won't see them anyway. Let's see how it goes.'

He needed no further prompting and scurried, with alacrity, to his favourite old chair, next to his cabinet of favourite guns, looking out over his favourite view of the front drive, the lawn, the sea and the boats beyond. The gunroom, like Belinda's sitting room, was to one side of the front door, with a view of all the comings and goings of this great house, so that they were in effect like a couple of weather people, poised either side to dart out. Truffle, who was in her basket in the corner, got up and wandered across to her usual position by his feet, where she collapsed. Perfect.

'Don't forget, you're in the driving seat here,' he told me, eyeing me beadily as I busied myself, getting my easel in position, changing from one window with the drive behind to the other, which put him sideways on and still gave me enough light. It was a better composition. I dragged up an old table for my paints which I was pretty sure wasn't precious; everything in here belonged to Roger. 'This is all your idea, savvy? You forced me. Dragged me in here kicking and screaming.'

I grinned. 'Don't you worry, Roger. I'll protect you.'

He wriggled happily in his seat and winked. 'That's my girl.'

I set about screwing my canvas to my easel, angling it slightly more to the right, then moving it again, then again, and always glancing back to my subject to check the shadows, the light, the effect. Roger sat stiffly and self-consciously at first, head erect, an ironic smile he'd no doubt practised in the mirror playing on his lips, but he was bored now. Realizing I'd be ages preparing, he took to settling back in his chair and staring dreamily at the sea, to the sailing boats beyond, the occasional speedboat whizzing by on the horizon.

As the sun caught his eyes and his handsome face relaxed, the effect was terrific. Oh, it wasn't hard to see what Babs saw in him. Roger was a very good-looking man. Tall, athletic – he'd played cricket for Cornwall in his youth and sailed tall ships in Australia – he was twinkly, naughty, and great fun. Years ago he'd been considered a huge catch and the fact that he'd married Belinda Chamberlain had been a source of great astonishment to the county. There'd been that lovely Fiona Driver, not to mention Coco H-B. But Belinda had been very, very determined, Mum told me. And Roger was biddable and open to flattery, and a tiny bit lazy, if she was honest. Fi and Coco played fast and loose and were up and down to London the whole time, and Roger hated London. They also played hard to get, although they definitely didn't mean it, and Belinda was – well, just there. Available.

Roger had quietly leaned across and unlocked the cabinet whilst I was squeezing Prussian Blue on to my palette, and was even now fondling a smooth, mahogany stock and gazing admiringly at it. Unless you're the sort of painter who gets off on a sour, uncomfortable subject, this was definitely what one wanted in a sitter's eyes: love. And this was surely the closest I was going to get to it, short of having Babs in here, and then I knew I'd get raucous laughter, tears streaming down faces, and that unmistakable spark of lust which they'd snap off in an instant in public and save for later. I'd seen it in the past and I didn't imagine much had changed. No, I was happy with the gun.

'English, of course,' he told me reverently. He rubbed a bit of imaginary grime away with his finger. 'Not a Purdey – got one of those – but same period. Nothing wrong with continental, of course. Got a lovely Spanish four-two. Like to see? No? But you can't beat a bit of English craftsmanship. Want me to put it down?'

'No, you're fine, Roger. I'm just getting the perspective. I'll be a while yet.' I was. He gazed beyond me, into the middle distance.

'Everything all right, Flora?' he said abruptly.

'Yes thanks, Roger. How d'you mean?'

'Well, I was thinking. Must be odd for you. Coming back.'

I glanced up at him from my palette. His eyes were waiting for mine. I smiled. 'I'm fine. But thank you for asking.' He nodded, satisfied. We were quiet again. Roger resumed rubbing his gun with his finger.

'Do you prefer it to hunting?' I asked, jerking my head at it. 'Shooting?'

'Lost my bottle for the chase, Flora. Had one tumble too many. Ended up having a brain scan in Truro General. Bab—Belinda said I was too old for it. Nothing like it, though, eh?' His blue eyes gleamed at me with such intensity that despite them being watercolours of their former selves, I saw his much younger self.

'Nothing. Particularly in country like ours.'

'Quite.'

We fell to silence, both in our respective reveries. He looked very far away, no doubt landing in some muddy field in his red coat with all the usual suspects. This last association no doubt led to the next, seeming non sequitur.

'You know Shona's on the box?' he exclaimed, glancing up.

I grinned. Reached for my box of charcoals. 'I do.'

'Couldn't believe it! There I was, boiled egg perched on lap for Sunday supper, and she came on with a ruddy great microphone outside the Eden Project! Reporting about some break-in! Shot my egg clean into the fire I sat up with such a jolt.'

I laughed.

'Roared for Belinda but she just paused by the door and said she'd already seen her. Ages ago. Imagine! She hadn't told me.'

I could imagine. I chose a small, stubby, well-used charcoal from the box. 'I haven't seen her yet, but Mum heard through Babs that she's really good.'

'Really good? Oh, but she's *splendid*, Flora. Regional news, of course, so you wouldn't get it where you are, just Devon and Cornwall. But there she is, bright as a button, pixie smile in place, all pert and pretty in a *very* fetching yellow frock, I must say. She looks heaps better than that terrible mousy girl we used to have who murders her vowels and mumbles so you can't hear a bloody word. *Speak up, you dismal woman!* Not our Shona. Crisp, distinct Queen's English. No messing about. I watch her every night at six thirty with my second Gin and French. Quite makes my evening.'

I grinned. 'I'll tell her. She'll be thrilled.' She really would, actually.

Roger stroked his gun barrel, staring into space. 'Slip of a thing,' he mused reflectively. 'Tell her not to mumble, eh?'

'I'll pass it on.'

We fell to silence. I started sketching him out with my charcoal, my hand moving quickly over the canvas, and time passed peacefully. After a bit, we both heard tyres on gravel at exactly the same moment – Belinda, back from her parish council meeting. Roger jumped to his feet and replaced the gun in the cabinet. As he sat down, he whipped a silk cravat from his pocket and put it round his neck.

'Bit smarter,' he told me with an enormous wink as he crossed his legs. 'She'll like that. Can always lose it later.'

The front door slammed. Footsteps could be heard moving down the hall to the kitchen. Then they approached, back down the passageway. Roger pursed his lips to suppress a smile, eyes wide and innocent. Moments later, the door opened and Belinda appeared. She was wearing another floral number, pink and white this time with a huge tulip pattern, and her grey-blonde hair was freshly waved and swept back in a great swoop from her forehead. She blinked.

'What are you doing in here?'

'It's my fault, Belinda. The light was terrible in Roger's study and he looked so stiff and awkward in his suit. I thought this might be more natural.' The truth, I find, works best in a tight spot.

'What about the drawing room?'

Bugger the truth, I lunged for the lie. 'We tried that, but the light was wrong. And also I thought it would be terribly inconvenient. After all, you use it, and no one comes in here.'

'Except Roger. How absurd.' She frowned. 'I can't imagine how it will look in the hall with all the other portraits. They're far more traditional. Most odd, I should imagine.'

Roger seemed to be shrinking down in his chair and holding his breath. I carried on mapping him out with the charcoal. No one spoke. I think she imagined we'd get up and move. 'Oh well, you know best,' she snapped eventually, clearly piqued. 'But take that ridiculous scarf off from round your neck. You look like a pirate.'

Roger dutifully removed it and she swept frostily from the room. She was truly cross and Belinda didn't do cross, she was far too controlled. She did disappointed. Or uncomprehending, even, at the strange ways of others. As her footsteps receded, Roger regarded me with awe.

'You were magnificent!' he breathed.

I sketched on, my hand, if I'm honest, a bit sweaty. We heard Belinda moving about the kitchen. Slamming about, let's face it, very noisily. Drawers were opened and shut. Cupboards banged. She obviously very much intended us to hear. Then a different noise. A regular, rhythmic, scything noise. One of steel on steel. Roger gasped.

'She's sharpening the knives!' he whispered. 'That's really bad news. Only happens in absolute extremis. You're for the high jump, Flora!' he squealed, utterly delighted, clearly thrilled it wasn't him.

'Well, she's hardly going to stab me, is she, Roger?' I said, sounding far more confident than I felt.

He lurched towards me in his chair. 'We can only hope!'

he whispered theatrically. Then he sat back, chuckling, inordinately amused.

Later that day, when I was exhausted by the concentration and so was Roger, I sought out Celia. She took some finding. I walked all along the cliff path above the estuary where Babs had suggested she position herself, but there was no sign of her. As I rounded the corner and gazed up towards the headland, only a couple of lone walkers strolled by with a terrier. Back I turned towards the cottage. It was only when I happened to glance below to the beach that I spotted her, perched halfway down the cliff, on a wide ledge. There she was, before her portable easel in her blue smock, beret on head – Celia always liked to look the part – palette in hand. It was actually a terrific spot for a seascape, if a little precarious, and she must have scrambled down a pretty rocky incline to get there. Celia was very much a lounge lizard and I was quietly impressed. I scrambled down to join her, the chalk crumbling with an aching familiarity beneath my fingers and my canvas shoes, a whole panorama of my childhood panning out in that single, simple sensation.

'Don't fall in!' I called, clinging to the tussocks of grass sprouting from between the rocks as I edged along to join her.

'Try not to,' she laughed. 'But isn't this marvellous? What a spot!' The wind was in her hair, her eyes alight.

'Well, it is today, but if you get a westerly tomorrow you might find somewhere more sheltered. You'll be blasted off the cliff.'

'Nonsense, I've got that protrusion overhead sheltering

me,' she jerked her head up. 'And anyway, this weather's set fair for ages, I checked my app. Look at that view!'

She waved her brush yonder and we gazed out across the estuary. Blue and shimmering in the sun, it was dotted with small bobbing boats, strips of golden sand bordering it on either side. Just a few children were building sand-castles, watched by their parents, the more popular beach being further on. The cliff on the opposite side rose palely to sloping green fields where cows, looking strangely large and out of proportion as they always did from this per-spective, grazed quietly. The distant hills beyond were hazy in the heat and just the odd wisp of cloud scud-ded through the bluest of skies above. I glanced at her canvas. She'd dived straight in as usual, no sketching for our Celia. Currently she was deep in the clear blue waters, her brush darting from blue to white to grey to silver on her palette – really getting to grips with the tricky way the sun shimmered on the surface of the water.

'That's good,' I said, meaning it, as she added a dab.

'Oh, it's not hard here,' she said, eyes shining. 'This is fabulous, Flora. I feel totally alive and driven for the first time in ages. I can imagine how Cézanne felt when he got to the South of France – the light! The amazing vivid tones! The translucent effect, the vivacity. And it's all here on a day like this – in sodding England! I can't tell you how energized I feel.'

She looked it, too. Her dark eyes were shining, black curls blowing under her beret, and her slightly sallow complexion was almost pink today.

'How did you get on?' she asked, still painting away, eyes narrowed at the view.

'Oh, terrific, painting-wise. But I changed the location and the clothing, and Belinda started sharpening Sabatiers in the kitchen.'

Celia shrugged. 'A few innocent vegetables for lunch? Skinning a mackerel, perhaps?'

'Perhaps. All the same, if I go missing, you'll probably find me in small pieces in the cellar. Or no, actually, she's got a few Gloucestershire Old Spots. If you can't find the body, check their sty for bones. Although apparently some pigs eat the bones, too.'

'Will do,' she said, not really listening, but I was genuinely a little perturbed.

'I saw Babs, by the way,' Celia went on. 'So sweet. She popped down to see how I was getting on and brought me a flask of coffee. And I met Christina, with her children. She was very cheery.' She glanced at me to see how this had gone down.

I made a face. 'I never really trust someone who smiles all the time and laughs too quickly, do you?'

She ignored me and painted on. 'Oh, and Iris was here, riding along the top. She gave me a wave. I've never had so many friends!'

It was true, Celia was a bit of a recluse in London: didn't really do groups of girlfriends, and could get a bit lonely and down in the dumps, what with our solitary occupation and Edward and his therapy chat. Terribly important, of course, to get to the bottom of problems, but rather sad and soul-sapping, too. Right now she looked as if her soul had popped right out of its socket, done a few cartwheels on the beach, and popped back in, scrubbed, gleaming and refreshed.

'And I felt so daunted a few weeks ago at the thought of filling half that gallery in Flood Street, but at this rate, and with this amount of inspiration – look at that *colour*, Flora, there, on that darling pink boat – I'll be ringing and asking for the whole bloody gallery!'

'Right.' I nodded, watching her paint on, attending to biting my thumbnail down to the quick. She wasn't a sensitive artist for nothing, though, and after a bit she paused. Looked me in the eye.

'Listen, Flora, this was always going to be hard. No one, except you, said it wouldn't be. Me, your mum, Peter even, once he'd got over his initial delight. But now we're here, it's actually fine. Better than fine. And Belinda will come round, you'll see. She's allowed to throw a hissy fit if she thinks she's been overruled in her own house, I would, too. Probably a bigger one than that. But she'll get over it. I suspect she's got far bigger fish to fry than which room you paint her husband in.'

'Meaning?'

She shrugged. 'I just feel she's quite – you know – manipulative. Controlling. Like there's stuff going on here under the surface, you know? A subtext. Absolutely nothing to do with us. Maybe family stuff, I don't know. I haven't quite sized them all up yet. But I'll let you know.' She grinned. 'There.' She lowered her brush suddenly. Stood back and gazed piercingly at her canvas. 'I'm done for the day.'

Celia was full of abrupt certainties like this, each one more irrevocably positive and truer than the last, be it time for tea, her stance on Brexit, or taking a violent dislike to the colour of someone's eyes. I was used to such pronouncements and often thought it was where I went wrong in life, being so uncertain. So full of wavering, shambolic dithering.

She was packing her bag efficiently with tubes of paint and rags. 'Here. You take this,' she commanded, handing me the rucksack. 'And I'll manage the easel. I'll keep the canvas screwed in for the moment, it's good and tight. Oh, you might take my palette, too.'

'I can't imagine how you got down here alone in the first place,' I said, gathering her stuff, but she was peering distractedly over the cliff now, moving along the ridge to get a better view. 'I'm surprised you made it.'

She wasn't listening. Her eyes were roving along the beach, until she found something, or someone.

She cupped her hands around her mouth. 'See you later!' she called down.

There was a pause, then:

'Need any help?' drifted up. A man's voice.

'No thanks, my friend's here now!'

I stared at her, but she wasn't meeting my eye. She'd already plucked up the easel then sidled round ahead of me. On she forged with her back to me, painting and easel outstretched in one hand, steadying herself on the tufts of grass with the other. I'd never seen her so agile and dexterous. She reached the little path and walked on up to the top of the cliff as I followed.

'Who's that?' I asked, as I joined her at the top.

'Hmm?' She pretended to be busy, unscrewing the canvas and setting it on the grass.

'Who were you talking to, Cele? Down there on the beach?'

'What? Oh, that's Ted,' she said nonchalantly, taking her backpack from me and swinging it on to her shoulders. She kept her eyes averted as she collapsed the easel and popped it under her arm. 'He's down here doing some conservation project. I ran into him up here on the cliff and he helped me down with all my stuff.'

'Oh. Right.'

I turned and gazed back down below. A tall, tanned, blond-haired man with windblown curls, very much channelling the beachcombing look in a faded blue T-shirt and old khaki shorts, grinned and waved. Celia beamed and waved extravagantly back. Still avoiding my eye, she picked up her painting and, holding it delicately with the tips of her fingers, easel under arm, she turned to go. Before she'd turned, though, I'd seen the light in her eyes. It had nothing to do with the vivid, sun-baked colours or the light glancing off the water. Nor the way the tints and the tones were speaking to her. Nothing to do with the way her painting was flowing off her brush, brimming, as she was, with creative impulse. It had nothing to do with any of that, at all.

8

Babs was just leaving our front door as we got back to the cottage, with Piggy trotting busily at her feet.

'Ah! There you are.' She stopped. 'I was just coming to look for you. Iris and I are going for a ride on the beach later – want to come?'

'Oh, I'd adore to!' I felt my spirits lift immediately.

'I thought so. Celia?'

'I won't, I'm afraid. I'm a suburban girl. My adolescent leisure activities revolved around the public baths, the library and cleaning out my budgie.'

'Ah well, there wasn't much else to do around here, was there, Flora? Apart from surfing.'

'Sounds idyllic,' said Celia enviously. 'Can you surf down there?' She jerked her head back towards the beach.

'No, darling, that's an estuary. But you can just around the bay, in Portmarrow, where I am. We'll go one day if you like. I'll see you up at the stables, then, Flora. About half an hour?'

'Perfect. And they won't mind?'

'Certainly not, they're delighted to have them exercised, as you know. I'm going like this and Iris has got plenty of hats up there, so don't dress up. See you in a bit.'

And off she sauntered to her red, convertible Triumph Stag, pert bottom swinging in white capri pants, and about to look even more fetching astride some huge, prancing steed.

'She is *so* cool,' breathed Celia as we watched her roar off down the track, blonde hair streaming. 'I want to be her when I grow up. In fact, I want to be her now. And still surfing.'

'She always used to go before breakfast. As did Roger. And then back to her cottage to warm up.'

'I can imagine. But not Belinda's thing?'

'Belinda never warms up.'

As I walked up to the stables later, along the rutted track between the fields, my boots and hat swinging in a basket, I wondered if Celia was right: that I was getting Belinda slightly out of proportion. Overreacting and losing perspective – it wasn't unusual. It was just that she had such inconvenient ideas for other people's pleasure, I decided, narrowing my eyes into the distance at the lowering sun. And was totally flummoxed when they disagreed. When we were first married, Hugo and I had found a sweet little flat in Clapham, which was near the Common for me to push a pram, and convenient for his office. We were all set to exchange, when Belinda arrived to inspect it and declared it was too damp for poor Flora and a baby and that I'd have no local friends. I tried, without success, to tell her I had at least two local friends and that the surveyor had said the damp was easily resolved, but in the blink of an eye she'd moved us to Fulham, where I knew no one (principally because no one could afford it – most of my friends were still drifting around in a post-university haze, bug-eyed at my marriage and imminent baby), and from where it was harder for Hugo to get to work.

When we'd moved in and I was two months away from giving birth, she'd arrived again, beaming and bearing gifts – beautiful cashmere for the baby and expensive bath oils for me – and we'd sat chatting cosily in the kitchen whilst Hugo was at work. I was thrilled. I thought she'd finally warmed to me. Her absence at our wedding still chilled me and it had never been mentioned, never explained. And yet here Belinda was, in her very best navy woollen dress with matching jacket and pearl brooch on the lapel, reaching for my hand over tea and banana bread – I told you, unnervingly tactile. She smiled excitedly.

'Darling!' she said, eyes shining, as if we were the best of friends. 'I have the most wonderful news.'

For an insane moment I thought she was pregnant too, and glanced down, but all looked normal, and anyway, she was sweeping on.

'I've found you the most marvellous maternity nurse.'

'A . . . sorry?'

'Maternity nurse, for when the baby comes. For the first two months. She's an absolute gem and comes highly recommended from Cynthia Palmer's girl, who says she simply couldn't have done without her. She's a complete treasure by all accounts and has a year-long waiting list – imagine! But by sheer luck a baby didn't quite go according to plan and so she has a gap.'

I couldn't help thinking the poor mother of the baby

that didn't go to plan wouldn't see it as luck, but I was still trying to get my befuddled pregnant head around the general concept.

'A nurse? Oh – but Hugo and I thought we'd manage, actually. And Mum's going to come up and help.'

'Oh nonsense, your poor mother has more than enough to do with all her work and I absolutely insist. You'll be exhausted. It's our present to you. Roger's and mine.'

She squeezed my by-now quite clammy hand which I hastily extracted, and smiled delightedly. Belinda, that is, not me. My head was swimming.

'But . . . so expensive, surely. And – and I'm honestly not sure I really want a-a—'

'Not a bit of it. I told you. Our present.' Her hand went up like a traffic policeman. Her eyes almost closed and then flickered, another unnerving habit. I'd mentioned money, too, of course, which was vulgar.

'And – and where will she sleep?' I said desperately. But I already knew.

'Why, in the spare room, of course. We'll clear it out.'

My painting room, she meant. My studio. Which she'd already communicated, via Hugo, she considered a health hazard because of the oil paints, not good for a tiny baby, even though I always kept the door shut and the window open and it was at the far end of the corridor. Dangerous, she'd even said on the phone to him once, which had alarmed Hugo and he'd repeated it.

I knew then I'd been outmanoeuvred and there was no point arguing. Hugo would agree with her because he did pretty much anything to keep her happy, principally because he was the only one who did. Roger appeared to but didn't, and Etta, by then, had moved to Australia, I was convinced, to get away from her mother. I'd run into Etta once, working in a wine bar in Covent Garden, and since I knew she worked in an advertising agency by day, had been surprised. 'I'm here every night. It's my running away money,' she'd told me, before returning briskly, tight-lipped, to the kitchen.

A couple of months later, in swept Pamela. She was from Edinburgh and she was very large, very pale, had orange hair, and ate for Scotland. I spent most of the time cooking for her. She was also ruthless in her insistence on a strict regime for Peter. I wasn't allowed to feed him when he cried; he had to go for four hours at a stretch before she would present him to me, clasped to her huge white starched bosom in a tight shawl, and then she timed him for exactly ten minutes each side, popping him off my nipple with a finger as she checked the second hand of her pocket watch, before announcing: 'Bairn's had enough!'

I went along with it in a haze of hormones and exhaustion, and so did Mum, initially. She'd sounded surprised when I'd told her what was happening, but then, as ever, said exactly the right thing: that it was terribly kind of Belinda and Roger. Mum never made trouble. But when, after two weeks, she arrived one day to find me sobbing in a heap at the kitchen table, Pamela meanwhile pacing her room with a screeching baby, she went in for a word and shut the door behind her. A few minutes later she appeared with a still-shrieking and hungry Peter in her arms and gave him to me. I can still see his red, tear-stained face as I unbuttoned my shirt and he pressed against me, fastening furiously to my breast, still making hiccupy sobs as he sucked, as if trauma lingered.

A few minutes later, Pamela swept down the passage in her coat, suitcase in hand. She clattered down the stairs without a word and slammed the front door.

'What will I say?' I breathed over Peter's downy head to my mother.

'Leave it to me. I'll speak to her. She'll understand.'

I never knew what she said, but Mum was made of deceptively stern stuff. She'd had to be, with Dad's job, and her own, unofficial role in those days of looking after the wives of Dad's men. Wives who were often alone without their husbands, scared, or even, on occasion, grief-stricken. So one Belinda Chamberlain, as was, of 26 Milverton Gardens, Truro, Cornwall, would not be a problem.

I'd driven there once, to Milverton Gardens; out of some sort of strange curiosity. It was in the days just after my divorce, when I often drove all the way to Cornwall in a sea of tears with Peter in the back; pretty deranged, not knowing what to do with myself, and occasionally doing the wrong thing, like turning up on the Bellingdons' doorstep. Oh yes, there's much I'd prefer to forget. Roger had been sweet. He'd sat on the beach and chatted kindly to me, but Belinda pretended not to be in, even though her car was there and she never walked anywhere. That was when I'd driven on to her childhood home, in Truro. It was one of five in a fifties cul-de-sac, neat and pristine with an immaculate front garden. A girl left the house next door in perfect tennis whites, swinging a racquet. I remember staring up at the windows, hoping for God knows what: some sort of epiphany about what had happened to me, what had become of my life. For some reason I always had Belinda at the centre of it all, the root cause, but I knew not why, had no idea why I felt compelled to get to the bottom of her like this. Later I'd drive back, exhausted, to London.

I shook myself now as I rounded the corner into the stable yard, a regrouping gesture. A shedding mechanism, wanting to rid myself of all that long-ago shame and detritus. Somehow I knew it was a skin I'd never quite slough off, but as I walked into the yard, the familiar smell of hay, feed, tack, hoof oil and all things horsey had its required, soothing effect. Below the clock tower where the loose boxes were, five immaculate mounts were tied to rings outside their stables, shiny bottoms towards me, tacked up and ready to go, head collars over bridles. Iris had her bottom to me too, bending and picking out the rear hind of the nearest horse. She turned. Raised her eyebrows.

'Dressed for the Bahamas?' she enquired, eyeing my strappy top and skinny jeans.

I grinned. 'Babs told me the dress code. And I've been inside all day, Iris, in this beautiful weather. Thought I'd get a tan.'

She lowered the hoof gently and stood up. 'Yes, well, Babs still rides in a bikini top so you shouldn't take any notice of her. I was just getting her ladyship's horse ready, heaven forbid she should do it herself.'

'You've tacked up five,' I said, looking along the line.

'Oh no, the other two did their own. We're a bit of a gang this evening. Ah, here she is. In time to finish the pedicure.' She waved the hoof pick at her friend as the red convertible swept into the yard.

'Sorry, darling!' Babs called to her as she jumped out. 'Got delayed watching Shona – I'm addicted! It's worse than *The Archers*!'

'Damn!' I hit my forehead with the heel of my hand. 'Six o'clock news – I forgot!'

'Oh darling, she's fab,' Babs turned to me breathily. 'Looks adorable, all pert breasts and shiny lip gloss and positively *pulls* you in with her gorgeous liquid brown eyes. She's mesmerizing!'

Iris rolled her own eyes. 'What she means is she's thoroughly competent, word perfect and never stumbles. What she looks like is immaterial.'

'And she's quite the local celeb,' Babs went on. 'Opened a fête in Manaccan the other day.'

'No!'

'Swear to God. Cut a ribbon and everything!'

For a moment I felt ridiculously jealous that others were more in the loop than me. Shona was *my* friend. I mean, obviously I didn't live here, but also . . . well. We hadn't kept in touch as much as we'd hoped, Shona and I. Busy lives, different cities – Shona had started as a reporter in Liverpool, then Manchester, now here. Some would say a backwater after those two, but I completely understood a primal urge to return to just about the nicest place on the planet.

'And does she love it here, now that she's back? Is she happy?' I asked, curiosity getting the better of me, despite wanting to hear all from the horse's mouth.

'I believe so, but you'll know more, I'm sure.' Babs turned. 'Oh, look at this for style! Putting us all to shame!'

I turned to see Tommy and Janey emerging from a back

door which led from the rear of the house. They were dressed in snowy white jodhpurs, shiny high black boots, crisp shirts, and looked far more professional than the rest of us. I took a breath to quell disappointment. Right. For a moment there I'd thought perhaps Hugo. Janey's blonde hair was tied back with a black velvet ribbon and she had bright red lipstick as a nod to glamour.

'Hi, Flora! Babs!' She gave us a cheery wave as she went across to her horse at the far end. Tommy's chestnut was beside mine. As he crossed the yard with his swaying, slightly swaggering gait which I was sure he put on, clearly going for the John Wayne look, his face wore its habitual mocking smile I remembered of old. So irresponsible himself, so judgemental of others.

'Flora. What a treat. Dressed for the occasion, I see?' He snapped a stirrup down and put on his hard hat, an elaborate affair with chin rest, strap and buckles. 'You clearly ride as you paint, in whatever comes to hand.'

'When have you ever seen me paint?'

'I went for a run this morning. Spotted you and Roger in the naughty room, disobeying orders.'

I sighed. 'Spying, as usual.' No longer the socially insecure ingénue of years ago, I was buggered if I'd be intimidated by Tommy Rochester. 'And you're right, I do rather swerve the sartorial element. I find people tend to hide behind it. Mistake it for skill.'

'Sartorial be damned, it's the safety element.' He fastened his chin strap tightly.

'Quite right,' I said, ramming my faded Patey on my head which would admittedly fly off in a catastrophic fall but was Mum's and looked great. 'And incidentally, there are some body protectors in the tack room if you're interested?'

'Also a fluorescent yellow bib someone gave Iris when they saw her riding at dusk?' Babs joined in, her mouth twitching as she swung herself easily into her saddle from a mounting block, still in her canvas shoes, six inches of skinny brown leg showing. 'I peeled the word "Horse" off the end, so it reads, "Pass Slowly. Young and Fresh." I'll get it for you, if you like?'

'Yeah, yeah,' Tommy grinned good-naturedly, aware he was being teased. 'Laugh now, but don't come running to me when you hit the deck and those two-bit bonnets fly off and the world's gone fuzzy.'

'Darling, the world goes fuzzy at midday in my house. I might not notice the difference.'

'Midday?' Iris raised her eyebrows as she rode up beside us on an extremely fresh, excited-looking young mare, who was snorting deliriously at this unexpected party. 'When have you ever made it to midday? I rode past your cottage yesterday morning at eleven and saw you sharing a cider in the garden with the postman.'

'Ah yes, but I'm the last house on Jean-Claude's round, you see, and he's thirsty by then. And after all he's French. I saw him panting up my track in his shorts and called out – "*Un petit verre, Jean-Claude?*" To which he gasped back, "*Oui, mais pourquoi un, et pourquoi petit?*"' Babs threw back her head and gave her throaty chuckle. 'We had a very jolly time.'

Iris raised her eyebrows. 'Practising your French *and* keeping my brother on his toes. What a surprise.' She swept past her friend and took the lead out of the yard under the arch. 'Over towards Farrow's farm via the headland?' she called back over her shoulder to all of us. 'Or down on the beach?'

'The beach,' Babs said firmly. 'Remember we wanted to show Flora something?'

'*You* did,' Iris said tartly. 'Up to your old tricks, as usual. But actually, the water will be good for Tommy's old boy. Soothing for his legs. And Flora, yours will appreciate it too.'

As we headed off in a group down the track towards the bay, it occurred to me that Babs was up to something. She really did have too much time on her hands.

At the far end of the path we took the quick way to the beach, through a sweet-smelling pine wood Roger's grandfather had planted years ago and which was now mature, and then took a rocky path down to the shore. My old mare had clearly ridden it a hundred times before and knew exactly where to put her feet, guiding me round the increasingly jagged rocks. I left her to it. Farthing had sadly died after a peaceful retirement in the pastures here two years ago, but this one had been her stable mate, arriving when Farthing was seven and could show her the ropes. Now she was almost an old retainer herself, and very sure-footed, whereas Iris's youngster was on her toes and inevitably stumbled. Iris soothed her with her voice to slow down. Babs was also on a baby, as was Janey, I noticed with interest. She'd clearly proven herself already and I felt slightly peeved, but to be fair, I hadn't ridden for years. As we reached the sand and wound our way around some larger boulders, I noticed the two glamour girls sizing each other up. Janey was looking Babs up and down, and Babs hung back a moment to check out Janey's riding, but Janey's friendly, open manner was disarming and her enthusiasm won Babs over.

'Oh God, the riding you have down here – this beach! You guys. Do you even realize how lucky you are? Back home I'm restricted to one measly bridle path which goes round and round in circles.'

'Where do you ride?' asked Babs.

'Central Park,' Janey said.

'Oh cool,' I told her. It was.

She shrugged. 'It's better than nothing, but it's repetitive and you have to go with a guide, much like in Hyde Park, which I've tried by the way. But at least in London you're left to your own thoughts. If I have to listen to one more lecture on the dredging and maintaining of the Jackie Onassis reservoir I swear I'll go nuts.'

'But New York's not really home?'

'No, Connecticut, where it's much better, obviously. But not like this.' We broke into a trot as we reached firmer sand. 'We're not allowed to ride on the beach, it's private.' She made a face. It was low tide, and the vast, almost empty beach spread out before us in a golden strip, the glistening water lapping it gently. My heart lifted inexorably.

'There's one guy who wouldn't be bored by the dredging and maintaining of the Jackie Onassis reservoir,' said Babs, riding up beside me and Janey as we headed for the water. She nodded towards a figure right in the corner where the rock pools were, waist-deep in a rubber wading suit that went up to his armpits and strapped over his shoulders. He was totally preoccupied, his hand suddenly plunging into the water with a jar. I didn't recognize him until he turned and stared.

'Yes, who *is* that?' asked Janey. 'I've spotted him down here before, mostly when I run, first thing. He's always got those jars of stuff, like specimens.'

'Ted Fleming. He's a conservationist,' Babs told her. 'He's on secondment to Truro from Imperial College, doing a special report for the government, apparently. It's to do with the environmental effects of toxic waste on the coast. He's a professor.'

'Cute,' Janey remarked. 'For a professor.'

'Very,' Babs purred, glancing at me.

'I met him earlier,' I told them. 'Or Celia did. She rather likes him.'

'Does she indeed,' murmured Babs, with a hint of irritation.

'That makes sense. He always seems to have a gang of students trooping along after him.' Janey nodded towards a sand dune where something resembling a camp had been set up: a gnomic gathering of earnest young people, mostly in hoodies, were hugging their knees.

'Jesus. What a load of hoydens you are.' Tommy rode up beside us at a collected canter, his riding skills – like his social skills, I'd noticed – somewhat improved. 'So that's the postman and the conservationist covered. Is there anyone safe from this alarming coven of sexual predators?'

Too late, he realized he'd set himself up. We turned on him in delight and chorused collectively: 'Yes – *you*!'

Tommy threw his head back and roared. The horses, sensing the mood, danced feverishly, fighting their bits, desperate for their heads. As one, we loosened our reins and gave it to them. Off they shot. We galloped through the shallow surf along the shoreline, the wind in our faces, water up to our boots, splashing up a storm, as we thundered from one end of the beach to the other.

9

When we returned from the ride, clattering into the yard, the horses on a long, relaxed rein and happy to be home, the back door opened. Hugo came out to greet us, having no doubt heard the hooves coming up the drive. He crossed the yard to talk to his guests first, asking if they'd enjoyed it, poking fun at Tommy's hat, admiring Janey's young horse, and why oh why did my heart still do that? When I so wished it wouldn't? Race away at lightning speed and make my chest tighten to accommodate its rickety-rackety pace? I watched out of the corner of my eye as the three of them laughed and joked together. He held Janey's horse as she dismounted. As he came my way I'd had time to summon up an easy smile and I was impressed with my jovial tone as I vaulted off backwards.

'Not tempted, Hugo?' Unfortunately, my horse moved suddenly, so my bottom was very close to his face as I said it.

I blushed as I turned, but luckily, Hugo's eyes were elsewhere, lowered as he flicked a horsefly off his knee. Only Babs shot me an amused look.

'No, I had things to do, sadly. Work, mostly. But I might come another time,' he told me eagerly, clearly so keen for this to work. My heart wrenched at his continual sweetness in the face of my eternal bitterness. Hopefully it didn't show, the bitterness. I loved Hugo too much to let him feel wretched on account of my pain, but the colossal effort this required was exhausting – no doubt for him, too. I felt for both of us, although a bit of me was aware that this was very good for us: learning coping mechanisms. Being more like my friend Josie – heavens, we might be going on skiing holidays soon, whizzing down slopes together. Not that I could ski. Or perhaps not, I thought, as Christina waved from the back door.

'*So* annoying!' she called. '*Wish* I could come.'

'She's allergic,' Hugo explained.

'Oh.' I raised my voice to reach her. 'Gosh, poor you! Rotten luck!' I realized I was inadvertently imitating her cut-glass accent, which is a habit of mine, no doubt in an effort to ingratiate myself with whoever I'm talking to. I can go from chav to duchess in moments.

'I did have one, actually, as a child,' she called. 'Daddy had to sell it. Brought me out in hives.'

'Ah!' I called back. It was quite hard, communicating at this distance, and I didn't trust myself to say more. Might bring out *rotten luck* again.

Nevertheless, she hovered on the doorstep. 'Must be lovely to be riding down here again?' she asked tentatively, as if worried that might be wrong.

My heart lurched for her a bit. She tried so hard with me.

'It was heaven!' I assured her with a grin, meeting her, hopefully more than halfway. She broke into a delighted smile and, content, went inside.

'Did you get Peter's text?' Hugo asked me, as I ran up my stirrups.

'No? What text?' I whipped out my phone, spinning round to face him.

'He sent it to both of us. Just to say he might be coming down.'

'Oh – how lovely!' I gazed at my screen in rapture and there it was. Addressed to both of us – very rare, as if we were married – and my heart stupidly gave a palsied leap. It was short and to the point:

Might pop down.

'I've said, great,' Hugo told me.

'Oh *yes*. *Definitely*.' I pocketed my phone. 'Great' wouldn't begin to cover it, though, and I knew I'd go to effusive lengths later composing an enthusiastic response.

That would make us a family, I realized as I removed my bridle from the chestnut's face, rubbing her sweaty ears and clipping on a head collar. Something we'd never been. Well once, obviously, briefly, and thereafter, let's face it, I'd always been the one who'd resisted. Yet somehow, strangely, it felt fine here. Maybe because we'd been a family here before, dangling Peter in the shallows in his nappy on that very same beach, watching him turn shells over in wonder with his podgy little hands. As I went to the tack room, saddle and bridle over my arm, the back lawn became visible to my right. I paused.

Hugo's two other children were playing on the monkey bars in the long grass by the trees. Christina was striding from the house across the lawn towards them with her hands in her jeans pockets. And the funny thing was, the more I saw of this evidently happy family, the easier I found it to be around them, I'd noticed. Yes, my heart still raced the moment I saw Hugo, but I hadn't lain awake for hours last night dissecting the evening as I did when I saw him on his own, at a parents' evening, or a rugby match. Replaying every line, every conversational gambit in my head. I hadn't felt a tiny bit sick today, either. I realized it helped to see them together. I'd built them up into a hugely glamorous couple, and they weren't. They were perfectly average.

Christina, who was now coming back across the lawn having no doubt informed her offspring of an imminent supper time, never wore more than jeans and a shirt, and not hugely fashionable ones. There was something graceless in her stride, I realized. She walked like a duck, feet out at an angle. And I'd seen her openly pick her teeth after supper last night. I didn't see that in the studio as I painted: I only saw her in that garden in Wales, seventeen years ago, swinging from a long rope across the stream. The only girl to do it. Landing on the other side with a whoop, turning and punching the air, Hugo's eyes shining. That's what I saw as I stood at my easel in Fulham, beside Celia. I certainly didn't see her throw open a window and shout:

'When I say now, I mean now! Not when it suits you!'

The window slammed shut. The twins exchanged a bored look, rolled their eyes, and slid off the bars.

Yes, this was very good for me, this little exercise, I thought as I went back to hose down my horse. A drip, drip dose of reality, not fantasy, which Hugo, talking to Janey now, as she rubbed her grey down beside me, helped by having a quick nose pick as Janey crouched to sponge the mare's legs. *And* he farts, *and* he's losing his hair, *and* his tummy's fatter and all those things, I told myself. Although he managed to ruin it, perhaps feeling my gaze upon him, by turning and flashing me that shy, Prince William at St Andrews smile, before shuffling inside.

Shuffling. Good. Another splendid observation, Flora, I thought later as I made my way back down the track to the cottage. I swung my basket jauntily. The sea sparkled brilliantly ahead of me, and pink campions studded the green banks beside me like little jewels. He doesn't stride – like his wife – he drags his feet. Always has done. Doesn't pick them up. I will, though, I thought with a grin. Pick them up. Those little defects. They'll mount up, you know. And soon, Flora, you'll have a bloody great mountain which you can pore over forensically at your leisure when you get home. It will do you the world of good.

As I turned the corner where the track forked into a long decline towards our cottage and the dunes, I saw the conservationist coming up towards me, rubber waders over his arm. Celia was right: he was rather attractive if you liked the beachcombed surfer look, which I'd obviously grown out of. And so should he have done, actually, I thought as he approached. On closer inspection he was older than me.

'Lovely evening,' I said, with a smile.

'For a ride, I suppose,' he said, eyeing my hat and boots in my basket. He stopped in front of me.

'Well, yes,' I agreed, a bit nonplussed by his tone. His face was set and tense and a muscle was twitching in his cheek.

'Which totally disrupted the beach clear-up operation we had in place for this evening. Very nice of you to churn up the entire shoreline, exactly where we were planning to trawl.'

'Oh, right. Gosh, sorry, we had no idea.'

'Oh really? The posters around the bay escaped your notice, did they?'

'Yes, they did, actually.'

'Which is odd, given that they were on every conceivable footpath and bridle path that leads down.'

'Oh – no, we didn't follow the bridle path.'

'No, you just came across through the private wood and down on to the beach from wherever you fancied, because the Bellingdons own the land and they can do what they bloody well like.'

I was thoroughly taken aback now. 'Look, I was just riding out and following Iris. I'm sure she had no idea.'

'I'm sure she didn't. But it is the supreme arrogance of people like that to live in a complete bubble and not feel they have to follow any of the normal countryside rules or conventions, isn't it?'

'Oh no, Iris isn't like that at all. She's frightfully hot on that sort of thing, closing gates and what have you.'

'Oh, she's frightfully hot, is she?' His dark eyes blazed into mine.

I gazed back then nodded slowly. 'Oh, I see. Yes, I get it. This is some sort of chippy class-war aggression, is it? Your beach party's been spoiled so you blame the toffs?'

'I blame the people who assume that because their land extends to the coast, they have a perfect right to treat the beach as theirs, too.'

'Well, why don't you go and tell them, instead of taking it out on me?'

'Oh, I fully intend to. I was on my way.'

'Good. Well, if you'll get out of mine, I'll be on my way too.'

I didn't wait, and instead, stalked around and past him. God. Bloody man. How *rude*. How dare he? I made myself not glance back. I mean, obviously he was cross, and I remembered now seeing the students in the dunes, no doubt ready with their buckets and – no, not spades – all manner of collection paraphernalia, nets and jars, perhaps. But to accost me when I clearly had no idea. *And* I'd apologized immediately. I knew I had. No manners. None whatsoever.

I opened the little gate that led to the cottage and strode up the path, annoyed that my pleasant evening had been ruined and that my admittedly always rather pivotal mood had been tipped the wrong way, just when it was inching so accommodatingly in the right direction. I shut the front door behind me with more vigour than I might usually. Celia was in the little strip of kitchen at the far end. The French doors were open to the garden, music was blaring, and she was cooking a stir fry, already halfway through a bottle of white wine. I flung my basket on the sofa and headed for one of the glasses she'd put ready on the breakfast bar.

'*Rude* man,' I told her, needing to share. She turned, surprised, spatula in hand.

'Who?'

'That conservationist chappie.'

'Oh really? Why?'

I told her. She turned back to stir the chicken and vegetables in the pan, thoughtful.

'Yes, well, I can see his point, actually. Especially if there were signs.'

'We didn't see the signs, Cele.'

'No, because, as he said, the Bellingdons aren't like normal people.'

'No, not because of that, because we simply came another way. That doesn't make them *ab*normal – *God*.'

'No, but that is the difference, isn't it? It's *why* you came another way.'

'You see what this is about, don't you? Not just a genuine mistake, but a seething great jealousy and resentment for people like the Bellingdons. And yet here you are, backing him up, but very happy to lap up their hospitality!'

I glared at her across the breakfast bar. There was a silence. Celia was sensible, though, and knew what this was about. Hugo and Peter were tangled up somewhere in the defensive armour I'd pulled on for the occasion.

'It's complicated,' she conceded eventually. 'But you must admit, there's a certain arrogance—'

'Iris is *not* arrogant.'

'Belinda is.'

'Yes, Belinda is,' I agreed. 'Since we're going off piste and including non-riders here, to support the argument.'

'Roger?'

'Oh Christ, why stop there – and actually, no, not at all. Roger does masses for the community. Chairs the local lifeboat charity, fundraises and what have you. Belinda too – in fact, she probably does more.'

Celia sniffed. 'Noblesse oblige.'

'Yes, OK, but you'd be pissed off if they didn't, wouldn't you? If they sat in their ivory tower and didn't get involved in raising money for the new classroom at the local junior school, but it's riding horses – *galloping* horses – across a beach where students have gathered that pisses people off. It reeks of privilege.'

'Because of the horses.'

'Exactly.'

'If they'd been bikes . . .'

I shrugged. 'Well, he'd have stopped us.'

'Motorbikes?'

'Illegal. But thuggish, more than arrogant.'

'Quite. Not sure where this is going.'

'Neither am I.'

'Drink?'

'Please.'

She poured me one and let me calm down. I perched at the bar and took a long glug of cold Chardonnay, watching as she drained the noodles, the steam rising in billowing clouds from the sink.

'Attractive, though, isn't he?' she said at length, still with her back to me.

'No, not at all. I don't go for that overgrown beach-boy look.'

'He's a professor.'

'So I've been told.' Who told me? I couldn't remember.

'Lovely eyes.'

'If you don't mind the craggy outreaches around them.'

'I don't.'

'He's spent too long outside. You could practically see the salt in those wrinkles.'

'A salty dog,' she purred, turning and sipping her wine. She smacked her lips and stared dreamily into space. Then she absently spooned our supper on to plates.

'Blimey, at this rate you'll be sailing away in a beautiful pea green boat. How's Edward?' I asked pointedly.

'Edward.' She sighed. Lowered her spoon. Her shoulders slumped too and I really wished I hadn't asked. She adopted her own defensive tone, similar to the one I'd just put on for the Bellingdons. 'He's fine, actually. But we've decided we need some space.'

'Oh, OK.' I nodded. 'When did you decide that?'

Edward, I knew, had decided it months ago, and had kept her dangling, and very much at his beck and call and imminent disposal, ever since.

'You mean when did I join in with his decision?' She gave me a knowing look as she resumed spooning the veg. I smiled.

'Yeah, OK.'

'This afternoon, actually.' She looked shifty. Then she grinned. 'When I came back from painting, I sent him a text. Told him it was over.'

My mouth dropped. I blinked in surprise. 'Really? Oh *good*. Good, Cele, I'm glad!'

I wanted to say, *Thank the Lord. He was never right for you, never treated you properly, always left you depressed and upset*, but I knew these things came back to haunt one. What was it girls said to each other in these circumstances which showed solidarity and boosted confidence but didn't entirely decimate the ex? Oh yes. I wrinkled my nose and looked thoughtful as we sat down to eat, perching on stools opposite one another at the bar.

'You could do better.'

She smiled and raised her glass. Twinkled at me across it. 'Thanks. I fully intend to.'

10

Babs sauntered down to the cottage the following morning. She'd clearly added us to her morning routine of surf, little tryst with Roger, shower, and then breakfast with the girls in their sunny back garden.

Her eyes were bright with mischief as she came through the back garden from the dunes. She sat down at the table, crossing her skinny brown legs in her shorts. Piggy jumped up on her lap. 'I say,' she said, helping herself to a croissant, 'you'll never guess what happened yesterday. You missed all the drama.'

'Oh?' I buttered my toast. 'The livid conservationist?'

She shot me an astonished look. 'Yes! How did you know?'

'I met him on his way up to the house. He wasn't particularly amused then.'

'I should say not. And, my dears, I can't tell you how impressive he was. Strode into the yard where we were all still hanging around, eyes flashing – he's got marvellous chocolatey brown ones – and really tore everyone off a strip. And not just about the riding, either. Apparently Hugo's company is holding back on filtration equipment and giving more money to shareholders instead, which is why the leakage here is so bad. He really gave it both barrels. And of course I know he's right because Roger's been worried about the shareholders getting greedy, not that he's got anything to do with the water these days.'

'Was Roger there?'

'No, just Hugo.'

'What did he say?'

'Well, you know Hugo. He stammered and went a bit pink – he's not exactly a natural orator – and said something about trying to find some middle ground and how hard it was to please everyone. Ted roared in with, "Yes, and you end up pleasing the pockets of your bloody board members!" Hugo said that wasn't true but that obviously he was under tremendous pressure from both sides – which didn't help. Then Tommy cruised in, rather smoothly actually, and said that as a shareholder himself, and, having been to the last board meeting, which admittedly was poorly attended, he was acutely aware of Hugo's efforts to turn the company around and be more environmentally friendly. He said a scientist and a marine biologist had been appointed to the board and at least two of the old guard had been sacked. He said that actually, Ted should inform himself of the facts before storming up here and complaining about one disaster, then conveniently tagging on another, which is far more complicated.'

'Excellent!' I purred, momentarily supporting the lesser of two evils. 'Good for Tommy.'

'And what did Ted say?' demanded Celia, rooting for her man.

'Ted said he was thoroughly informed, actually, because one of the marine biologists was an erstwhile colleague of his at Imperial College who'd said his appointment to the board was pure tokenism. He said he didn't have a voice and that it was a gesture from Bellingdon Water to appear environmentally committed, but that they weren't interested in what the experts had to say at all, only profits.'

'Splendid!' said Celia. She sat bolt upright, her face glowing.

'And Hugo?' I asked urgently.

'Oh, well, Hugo was sweet, of course, as always. He said he would absolutely promise to look into it, and if Ted would like to come up to the house for a proper meeting tomorrow, he'd listen to all he had to say.'

'You see? Lovely.' I sank back happily in my chair.

'That didn't mollify Ted,' Babs said. He spat, "Listen, sure, but you lot never *do* anything. I've heard it all before." And then he turned on his heel and stalked off.'

'*Rude* man,' I said angrily. '*Again!*'

'But passionate,' sighed Celia wistfully. 'Such tremendous passion. For the environment, for marine life, for ecology – all that wonderful, worthwhile stuff.'

'Like *Blue Planet*,' I reminded her. 'Which you hate. Saying it's too blue and too fishy.'

'That was before I got hooked.'

'I'll say.' I raised my eyebrows.

'No, I mean before I really concentrated and listened properly to Saint— Sir David,' she said firmly, looking me in the eye and warning me not to let her down, should a certain marine-life lover come wandering over the dunes for a drink.

Babs was looking from one to the other of us, clearly increasingly perplexed at the line this conversation was taking.

'Hang on . . . you've written him off after one little encounter, Flora?'

'I hadn't, actually. I'll give anyone a second chance. But I have now I know he had such a go at Hugo. Celia, as you can tell, feels differently.' I waggled my eyebrows and grinned. 'Coffee, Babs? I'll put the kettle on.'

'Oh . . . um – yes. Please.' She frowned. Looked a little displeased.

I got up and went inside. Filled the kettle at the sink. The radio was on quite loudly, but after a bit, I could hear fierce mutterings and hissings coming from the garden. I went to the loo while the kettle boiled. First I had to find some more loo paper, though. When I finally came out with a tray of mugs and a percolator, they both looked rather hot and cross. Celia's face was flaming with indignation and Babs was tight-lipped.

'Problem?' I blinked, setting the coffee down.

'No, no,' Babs soothed. 'Celia just . . . just took one of my ciggies. It was my last. She – she didn't realize.'

'I didn't realize *stealing* was even possible,' snapped Celia. She gave me a thin smile. 'I didn't realize the con-servationist—' her face momentarily twisted with rage, before she composed herself, 'the *cigarette*,' she enunciated elaborately, correcting herself, 'had been reserved for you.'

'I don't smoke!' I spluttered, confused.

'You don't do anything naughty since Hugo, but appar-ently, it's high time you did. Apparently it's *your turn*. And I'm to stand down. Your need is greater. Well, good luck with that. I'm off to start work. Can't sit here nattering all day, I've got a gallery to fill.'

And with that she went into the cottage to collect her

easel and paints, leaving me staring after her, my mouth open. A moment later she came out and stalked back past us. She marched down the path that led towards the cliffs, rucksack on her back, easel under arm, canvas in hand.

'What on *earth* was that all about?' I exclaimed.

'Oh, don't worry about her,' Babs said airily, waving her ciggie in the air. 'She's sexually frustrated. I know the signs. Comes out in temper.'

'Yes, but—'

'She needs to get laid,' she said firmly. She narrowed her eyes at Celia's departing back. 'Callum Murray's just left his wife. He's awfully good fun.'

I snorted. 'Callum Murray? Celia's a sophisticated London girl with an important exhibition coming up. She's not looking for a bunk-up with a local farmer – Callum's got straw between his teeth. And anyway, I think she's rather set her cap at Ted.'

Babs took a long, thoughtful drag of her cigarette. Blew it out in a thin blue line. 'Yes, but Ted may be otherwise engaged.'

Later that morning, as I waited for Roger in the gunroom, I reflected that Cornwall did rather have this effect on people. It brought out the holiday spirit, even if you lived here, and with that came frivolous concerns like holiday romances and ridiculous crushes. The first of which, Celia, if I remembered, had had on Babs. Now they seemed to be sniping at one another. I sighed. Ah well, she'd settle down. She'd soon realize tedious normal life went on down here just the same as it did everywhere, even if one was ambushed by glorious views at every turn and the sound of the waves crashing on the sand, which got the old hormones going. In the fifties, apparently, film directors would cut to pounding surf to suggest an orgasm. I gazed out of the gunroom window trying to remember when I'd last had one of those. The huge cedar tree on the lawn spread its green skirts and cast a dark shadow across my thoughts. But not enough to obscure the view beyond. The banks of shocking pink rhododendron bushes gave way to a strip of shimmering turquoise water. I smiled. Always there in the distance. Always a glimpse. More so in Cornwall than anywhere else. Always hope.

Making their way towards that very same vista across the lawn this morning, right on cue, as if that same, unseen fifties director had whispered 'action', came a party of attractive specimens to grace it. The twins were first, in shorts and T-shirts, blond, skinny and brown. Theo was keeping a ball in the air with a plastic bat, and Ibby was maintaining a regular skip beside him, so that although he ran ahead in between batting he dropped the ball a lot and she steadily skipped past. They were followed by Christina, a beach bag swinging from her hand, the habitual jeans replaced by utilitarian shorts and bog-standard flip-flops. Quite long, those white shorts. Big side pockets. Not my style, but there you go. In contrast, Janey, behind her with Tommy, was certainly not foregoing her pink lippy and gold sandals, and was wearing a very fetching navy mini skirt together with a red polka dot bikini top. Beside her, Christina looked . . . well, a bit frumpy, I realized with a start. Janey wasn't a mum, of course, that helped enormously, but all the same. Christina had lost that joie de vivre, that edge, that I remembered. It was as if Janey, in this particular little vignette, had stolen it. I watched her teasing Tommy, pretending to link arms but actually linking her leg around his so he very nearly fell over. I laughed as he stumbled, my voice echoing in this tall room.

He'd done very well, I thought as he mock-cuffed her hair: he was clearly very successful. He had that expensive, American look and had grown into quite an attractive, rangy man, albeit very much in the preppy Brooks Brothers mould, swaggering off in his predictable Ralph Lauren shorts and polo shirt to the beach. Not much he could do about his foul mouth, bad temper and red hair, though. I watched them disappear from view.

No Hugo, I realized. He must be working. Poor Hugo, he worked so hard, always had done. He was so conscientious, which was why it was deeply unfair for some outsider to criticize him, I thought, bristling with fury. What did he know about long office hours and City life? The intolerable conferences, the all-nighters sometimes. Peter told me they even had pods in the office now, so they could leave a meeting at two a.m., grab a few hours' sleep, then start again at seven. Oh, they were well paid for a reason. It certainly wasn't as relaxing as looking for plastic bottle tops in your shorts on the beach and getting all hot under the collar about – hello. Talk of the devil. Ted Fleming himself was approaching from the same direction the others had disappeared in, walking up from the beach to the house. But not in shorts or waders this time. He was wearing pale biscuit chinos, a blue shirt and had a leather folder under his arm. Ah, right. Clearly he was taking Hugo up on his offer of a meeting, which was interesting.

A few minutes later, the doorbell rang. Belinda was out, I'd seen her car leave as I arrived. I waited for Hugo's footsteps down the hall from the study. Roger's, even. The doorbell went again, so after some hesitation I walked slowly down the hall hoping someone would beat me to it. No such luck. As I opened the door, the surprise was on him, which at least gave me an advantage. I smiled, but didn't say anything, which I could tell wrong-footed him.

'Oh – er . . . I came to see Hugo.'

'Come in.' I stood aside. 'I'll see if he's in.'

'Right. Thanks.' He looked awkward and it occurred to me to wonder if he thought he'd offended the hired help yesterday, now in scruffy work clothes on door duty, and not some posh totty galloping through the surf.

'Oil see if Mr Bellingdon's about,' I said, giving it my best yokel brogue. 'If you'll jaast wait here . . .'

'Yes. Yes, of course.' He reddened, astonished. He'd heard me speak yesterday, and I could tell he was confused.

I didn't exactly tug my forelock but I shuffled off and gave it a bit of a limp. Round the corner I knocked on the study door. No answer. I popped my head round. Nope. Empty. Not a soul. As I came back, I heard a door slam and voices. Hugo and Roger were coming down the passageway towards the front door, from the kitchen. Roger was looking wicked and Hugo was rushing ahead, flustered.

'I am so sorry, Mr Fleming, to keep you waiting.' He hastened to shake his hand. 'But I had to locate my father. I knew Flora would be waiting for him, you see. Sorry, Flora, I've tracked him down for you.' He handed Roger over as one would a naughty child, or an unexploded bomb. 'Now, Mr Fleming, shall we go to my study?' Hugo extended an arm and led the way past us. 'See if we can iron this out.'

As they swept away to do business, I realized I now looked like the hired nurse, about to spend the day with my charge, a permanently bewildered senile father who habitually wandered off. Splendid.

'Sorry, my dear,' purred Roger, stroking an imaginary moustache like Terry Thomas. 'Got caught up in my aviary. The love birds are breeding and I was just sorting out their nesting boxes.'

'Is ten o'clock too early for you, Roger?' I asked, as we made our way to the gunroom. 'Make it half past?'

'No, no, it's perfect. Been up since six. It's just, well, I was thinking, my dear.' We went in and he hastened across to sit in his chair, in the wrong shirt and trousers, I noticed, but beggars can't be choosers. Getting him to change would take forever. 'Must we do it *every* day?'

I smiled. 'We're not doing it every day, Roger, we're pausing for Fridays and weekends. And it's only eight sittings.'

'Eight!' His shoulders sagged dramatically and he let his head droop theatrically. 'So *boring*! All I do is sit!' He really was like a small child.

'Well, you can listen to the radio—'

'Read the paper?'

'No, that would get in the way, but—'

'Watch the box? *Loose Women*? I like that Penny Lancaster. Feisty bird. I'd have a go.'

'It doesn't really work, Roger.' I'd been asked this before. 'The eyes go a bit glazed. It all looks a bit – day room at the loony bin.' I realized I became desperately un-PC in Roger's company.

He pouted. 'Only the eyes. You could pop those in later.'

I smiled. 'Tell you what, let's see how it goes and if you get a bit fidgety we'll make it a short morning, OK?'

He sighed. 'Righty-ho. You know best. Only it's dull, dull, *dull*.' He pouted glumly out of the window.

I suppressed a grin as I cleaned my brush, wondering how Belinda coped. Well, she didn't, Babs did, and she was like a child herself. I ignored him and painted on happily for a while, my sketch good, I realized, which was a relief. Indeed, I was really getting into Roger: really getting a feel for the breadth of his shoulders and the muscle that was evidently still there – after all, he'd once been a very fit man, could still chop logs all morning – and that all-weather look was still in his face. It wasn't all pouts and smiles. There was the great outdoors and an enquiring intelligence. A love of nature, too, particularly birds, which he'd always had, and that was in his eyes right now as he watched a sparrow-hawk sail across the sky and settle on a bough of the cedar tree. Marvellous. If he could just hold that look, that light, I'd be—

'Flora?'

'Hmm?'

'Fidgety.'

I paused. His eyes were wide and innocent.

'You did say . . .'

I sighed. Lowered my brush and looked at my watch. 'We've done precisely twenty minutes, Roger.'

'Harrumph.'

I carried on, ignoring him.

'Would you settle for an hour?' he asked.

'I'll settle for an hour and a half.'

He rolled his eyes but I knew I'd got a deal. I painted faster. If I could just get a bit more done I could take a photo and work from that for a bit, but I wasn't telling Roger that. And it wasn't something I generally did *instead* of sittings. It was as well as. I'd have to be firmer.

Luckily more birds had caught his eye through the window, because that special light had returned, but, when he sat up very straight and I glanced out, I realized it was of a different variety.

'Pretty girl,' purred Roger. Janey was coming back up the lawn from the beach in her bikini. I smiled and wondered if I could poke my head out and persuade her to linger, do a few cartwheels. I painted on.

'*Very* pretty girl,' he murmured. Out of the corner of my eye I realized she'd paused to look at her phone.

'And very nice, too,' I said.

'Isn't she?' he agreed quickly, instantly perking up. 'Smart as a whip. I like her enormously.'

'Me too. She's got wit.'

'That's New York for you, of course,' he told me confidingly. 'Sparky bunch.' He crossed his legs as he warmed to his subject, which was not ideal as it shifted everything about, but at least he was still here. 'Full of wisecracks and smart-alec remarks. I lived there, you know, for a bit.' I could sense a bit of misty-eyed reminiscing coming on, which didn't hurt. Better than a sulk. 'Back in the seventies. Surrounded by girls like Janey in the office. Up to here in fanny.' He pointed to his armpits.

'Roger . . .'

'Sorry. Can't say that these days. Back then you could, and get a smarter remark back. They'd whip you every time. Ha! One girl, Lauren, used to perch on my desk in a very tight skirt and stare at me for ages. Frightfully disconcerting. "What are you doing?" I'd say. "Roger, honey, one day, guys like you will be extinct. I'm getting an eyeful of an endangered species while I can." Ha!' He barked. 'Splendid! Ah look – she's off.'

Janey was popping her phone in her basket and sauntering on again. She suddenly saw us and waved. Came across to the open window.

'Look at you, for God's sake. Creating, while the rest of us can only gape in wonder. Am I disturbing?'

'Not at all, we've nearly finished.' I smiled. 'Roger's got ants in his pants.'

'Oh really?' She looked at him sternly in her bikini. She had a very full bosom and she folded her arms under it to swelling effect. His eyes shone. 'Well, you sit tight, Roger the Dodger. You're the one who's commissioning this portrait, right? How's Flora supposed to paint you if you're jumping around all over the shop? Ten more minutes,' she told him firmly, wagging her finger at him. 'Then I'll beat you again at tennis.' She gave him an enormous wink and sauntered off.

Roger sank back weakly in his chair, defeated. 'She's a goddess,' he whispered. 'I'm putty in her hands. But I'll beat her, don't you worry. Only lost by one game yesterday.' He gazed dreamily into space, a slight smile on his lips. I made the most of his haze.

We both came to at the same moment. The study door opened down the passageway. Muffled voices could be heard coming down the corridor. Roger stiffened. He sat up straight and cocked an ear, alert as a pointer.

'Bloody know-it-all,' he seethed. 'Coming up here and telling us how to run the show.'

'He's only trying to save the planet, Roger,' I said, playing devil's advocate.

'Oh, I'm aware of that. And I'm as environmentally conscious as they come. Scratch me and I'm very green. Why d'you think I maintain and replant all the hedgerows? Pick up litter on the beach — most mornings I'm down there bagging the stuff. And remember the tar? Remember that terrible oil spillage? The tanker? That Bulgarian bastard, illegally washing out his fuel tank at sea, releasing all that oil then steaming on to avoid charges in port?'

'I do.'

'Who was it who took a sample from the oil, eh? Got it analysed and traced it back to the country of origin. Even found out which tanker was responsible, not that the buggers did anything about it.'

I nodded. There was a more furious light to his eyes now, but a light nonetheless. I worked with it.

'Remember down on the beach that night, after Alvern Tremain had come running up to tell us? Woke us all up?'

I was silent. I did. And I remembered Roger instantly throwing on his clothes and running down.

'Tried to get Hugo to come.'

I worked on silently.

'He never did like the water.'

I didn't say anything. It had been a huge bone of contention, Hugo's lack of enthusiasm for anything aquatic. His fear, even, of the sea, whilst Roger practically lived in it. And I knew Roger had worked day and night during and after the spillage, whereas Hugo had . . . well, he'd manned the phones. Somebody had to. It was bedlam here. Coastguards, police, journalists, camera crews, and since Hugo hadn't gone down that night, I had, with Mum, Babs, Iris and all the locals. Even Belinda had been on the beach. And he'd looked after Peter. Somebody had to. Pointless both of us staying behind. And I was good in the water, and didn't mind it at night, either. I remembered being in a boat with Roger and Babs, just one light on the prow. How he'd reached right in and brought up a baby seal in his bare hands, covered in oil. I remembered how he'd actually cried. Sworn a lot, too, but cried, nonetheless, as we'd desperately tried to clear its airways, Babs crouched in the bottom, breathing into its nostrils as she tried to resuscitate it. Oh, they'd had their adult moments, those two. But Hugo had been good with the TV people, assuring them of no risk to the filtration plant, whereas Roger, tall and commanding and covered in tar and oil coming up from the beach, had just roared at them. Told them all to bugger off. As I'm sure Hugo was being good now, I thought. Polite. Diplomatic. Soothing. Roger's ear was still cocked and when he heard the front door shut, he gave a loud shout.

'*Hugo?*'

He shot me a defiant look. I lowered my brush resignedly. Hugo's head appeared around the door.

'Well?' Roger demanded.

'I've invited him to come to a board meeting. Let him see for himself.'

'What!'

'It was Tommy's idea,' he said, slightly sheepishly. We exchanged a glance as Roger fumed. Hugo shut the door.

Roger affected a high, silly voice. 'It was Tommy's idea,' he mimicked. 'Grrr . . . got no *bite*, that boy.'

He drummed his fingers furiously on the arm of the chair as I painted on. But after a moment he got to his feet.

'Right – that's it,' he declared. 'I've had enough.'

And out he marched.

11

Peter arrived by train a couple of days later and I went to Truro to meet him. Hard to describe my skippy excitement. Ridiculous, really. My son, who I could contact as much as I wanted, and who was good at responding although I deliberately didn't text him too much, so why the beaming smile? The jaunty gait? The truth was I didn't see nearly as much of him as I would have liked these days. For all the right reasons, obviously. He was off. Grown up. Independent. Exactly how it should be at seventeen – eighteen next month – having left school a matter of weeks ago. It was a good age, I reflected, as I watched the train pull in. Just clear of the awkward, adolescent, grunting stage – although Peter hadn't done too much of that – and heading towards the slightly loftier ground of further education, which in Peter's case meant knuckling down big time, hopefully with like-minded, similarly industrious souls. But Peter was no swot and I knew he'd also have time for some cricket, which he loved, and – I don't know, punting perhaps? May balls with pretty girls? Or had I swerved into *Brideshead* territory? Anyway, whatever it was they all did there, I was quite sure it would be on his agenda.

As the train came to a hissing halt before me, there was a pause, then the doors opened. The train was destined for Penzance, so only about a dozen or so people alighted. I saw him immediately, down at the far end of the platform. Tall – very tall – skinny, blond and so like his father. My hand shot instinctively into the air but I managed to resist shrieking: 'Darling!' Instead I walked slowly towards him and said it more quietly as he gave me a hug, towering over me, adding, 'Lovely to see you.'

'You too, Mum. And such a relief to get out of London – it's baking. Heaving, too, thousands of tourists.'

I smiled as we made for the exit. 'You sound like some jaded old businessman who's commuted for years.'

'I *feel* like it. God. Six weeks in that bank has shown me how the other half lives.'

'Enjoying it?' I asked with interest as we threaded our way through to the car park. I didn't really mind what Peter did as long as he was happy, but money was always useful and banking surely provided that.

'I'm not sure "enjoy" is quite the right word,' he said wryly. 'But it's interesting, if only from an anthropological angle. Some properly weird characters.'

'Oh really? You mean higher up? The chiefs, or the other Indians?'

'Mostly the other interns. The guy I'm paired with, right, has clearly modelled himself on Gordon Gekko. We're talking slicked-back hair, braces, a proper pin-striped suit, and he's already bought a briefcase which has probably got cigars in it. He's my age!'

'That won't do him any favours.'

'The whole thing is a bit like that Tom Cruise film, *The*

Firm, if I'm honest. Pizza arrives at your desk for lunch, supper even, and they get you a taxi home at some ridiculous hour, and there's a gym you can use, but I could tell it was frowned on when I met Adam for a drink at lunchtime. It's like they own you.'

I made a face. 'Sounds a bit soul-destroying to me.'

He threw his bag in the boot of the car. 'Yeah, maybe.'

I could tell he was a bit disappointed. It had been something of a coup to get a summer internship in the City, and Peter had had to jump through a few hoops and do tests and have interviews to get there. He hadn't expected to be anything other than pleased and excited at having completed it. We drove for a bit in silence.

'Well, you've got ages to decide yet, you haven't even started university.'

'Oh God, yes, I know.'

Peter liked things tied up, though. He liked a plan.

'Publishing, maybe?' I ventured. 'You've always loved reading and it's what you always intended to do?'

It was Peter's turn to make a face. 'Except that's the sublime to the ridiculous. There's no money in that, apparently. Adam's uncle is like, right at the top of some big publishing house and he earns jack shit. I've heard it's one for the chicks.'

My eyebrows shot up. 'Is it, now? Darling, for the first time in your life you're about to be educated with chicks. I think you'll find them a surprisingly brainy bunch.'

'And I think you'll find I was employing heavy irony there, Mum. Sorry I didn't create the quotation marks in the air to alert you.' He grinned. 'Trust me, I've met plenty of ball-crushing girls.'

'Ah. Right. Too slow.'

'Just a bit.'

Peter wasn't remotely sexist, I knew, but nonetheless, it was also the right time to leave that school, I reflected. I'd noticed his tone had become – not arrogant, but, well, more confident. Sandy, who lived next door to us in Fulham, had raised her eyebrows when I'd mentioned this and said: 'And Jamie isn't?' Jamie, her son, the same age as Peter and a great friend since toddler-hood, was at the local comprehensive and positively swaggered with confidence. Charm, too, I thought, although Sandy would groan if I said it. 'It's got nothing to do with the school, Flora, or his advantages; it's the age they've been born into. I call it The Age of Entitlement. Poor buggers. They'll get the shock of their lives, soon, when the real world hits them.'

It had already hit Peter, I thought with some amusement. Six weeks in an office and he was world-weary already.

'So what's the form?' Peter turned to me, eyes shining. Living in the moment as the Entitled Age did, he'd already completely forgotten the office. The undulating green hills we'd plunged into told him where he was heading and there was even a flash of blue in the distance. That was enough. 'I can't wait to have a swim. How is everyone?'

I could tell he'd deliberately couched it as if this was a perfectly normal situation. As if we did this all the time, he and I, visiting his grandparents. My heart lurched for what he'd never had: for what he was pretending he had now.

I pretended along with him, and gave him a – hopefully – light-hearted appraisal of everyone present, but majored on his grandfather, whom he adored, and who was always good value.

Peter guffawed, bent double in his seat with delight. 'God, I can just imagine him – Grandpa's never sat still for two minutes! What possessed him to do it?'

'Your grandmother,' I said archly, but hopefully not too tartly.

'Ah.' He grinned. 'Well, I'll get the Wayfarer out tomorrow. You won't see him for dust.'

'Do not!' I said, horrified. 'I mean do, by all means, but don't tell him! I'll never *see* him again.'

'Or the Laser. I'll crew, he'll helm, just like the old days.'

'Seriously, Peter, if you do that there'll be the most tremendous bust-up and Granny will be livid and I'll lose this effing commission.' I raked a hand through my hair.

'Relax.' He laughed. 'I'm joking.' He grinned out of the window. 'A bit.'

I smiled over the wheel as we drove on through the lanes that led to Trewarren and, as the scenery opened up and the sun came out, Peter turned up a song we both liked on the radio, Talking Heads. I sang along at the top of my voice which I complained children these days never did, too cool, and he made a mock horrified face. We laughed. God, it was good to see him.

'How long are you staying?' I asked casually.

'Not sure,' he said equally casually back, and I knew he was thinking: I'll see how it goes.

'There's this festival in Wales . . .'

'Oh yes, you said . . .'

'If I can be arsed.'

'Who's going?'

'Alex, Adam, Sam, the usual.'

'I haven't met Adam?'

'Oh no, he's a friend of Sam's. Different school.'

'Ah.'

There was a silence.

'So . . . what is the form, Mum?'

'What d'you mean?' But I knew what he meant. And he'd asked earlier, when we'd set off, but I'd dodged it and moved swiftly on to his grandfather's idiosyncrasies.

'How's this all panning out?'

I licked my lips. We were pulling into the long wooded front drive now, not the way I'd approached with Celia. It was a mile in length, and darkness fell as we plunged through the trees, then suddenly rose again, surrounded by banks of glossy pink rhododendron bushes, livid flashes of fuchsia, blush and white.

'Well, we all had lunch together on the first day . . .'

'Excellent,' he looked at me admiringly.

'But other than that,' I said quickly, 'I just – you know – pop in to paint. But Granny has asked Celia and me to supper tonight.'

'And you're coming?'

'Yes. We're coming.'

He smiled. 'Well done, Mum.'

I didn't answer. Couldn't really. My throat felt a bit blocked. This had been Peter's dream since he was a small boy: for his parents to get on properly, not just present a united front at school, and I selfishly hadn't given it to him. Until now. It's not much to ask, is it? But I'd found it a lot. Peter was fiercely loyal to me, I knew that, and protective of my feelings, so to have me come here, of my own volition, with no persuading from him, in the house he liked to visit most of all, and to which he would bring friends to sail and swim, was very special. It occurred to me then, as if I'm honest it had done before, that of course Josie didn't necessarily want to go on holiday with her ex-husband, that she wasn't thinking of herself. She was bigger than that.

And I'd made up my mind to be more like that: had made a conscious decision yesterday, actually, just before, coincidentally, Belinda had intercepted me in the hall – minus the knives, I was relieved to notice – and after I'd had a slightly more successful session with Roger. The test match had started, glory be, and the radio provided a good few hours of calm. She'd breathlessly presented me with the invitation for tonight's supper with all her gushing generosity, like a well-behaved child with a special treat to share.

'We would so love it, Roger and I, if you would join us, Flora.' She always said that. Roger and I. Like the Queen. My husband and I. 'Everyone would love it, honestly.'

It was as if she'd canvassed opinion. Said at lunch, her face concerned and caring: 'Now, listen, everyone. I feel we *have* to invite Flora and her friend. It would be too awkward not to, with Peter here.'

Grave nods round the table as the family Did The Right Thing. I'm probably wrong. Not about Belinda, but about the rest. Hugo had always encouraged my presence and Christina had only recently sent me a Paperless Post invite with a little note attached, explaining there were loads of people coming – i.e. not too stressful, well diluted – and that it was a barbecue – i.e. relaxed. She hoped I'd come. I hadn't.

Peter and I had even argued about it. 'Move *on*, Mum. Jesus, it was fifteen bloody years ago! God, you might even meet someone there.'

'I do meet people. And anyway, there's Tim and Rupert—'

'You hide behind Tim and Rupert. Tim's a friend and he's always been just that, and Rupert is fun but too weird to have a relationship with, you told me that.'

Where had I heard all this before? Ah yes, Celia. I'd been tight-lipped. Said nothing.

As we crested the brow of the hill now and swept into the front drive, I stopped the car on the far side of the fountain, away from the front door. I turned and gave him a wide smile.

'I'm going to drop you here, darling. See you later.'

'Yeah, yeah, good plan.' Excited eyes were on the house now, delighted to be here, on a beautiful day. The sea was glistening enticingly and he was itching to get in it. He leaned across and gave me a fleeting kiss, then got out and went round to the boot for his bag. As he went to go inside, though, he remembered. Turned.

'Oh – Granny A sends her love.'

'Oh *Peter*!' I chided him.

He grinned sheepishly. 'Yeah, sorry, I forgot. I had lunch with her the other day.'

'What a time to tell me! Forty minutes in the car!'

The front door had already opened, been flung wide, and Granny B – you can imagine how that went down, hence it staying Peter's and my private joke – was already hastening down the steps in another floaty floral number, arms outstretched. 'Darling!'

Peter grinned and slouched towards her, submitting to his grandmother's embrace. But as she hugged him, over his shoulder, she had the grace to lift her hand in greeting. I raised mine back. Then they went inside and I drove away. Strangely, I felt happier than I had done for some considerable time.

12

Supper that evening was redolent of an al fresco Mediterranean affair, certainly in respect of the balmy temperature and the setting, if not the detail. Outside on the terrace a long table had been beautifully laid with white linen, crystal and silver. No IKEA cutlery and cork mats for Belinda; everything was always done properly. Too properly, Babs would say.

'It's as if she's got the rulebook out, it betrays her social insecurity.' She said the truly grand didn't bother about things like that – and by that she meant herself; Babs' grandfather had been an earl. She said they had the confidence to shove whatever they liked on their table, and that all Belinda's relentless white linen and towels reminded her of the Ritz, which only a desperate arriviste would think was the height of good taste. Sprays of white jasmine in little glass vases tumbled down the middle of the table and long beeswax candles were alight in proper silver candelabra from the dining room. I thought it looked lovely. Most would say she'd made an effort on her grandson's first night, and only the most cynical and curmudgeonly would find fault, but, as we made our way to the table from where we'd gathered further along the terrace for drinks, I could see Babs' grinning face.

Knowing I was nervous, I'd determined not to drink too much. I'd only sipped the champagne I'd been handed by one of Belinda's apron-clad flunkies – oh yes, this was catered – so I still had a pretty full glass as we made our way to the table. I was placed between Roger and Tommy, which could have been worse, I decided. I absolutely wouldn't have wanted Hugo beside me, and Peter and Janey were opposite, which couldn't have been better. My son's delighted face at this truly extraordinary family gathering shone like a beacon above his pink Ralph Lauren shirt and once again, I felt a lurch of shame at not having provided him with more delight sooner. Better late than never, I decided, as I smiled up at Roger, who'd pulled my chair out for me. Some divorced couples didn't speak until a child got married, and even then avoided each other at the wedding. At least I'd made it before that.

Roger beamed and chatted away beside me, with the occasional hand pat, and I knew he was going out of his way to make me feel at home. And he was so easy. I could listen to his increasingly outrageous anecdotes and patter all night, and smile and nod in the right places, even properly laughing. He could be very amusing. Belinda, happily, was at the far end of the table, but as we'd sat down she'd bustled round to assure me, in a confidential tone, that she was happy on the end because she'd had a long chat with her grandson earlier, which if I'm being churlish, suggested she was making a huge sacrifice by letting him sit next to Janey. Janey, who couldn't help but overhear, had felt obliged to say: 'Oh – surely you'd like to sit next to your grandson? I'll sit on the end, really.'

'No, no!' Belinda had fluttered away to her seat, hands waving, as if no amount of persuasion would make her change her mind, taking the martyr's crown with her. Just as Roger went out of his way to make people feel comfortable, Belinda went out of her way to do the opposite, and, before she'd gone, she'd touched Janey's arm with her fingertips, bestowing on her that kind, selfless smile.

Janey obviously didn't take shit from anyone, though. Whilst Roger was busy chatting to Christina on his other side, she'd lowered her voice and said to me: 'I'm sure your boy's delightful, Flora, but frankly I don't give a damn who I sit next to. Don't do *me* any favours, Mrs B.'

I gave a snort of laughter and was then horrified to see Belinda's back stiffen before she sat down.

'She hates you calling her that,' I told her as we took our seats. And then I leaned across and quietly told her about the grannys' names.

'Oh, *irresistible*,' Janey agreed under her breath. 'And I know she hates it, incidentally – she keeps saying, "*Do* call me Belinda." But the thing is, when we arrived, she originally introduced herself as Mrs Bellingdon, wafting into the drawing room where she'd kept us waiting for ten minutes, hand outstretched. Kind of putting me in my place, if you know what I mean—'

'I do.'

'And then after a couple of days she got all confidential and cosy and said, "Call me Belinda." Like I'd passed some sort of test. So I kicked off with the Mrs Bs. When she tries to insist, I contrive to look terribly confused, and

163

say my mother would not approve of that, and that my brothers still call my father sir, like we're some kind of Waspy, Westport family. She gets in a hell of a fluster.'

I grinned, pleased Janey had Belinda's measure. I watched Janey now as she chatted with Peter, who looked like all his Christmases had come at once, his face the same colour as his shirt. Janey talked to everyone like this, of course, making them feel special and important, which was such a gift, but he was enjoying every minute of this beautiful, charismatic young woman's company and his moment in the sunshine. Celia caught my eye and we grinned before she turned to Hugo. Ah, right. I'd grill her later. As Janey asked Peter what he was up to, Roger overheard him bemoaning his lack of a gap year.

'Gap year?' he roared. 'Whoever invented the bloody things should be shot! Only used to happen when you sat an Oxbridge exam, and even then it was only nine months. Certainly didn't involve bungee jumping in Thailand. Absurd!'

'Except you did actually go to the South Seas, Pa,' Hugo reminded him with a smile.

'Yes,' he conceded, 'but only when I'd worked in the family business for six months. *And I paid for it.* My father was none too pleased when I got back.'

'Why?' asked Peter.

'I'd sent him a telegram. *Having the most splendid time. Coming back Wed.* He thought I'd got married.'

'Oh!'

'Met me off the boat. Purple faced. "Well?" he bellowed. "Where is she?"'

'God, how awful, Grandpa! Imagine if she'd been there?'

Roger blinked into space, considering. 'Yes. Yes, never thought of that,' he mused.

'He must have been delighted when you introduced him to Belinda, then?' Janey said naughtily.

Roger paused. 'Absolutely. Yes, he was.'

But the pause had escaped no one. Janey shot me a wink. 'I'll bet Mrs B had all the men in the county after her, didn't she, Roger?'

I held my breath. We all inadvertently glanced down at Belinda, who, rather hot, her nose red and shiny, was not looking her best. I saw Tommy flash Janey a warning frown.

'Naturally she did!' Roger agreed gallantly, quicker off the mark this time. 'As I'm sure you do, my dear!' He leaned across the table. 'In New York? Like flies to the honeypot?'

'No flies on me, Rog. I swat them away pretty sharpish, I can tell you.'

'I bet you do!' declared Roger, delighted.

Peter was intrigued. 'Is that where you work, then? New York?'

Janey turned to him properly, and as she chatted away about Manhattan, filling him in on all the Big Apple had to offer, I saw Peter's colour rise again and his eyes light up.

'Janey's working her magic,' murmured Tommy beside me.

I turned to him with a smile, prepared to be civil to anyone on this rather momentous evening.

'He can't believe his luck. She's a lovely girl, Tommy.'

He mock-blanched, holding the edge of the table. 'Said like I'm undeserving!'

'No, I just meant—'

'Relax, I'm kidding. She's not mine, anyway.'

'Not your girl? But I thought—'

'No, you assumed. Janey's an old friend. Oh, we had a brief liaison some years ago.'

'Ah. She dumped you.'

'A gentleman's code means I'm not at liberty to comment. But let's just say our hearts weren't in it. She's too sparky for me.'

'Being sparky yourself?'

'Sure, maybe. They certainly flew. But it was pretty great while it lasted.' His eyes twinkled at me as he raised his glass.

'I'm sure it was.' I sighed. Rolled my eyes despairingly. 'I'm afraid your reputation goes before you, Tommy. I gather there's no hope. You really are a marvellous role model for your godson.'

Tommy threw back his head and laughed. 'Well, good! I like to think our little lunches in London are instructive!'

I never quizzed Peter when he returned from meeting Tommy when he was over, looking flushed and rather pleased with himself, having been somewhere rather smart and grown-up. I looked into Tommy's grinning, irresponsible face now and wondered just how many girls had succumbed to his rather too obvious charms. It pained me, on behalf of the sisterhood, to believe it might be plenty. Tommy played the-boy-can't-help-it card beautifully, but there would surely come a time when it would become a bit worn at the edges? When perhaps, literally overnight, he might wake up in yet another strange bed, transformed inexorably from lovable rogue to seedy old dog? Happily it was not my problem.

'And how are your parents?' I ventured politely, feeling we'd wandered too far into Tommy's specialist subject and deliberately putting us on more formal ground. Tommy's parents had visited London when Hugo and I were first married and we'd gone to Rules for lunch with them. They'd been surprisingly delightful. Very much the sort of Westport family Janey had been describing earlier.

'Dad died,' Tommy said shortly. 'Two years ago.'

'Oh. I'm sorry.' I was. 'He was a lovely man.'

I remembered his kindness to me that lunch: telling Hugo what a lucky man he was as he beamed across the table at me, asking after Peter, who was nine months old at the time. His wife, Lillian, too. So gracious, generous and intelligent, a painter herself. I recalled Tommy's delighted eyes on me at that meal, knowing he'd caught me out: knowing I was thinking, how can a man like that have parents like these? When his mother had asked shyly, when the men were talking, if she could possibly see my work, I'd found myself going round to sit next to her. I'd shown her bits of my portfolio, which I'd had with me because I'd been on my way to a commission. She'd admired them, but properly. Critically. Agreeing when I'd pointed out flaws, which most people didn't. She'd had a few postcards made up of her own work, beautiful tulips, mostly overblown, very close-up. When I'd genuinely enthused about them, she'd made a face and said how well paintings always photographed, which was true. Tommy's father overheard and broke off his conversation to disagree.

'They're heavenly, Flora,' he assured me. 'Everyone says so, and those postcards don't do them justice. Huge great canvases, they are, very powerful. But can I get her to exhibit? Not a chance.'

'Oh, but you don't know anything, Michael,' Lillian had

laughed, quickly tucking her postcards away. 'You'd like anything I did, and so would my friends. I need an object-ive, professional eye, like Flora's.'

She'd come alone to my studio the following day and I rarely let anyone do that. I think I was happy to do it because she was a fellow artist and also she was going back to America. But maybe it was something else. Maybe I'd spotted something sympathetic within her; something deep and quiet.

'She's painting like fury,' said Tommy, as if reading my thoughts. 'All day, every day. And my sisters have been amazing. Kit-Kat, the eldest, has a cottage in her garden, a converted boathouse. She's trying to get Mom to move in there, but she won't. She says she's not done parenting yet. Doesn't want to be in the granny annex.'

'That'll be you,' I told him.

'Oh sure, the baby she despairs of.' He grinned and reached cheerfully for his glass. 'Keeps her on her toes.' He winked. 'She's happy about that. I'm doing everyone a favour.'

'I'm sure you are. Give her my love.'

'I will do. She liked you.'

I knew this to be true, but nonetheless, a genuine compliment like this was rare and I glanced up at him, surprised.

'And yours?' he said smoothly, moving on.

I'd forgotten he'd met Mum and it momentarily wrong-footed me. Suddenly, we were seventeen years old again, back in my family home, Mum making tea for him and Hugo when he'd come to apologize after the hunt. I real-ized he'd have met her at our wedding, too.

'Oh – she's fine. Really well. But actually, someone's seen her far more recently than me.' I leaned across. 'Peter, how was Granny?'

My interruption gave Janey an opportunity to turn to Hugo on her other side. Peter wasn't quite old enough to realize he was monopolizing her, and Janey shot me a smile as she turned. Belinda had also broken off on hearing what she thought was her name. She beamed eagerly and expectantly down the table.

'Really well,' Peter replied. 'She's got lots of students, so that's good. But London's the pits at the moment, it's so hot. I thought she might be able to come down here?' He turned to his other grandmother.

'Oh, *your* mother, Flora,' said Belinda. 'I heard "Granny". Oh, I *am* glad she's busy, such a worry for you, making ends meet. Yes, well, Peter, if your mother and her friend could share—'

'I'm sure she's far too busy,' I said quickly. I'd known Peter had meant to stay here, in the house, and that Belinda hadn't even entertained it. And 'your friend' again, not 'Celia'. I felt myself burn.

'Ah, your lovely ma!' Roger roared in, oblivious. 'Now she really *did* get the county buzzing. Everyone was mad for her – what a beauty! Did you ever meet her, Tommy?'

'I did.'

'Sweetest, kindest thing, too, not a bad bone. Just like you, my dear.' He squeezed my shoulders and I actually wanted to snog him. *God*, Roger was nice. And *God*, Belinda was a cow. I saw Celia looking at me, a half-smile on her face, her eyes saying, *I don't give a toss what she calls me, Flora, calm down.* So I did. Deep breaths. Why was my mother a worry, why? She wasn't. Never had been. She was relentlessly cheerful and capable and only ever thought about other people.

Tommy got to his feet and, leaning around the table, topped up all the wine glasses. Something about his arm, moving between us, drew a convenient veil. I'm not sure if he did it deliberately, but I was grateful nonetheless.

'So are you over here on business?' I asked him, as he sat down. I knew normal conversation would help. That I was too quick to overreact.

'A bit,' he said shortly. 'But not my business.'

'Oh, OK.'

He didn't say any more and I was aware he was being cagey. As one often does when one's been slightly snubbed, or at least I do, I bit back.

'Shona's on the television these days, you know,' I said casually, knowing her name would make him sit up.

'Yeah, I know. I saw her the other day.'

'What – doing the news?'

'No, opening the fête.'

'Oh, right, you mean it was on telly?'

'No, I went to the fête.'

'Why?'

'To see Shona.'

I stared in astonishment as he calmly carried on eating his lemon tart. A smile tugged at his mouth.

'Cream?'

'What?' He was offering me a jug. 'Oh, no thanks.' I blinked, amazed. 'Why did you go to see Shona?'

'Why not?'

'Well – do you keep in touch?' I blustered.

'Oh yeah. All the time. Don't you?'

My mouth was hanging open. 'But – since when?'

'I don't know. Since way back.'

'She never said!'

'So do *you* keep in touch?'

'Not enough,' I admitted. 'And when we do, it's mostly emails. And I suppose it's mostly about ourselves.'

'Exactly.' He was grinning now. 'Why would she mention me?' His eyes widened innocently. He was so pleased with himself it was infuriating. 'But you've seen her since you've been down here, right?' He adopted a serious tone. Oh, he was enjoying this enormously.

'Well, no, I've only been here a few days.'

'Oh, OK.' He contrived to look sad. 'A week, maybe. But you know best.'

'And I'm working, for God's sake! Unlike you!' My voice must have carried.

'Is there a problem, Flora?' Belinda's voice cut in like ice, from the other end of the table.

'No – no, of course not,' I flustered, horrified.

'I'm teasing her, Mrs B,' Tommy said smoothly.

'Oh, Tommy, not you, too. You *know* it's Belinda!'

'Course I do, ma'am.'

She wasn't sure how to take this, but I could tell she preferred it.

'Well, come along, then,' she said decisively, at this pause in the conversation. She dabbed her mouth with her napkin and pushed her chair back. 'I think we've all been sitting here long enough. And it's getting chilly. I tried to catch a few eyes earlier,' she murmured reprovingly. 'We'll take our coffee inside. Leave the men to their port.'

She rose like the queen and I immediately rose too, as did Christina beside her. But Celia and Janey's eyes were huge. Celia glanced at me, and after a moment's hesitation, slowly got to her feet. Janey stayed put.

'I'd like some port, too, if I may,' she said pleasantly. I saw Celia's bottom itching to rocket down again, but I shot her a look.

There was a silence. Then: 'Of course,' said Belinda quietly. But there was steel in her tone.

Without further ado she drifted away from the table, hands trailing behind her. She sailed majestically through the open French doors to the drawing room. Her female disciples followed mutely in her wake. Judas sat firmly at the table.

In front of the fireplace, on a vast, creamy, fringed stool, a waitress, as if by magic, was just setting a tray of coffee, a pot of mint tea, and a plate of home-made truffles. She glanced nervously at Belinda who nodded curtly, still clearly put out. Then she disappeared.

We sat down on the edge of the sofas and quietly helped ourselves to coffee. Belinda wrinkled her nose. At length, she spoke. 'Funny little thing, isn't she?' she said softly. She took a sip from her tiny cup.

'Who?' Celia asked innocently.

'The American girl.'

There was a silence. Celia set her cup down in her saucer and looked Belinda in the eye. 'I was always taught it was impolite to discuss other guests so I couldn't possibly comment. Where might I powder my nose, Mrs Bellingdon?'

Belinda stared at her, astounded. 'Well, I—' Then she

gathered herself. Sat up straight. 'Down the corridor,' she said tartly. 'Second on the left.'

'Thank you.' Celia rose and disappeared.

Belinda looked most put out. She gathered her pink pashmina shawl closer around her shoulders. '*Well*,' she said at length. She shuddered ostentatiously. But then abruptly, her face puckered. Ridiculously, I found myself feeling sorry for her. I sank into my coffee. When I looked up, Christina's eyes were upon me. She looked upset, too. We exchanged knowing looks and drank our coffee. We had a great deal in common, Christina and I. We obviously had Hugo, but more pertinently, we had Belinda.

13

'She's insufferable,' Celia told me later as we walked home. 'It had to be done.'

'But we're *guests*, Cele. It makes it awkward, don't you see?'

'Well, I won't be, again. A guest. And we're renting the cottage so, no, not really. I don't care if I offend her.'

'We're renting the cottage for a pittance, nothing like the usual rent, and only because I insisted.' She didn't answer and we walked along in silence. At length, I sighed. 'Oh God, d'you know what? You're right. She's a bloody nightmare. And I don't want to talk about Belinda, anyway.'

'Quite. Let's not give her the pleasure. She thinks the world revolves around her as it is.'

'How did you get on with Hugo?'

She paused. We were picking our way along the rutted clay track towards the sea in the dark and she bent to get a stone out of her shoe, but I knew she was considering her words. She straightened up. 'Well, I'm loath to say it, but he's a very nice man.'

I glowed beside her in the dark, the terrible, shining beam of true love for a false god. 'I knew you'd say that. If you were honest. Knew you couldn't possibly say otherwise.'

Celia hadn't really met Hugo before, apart from at the odd school play of Peter's. She'd arrived in my life just after he'd departed, when I'd put an ad in the *Art Newspaper* offering half a studio for rent, to an artist who kept to themselves. I'd even said that. I hadn't wanted to talk. I had sitters, obviously, so a chatterer wouldn't have worked, but I didn't have the words, at the time. A garrulous, Bluebeard the Pirate type with copious facial hair, a booming voice and no doubt canvases as big as his personality had arrived, and then Celia, who painted small, delicate pictures back then, and who, unbeknownst to me, had just split up with her boyfriend, had a row with her parents who wanted her to be a lawyer, and didn't want to talk either. We'd painted in companionable silence for weeks, and she never asked about the father of the child I appeared to have: the one that had gone by the time she arrived, but appeared at about four o'clock each day when Mum brought him back.

My mother sold the house in Cornwall immediately when Hugo left me. She'd rented at first in London, while she looked, then bought a flat a few roads down from me. I didn't argue with her. Didn't beg her not to come, to stay where she'd grown up, with her friends, her work, insist I was fine, because I knew she wanted to come and would be deeply unhappy if she didn't. Love is like that. And Celia didn't comment on the juggling act we performed that first year as the phone would ring and I'd shoot off to meet Mum somewhere, to take Peter to the park while she taught for an hour, then dash back to the studio. I knew I had to paint for my sanity and my mother knew that, too, and enabled me to do it. It was all that kept me from pills or drink, or whatever people normally did. When Peter went to bed I'd start again, often into the small hours. Sandy, next door, who's a writer, says the same. Says it saves a fortune on therapy.

I also wanted to be entirely financially independent from the Bellingdons. The flat I couldn't do much about, nor later the school fees, but despite Hugo's insistence – and Roger and Belinda's, too – I took no maintenance for Peter, and nothing for myself. Roger had even made a surprise visit one day, begging me to accept a handsome sum, but I wouldn't. I was selling paintings, I told him, portraits. I showed them to him in my studio, some already framed, waiting to be collected, already paid for. I could tell he was impressed. He even knew one of the generals I'd done recently. He'd gone off to his club, and then home on the train from Paddington, slightly appeased, but still fussed about the situation.

Gradually, of course, Celia and I had talked. And eventually, I told her everything, as she did me. About her overbearing parents – both professors – her excellent grades, her degree from Cambridge and their horror that all she wanted to do was paint. At least I'd never had any opposition to my career of choice. Instead, I told her about my dad, and then about Hugo. How it had felt to be bereaved all over again. Back then she hadn't slandered him at all, knowing I was far too fragile; she just listened. Later, of course, being Celia, she'd been more expansive on the morals of a man who could persuade his pregnant girlfriend to marry him and then abandon her with the baby, and I knew some of the attraction of coming down here had been to size up this mythical, demonic creature in the flesh. This was some admission, then. No wonder she'd paused before answering.

'I knew you couldn't fail,' I told her, trying to keep the smugness from my voice. It vindicated my enduring love, you see, all these years. Made sense of my tremendous emotional hiatus. A peculiar warmth and light radiated through me. I was so grateful for her endorsement. I walked quietly beside her in the dark, waiting for her to go on. Willing her to elaborate and exonerate me.

'He has Peter's gentleness, which is lovely, and that same endearing way of never quite looking at you, but shyly asking all the right questions. And not in a practised, nosy way, just in a genuinely interested way.'

'I know.'

'I even found myself talking about my mother's obsession with antiques, how weird is that? How she has to polish everything lovingly every day, as if with every layer of polish she adds more value. How everything in her life is a means to an end, never mind how you get there.'

'What did he say?'

'He said materialism often got confused with joy, and he thought it was because some people lacked hope. He said he'd been guilty of it a bit himself. I said: "That's true. My mother is the enemy of hope."'

'Oh, you went deep.'

'I suppose we did.'

'Did you tell him about Edward?'

'A bit.' She scratched inside her wrist where she had a bit of eczema. 'Yes, OK, a lot,' she conceded. 'And he didn't even ask. I don't know why I did.'

'What did he say?'

'He said sex isn't everything.'

I stopped still. 'Oh, you told him about *that*.'

She shrugged. 'You know me.'

We walked on in silence. Our feet moved in synchrony for a bit. Sex isn't everything. Interesting. Illuminating, even, in view of our own sex life.

'But the point is,' she went on, 'we talked about me, and I'd so wanted to find out more about him.' I gave this a knowing smile in the dark. 'By the time I realized I'd monopolized the conversation and tried to talk about him, Janey had joined us.' She made a face. 'Sorry about that.'

I laughed. 'Oh, I wasn't hoping you'd glean anything, I'm just so pleased you liked him. I'm so tired of trying to explain my addiction.'

'Yes, well it explains it, but it doesn't justify it.'

I didn't comment. Didn't want to ruin anything by arguing. I liked what I had, what she'd given me. It was enough. I'd enjoy it later, in bed. We walked on.

'His relationship with Belinda is weird, though,' she said. 'It's as if he's always trying to protect her, to stop everyone from seeing what she really is. He constantly reimagines her.'

'Yes, I know.' Celia had cottoned on to this family remarkably quickly.

'She told Christina, at drinks, for example, that Theo might like a dog, he seemed so attached to Truffle. And Christina said unfortunately she was allergic to them – which, let's face it, Belinda must have known – and so Belinda suggested a cat. Christina said awkwardly that she wasn't mad about them and Belinda said: "Nonsense, everyone loves a kitten, Theo would adore it."

Hugo stepped in smiling and said the thing was, Belinda couldn't imagine anyone's home without a pet, which makes her sound lovely and cosy, when in fact she was twisting Christina's arm.'

'I know.'

I did know. I knew all about the things Belinda gently suggested. And the way Hugo explained them, spinning them to something good. A couple of years ago she'd decided Peter needed a hobby, and although he loved boats we rarely got to the sea. So she sent a very expensive set of golf clubs to his school.

'Really kind of Granny,' Peter had said anxiously when he'd rung me, 'but when will I use them? I'm up to here with revision. And there's the school play . . .'

'Well quite. Don't worry, darling. Perhaps keep them in Cornwall for the holidays?'

'Yes, perhaps. Not really my thing, though. I'd rather sail. And she did ask, last time I was down there, if I'd like to take it up, and I said no, I wasn't interested. I think I even said it was boring.'

'Right.' I swallowed hard.

Peter had never used the clubs, but had then felt bad when his grandmother asked, so he'd said, occasionally. She'd written and asked which courses he went to. He hadn't replied and she'd sent another letter saying she was rather disappointed in him. I'd had to leave the room when Peter told me in case I threw my mug of tea against the wall. Hugo had ironed it out as usual and used the clubs himself, saying he'd always wanted to take it up.

'Cele, I think I'm going to pop down to the beach for a bit.' I looked up at her in the moonlight. We'd reached the cottage gate by now, were about to go up the path. 'I'll see you in the morning.'

It was a beautiful warm night and not that late. I saw her face light up at the idea. But then she saw mine and knew at once.

'Good shout. I'll go up. It's about time I had an early night.'

We hugged and I walked on. Further on, the track ended as it met the dunes. As I picked my way through the cold sand, my feet sinking lower and lower with every step, sharp tufts of grass scratching my ankles, I thought, you see? She knew I wanted to be alone. No spiritual myopia for Celia. She was as clear-sighted as they come, unlike Belinda, who deliberately only saw what she wanted to see.

It was a clear night and the moon, almost full, and high above the sea, reflected a rippling white path towards me across the water. The tide was out so the beach was peppered with marooned boats, which I always thought looked peculiar, embarrassed to be so exposed, their muddy bottoms at wobbly angles, not bobbing brightly on the water as they would be in the morning. Small, seaweed-strewn rocks dogged my path but I knew this beach well, had played on it as a child, and I picked my way easily amongst them like the eight-year-old I'd once been. Back in those days the Bellingdons were a distinctly mythical family, and the house – I stopped and glanced back at it now, standing white, proud and isolated, high up on the cliff – had been emblematic of all that stately grandeur. We knew of parties on the lawns, tennis matches, croquet, and in my childish mind's eye I always had them in long Edwardian dresses.

As I gazed back now, I wondered if tonight's party had broken up. The lights strung above the terrace were still shining. Perhaps Janey, Tommy and Roger would still be drinking and chatting around the table, but Hugo and Christina would have gone up, I was sure. I saw them mounting the stairs companionably. Brushing their teeth, doing all the cosy, familiar things together. Reading for a bit, maybe. Then the lights would go out. Then what? *Sex isn't everything*. Would he squeeze her hand, murmur something soft, then roll over and go to sleep, as he had done with me?

I sat on a rock and drew up my knees, wrapping my arms around them. Then I allowed myself to indulge in something I very rarely did these days, but for which I felt Celia – the caustic, demanding Cele – had given me a green light. I had a proper think about Hugo. As I gazed up the path of the moon, I let him flood my mind, knowing, once the sluice gates had opened, he'd be there in glorious Technicolor. But for some reason my guilty pleasure wasn't entirely satisfactory. Because the thing was, the qualities Celia had complimented him on – his gentleness, his compassion, his ability to listen – suddenly became suspect. Because she'd also so neatly skewered his ability to remould his mother. The kindness and loyalty in those circumstances were misplaced, which suddenly put everything else at a skew, too. I also recalled him catching my eye as I talked to Tommy, in a considerate, caring way, making sure I was OK. Knowing Tommy wasn't my cup of tea. It was something I would normally have chewed salaciously over later, like a tasty bone. But the thing was, I really was OK. Was totally up to Tommy. Really didn't need him asking. So disorientated was I by my unfamiliar thought pattern, by my feeling that Celia's objective eye had cast a shadow she wasn't even aware of, that when a male voice rasped loudly in my ear behind me, I actually toppled right off my rock on to the sand.

'*Orright, my loverrr?*' had trumpeted behind me, at full volume.

I picked myself up from the sand and spun about, heart pounding. I was startled beyond belief. My eyes made out a shadowy figure looming over me, his back to the dunes. As I focused properly, and with the help of the moon, I realized it was Ted Fleming. He was grinning from ear to ear.

'What the *hell* . . . ?' I clutched my heart which was still hammering.

'Oh sorry. Did I startle you? I thought a traditional Cornish greeting would be just the ticket for a girl steeped in the dialect.'

I stared at him, flummoxed. Then my mind flew back to our little exchange in the hall the other day. The dawn began to come up. I nodded in acknowledgement. Smiled thinly. 'Ah. Right. Touché.' I notched up a point in the air to him with my finger. 'Well done you.'

He inclined his head in gracious acceptance of his victory, still grinning.

'Tell me,' I asked at length when I'd composed myself. 'Do you conservationists never sleep? Is your cause so urgent and worthy that you have to comb the beach all night?'

'You make that sound like a bad thing. Easy to poke fun at good causes, of course.'

I folded my arms. 'I just wish they were done with a little more joy, that's all.'

'Really?' His eyes widened, theatrically stunned. 'What – *all* worthy causes? Dropping aid from planes in Ethiopia whilst singing a merry song? Handing out medical supplies in Aleppo and dancing the hornpipe?'

I managed not to smile. 'No, OK. Not all. You surprised me, that's all. I was miles away.'

'Well, only one.' He jerked his head back to the house. Then he looked at me. 'You were up there.'

I followed to where he was suggesting, disconcerted. 'Fair enough.'

'With your ex-husband?'

I frowned. 'How d'you know he's my ex-husband?'

'Oh, Babs is full of chat. I had a drink with her. She seems to have slightly adopted me, didn't you know?' He grinned. Then he shrugged non-committally. 'He's a nice man.'

I nodded slowly. 'Of course. You had a meeting with him.'

'Nice, but malleable. The intention is there, but the decision-making isn't.'

'Are we talking about beach pollution *again*?'

'So wearying.'

'There are other things?'

He regarded me carefully a moment. Then he moved to the rock I'd been sitting on. Perched on it. Patted the space beside him. I hesitated, then went and sat down.

'There are, admittedly, other things. But right now it's pretty pertinent. Particularly here. Particularly with that family being so involved.'

'It's not Hugo's fault,' I told him defensively. 'His hands are tied.'

'Of course it's his fault. He's the CEO. His father's hands were never tied, I've checked.'

'Roger's a different person.'

'You mean he's his own person.'

'That's a cretinous expression. Everyone's their own person. It's just whether or not you like what you see.' I was horribly aware, though, that this man was spookily echoing thoughts I'd had myself, only moments earlier. 'And anyway, what d'you mean, you've checked? What are you, the police?'

'When Roger was in charge there were plenty of contentious decisions. Too much sewage being pumped into the wrong places, or ignored at sea. Not enough filtration – the waste water treatment in Plymouth is wholly responsible for Bio-Beads, incidentally, those minute things we'd carefully gathered into piles and which you galloped gaily through the other day. Even Roger would admit that. Although he'd also say they were unaware of the dangers back then, and he's right. Mistakes were made through general ignorance. But everyone is so informed these days, there's no excuse. But it's not just that. Crucially, in Roger's day there were far fewer anomalies.'

'What d'you mean?'

'I don't know, exactly.' He narrowed his eyes and gazed out to sea. 'I'm not sure yet. But something here doesn't quite stack up.' He was quiet for a while. After a bit, he sighed. 'I don't know. Perhaps I just want someone to blame for something I care deeply about.'

I grinned. 'Ah, at last. A glimmer of self-knowledge.'

He didn't smile, though. Looked depressed, even, and I rather regretted my barb. 'You can't help having a passion,' I offered in recompense. 'Hate that word, by the way. It's so overused and devalued.'

'Used as an excuse for anything.'

'Exactly. Shopping, exercise – any selfish activity people want to do to please themselves for hours on end.'

'So you wouldn't apply it to your art?'

'I wouldn't, actually. I was thinking about it earlier. Painting is what keeps me grounded. In control. Even though, paradoxically, I'm out of control when I'm doing it. Exposed and completely at its mercy, if you see what I mean. It nevertheless roots me. I can't really explain.'

'You're doing very well. And I wouldn't begin to compare my joyless, beachcombing activities with anything truly creative, but losing myself in it comes close to what you describe. I do become consumed.'

I remembered his concentration when I'd first seen him, wading and gazing forensically into the shallows, container in hand.

'Which is healthy, I feel.'

'Quite.'

We were silent a moment. A light breeze ruffled our hair.

'I feel we got off on the wrong foot, when we first met,' I said abruptly. 'Sorry about that.'

'My fault, too. Seem to remember I had a go at you about something. Ah yes, the riding.'

'Well, you're your "Own Person",' I said ironically. 'That's pretty much a licence to kill.'

He smiled down at his knees. Nodded. 'Truce?'

'Truce.'

'Drink?'

I blinked. 'Sorry?'

'Well, not now. I'm going to bed. But tomorrow maybe? In the Mariners?'

'Oh.' I thought for a moment. 'Well. Yes. All right. Why not?'

'Don't panic, Flora, it's a drink in the Mariners. Not a hot date. I'm usually there with some of my students at about seven. They like to ponce a drink off me. Babs is often there, too.'

'I might bring Celia along,' I said, remembering suddenly.

He nodded. 'I'll see you then.'

He got down off the rock and dusted his hands. Then, without looking back or saying goodnight, he walked away. A tall, solitary figure, roaming steadily back down the beach. He had a certain presence, I'll give him that. I watched until he was around the corner of the bay and out of sight.

14

The following day, however, a more pressing appointment was first on the agenda; one at lunchtime, in Truro.
The restaurant was crowded and much bigger than I'd
imagined. I'd had trouble finding it because I'd nonchalantly assumed I knew everywhere there was to go in this
city, only to find that the whole place had changed beyond
recognition behind my back. It had always bustled and
thronged with people, but in my day they were shuffling
in and out of McDonald's and Greggs in pac-a-macs, not
sprawling indolently in cutting-edge fashion all over the
Cathedral square which appeared to have got itself up like
an Italian piazza. In the surrounding streets, café society
spilled from every conceivable eatery orifice, of which
there were many, everyone sipping rosé and cappuccino
and taking the mezze option or the sharing platter, not an
egg sarnie or a pasty in sight.

The restaurant to which I was headed was off the main
square and in a similar vein, although we seemed to have
moved seamlessly from Italy to France. I pushed through
the revolving glass door into a long, bustling bistro. Its
white walls were crowded with black and white photographs, and pedestal lamps were suspended from the

ceiling. Shiny brass railings and wooden compartments sectioned off little areas of leather banquette seating and white linen-clad tables. The acoustics were presumably intentionally dreadful to give the place instant atmosphere, which it certainly did. It was mostly full of young, thrusting executives having noisy lunches as even younger waiters wove amongst them in long, crisp aprons, expertly balancing seafood platters on one hand above their heads. Oysters on a huge tray of ice swept past my nose. I mean for heaven's sake, what did Truro think it was? Oh, OK. Bang next to a fishing port.

The maître d' was already leading me efficiently across the wooden floor, but I saw her before he did. My hand shot up in delighted recognition as she simultaneously saw me and got to her feet, waving both hands above her head in wonderful abandonment. She looked even more glamorous than I remembered. She was wearing a silky blue wrap dress and heels, whippet thin as ever, and her hair was neatly tied back in a velvet bow. We held out our arms dramatically. Grinning from ear to ear, we hugged each other tight. The maître d' smiled and left us to it as we failed to unclench.

'Too long,' said Shona finally, as we eventually released one another. '*Far* too long.'

'My fault,' I told her truthfully as we both dabbed at our eyes with our napkins, mine properly streaming, which made us laugh.

'Yes, *all* your fucking fault, you're a hopeless correspondent. I'd have been better off with a carrier pigeon.'

'But all *your* fault for moving about the country so much. Liverpool, Manchester – what the fuck!'

'Yes, OK, but when I *did* come to London, you weren't bloody there!'

'I never usually go away. I could have cried. Knew there was a reason why I didn't. What was I thinking?'

'Fuck knows. I mean, Paris in the springtime – who needs it?'

Shona swore quite a lot and, sheep that I was, I always joined in as if it was something I routinely did. I found it funny and relaxing and sank into it contentedly now, along with our mutual past and the palest of pink wines which she had already ordered.

'Peter needed the break after his exams. And we only went for three days. But give me more warning next time, there's a doll?'

'Can't, I'm afraid,' she said ruefully. 'It's the nature of the current affairs game, the clue's in the title. And anyway, I'm rarely in London. It's only if a Cornish story breaks and transfers dramatically like that one did – which couldn't have ended up being more parochial, by the way. Boy gets shell stuck up nose on Rock Beach and is flown by private helicopter to Great Ormond Street because Russian oligarch parents don't think Newquay Hospital is up to it.'

'Stop it.'

'Swear to God. So your trusty, probing reporter was rushed to the bedside. I bloody nearly whipped out my tweezers and hooked it out myself as we waited for the doctor, it would have been quicker.'

'But at least you're fronting it all now,' I said admiringly. 'I mean, anchorwoman. How cool is that?'

'It's better,' she admitted.

'And down here! Presumably this is the gig you wanted? You must have been thrilled when it came up?'

'Oh, hundred percent. Dream come true. Totally where my heart is. Not that I hadn't lobbied for it, of course. It didn't exactly come up. I shoved.' She grinned.

'You don't say.'

Shona pretty much got what she wanted in life.

'And to be fair, no one else did, they all wanted London.' She sipped her wine and her dark eyes flashed at me above the rim. 'But in ten years' time they'll all want this, of course, and I'm not budging. Oh – mussels, please,' she glanced up at the waiter who was hovering expectantly. 'And chips. They're brilliant here,' she told me.

'The same, please.' He departed. 'And Paddy? He likes it here, too?'

'Paddy's happy if I'm happy,' she said airily, breaking into her bread roll. 'Which sounds arrogant and probably is, but temperamentally he could live in a cave, he doesn't really notice his surroundings. And also, realistically, he can work anywhere, which I can't. And the kids love it. Can't keep them off the beach.'

'And he's working? Writing?' I asked cautiously.

'Just had his second book accepted by Heinemann. And the Tate are backing it up with an exhibition – it's a biography of Charles the First, who was a demon art collector.'

'Oh wow, that's amazing.' It really was. Paddy was a huge, handsome academic. A lovely man she'd met at Durham who wrote biographical history, but it wasn't always lucrative. Shona pretty much kept the financial wheels on the bus, but this sounded promising.

'That's the Tate St Ives, not *The* Tate,' she told me dryly.

'But still. He's got a two-book deal. And he's unofficially been offered History professor at Exeter University. He hears for sure next week.'

My eyes popped dramatically at her across the table. I let my jaw drop. 'Shona – that's huge!'

She was deliberately underplaying it, but I could tell she was thrilled. A smile escaped her. 'Well, it takes us to a dual-income family, which I agree is pretty huge.'

'We should have ordered champagne.'

'God, no. I'm still touching wood about next week. Shit – quick.'

We hurriedly found a table leg each, shut our eyes, took our feet off the floor and counted to ten, as we had done since childhood. Then we laughed and sank into our rosé.

'And you?'

I told her much of what she knew already: we'd emailed now and then even though we hadn't seen much of each other. I told her about my painting and I told her Mum's news and about Peter's success at Oxford. She listened. Then she frowned and leaned forward, arms folded on the table.

'OK, well, that much, apart from Peter, I pretty much already knew. And huge congrats to him, by the way, I'll send him a text. But what about you?'

'What d'you mean?'

'Well, have you moved on? Found someone else?'

I laughed and took a nervous sip of wine. 'You sound like Peter.'

'Well, good. I'm glad he's on it. Shit, you're not even Catholic, like me. What's the problem?'

'There isn't one,' I said stubbornly. I was about to

embark on my tedious Tim and Rupert lies but found I didn't have the energy. 'I hear you saw Tommy,' I said, changing the subject.

'Yes, he came to the fête.' She sat back and smiled. 'I mean, opening a fête, can you believe it? I nearly fell over when they asked me.'

'You'll be launching ships next,' I warned.

She made a face. 'Talk about scraping the barrel. And Tommy was no help. He insisted on Whipping Up The Crowd, as he called it – such as it was, three men and a dog – clapping and wolf-whistling *very* loudly when I'd done the deed with the scissors and ribbon. He even brought along a stash of booklets I'd written years ago on Cornish tin mines – fuck knows where he found those – asked people if they'd like them autographed. They bloody did, too, it was beyond embarrassing. So Tommy's dissolving with laughter, OK, as I have to inscribe one to Maureen, whose sheepdog howls with delight whenever I come on the box, apparently. I told Maureen her dog is probably allergic to me and should be allowed to leave the room.'

I laughed. But I was surprised all over again. 'I didn't know you and Tommy were such mates?'

'Oh, we've kept in touch. Years ago his mother got him to write to me, you knew that.'

'Did I?'

'Yes, after that whole hunting debacle. When he went home she could tell something had really upset him and she suggested he wrote. I see him when he's over. He's a laugh.'

'You never said.'

'Oh, and when *would* I have said, you bloody recluse? And anyway, on the odd occasion I do see you, we only seem to talk about Hugo.'

I nodded down at my mussels, which had conveniently arrived. Popped in a chip. 'Yeah, well, that's all changing,' I muttered. 'This holiday has seen to that. I'm embarrassed, actually, Shona. Don't know what the fuck I've been doing with my life.'

'Well, that's progress.' She looked surprised, and, if I'm honest, my words surprised me, too. I determined to believe them, though. 'Tommy told me to work on you but I'll be delighted to report I didn't have to. Here's to a new dawn.'

She lifted her glass and met mine, mid-air. I sipped thoughtfully.

'Why did Tommy ask you to work on me?'

She shrugged. 'I don't know. Because like the rest of us he can see you're wasting your life, I imagine. Thinks the early Christian martyr look doesn't suit you, perhaps?'

'Tommy.' I snorted. 'What does he know? I hadn't seen him for years.'

'He sees Peter. And me, of course, and I'm not protecting you, so don't get any big ideas.' She hesitated. 'And if you must know, I think he feels a bit responsible. Thinks he should have tried harder to stop Hugo marrying you. Because of Christina, I guess. He feels guilty, OK? Is that so weird?'

I remembered Tommy and Hugo in the ante-room of Marylebone Registry Office. The fierce determination on Tommy's face as I interrupted them. That had nothing to do with Christina, he just didn't like me.

'So if I whip off the sackcloth and ashes and start putting it about as much as he does, he'll feel better, is that it?' I said lightly.

'Don't be glib, he's not like that.' I'd been extracting a mussel but I glanced up at her tone. 'And anyway, he's been a star as far as I'm concerned. He got my niece an internship at Christie's in New York which was super kind – his sister knows someone there. And he's offered us his apartment if we ever want to stay. If I can ever get Paddy away from Charles the First's personal possessions, that is.'

'Right.' I felt a peculiar stab of jealousy though. And betrayal. Ridiculous. But it was as if a whole subplot and storyline had been going on without me, behind my back. The Tommy and Shona show. But the truth was I'd been too self-absorbed to notice, or even care. And what I did, painting, only encouraged that inner life. Celia and I knew that. We could go for weeks – months, even – without talking to a soul, and because we had each other, and I had Peter and Mum, it always seemed OK. It wasn't. I'd neglected friendships. Well, this one, anyway. What else, I wondered?

The waiter removed our bowls of empty shells and gave us water bowls for our fingers. I swirled mine about thoughtfully.

'Shona, have you had any stories hit your desk recently about the water down here?'

She put her head on one side and dried her fingers with her napkin. Took a moment. 'Why do you ask?'

'You have.'

She made a non-committal face. 'The water's always been dodgy down here, you know that. They should bloody nationalize it. Fucking privatization, makes me puke.'

'But the Bellingdons, specifically?' I insisted, ignoring her polemic and already knowing her politics.

'Well, they run it, Flora. This patch, anyway. Can't get more specific than that.'

'So you have,' I said anxiously. 'It's just that – well, I know it's hugely contentious at the moment, but Hugo is so hard-working and dedicated and—'

'Oh, *Hugo*.' She threw down her napkin, exasperated. 'I thought we were forgetting about him?'

'Well, it concerns Peter, too,' I said defensively. 'By extension.'

'Only if he goes into the family firm, which I bloody hope he doesn't. Do I need to have a word?'

I shook my head. 'No, he doesn't want to. He's sure about that. Actually, I think he'd make a good journal-ist. So maybe you should?'

'I'd be happy to. Send him my way.'

I smiled wryly. 'Although I'm told the BBC is none too keen on public schoolboys these days. Reverse discrimin-ation and all that?'

She shot me a sharp look. 'They can take it.'

'Well, quite,' I said quickly.

'But you're right, legend has it Frank Gardner was deemed too posh to be a newsreader so he became a for-eign correspondent, then got shot, poor guy. Everyone's got an opinion. I had complaints in Manchester about my accent being too West Country – I'm bloody Corn-ish, what do they expect! Shit.' She glanced suddenly at her watch. 'I've got to run. Got a production meeting in literally three minutes – bugger.' She stuck up a hand and waved extravagantly for the bill. 'Oh Flora, I'm so sorry!' she wailed, eyeballing a waiter and scribbling in the air. 'Forty-five minutes, we've had – this fucking job!'

'I'll do it, Shona, you go.'

'Certainly not, you're the impoverished artist. I'd never have suggested coming here and letting you pay, and anyway, I've got a work account. I'm interviewing you about your important new commission.' She winked.

The waiter hurried across and she quickly signed the card he gave her.

'Look at you,' I said admiringly as she got to her feet and shrugged on a jacket. 'Quite the high-flying exec.'

She made a face. 'Sorry. Not trying to show off, but it's pretty much the works caff. The office is next door. And let's not get ahead of ourselves, it is only Truro.'

I got to my feet to hug her as she came round the table. But it was a different sort of hug to the one when we'd met, which had been one of unadulterated joy. This one had a bit of tension in it; from both of us. Her exasperation with me and my defensiveness had snuck in, despite our best efforts. But it was better than the last time, when she'd been in Manchester and we'd met halfway. At that Italian. When, actually, we'd had words. Or she had. This was better. Had been better. The trouble was, we knew each other too well to pretend. Not knew, loved. We loved each other much too much to be disingenuous: to dissemble and agree, for form's sake, when we didn't. Which might explain my lackadaisical approach to emailing. And why I hadn't always picked up the phone when I'd seen her name on my mobile. Sent a text afterwards. 'Sorry – I'm painting, will call later!' And hadn't. Shona was rigorous. Ruthless with me. Far worse than Celia. Yes, it was why we'd become – not estranged – but distant.

'Come for supper,' she said urgently. She held my shoulders, her eyes searching my face. 'And bring Peter. Come next week – you'll still be here?'

'Yes, I'll still be here.'

'And you can say hello to my lot. God, is there no peace?'

A hugely overweight woman with a young man in tow was making for the door from another table, jerking her head urgently at Shona. Shona nodded back. 'My editor and my sub. He's heaven, she's an oversexed nympho. She looked me in the eye the other day and said, "The thing is, Shona, I think about it *all the time*." I said – thinking I was being caring – "Maybe you should see someone? There are sex-addiction therapists, you know?" Turned out she was talking about food. Wasn't a great moment. Oh look, he's waiting for me, the love, I told you he was heaven. I'm going to have to fly.' The young man was hovering anxiously by the revolving door. 'I'll text you about supper.'

She left, sweeping elegantly through the tables. As she went, heads turned, certainly at her beauty, but many in recognition. The man on the table beside me turned to his fellow diner and smiled, whispering her name.

'Really? Shona Okafor? Where?' Her head spun round to look.

I watched as the young man grinned and grabbed her hand when she reached him, and then they squeezed, laughing, into the revolving door together. Through the huge plate-glass window I saw them race down the street, still laughing. Shona's face was alive and joyous. Vital. That was the word I was groping for. I sat down slowly and reached for my glass. Sipped from it. The wine was warmer than one might have wished for.

15

The Mariners was already in full Saturday-night swing when I arrived. All the tables on the terrace were taken and the pavement was rapidly filling up with the overflow, as standing room only began to apply. I pushed through the throng and went inside to the saloon bar. The small, oak-panelled room, hung with nets and rods and lobster pots and all manner of fishing memorabilia, was already at least ten deep at the bar and hot as hell. Through the crowd already at the bar placing an order, I could see Ted, towering above the rest. He was waving his arms as if conducting an orchestra, surrounded by students. Babs was there, too, helpfully handing out the drinks.

'Coo-ee, darling!' she cried. She waved extravagantly, clearly loving her role as magician's assistant. 'Just like old times, isn't it? Just getting them in – what'll you have? One of these?' She held up what looked like gin with a tonic bottle.

'Please!' I called back as I retreated to the periphery of the crowd.

Ted was dispensing more drinks to the youngsters behind him, rolling his eyes as they jumped on the bandwagon with huge endearing smiles. Then with a sudden – 'That's your lot!' – he handed the barman a fistful of money and pocketed the change. Holding the glasses high, he muscled his way through to me.

'Bloody freeloading yobs,' he muttered, handing me my drink.

I grinned. 'And you wonder why you're so popular.'

'Oh, total cupboard love, I agree. I'm under no illusions. Come on. Let's get out of here.'

'This place has got worse – it's absolutely heaving,' I complained as we jostled our way through the crowds on the pavement, trying not to spill our drinks.

'Rather pejorative, surely?' Ted enquired with a grin. '"Buzzing" or "happening" could also apply.'

'Only if you're a tourist,' I said wryly, as we made our way, with Babs in tow, to the sea wall on the other side of the road. 'Trust me, the locals like their peace and quiet.'

'You speak for yourself,' Babs objected as she and I went to perch on the wall together. Ted stood facing us, gazing out to sea, a view I could tell he was happy with and would easily forgo a seat for. 'If you live down here full-time it gets jolly quiet in the winter. I don't mind the merry throng at all.'

'And you can bet the locals don't turn their noses up at the dosh the tourists bring, either,' Ted remarked.

'Well, quite. Ken behind the bar didn't look too distressed when you handed him a wodge.'

'Hang on – I live here! I mean, only recently, but I'm not a bloody tourist. Cheers!' He raised his glass and we raised ours back.

'Cheers.' We all sipped together.

'No Celia?' asked Ted, wiping froth from his mouth.

'No, she said she wanted to work late. She's somewhere along the coast waiting for a Turner-esque sunset.'

What she'd actually said, when I'd told her slightly nervously that I'd bumped into Ted for two seconds on the beach and he'd said there was always a crowd at the Mariners and why didn't we come along, was that firstly she was painting late, but secondly, she'd decided Ted was too outdoorsy for her. Too hearty. A bit big and bear-like. I was used to Celia's sudden and dramatic changes of heart, but nonetheless I was surprised.

'Really? I thought you liked him?'

She'd wrinkled her nose over her muesli. 'Bit too Fisherman's Friend and Aran jumpers for me. Too much of a Barnacle Bill. I'm more of a Larry the Lounge Lizard girl. Can't really see him at the Donmar, can you? I might pop along later, but don't wait if you're going out to eat. I might still be at my canvas.'

I told this to the others now. The last bit, about not waiting. Not the Barnacle Bill, obviously.

Babs smiled into her drink. 'Sensible girl,' she murmured.

I frowned. 'Why?'

She widened her eyes innocently. 'Making the most of being down here. You don't get that view in London, do you? Why waste it? Anyway, Flora, what have you been doing today?'

I had an idea she was up to something, but Babs was always up to something, so I told them about going into Truro for lunch, and my astonishment at its total transformation from my youth. How old I felt suddenly. Then I told Babs about Shona, filling Ted in on what she did and how influential she'd become. 'She might be reading the

autocue in a smart suit but she's still very much the investigative reporter with the social conscience,' I told him.
'She's like a bloodhound, always has been.'

'*Love* Shona,' enthused Babs, who was wearing a very
chic denim jumpsuit together with pink canvas shoes.
'I bet she sorted you out.' Her blue eyes twinkled at me
above her gin.

'We had a delightful lunch, thank you,' I told her evenly.
'And how exactly did you fill your day?' There was more
than a touch of thrust in my retort, slightly bored as I was
with the whole world jumping on my case and not necessarily examining their own ostrich tendencies first. Mum
said Babs had been left so much money by Filippo that
she never had to do anything, but she always claimed to
be frightfully busy. Never a spare moment in the day. She
ignored my dig.

'Ted and I went to Porthchapel, didn't we, darling?'

Ted rolled his eyes. 'Babs maintains I give Cornwall
a bad press and wanted me to see a pristine, plastic-free
beach. She says the problem is not home-grown at all,
and it's all to do with the Mexicans. Which of course is
bollocks.'

'Except where we went today was indeed litter free,
agreed?' she insisted.

'Agreed.'

'Because it's in the thermal tide surge, which means
that any debris comes from the UK – i.e. none. Whereas
Portethal, for instance, where you're mostly working and
finding all that crap, takes in the current from the Gulf of
Mexico. They're absolutely dreadful about chucking their
tacos wrappers about. A crisp packet from Guatemala was

washed up the other day – imagine! *So* irresponsible. Tell me I'm wrong,' she demanded.

'You're not wrong,' he agreed. 'And that story was indeed reported in the *Daily Mail* recently, that great oracle of truth. But without wishing to be patronizing, the oceanography is a great deal more complicated than that and it's got nothing to do with the thermals. Oh, hello there.' He broke off to greet a couple of students who'd come up to say thanks for the drink. I watched him joke around with them, well liked beyond his wallet, clearly. A couple more drifted across to join in and Babs and I stepped back to accommodate them. He threw back his head and roared at a joke.

'Frightfully attractive, isn't he?' murmured Babs, following my eyes.

I shrugged. 'He's all right.' I sipped my drink.

She was about to object, when suddenly she grabbed my arm. 'Oh darling, *do* look over there,' she hissed. 'There's Peter, with that lovely Janey.'

I glanced across to a table at the far end of the terrace, where Peter and Jancy were indeed perched on the edge, having a drink.

'Oh great! I'll go and say hi.' I made to go.

'No, no,' Babs whispered, keeping her hand on my arm. 'He's having a lovely time, leave him. Been sailing with her all day, just the two of them in the Wayfarer. I saw from the beach. Lovely.' She smirked.

I laughed. 'Oh, don't be ridiculous, Babs. She's in her thirties! He's seventeen!'

She made her famous face: the one with the arched eyebrows and the dancing, irresponsible eyes. Lit a cigarette and inhaled deeply. 'What's age got to do with anything? I went out to dinner with a very young man recently.'

'You're turning into Emma Woodhouse,' I told her, as Janey, having spotted us, came weaving across.

'Your son saved me from a very tiresome day today,' she confided when we'd greeted one another. 'Your ex-mother-in-law wanted me to make up a bridge four, which I have to say, did not have me salivating at the mouth. Happily, Christina fell on her sword, and Pete and I vamoosed and went sailing. He's great company. You've done a terrific job, Flora.'

'Thanks.' I beamed. 'What about the others?'

'Tommy and Hugo were holed up all day in his study, can you believe it? On a day like this! We're supposedly meeting them in the Lobster Pot later for supper, but I'm not holding my breath. And I say "we",' she glanced behind, 'but Pete's just met some of his buddies. So now I've probably lost him, too.' I looked across to where Peter was standing up and chatting animatedly to some boys his age, his cheeks flushed. I recognized one from school. 'Can I persuade you two to come along instead?' She leaned forward conspiratorially, including Babs with her darting eyes. 'If I'm honest, I've got the most horrific cabin fever. If I have to stay in that house another night for dinner, I swear to God I'll top myself. I was tempted to look you up, Babs, see if you fancied another ride.'

'Oh, any time. I'm your girl. And frankly I'm astonished you can stay in that woman's house at all.'

Janey laughed. 'Oh, woah, I didn't *quite* say that. And anyway, it's Roger's, too, surely?'

'*Well* . . .' Babs needed no further prompting. In my

peripheral vision, I saw Ted rolling his eyes at me in despairing apology, trying to disentangle himself from the young, so I left Babs and Janey to it. I was reasonably sure Janey had deliberately asked a leading question and wanted all the dirt. Those two were not dissimilar. I made my way towards him.

'I'm besieged!' Ted wailed as we moved along the wall and found a quieter spot.

'It's *Goodbye, Mr Chips* all over again,' I told him. 'You've lost all authority and become one of the gang. Slippery slope, I'm afraid.'

'Not entirely sure that's what happened to Mr Chips, but I know what you mean. Trouble is, I find them much more entertaining than some of the fossils in my department.'

'That's because the fossils have all got spouses and children and you're still living the single life, like this lot.' Ah, clever Flora. Investigative stuff. Shona would approve.

He made a face. 'Up to a point. I was married, actually.'

'Oh, right. I'm sorry. Ended in tears?'

'Sadly, yes.'

'Whose?'

'Both.' He hesitated. 'But hers mainly, I guess. I mean, obviously I was sad. But I just wasn't ready. We were students together. Got married far too young.'

'Yes, me too, I suppose.' I realized it was the first time I'd admitted it might have been a mistake. Both to myself and someone else.

'You regret it?'

'Well, I certainly don't regret Peter.' I nodded across the sea of heads in his general direction. 'Tall, blond, stripy blue shirt.'

He followed my gaze. Then his eyes widened. 'God, you *did* marry young.'

I laughed. 'He looks older than he is. He's only seventeen.'

'Still. Don't know what I've been doing with my life.' He sank gloomily into his beer.

'None in your camp, then?'

'No, thank the Lord. I mean, not that I don't love children. But it does rather complicate matters.'

Peter had intercepted my glance and was coming across. 'Hello, darling. I see Tom's here?'

'Yeah, and Adam,' he nodded at a tall, dark-haired boy, 'who I was telling you about.'

'Well, this is Ted Fleming. He's a marine biologist.'

'More of an environmental scientist, actually, but I'll take that. Hi.' They shook hands.

'Oh, right, that's what my friend Sam wants to do, when he goes to university,' Peter told Ted.

'Oh, OK. Where's he applied, d'you know?'

And off they went; waffling on about courses and different degrees and what have you, and I noticed how well Ted clearly got on with young people. Well, he worked with them, for God's sake. It would be like me not getting on with a paintbrush. But also how, a few minutes later, when they'd finished their academic man-chat, and Ted had offered to have a word with Sam, and Peter had thanked him effusively and then gone back to join his mates, having shaken Ted's mighty paw heartily, Peter had given me an admiring look. A look that clearly said, *Much better, Mum. Go for it.*

I hoped to God Ted hadn't seen it, but there's precious

little subtlety about a seventeen-year-old. I became absorbed with my drink, pretending it was absolutely crucial to extract my lemon and give it a little suck, something I can't imagine was that attractive to witness.

'So are you Lobster Potting with the Bellingdon crew?' he asked, when I finally dared to drop my lemon and meet his eye, which, annoyingly, was amused.

'No, I don't think so. It's horribly expensive.' It was, but Peter would no doubt be paid for by his father if he turned up, and Janey, who'd invited him, if he didn't. 'Anyway,' I lied, wishing I hadn't mentioned money, 'I see enough of them during working hours, as you can imagine.'

'Fisherman's Retreat?'

'Oh – you mean . . . ?'

'Why not?'

'Gosh. Quite the discerning local. How d'you know about that?' The Retreat was a closely guarded secret. Tucked away down a side street, it was in a deceptively grotty part of town.

'Babs took me.'

'Ah, yes. She would.' I hesitated, glancing about. 'It's just . . . I'm a bit worried about Celia. She said she might come down later, but—'

'She's over there.'

He pointed through the crowd towards the pub. Celia was indeed standing talking to Babs and Janey, smiling and laughing. She saw me, waved and grinned. Phew. I was relieved.

'OK,' I agreed. I put my glass down on the wall. 'Lead on, Macduff.'

He scratched his head and looked perplexed. 'Ah. Well.

There you have me, I'm afraid. I talk a big locals' game, but I'm not *entirely* . . . up the high street, peel off left somewhere and head back along the cliff?'

I laughed. 'Not even close. Why would we go into town to get back to the coast, Mr Seashore Man? Follow me.' I vaulted, rather neatly, I thought, over the low sea wall to the beach, and brushed off my hands on my jeans. After he'd followed suit – almost as neatly – we strode off along the beach together, into the gently gathering gloom.

I'm not entirely sure we needed two bottles of wine at supper, one with the prawns and one with the steak, but, as is so often the way when you first meet someone and sit down to break bread together, it oiled the wheels. I was also quite pleased to see he seemed – not nervous, that's the wrong word – but as apprehensive as I was. Not a seasoned dater, I'd hazard. For a date, I'd realized as I sat down, this surely was. At Peter's age, and for some years beyond, the same scenario can easily be interpreted as a casual supper with a new mate. But when two people of a certain age sit opposite each other at a small table, so small their knees are almost touching, in a candlelit, crowded restaurant – he'd clearly booked – and share their past, their chequered histories, and are open and frank with one another about their mistakes, their disappointments, their failings, as well as their successes and sources of happiness, it comes under a more intimate heading. On the success and happiness front we both reaffirmed that we'd been lucky enough to have fulfilling, absorbing careers that we adored, and whilst I admitted mine had occasionally given me an excuse to withdraw from the evolutionary struggle, he told me his had very definitely contributed to the break-up of his marriage.

'Jilly asked me one morning, as I set off for the Summer Isles for the third time that year, if I preferred them to her.'

'Oh. And?'

'I had to admit, I did. She said she thought she should leave and waited for me to say "Please don't." I didn't exactly pack her bag but I certainly didn't dissuade her. And I remember feeling . . .' he hesitated.

'Relieved?'

'Yes, relieved. When she left. Sobbing. Awful.' He did look thoroughly ashamed as he wiped a chip gloomily around his plate.

'Not awful, you can't help how you feel. I'm sure Hugo felt exactly the same when he finally told me he was leaving me for Christina. And I'm not convinced she should have asked you to choose like that. It's not an either–or situation.'

'Except I was secretly pleased she'd made it one. And she knew I was. She was the one with the courage, eventually.'

'Ah. Yes. I see. And I wasn't. I knew, too, you see. And I didn't give Hugo an out.'

'You had a baby.'

'Not when I knew for the first time, I didn't. When he first met her.' Sailing across a river on a rope. Wide smile.

'Oh. Right.'

I looked over his shoulder at the bar: people were perched on stools with late-night cocktails. My eyes came back to him. 'In fact, in the spirit of full disclosure, Ted, I'm not sure I'm a very nice person.'

He laughed. 'And *I'm* not sure you can be the judge of that.'

'No, but it's true. Jilly called time and gave you your freedom. She wasn't grasping and greedy, like me. Hanging on in there.'

'Which could also be interpreted as desperately in love and frightened to death.'

Our eyes locked. It was the last word that had done it.

'Yes. I was.'

'But you never . . . ?'

'Only on one occasion. When I was driving. Peter was in the back and a wall loomed up suddenly around a corner. I remember thinking, I could just drive into that, very fast. But no. It was a moment. Nothing more. Painting saved me. And Peter.'

'Whereas Jilly had nothing,' he said sadly. 'Oh, she worked in a marketing consultancy, but it was a job. She didn't love it.'

I could hear both of us wondering whether that made us more compatible: because we both had absorbing careers. Whether I'd say 'yippee' if he went to the South Pole for months on end, whilst I holed up in the attic with my easel and plenty of canvases. Yes. Probably. In fact, definitely. The cogs were whirring too loudly, though, and in another moment, I'd instinctively shied away. Found myself looking at my watch. I think he might have been about to suggest a cocktail at the bar but instead he said:

'Time to go?'

I was relieved but cross with myself. Come *on*, Flora. Join in. *Lovely* man. Unattached, clearly likes you, very attractive, too, as Babs had so succinctly pointed out. In fact, as he paid the bill, it struck me rather forcibly that I wasn't at all sure I would mind him kissing me. I inwardly boggled as he smiled up at the waiter, pocketing his credit card. Lordy. Had I really thought that? This was surely progress.

As we wandered outside into the cool night air, a canopy of stars twinkled down from above. The estuary glittered with lights from the boats. Suddenly I was bold enough to say:

'Walk along the beach?'

He'd been looking around futilely for a taxi, but he glanced down at me, delighted.

'Capital idea.'

Yes, lovely man. He could easily have suggested it himself, but was taking his cue from me, not pushing anything. I liked that. I realized that if I was attracted to men at all these days, it was men like this, who didn't push, and who let me slowly come to them. And there was plenty of time, I reasoned. The winged chariot was not at our backs, if neither of us wanted it to be. When we reached the beach, and walked down the steps on to the sand, he put his hands in his pockets and didn't even attempt to take my hand, or even my arm. As we chatted and meandered along the seashore, laughing as we stopped occasionally to skim stones, or as a wave nearly reached our feet and we had to hop out of the way, it occurred to me, that since I was here for the duration of the summer, and he was going nowhere, we really did have world enough and time. And that gentle consideration and slow progress were not, for once, a prevarication. A stalling of real life. But a luxury I could, and should, afford.

16

As Ted and I rounded the corner to where the rocks crept in towards the sea, we both saw the camp fire ahead of us at the same time. Flames leaped into the night sky and snapped and crackled in the darkness. A party was in full swing around it. Silhouettes of darkened figures surrounded it, and music was playing, no doubt from an iPhone, but pretty loudly. People were sitting or standing, swaying or half dancing, glasses or bottles in hands, cigarettes glowing.

'Is that still allowed?' I asked in surprise as we made our way towards it.

'What, the fire or the music?'

'Both, I suppose.'

Ted shrugged. 'I imagine the music is fine until someone complains, and the fire is OK unless the beach is privately owned. Which I gather has always been the Bellingdons' bugbear.'

I caught the satisfaction in his voice and glanced up at him. 'I'm a Bellingdon.'

He smiled down at his shoes. 'Yes, OK. Point taken. I'm being chippy. But they must be sore as hell they sold it.'

'Actually, Roger's grandfather donated it to the village; he was quite the philanthropist. But no, I don't imagine Belinda's ecstatic about it. Iris told me she never comes down because it grates too much. If she did own it, of course, it would gleam like a new pin. She'd have the Hoover out twice a day, no litter at all, so maybe private ownership is a good thing?' I ventured mischievously.

He grinned good-naturedly. 'And she'd sit on her pristine beach in splendid isolation with not a hint of hoi polloi in sight. Speaking of which, don't we know those two reprobates?'

I followed his gaze. As we got closer to the fire, I saw Babs – oh, and Celia, too, good. Amongst the milieu of almost exclusively young people who were swaying laconically to the music, Babs and Celia, ciggies aloft, were very definitely boogying on down with gusto around imaginary handbags. Singing along at the tops of their voices to whatever song they were thrilled enough to recognize, all angst between the two of them clearly forgotten, they turned their faces up to the sky and foghorned the chorus to 'Brown Eyed Girl' out into the night.

'Shit-faced,' observed Ted.

'Oh, completely.'

'And the rest are my lot, of course,' he added, glancing around. 'Who will be in a similar state, but far more used to it.'

I made a considering face. 'Babs has had a bit of practice.'

'True.'

We were nearly upon them now. The bass note from the speakers throbbed in my ears. Young girls in tiny shorts and cropped tops flirted and half danced in boys' faces. I could feel the drink-fuelled electricity from here: the snap and crackle of impending sex.

'Darlings!' Babs suddenly spotted us. She threw up her hands and ran to meet us. Celia saw us and followed. 'Isn't this fun? It's years since we've done this – remember how we used to, Flora?'

'I do.'

It brought a bit of a lump to my throat, actually, albeit recalling a very different sort of party. Usually my father would light the fire, but always in a pit, surrounded by rocks, well supervised and military in fashion. We children would eat baked potatoes cooked in tin foil from it and poke them with sticks. Mum and Iris would fry sausages on a primus stove and a local boy, Gideon, would play the guitar – Cat Stevens, Leonard Cohen – and we'd all sing along. This was a very different sort of event. Not louche or out of hand, though, by any means, I thought, as I saw a group of students sitting in a huddle having an earnest discussion. Another group, all girls, were in a circle, singing along softly together. As Ted had observed, there was certainly more decorum amongst this age group than our peers. Two rather pretty blonde girls suddenly spied their professor. They leaped up to dash barefoot across the sand to lead him, protesting, by the arm, to their little singing coterie.

Babs' face was instantly in mine. Her eyes were bloodshot and her breath billowed like a furnace.

'Well?' she hissed.

'Well what?'

'Are you having a lovely time?'

'Very pleasant, thank you, Babs.' I stepped backwards to escape the fumes.

'Very pleasant? *Very pleasssant!*' she slurred. 'You're not at a garden party! You've got to fuck him, hasn't she, Celia?' She turned to her new best friend. Celia was somewhat insensible, though. She swayed, mute and glassy-eyed, beside her. I hoped she wasn't going to puke. Babs took her arm and shook some life into her.

'Tell her, Cele!' she insisted.

Celia could barely talk. She tried to focus on my face. Remember who I was, maybe. She opened her mouth to speak. Shut it again. Finally she made contact with her vocal cords.

'*Fuck him,*' she agreed loudly.

'Because if you don't,' Babs swayed back into my face again, and then out. She staggered a bit. '*Someone else will!*' Widening her eyes for dramatic emphasis, she swung her arms about extravagantly, magnanimously including all comers. Then her chin disappeared into her neck as she regarded me disapprovingly. I hoped that was the end of it, because one thing is absolutely certain: you cannot argue with a drunk. When pitted against any sober individual they have complete autonomy. It was just crucial these two particular inebriates were not overheard. Celia was taking a breath and looking as if she was gearing up for a very loud second wind.

'What you've got to do is *fu—*'

'Shall we sit over here?' I interrupted urgently. 'Look! Let's join in.' Seizing both their arms I led them firmly to some students, admittedly of the intense, male variety which wasn't ideal, but well away from Ted. A glance at the girl group told me he was already looking around for me. Once located, he gestured with a long arm for me to join him.

I held up my fingers. 'Five minutes,' I mouthed. Then I rolled my eyes at my two companions, indicating I was chaperoning. He grinned, nodded and went back to the young.

'Why here?' Babs was wailing, more at home amongst the dancers than this earnest, cross-legged group of boys. I made them collapse – not difficult. 'Why not over there with—'

'No, because *here*,' I improvised urgently, 'is much better.'

'Why?' Babs pouted like a two-year-old. She made to get up again but her legs were weak. I pulled her down.

'Because here . . .' I glanced around for inspiration, desperate for some extraordinary washed up sea urchin with which to distract these petulant toddlers. Unfortunately, Babs had spotted something far more fascinating. It was long, fat and white and burning between the fingers of the boy sitting beside her. He took a drag and the paper glowed brightly in the night sky. She stared, hypnotized.

'Drugs!' she breathed in wonder.

Celia came back from the dead and followed her eyes. 'Weed,' she informed her gravely.

The boy overheard and turned. He smiled. Offered it to her. Celia took it, and old hippy that she once was, took a professional drag. She paused, and then took another, before passing it to Babs. Oh dear. I was reasonably sure she didn't indulge, but on the other hand, who knew? She lived by the sea, drank like a fish, and it seemed that when

Roger wasn't available she went out with younger men. Plus she was about sixteen at heart, so for all I knew, she was off her head every night.

Something about the way she handled the joint, though, not with trepidation, but with fascination: and her childish excitement – sniffing it first – made me feel this was surely a baptism by spliffy fire. She raised it to her lips and took a drag. But it was a small, experimental one. Then, she frowned, as clearly nothing appeared to be happening. She took a much bigger drag, right down to her pink canvas shoes, then let it out. Her eyes widened as she waited for the psychedelic dawn to come up, for Woodstock, for the Beach Boys, for flowers to appear miraculously in her hair. When they didn't, she raised it eagerly again, but I was too quick for her.

'My turn,' I told her firmly. I whipped it from her fingers. 'You've had your go.'

For some reason I'd rather missed the stage of my life when I should have been entertaining this hobby. I'd been too busy, in a respectable, good-girl way, either riding my pony and painting seascapes, or getting married and having a baby. And despite having been an art student in groovy Glasgow and seeing a fair bit of life, I'd lived with similarly well-brought-up girls who, likewise, didn't indulge. Well, there was always a first time. And frankly, I'd always slightly regretted my well-spent youth. I took a small drag, but as I did, Babs and Celia watched intently. I'd hoped Celia might have collapsed by now. Died, even. I had no choice but to take another one.

'And again,' said Celia sternly.

'I've had two.'

'That first one didn't count.'

'It's not an exam,' I snapped, glaring at her. Nevertheless, I went back for more. Rather defiantly, I took an absolutely humungous inhalation this time.

A vast snake, a python of smoke indeed, swirled luxuriantly down and around my lungs. It filled them completely, finding its way into all manner of nooks and crannies I didn't know existed: it was like a Victorian pea-souper, swooping low and triumphantly, claiming the entire geography, transforming the landscape. Such a novel, and not entirely unpleasant experience was it, that I delayed exhaling and held it down. Well done me. Meanwhile, I cannily passed it, without looking at the recipient, keeping my eyes firmly on Babs for signs of grabbing, to the next lucky customer.

'Somehow I had you down for a cocktails-at-six girl,' said an amused voice in my ear. Ted was crouched beside me and had relieved me of the joint. He took a drag, then passed it on. 'Things *are* looking up.'

I stared, horrified. 'Oh – no, no, they're really not,' I said, aghast. 'I don't, actually. I just did it because—'

'She does,' Babs interjected firmly. Her head lurched drunkenly between the two of us. 'She does everything. She does drugs, she does sex, she does—'

'Rock and roll!' I said desperately. Getting to my feet, I dragged Ted, who luckily had only been crouching, up with me. 'Come on,' I said, holding firmly on to his arm. 'Let's go. Over there, where the music is.'

Ted, looking totally bemused, nevertheless allowed himself to be led to where the dancing was certainly more concentrated. It was quite some distance, beside some makeshift speakers, on the other side of the camp fire, well away from Babs and Celia. As we joined the throng and swayed along to Coldplay, I saw some of his students on the sandy dance floor nudge each other delightedly. They danced up close to us, grinning, mobbing him up. He grinned sheepishly back. After a bit he leaned in.

'Not sure I'm quite drunk enough for this!' he confided loudly, above the din.

I wasn't entirely sure I was either, but Babs and Celia – I glanced over my shoulder – had at least stayed put, so needs must. I grinned and nodded as if I couldn't really hear him. We swayed along to another number, and then actually, suddenly, as if by magic, I *was* drunk enough. I began to feel most peculiar, in fact. Remarkably mellow and – yes, graceful. I waved my arms high in the air, swaying along. Ted looked amused and I hoped it wasn't because I was displaying too much bingo wing, but no, he must surely see that what I was actually doing was reaching for the stars, which I grasped, and which then turned to sparkling gems in my hands. I stared at them in wonder. I really was up there, with Lucy, in the sky with diamonds, how *extraordinary*. And it was slanting slightly, the sky, which made grasping that much easier. I leaped about like a gazelle, seizing sparklers, in fact . . . golly, I *was* a gazelle, I realized, as my legs grew long and bony, with hocks and hooves. I stood still.

'Look!' I implored Ted, tugging his arm as he danced. 'Look at my legs!'

He gazed down, surprised. 'Very nice.'

'But I'm an animal – can't you see? In fact . . .' I gazed down incredulously. 'I'm an impala,' I told him importantly.

Ted laughed softly. He took my arm. 'So you are. But I've obviously had less impala puff than you, which puts me at something of a disadvantage. Why don't we retire to that quiet spot yonder by the rocks, where the youth have conveniently left a bottle of plonk and some cups, and see if I can catch up?'

It seemed a reasonable enough suggestion under the circumstances and he led me away. But I had to trot, obviously, because I had hooves. And shake my head. As I settled down beside him on the vast sandy plains of the Maasai Mara, folding my long back legs beneath me, I gazed about admiringly. Ted was pouring me a plastic cup of wine.

'Won't they mind?' I asked, some clarity briefly returning as I took it.

'Mind? God, they take enough drinks off me, fucking students.'

'Fucking students,' I repeated slowly, consideringly. I enjoyed the sound of it. 'I don't swear enough, Ted. I'd like to do it more.'

He laughed. 'You *are* away.'

'No, but seriously. I will. You'd like my friend Shona, she swears a lot.'

'I don't think I *do*, that much!' he protested.

'No, but still, you'd like her. Works for the BBC.'

'So you said.'

'Big microphone. Furry one. Big job. Tiny girl. Like these. These tiny grains of sand.' I gazed in wonder as I took a handful and let the grains pour through my fingers. 'Look! Look at all the little animals! Crabs, beetles – turtles!' I showed him a miniature turtle on the palm of my hand in fascination.

He laughed. 'Come on. Time to get you back, I think.'

I gazed at him, at his handsome, smiling, slightly craggy, good-natured face. 'Not until I've kissed you,' I informed him gravely. I took his face in both my hands, brought it towards me, and kissed him, very seriously, and very thoroughly, on the lips. Actually, not kissed, snogged.

'There,' I said when I'd finished. I returned his surprised face to its rightful position. 'That's better. I thought it would be a good idea earlier, in the restaurant, and it was.'

He threw back his head and roared. 'Well, I certainly found it more than just A Good Idea. But to be continued, I feel, at a later date. Let's get you home.' He got up and helped me to my feet, which were wobbly and not quite so gazelle-like now.

'*Oi – Ted! You bastard – our fucking bottle!*'

A few outraged students ran across from the dance floor and swarmed around Ted. He laughed and held up his hands.

'Literally, barely had a sip. But frankly, if I'd known it was yours, Shaun Casey, I'd have finished it. I've kept you in beer for three years!'

More jokey banter ensued as they pooh-poohed this notion, and reclaimed their bottle, with much discussion about who drank more, the professor or his students. Then a girl approached, one of the two pretty blonde ones who had originally rushed up to drag Ted away, and she said something sharper to Ted, something cutting. A couple of the boys had to calm her, tell her to pipe down, but I didn't really take much notice because I was somewhat distracted. As Ted broke off from them and came back towards me, I was staring away into the distance.

I realized I'd recognized a couple walking away from the fire in the opposite direction: back along the beach towards town, where Ted and I had just come from. The figures had gone now, they'd disappeared around the rocks of the headland. But I was absolutely sure I'd seen Peter and Janey, arm in arm.

17

The following morning, Celia and I both stumbled out of bed at exactly the same time, midday. Passing each other on the landing we staggered to the bathroom where we held a lot of porcelain. Obviously we didn't speak. Finally we tottered downstairs, still with no words having been exchanged, just the occasional groan, clutching one another. There, at the bottom of the stairs, an extraordinary sight met our eyes. Stopped us in our tremulous tracks. We swayed gently on the Cornish slate floor, in our bare feet, strappy tops and PJ bottoms, surveying the chaotic scene beyond in the kitchen.

'Dear God,' Celia finally said, faintly. 'Have we been burgled?'

Every kitchen drawer was open, every cupboard door flung wide: dirty pans and plates tottered at a precarious, uneasy angle in a pagoda in the sink, and every work surface was covered with empty packets of foodstuffs, mostly of the artery-clogging, fry-able kind.

'Wait.' I put an unsteady hand to my head, which was throbbing dully. 'It's all coming back to me.' I tottered to sit on a stool at the bar, clutching the furniture en route. 'When I got in, you were busy eating your own bodyweight in breakfast fare. There were eggs and sausages and bacon sizzling in every pan.'

'That's it,' she agreed, remembering. She groped her way to sit beside me. 'And you joined in.'

'I was starving,' I told her in surprise. 'Really ravenous. And I'd been out to dinner.'

'That's what happens,' she told me gravely, 'when you dabble in illicit substances.'

'Ah.' I nodded. 'Yes, of course.' I paused nervously. Some of the highlights of my evening were returning rather too vividly and gloriously. 'Did . . . Ted drop me off?' I hazarded.

'He did.'

'And was I . . . you know . . . OK?' I asked anxiously.

'Define OK.'

'I mean, did I . . . you know – comport myself, um, decorously?'

'I think you made your intentions pretty clear when you invited him for a naked swim.'

I put my head in my hands and moaned low.

'Oh, don't worry, he knew you were out of it. He disentangled himself from your clammy clutches and bid us a cheery goodnight.'

'Right.' I raised my head. 'Super cool, then.'

'Well, not you.'

'No. Quite.'

'Oh, I shouldn't worry. You've lost none of your allure.' Was there an edge to her voice? I couldn't tell. 'He seemed pretty taken with you, if you ask me.' She heaved a great sigh up from her bare toes.

I regarded her in alarm. 'Cele, if you've changed your—'

'No. Hundred percent haven't. Just got a thumping headache.' She gazed bleakly around the kitchen. 'Bacon and eggs?'

I gave the greasy mess a considering look. 'D'you know, weirdly, yes. Should we wash the pans first?'

'I think that would elevate us from the student gutter to the more mature, scatty artist level.'

We pottered about gingerly, slowly clearing up the kitchen. I turned the radio on very low, but Celia turned it off again.

'Speaking of which, are we working today?' I paused at the sink and frowned, up to my elbows in suds. 'What day *is* it?'

'Sunday, so no. Personally I'm going to lie in a darkened room until the gaudiness of last night's excesses recedes into the very distant past and all memory of—*God!*'

We both froze. Cringed low as our doorbell rang at full volume. *Brrrrrrrrrrr!!* When it finally stopped, I turned, arms still in the water. Celia had her hands over her ears.

We gazed at one another in horror. 'Did you even know we *had* one?' she whispered, removing her hands gingerly from her head. 'Don't people down here just push on through?'

'Shouting coo-ee, yes.'

'So who is it?'

'No idea.'

'Who would do that?' She looked worried.

'Don't know, Cele. Can't see through doors.' I removed my hands from the sink and wiped them on a tea towel since she clearly wasn't going to make a move.

'We don't *want* anyone like that,' she said petulantly. 'The police?'

'Oh, don't be silly!' But suddenly I was marching very quickly to that door, Peter springing instantly to mind, together with the usual maternal nightmares to do with teenagers, the sea, copious amounts of alcohol and various notorious horror stories. But something else about Peter and last night, which was coming back to me, made me open the door with even greater alacrity to the morning sunshine.

A familiar figure stood silhouetted on the doorstep. But it was one I hadn't seen for quite some time, so I was wrong-footed. A pale, sandy-haired man with freckly skin and tortoiseshell glasses, behind which he blinked a great deal, was facing me. He was clutching what can only be described as a man-bag. I would get there, I would. But it was taking me a moment. Celia, coming up behind me, got there before me.

'Edward!' she called in surprise.

That's it. Edward.

She joined me at the door. 'What on earth are you doing here?'

'Well I – I just thought I'd come down and see how you were – you know,' he faltered, 'how you were getting on.' It was quite a long sentence for Edward. He blinked rapidly with the exertion.

'Well, what a lovely surprise, come in, come in! You've come miles, for heaven's sake – have you come from London? Surely you haven't come down for the day? And how come you're not working? I thought you were working? By the way, we don't normally live like this – here, sit here.' She guided him to a barstool, still firing questions at him and not waiting for an answer. She flew around the kitchen like a whirling dervish, on a mission now, to make it gleam like an operating theatre.

Throwing open the back door to the garden, she then changed her mind about the stool and told him to go outside and look at the view. She generally bossed and scolded him, telling him he looked pale and to get some sun and that she'd bring him a coffee and to sit at the table – no, not in the shade, in the sun – talking at a million miles an hour.

I gave her a hand as she buzzed around, hangover all forgotten, nothing artistic or fey about her homemaking now.

'Did you know?' I murmured, throwing a handful of empty eggshells in the bin.

'No!' she hissed.

'So what's he doing here?'

'Search me.'

'Shall I make myself scarce?'

'Yes!'

Right. That was fairly unequivocal. Abandoning whatever greasy pan I'd been about to wash up, I crept upstairs, needing no further prompting. No tragedy at all, actually. I very much needed a lie-down. I stole gratefully back to bed, snuggled under the duvet and hunkered down. I shut my eyes. Edward. Golly. Celia usually had to make an appointment to see him, weeks in advance. And even then he generally cancelled if he was feeling too sensitive. Edward was a very sensitive playwright, frightfully talented, Celia always told me, although it seemed to me the sensitivity kicked in mostly when his plays were panned, or pulled, or not produced at all, which appeared to happen with increasing regularity. Maybe because they were too bloody difficult? I'd loyally been to see a few, usually in some converted warehouse in Tooting, or Peckham. A particularly memorable one involved a man lying naked on stage for two hours whilst various cast members – well, the other two – had a long and boring discussion about him. Celia told me it was very exciting and provocative, but it seemed to me Beckett had done it all years ago.

My thoughts turned, somewhat frivolously, away from Celia and Edward, to what I might even be so bold as to call my own love life. To Ted, on whom I hoped I hadn't made too disastrous an impression. And about whom, actually, I was beginning to have some rather warm, glowing feelings, which were remarkably pleasant, and which I hadn't experienced for a very long time. A small smile escaped me under the duvet and I opened my eyes a touch. We're not talking thunder bolts here, or a karate chop behind the knees, nothing like that. Just a warm, rosy glow, rather like – yes, rather like a cosy four-ply Aran jumper, if I'm honest. Disappointingly, though, as my mind roved back to kissing him on the beach, which possibly hadn't been my finest hour but had at least got the ball rolling, the rosy glow didn't last. Because some-one else, also on the beach, loomed large and took centre stage. Peter. I'd thought he was with Janey, but could it equally have been a young student? I frowned. I hadn't noticed him at all at the party, but he'd obviously been there. Had he met someone?

I sat up abruptly and reached for my phone. Sent him a text.

> Hi darling – hope all's well.
> Think I saw you last night at
> the beach!

I waited, ridiculously, impotently, because of course the young don't text back like we do. They don't have their phones on volume or they'd be beeping away boringly all day, unlike those who get positively exercised by their occasional music. But then, amazingly, he did. I jumped. Gazed at my screen.

> Yeah, I saw you too. Kissing
> and taking drugs – look at
> you!

I dropped the phone in horror. Both hands went to my mouth. God. How *awful*! I was about to text back and say I was doing nothing of the kind but that would, of course, be a thumping great fib.

Instead, after I'd unfrozen, which took a few moments, I scuttled to the bathroom in shame and shut the door. I'd left the offensive phone on the bed where I couldn't see it, and I crept now to run a hot bath with lots of bubbles. Had he been jocular in tone? Not embarrassed and aghast? Yes, of course he had. Still. I could hardly ask him now if he'd been walking along the beach with Janey, could I? It seemed positively tame in comparison to my antics. And anyway, so what if he had? They hadn't been arm in arm, I persuaded myself. I don't know why I'd thought that. No, it was just an innocent stroll, that was all. Golly, you do overreact, Flora. I gently peeled off my clothes. Slowly I immersed my poor, bewildered, traumatized self in the steamy water, hoping not only for a cleaner body, but a cleaner mind, too.

Celia and Edward were sharing a moment when I came downstairs. I popped my head out of the French windows into the garden. Eyes were locked, cheeks were pink, hands were clasped across the table. He was playing with her fingers: making up little stories about what they were up to in a this-little-piggy sort of way – and who hasn't found themselves succumbing to such inanities in their time? I popped my head smartly back inside and wondered where else I could make myself scarce. Celia had seen me, though, and was inside in a trice, principally to seize a bottle of wine from the fridge, but also to turn the radio on to cover our voices as she informed me of my duties.

'It was the text I sent,' she whispered. 'Dumping him. The one about meeting Ted and not needing him any more. It made him super jealous and he realizes now how much he loves me and doesn't want to let me go. He's beetled all the way down here just to see me, can you believe it?' She had the bottle between her legs and, with an old-fashioned corkscrew, was manically attempting to uncork a screw-top lid. I took it from her, untwisted it and handed it back.

'No. I mean – yes. Of course I can believe it.'

'So listen.' She came closer, much closer, clutching her bottle. 'He's horny, OK, which, as you know, is rare. Really rare. And I badly need a bath. So this is the plan. You go out into the garden and sit, and chat, and have a glass of wine, till I come back. But not too much wine, OK? We might lose it otherwise, right?'

'Lose what?'

'The stiffy.'

'Oh. Right.'

'So keep it chatty and light. Nothing deep, got it? And don't ask him about his plays.' She shoved the bottle into my hands.

'Right. So ... what should I ... you know ... chat about?' I asked nervously.

'Oh God – anything! Make it up. The London social scene, the weather, whatever. But don't flirt,' she hissed, her face very close to mine. 'Or maybe a tiny bit,' she said, eyes sliding away, considering. 'To keep it there, till I get back.'

'Sorry – Celia, am I sitting in the garden helping a man maintain an erection?'

'Of *course* not, don't be ridiculous.' She dithered a moment. 'Yes. OK. A bit.' She took two glasses from the cupboard and thrust them into my hands. 'Just don't cock it up, all right?'

I muttered something about this being an unfortunate analogy under the circumstances, but she was already away. Taking the stairs two at a time in her PJs, wild curls springing from her head, her face aglow, eyes shining, something I hadn't seen since – ah. Yes. That first day. Painting on the cliff, with Ted below on the beach. Right. Golly. *Quite* a responsibility. No pressure, Flora. Nervously, and with much trepidation, I went gingerly out into the garden.

Edward was no longer sitting, but standing, hands

in trouser pockets, facing the house. Facing me, in fact, and – oh dear God, there it was. Head down and eyes averted, I scuttled to the table, bottle in one hand, glasses in the other.

'Edward, how lovely to see you,' I said, keeping my eyes firmly on the refreshments. My hand shook a little as I poured a glass and it seemed to me my voice was different, too. More high-pitched. Squeaky.

'*So* glad I came,' he said, rather assertively for him, and with, when I dared to glance, an alarmingly wide smile. 'I thought it was a good decision. But you never quite know till you get there, do you?'

If only he'd take his hands out of his pockets and stop rocking back on his heels like that.

'No – no, you don't. Um, Edward, shall we sit down?' I already was. Firmly. I meant him.

'Yes, OK.' He came across, still beaming, but disconcertingly, didn't sit. I handed him a glass without looking. Luckily it made contact with his hand.

'You're looking so well, Flora!' he told me admiringly, with – yes, I had to glance, rude not to – a disconcerting gleam in his eye.

'Oh – well, yes, gosh. I have been ... well,' I said, keeping my eyes low and licking dry lips. 'Threw off that dreadful cough I had for ages.' I was keen to get away from the aesthetic connotations of Looking Well and on to the more mundane ones of Being Well. He looked a trifle miffed at this and I remembered to flirt a tiny bit.

'But I was just thinking the same about you, Edward. You're positively glowing!'

The beam returned instantly and I prayed he'd sit.

Just . . . effing well . . . sit. Just as he did – finally, thank the Lord – a loud 'Coo-ee!' trilled from inside the house. The front door slammed and I swung around in relief. I was fairly sure Edward and I would dry up in seconds on the London social scene, which neither of us participated in, and Babs could surely be relied upon to jabber away flirtatiously until Celia appeared. It was what she did best, after all.

'How are you girls this morning?' she was calling gaily as she came sailing through the sitting room. Out through the French windows she breezed. She was wearing a gingham sundress and white gym shoes. 'Have you recovered from your night on the tiles?'

'Yes thanks, Babs. And you, too, I hope?' I asked pointedly, but her eyes were already on our guest, who was politely, and rather disappointingly, getting to his feet.

'Um, Babs, this is Edward. He's a – a great friend of Celia's,' I finally plumped for, by way of introduction. Babs' eyes had already travelled low.

'Um – Babs, drink? Do sit, honestly, everyone sit. I'll get another glass.' I scarpered inside. Once in the kitchen, I peered back through the open doors. I could see Babs talking and undoubtedly flirting, but was she being dismissive and scary, too? She could be. She often was. I grabbed the glass and scuttled back. Still Edward was on his feet – was he oblivious to his condition? How could he be? Or proud? Encouraging everyone finally to be seated, I kept the conversation light and general. Babs was sizing him up in silence. She lit a cigarette and peered at him through smoke and narrowed, highly amused eyes. Meanwhile I laboured on about which route he'd taken, and the joy of finally getting to Stonehenge. How it took me back to my childhood every time. How, in my day, there were no ropes cordoning it off, and we'd perch on the stones to eat our sandwiches. All the time Babs looked on, and smoked and stared. Finally she cut in.

'So what is it you do, Edward?'

I nearly lowered my forehead to the table. Indeed, it's possible I did. Edward's smile faded and it seemed to me the sun went behind a cloud. The birds stopped singing in the trees, and an icy chill fell upon the garden.

'I'm a playwright,' he told her.

'Oh, how fascinating! What have you written?'

He told her and she frowned. 'No. Sorry.'

'But Edward's shows are mostly in London,' I told her quickly. 'They're not provincial.'

'I come to London. Do you get good reviews?'

By the time Celia came down from her bath, it was all over. Babs had gone through every one of his plays – three – and asked why he thought they hadn't worked. Why the critics hadn't liked them. As he'd told her, at rambling, juddering, stuttering length, she'd finally got bored. She glanced at her watch, drained her glass and said she'd had a lovely time but she really must be going. She was going sailing with Roger. Blowing us dinky little kisses, she got up and swept away down the garden and through the little picket gate, taking the sandy path to the dunes, and the beach below.

Celia came out into the garden, beaming. She was look-ing ravishing in a pretty yellow summer dress, her arms already brown from the sun. Smelling gorgeous, she had a touch of eyeliner on, some lipstick, but not a slap job. She was altogether looking hopeful, expectant, and delighted with life. I got to my feet.

'Um, Babs has just been,' I told her carefully, looking her in the eye. 'She was asking Edward about his plays. I'm, er . . . going down to the beach. For a swim.' I abandoned all further eye contact and turned, cravenly, to scuttle after Babs. No costume, no towel, no nothing. Too lily-livered to dart upstairs to fetch them. Because by the time I came down, the music might well have started. I turned, made haste, and fled.

18

Did I mention I was barefoot, such was my haste? Happily it didn't matter because I was heading to the beach, but, as I did, it occurred to me that I was also incredibly hungry, and, not only did I not have shoes, I didn't have the wherewithal to silence my rumbling stomach. Since I might have to be gone for some time, this could be a problem. There was a tiny beach café just a bit further along, where they served delicious coffee and toasted sandwiches. I wondered, as I made my way towards it, if I could possibly prevail upon the patrons to advance me a morsel of lunch? Which I would obviously reimburse them for as soon as was humanly possible?

The café operated out of a pale blue Volkswagen camper van. The small fenced garden was already well populated, the clientele mostly of the young, wave-riding kind. Plenty of wetsuits were being sported and there were a few boards piled up in the corner: music was playing. I went through the garden and tested my idea on the two young surfing dudes who were behind the makeshift counter in their blue-and-white stripy butchers' aprons. Their bright, welcoming, toothpaste smiles, which had flashed up so promisingly when I'd approached, faded.

They looked genuinely upset. The blond boy scratched his woolly, wave-tossed hair.

'You know, we'd really like to say yes, because you're so obviously kosher, and you've told us where you live and everything, but the thing is, we've been stung once too often. So we now have this policy? That we don't run a tab?'

'Last summer,' added his friend who looked as if he'd been through the washing machine with a tub of Vanish he was so bleached, 'I'm not gonna lie, not one person came back to pay.'

'Oh, that's appalling. How dreadful. Yes, of course. I do see, absolutely. No, well, I'm sorry to have asked. Sorry to have put you on the spot.' I made to move on, thoroughly embarrassed and pretty pink now because there were a couple of people behind me. I was far too old for the begging, urchin look. I should have gone, I realized, to Pam Maynard in the bakery, who'd known me since I was born, although that, of course, would have involved a barefoot pilgrimage down the high street. I turned to go, when suddenly a large, tanned paw came from nowhere, between me and the counter, clasping a tenner. A familiar voice in my ear said:

'Cheese and pickle?'

I already knew it was Ted. His voice, which was strong and reassuring, had, if I'm honest, sent something of a girlish frisson up my spine. I turned and bestowed what I hoped was my most dazzling smile. His eyes sparkled into mine: they were highly amused.

'Please. But hold the pickle. I'm in enough of one already.'

'Add to that a toasted cheese and ham,' he told the boy. 'And a cappuccino?' he offered, with an enquiring smile.

'Perfect.'

The boys looked relieved, and, if I'm honest, rather admiring. I mean, how lucky was that? Talk about a knight in shining armour. They told us they'd bring it straight across when it was ready, and we moved away to sit at a table that was just being vacated, in pole position, right at the edge of the garden. Take one more step and you're in the sea. Just then the sun came out from behind a very tiny cloud. Perfect.

'Yet again, Mr Fleming, I am indebted to you,' I said as I sat down.

'Think nothing of it, Mrs Bellingdon. And I don't think it's Yet Again, is it?'

'Well, by all accounts you delivered me safely home last night and didn't take advantage of my riotous condition, which, according to Celia, I gave you every opportunity to. Indeed every invitation.' I rolled mortified eyes.

'Ah yes.' He laughed. 'The skinny-dipping. Which under normal circumstances I'd be more than up for. Do ask again.'

His eyes held mine. They were warm and tender, not mocking. But although I was enjoying it, I was out of practice and couldn't do it for long. Mine slid away to the sea.

'This your usual haunt?' I asked casually.

'Most days, actually. The boys used to be students of mine. They're nice lads trying to run a business on a shoe-string, so I patronize it as much as I can. They could do more with their degrees, but some people, particularly marine biologists, can't bear to be away from the sea even for a minute. I get it.'

My eyes came back to him. 'And the same goes for you? You have to be by the sea?'

It sounded a bit as if I was canvassing him on where he might settle down with me some day, but I'm increasingly aware that I'm alone in such hypersensitivity. He certainly didn't treat the question as a loaded one.

'No, actually, not necessarily. But I do need water. Where I live now there's a river at the bottom of the garden – that's enough for me. You get all the wildlife: the wagtails, the kingfishers, herons, otters. I even saw a water vole the other day. I can sit there for hours.'

'Sounds idyllic.'

'But you prefer London?'

'No, I'm very definitely a country girl. And, actually, in an ideal world I would want to be by the sea, it's where I grew up. But Peter's school is near London.'

'But he's left school, surely?'

'Yes, but his life will be there, I can tell. He's a clever chap. And I want to be near him.' May as well iron out that little crease straight away: some things are non-negotiable.

He nodded. Looked thoughtful. 'Although London doesn't have a monopoly on attracting clever people?'

'I know. But the sort of place he'll want to apply to does.'

'Oh, OK.' He grinned. 'So – what? Make a pile of dosh before retiring to the Home Counties to hobby farm? Send his children to private school and take up shooting?'

I laughed. 'You make that sound like a bad thing.'

He shrugged. 'No, not necessarily. Just a trifle . . . formulaic.'

I swallowed. I could explain that my own life had been anything but formulaic. That I fervently wished it had

244

been. Wished I'd been to the right schools, that I'd had all the advantages Christina had had: played in all those lacrosse matches, been captain of the tennis team. Or at least, had the opportunity to turn it all down. And how a ridiculous part of me wondered if that was what I'd lacked, for Hugo. Polish. Once, when Christina and I had had a nerve-wracking chat at speech day at Peter's school, she'd told me how she wished she rode, and how good Hugo said I was. I knew she was being kind and I appreciated it, even though I hated it, too; this crumb from the rich man's table that my feet should by rights have been under. But I was interested that this was what Hugo had chosen to praise about me. Not my art, or even my mothering skills, but my prowess in the saddle. Or perhaps I was reading too much into it, as was my wont. As for ensuring a formulaic life for my son, Peter had already turned his nose up at banking, which I'm sure Ted would applaud, but with every fibre of my being I wanted to be on hand to personally supervise any future enablement. For him to be party to all the best choices, even if he refused them. And yes, Ted, this powerful maternal force, perhaps the most powerful force of all in the natural world, that world you love so much, would therefore prevent me from settling by my beloved seashore, which constantly called me back and which I so longed to call home once more.

I shrugged. 'I can take it or leave it, frankly,' I told him. 'I saw enough of the sea in my youth.'

Our sandwiches had arrived, and I bit into mine, wiping hot cheese away as it dribbled down my chin. Ted regarded me with curiosity and I'm not entirely sure I got away with it. The lie or the mess on my face.

But he didn't pursue it. We chatted on. Nothing deep, just observations about how the place had changed since I'd grown up here, which was not that much actually, and a bit about some new research he was doing. When we parted, an hour or so later, him to supervise a field trip and a clear-up operation further along the coast, and me to achieve something I'd been meaning to do since I arrived in Cornwall, I thanked him again for my sandwich.

'That's the second meal you've bought me in two days,' I told him as we walked towards the car park together. 'I'm beginning to feel like a kept woman.'

'Is it a role you could get used to?'

'Will I need a poodle and a feather boa?'

'Only if I grow a handlebar moustache and drive a Morgan, so probably not. But it does rather cast a shadow over my next question.'

'Which is?'

'Well, I wondered if you'd like another meal, but I'm beginning to sound repetitive.' He stopped by his car and scratched his head. 'You try being a man. I don't like bowling, and who wants to sit in a cinema where you can't talk?'

I smiled. 'I could cook?'

'Can you?'

'Not terribly well, actually. But I'm told my fish pie is edible.'

He smiled. 'My favourite, as it happens. When would suit? Tomorrow? Or is that too keen? It's just I'm around at the moment, and I'm not always.'

'No, that should be fine,' I said slowly, remembering Celia and Edward. 'Tell you what, tomorrow, unless I text. It's just Celia could be entertaining, too.'

'Blimey, you're both at it. Who's Celia found?'

I explained. 'Jealous?' I asked him.

He had a shout of a laugh which involved his head being thrown back and a hoot up to the sky. I liked it.

'No, Flora. If I was, she'd be making her signature dish for me.'

'The arrogance!'

'Oh, she made her intentions clear when I helped her down the cliff with her easel.'

I looked incredulous. 'You think?'

'Don't pretend you don't know that. I'll think the less of you.'

'Well, we can't have that, can we?' I said lightly, but I knew he was right. 'OK, put my amazement down to loyalty to my friend.'

'I already did, my love.' He grinned. 'And I liked you for it. See you tomorrow.'

He pulled out his car keys along with his phone and we swapped numbers: and then I turned and walked away, mostly to hide my ridiculous smile. And my high colour, which always happens when I'm having a nice time. I don't think I'd been called 'my love' before. I rather liked it. Hugo had called me darling, Tim, too, and Rupert didn't call me anything, barely even Flora. I knew, too, I'd feel a thrill of excitement when we messaged each other to confirm our plans. Knew he was making me feel about fifteen.

I left the beach car park and walked up the long flight of steps to the cliff path, clouds racing above me, salty wind in my hair. I really wished I had shoes on, though. I paused for a moment to consider. It wasn't far, but the grass here was coastal and spiky and my feet weren't

Cornish hard yet. I decided to persevere. But I kept to the sandy path which was gritty but manageable, and obviously kept an eagle eye out for dog poo.

Some time later, as I rounded the bend around the headland into the estuary, I saw a familiar figure ahead, on the intersection with the bridle path. Iris was silhouetted against the bright blue sky on the large grey mare I recognized from the other day. Her reins were loose, one hand was resting on her knee and she was gazing out across the mouth of the estuary. It struck me that if I ever painted Iris, which I'd dearly like to, this was how I'd want her. In the saddle but with the sea behind her, at one with horse and nature. She saw me and turned. Waited for me to come up the hill.

'That makes a fabulous tableau!' I called, puffing a bit as I approached. 'Very Demelza Poldark!'

She laughed. 'Yes, except for the Pre-Raphaelite hair, the low-cut dress and the youth. The absolute spit!'

'Still, I'd love to paint you there.'

'This one would never stand still for long enough,' she said, patting the grey's neck as she danced a bit. 'How does anyone ever paint animals?'

'They cheat and photograph them. But that's OK, because sometimes you need props to capture someone's personality, or at least their great loves. I always think the Queen should either be covered in corgis or on a horse. And I'd certainly need a horse, the sea and the sky, with you.'

'In that case you should probably paint my brother out here, rather than inside.' She grinned and inclined her head out to where she'd just been gazing. I followed her eyes.

Out in the relatively calm waters of the estuary, a little blue boat with a green sail was slowly gliding through the water, but even at this distance we could hear the shouts of laughter, the banter. I could see the boat rock occasionally as if with mirth, and practically hear the gin bottles clinking as a gingham dress and a stripy blue polo shirt toasted one another.

I smiled. 'It had occurred to me, actually. But the logistics are pretty impossible. Would you say that's everything he loves most? The sea, a boat, and Babs?'

'These days, yes. In the old days, no.'

'Ah. Belinda would have featured?'

'No, a horse would have featured.'

I giggled. 'That's awful, Iris. Did he really never love her? Belinda?'

'Oh, I'm sure he did, in his own way. Probably still does. But is it really love, if it's that milky and diluted? I think few people are ever lucky enough to really find it, Flora. And many settle for less.'

I was fairly sure this was why Iris had never married. Mum had always said she couldn't brook compromise and I was silenced by the quiet authority of her words. And the confidence. You needed that, to be completely on your own. Some would say I had it, but I'd always had Peter, and I'd also had, in the past, pluperfect sense, Hugo. I'd obviously grilled Mum about Iris and had longed for her to say, ah yes, well years ago there *was* this dashing young hunt master/naval captain/stable girl, perhaps, who broke her heart, but she never did. Iris remained an enigma: happy with her horses, her flat above the coach house, her life. Integral to, but always separate from, the Bellingdon clan. A spectator. I wonder if she also knew that her happiness – not just contentment – unsettled people.

'How is everyone back at the ranch?' I stroked the mare's silky, warm neck. 'Peter OK?' I added casually.

'Gone surfing with his mates, round at Porthlemon. Quite a way. They drove up this morning to collect him. School friends, I gather.'

'Oh good! Yes, that's right, he met some of them at the pub. Good, I'm glad he's having fun. Otherwise it's all rather old for him up there, don't you think?'

Iris narrowed her eyes speculatively across the bay. She took her time to reply. 'Oh, Peter can look after himself.' Then she shortened her reins. 'This one's getting fidgety, Flora. I'd better move on. Give him my regards.' She jerked her head further on, up the hill.

I glanced to where she'd gestured, where I was going. 'How did you . . . ?'

But when I turned back she'd already gone. I watched the flanks of her young grey mare, spooking at the rabbit holes she was being asked to navigate, with every assurance from her rider that there were no tigers in them. In a few years' time she wouldn't give them a second glance and would be tripping nimbly down here in the dusk, knowing exactly where to put her dainty hooves, thanks to the expert guidance she'd been given. I watched her progress for a bit then walked on.

The tiny grey church on the headland seemed to rise out of the very ground it was forged from. Ancient and granite, it crouched there on the hillside, the exact same colour as the rabbits that hopped away the moment I approached, their white tails flashing. I went through the little iron gate and around the side to where the hillside slipped dramatically away to the sea. The gravestones, over the years, had leaned right back to accommodate the incline, some almost touching the grass behind them. This one would go that way too, one day, I realized as I crouched down beside it. For the moment, though, it was straight and strong and steady, as he had been. I gently stroked its rounded top with my fingertip. Then I took a deep breath and let it out slowly. No need to read it, imprinted as it was on my DNA, but I did anyway.

WILLIAM HENRY PENHALLOW. KILLED IN ACTION. 1944–95. BELOVED HUSBAND OF MAGGIE AND FATHER OF FLORA. WE MISS HIM DREADFULLY.

The funeral director had glanced up at us in surprise as he wrote this down on his pad. 'Not – sadly missed?'

'No,' said Mum. 'We miss him dreadfully. So that's what I want to say. Sadly missed sounds like . . . I don't know. Kind regards. Pat. Trite.' She stiffened, as did our man behind the desk, not used to having his expressions of sympathy dismissed so. But Mum and I felt it bound the three of us together for ever. Made it quite clear who, exactly, missed him dreadfully. Others might miss him in a more general sense; in the officers' mess, sitting on the parish council, taking Year Eleven on their annual trip to the rifle range at Bodmin, but not like we did. Not as deeply, painfully, and yes, dreadfully.

After a while, my knees began to stiffen. Hard to know how long I'd been crouched there. I straightened up, with difficulty.

'Iris sends her love,' I told him.

I'd told him a lot more, too, silently, when I'd been low and close. About how I thought he might be more pleased with me, these days, for moving on. About how sorry I was that the last time I'd been here, I hadn't come to see him. How I'd been too ashamed. It had been at the height of my madness. I told him about how, maybe, just maybe, I could be here more. Talk to him more. Do a bit of both. A bit of Cornwall, a bit of London. Who knows? I could only tell my father things like this. Nonsense, you might call it, but what was in my head. Let's face it, it was going nowhere.

My father had habitually given far more advice than my mother: given much more of a steer. He believed, for instance, that resilience had to be cultivated, and would tell me so. When he'd died, one of the things that had shaken me most was the realization that he was no longer saying things like that, no longer telling me to step up to the plate, be brave – *courage* was a word he used a lot – that he was no longer attentive. Mum was there, of course, but she was more laissez-faire, relaxed. My life was going by now, unobserved. These days any form of vigilance goes by the unfashionable, derogatory word of *judgement*, usually by those who want to avoid its eye. But at its best, it's about love and care. And the very best sort is so ingrained, it becomes invisible. In my heart I knew that had Dad lived, I wouldn't have wasted so many years of my life. That he wouldn't have let me get away with it. Not in any stern, draconian way; he might not even have said anything, but knowing his eye was upon me, I couldn't have let it happen. Couldn't have taken the path of least resistance.

I knew, too, that if I'd taken that difficult route, forced myself to have more of a life, found someone else, married even, when I was still young, had more children instead of indulging my emotions, wallowing in my misery, sooner or later, everything would have been fine. He'd taught me that, as well. Taught me that if you go through the motions, force yourself, eventually the motions become real life. Without him standing by, I hadn't done it. I'd cheated.

I took the deepest of breaths. There were gulls circling overhead, but they weren't calling to each other as usual and the sea was millpond still. All was strangely silent. The quiet little churchyard sounded very loud to my ears, though. I'd lost my father long ago. What I shouldn't have lost was the courage to believe that one day someone else might love me in a similarly concerned and careful manner.

I kissed the tips of my fingers and touched the top of his headstone, my eyes full. Then I turned and made my way back through the churchyard to the cliff path, and embarked on the long walk home.

19

Trewarren was bathed in sunshine when I walked up the hill towards it the following morning. Facing east, as it did, to the sea, all its windows seemed to glitter with salty satisfaction as it stood, large, square and proud at the top of the huge sweep of gravel. The front door gently opened at my crunching feet and Truffle, old and with a grey muzzle, but clearly very sound of hearing, came arthritically down the steps to meet me, waving her tail apologetically for being so slow. I fondled her ears and crooned to her. A puppy when I'd first met her years ago, she'd pranced around Peter as he took his first steps here in the garden, cheering him on as she gambolled beside him, showing him how it was done. I'd often find Peter in her basket, which she chewed ferociously, letting him take the broken wicker pieces from her mouth and then – oh Lord – have a chew himself before I'd rush and retrieve them. I wouldn't retrieve the boy, though: he loved it in there and I loved to see them playing together in her bed, even though Belinda said it was unhygienic. I patted her grey flecked back and she followed me slowly inside.

The hall was cool and quiet. Only the long-case clock ticked under one of the two flights of cantilevered stairs which, having risen centrally as one, separated on to the landings. The pale-yellow walls were hung with familiar family portraits, all pioneers of Bellingdon Water. 'Trade', Babs would say with a smirk to Roger, who would roar with laughter. I gazed at them now. Some terrible, some very good. All male. And of course, mine of Roger would hang here one day. And, no, it didn't daunt me. I have a lot of problems, but confidence in my work is not one of them.

I turned down the passageway away from the formal rooms and pushed on through the green baize door at the end. More through hope than expectation I poked my head around the first room I came to but, naturally, the gunroom was empty. I carried on down to the kitchen with a slightly sinking heart. If only it would rain, or at least not be quite so spectacular weather-wise, I might corner my prey. Yvonne, Belinda's daily, had her back to me in her apron. She had her mop out and was giving the floor what she'd call 'a jolly good seein' to', so I perched in the doorway on the threshold of the wet tiles and called a loud 'coo-ee!' above *Woman's Hour*. She turned.

'Hang on!' She flew to the counter and deftly put some pieces of newspaper down for me. I treated them like stepping stones and arrived to give her a hug. She gave her usual, nervous, infectious giggle as Truffle declined the paper and padded up.

'Old dog, new tricks,' I told her as Truffle flopped down beside Flurry, the Border terrier, in her basket.

'Except she used to. I taught her once, but she thinks it's beneath her now.'

'Quite right. She's an old lady.'

'Aren't we all.'

We perched on stools at the island, but only one buttock each, in case Belinda came in, and I told her I'd missed her last week, and she told me she'd been on her annuals in Newquay. Seeing her sister, but she wouldn't be going again. Too kiss-me-quick and she missed the dogs too much. I knew she meant these two, who she treated as her own. Years ago Yvonne had cleaned for friends of Mum's in the village, but Belinda had decided she didn't like the tittle-tattle and wanted Yvonne exclusively for herself. She threw money at it and Yvonne wasn't stupid. But the tittle-tattle continued, only more so, since Yvonne was here every day and had more to tell. She asked about Mum and I told her she was well.

'What's up with Flurry?' I pointed to the terrier, who'd failed to greet me. She was in her basket, shivering gently.

'Phantom pregnancy. I took her to the vet cos her ladyship wouldn't, and they gave her some canine Valium, for the nerves. I slipped one in Belinda's tea to see if it would make any difference.'

I giggled. 'Stop it. And it's Mrs Bellingdon to you, you've only worked here twenty years. Is she about?'

I glanced around nervously, expecting her to waft in, in all her floral glory, at any second. Yvonne got up and resumed her moping.

'She and Hugo have gone out for the day. An arboretum or something then lunch. Don't ask me. Christina and the kids have gone swimming, and Peter's gone out with some friends, far as I know.'

'Oh good. And Roger?'

She grinned. 'You'll be lucky. Gave me a message. Said

he was just going to get his boat out of the water and he'd be back in a jiffy. To be fair, I thought I heard someone in the study earlier, so he might have crept back in.'

'Thanks, I'll have a look.' I surveyed the newspaper pieces which Truffle had scattered, rendering my return journey more tortuous.

'Go on, you can do it!' laughed Yvonne as she leaned on her mop, watching. 'Twister! You remember that!'

Back on the other side of the front hall, the study door was shut. I knocked softly and went in. Empty. Damn. Except – hang on. The long leather Chesterfield sofa with its back to me had feet sticking out from one end, over the arm. Grey-socked, and male. I crept in and around, expecting to surprise Roger, doubtless just settling down for a read of the newspaper and a cup of coffee, which under normal circumstances he'd do in the gunroom but who wants to be disturbed by that wretched girl and her paintbrushes. Instead, fast asleep, I found Tommy. His normally ruddy face looked washed out: his forehead was creased and his wavy red hair, greying at the temples, stood on end. His mouth was open and drooped dramatically at the sides. It struck me he'd slept in last night's clothes, chinos and a smart shirt, not daytime wear. He looked strangely vulner-able, for Tommy. All around, on the floor and the sofa, lay a sea of papers. Enormously surprised, I nonetheless crept away. Although clearly, not quite quietly enough.

'Hello?'

I'd reached the door. I paused. Turned. Came back round, where he could see me.

'Sorry. Didn't mean to disturb.'

On seeing me, his eyes, which had been cloudy, cleared instantly. He swung his legs round and sat up. Rubbed his face vigorously with the palms of his hands.

'What time is it?'

'About ten o'clock. Sorry—'

'No, no, stay. It's fine.'

I hovered uncertainly.

'Sit, even.'

I glanced at the chair at Roger's desk. Swung it round and perched even less of a buttock than I'd rested in the kitchen.

'Were you . . . working in here?' I asked hesitantly, looking around at the papers.

'Oh.' His eyes followed mine. 'Yes. Till far too late, I guess. Lost track of time.'

'You slept here?'

'Well, I didn't intend to.'

Even upside down I could read *Bellingdon Water* on a few of the letterheads. Plus a wavy blue logo I was familiar with.

'Helping Hugo?'

'Yeah. Trying to. And getting somewhere, until my eyes closed. I guess I'll go again later today.' He smiled sheepishly and began shuffling the papers together. They were mostly awash with figures.

I frowned. 'Does he need your help? I mean . . . Hugo's usually so on top of things.' I suppose I might have sounded slightly defensive, as if I suspected Tommy of interfering.

Tommy glanced up from paper-shuffling, blue eyes sharp. 'That's right, Flora. Hugo is on top of things. And he works so hard, as you, his mother and Christina are fond of telling me.'

'Well . . .' I was flummoxed. 'He does work hard.'

'Agreed. He does.'

His tone was harsh, but worry made me fail to retaliate. 'Is he in trouble?'

'Define trouble.'

'Well, you tell me, Tommy. I know he faces accusations of spillage and sewer leaks. Is it that?'

'Let's put it this way. It doesn't help.'

He wasn't expanding. He went back to the papers. He was being very taciturn.

'And . . . you'll sort it out?'

'Doing my best, ma'am.'

I licked my lips as he continued to busy himself. His eyes remained firmly on the task, avoiding my searching ones.

'Tommy . . . is that why you've come? To help Hugo? Is that why you're here and not in London?'

'Well, in this heat it's a nicer place to work than—'

'Please tell me,' I interrupted urgently.

He caught my tone. Glanced up. Our eyes locked and he nodded. 'Yes, that's specifically why I'm here.'

My heart began to thud. All my nerves tautened and I felt my mouth dry. 'Oh God, is he in serious trouble? I mean – not him, but the company?'

I must have looked scared because he instantly laughed and said, 'Of course not!' He got to his feet and I saw how creased his shirt was. I wondered what time he'd finally fallen asleep. I cleared my throat.

'Tommy, I didn't mean to ask you in that pathetic little voice. Tell me. I can take it. I promise.'

His blue eyes came round to meet mine, heavy from lack of sleep. Years of resentment existed between us, but in that moment, all that prevailed, in the steady gaze we gave one another, was concern for a man we both cared for.

'I know you can, Flora. At least – please God, after all these years – I think you can. I think you've found some detachment. But I can't tell you. Not right now. But trust me, I'm doing my best.'

I stared at him. My mouth was devoid of saliva now, but I knew he spoke the truth. That he couldn't tell me, and would do everything in his power to help Hugo.

'Thank you,' I said in a small voice. It wasn't nearly loud enough, but at least I'd said it. He nodded and I knew he was acknowledging my gratitude, but also dismissing me.

I went back down the corridor, biting the skin around my thumbnail, deep in thought. More through routine and reflex than with any real consideration, I continued on through the green baize door and into the gunroom.

'Where've you been?' roared Roger. His bottom was just about to hit the seat of his chair. He looked bright-eyed and delighted but smelled of fresh air and the sea. He'd clearly just arrived. 'Been here ages!' he boomed. 'Looked everywhere for you!'

'Oh, shut up, Roger. I was in here ten minutes ago so don't give me that.' I managed to smile but I wasn't in the mood. I was worried.

'Nonsense, been here hours,' Roger chortled, still enjoying his joke. He rubbed his hands gleefully. 'Must have missed each other when I popped to the downstairs lavvy for a precautionary. Thoughtful fellow, me. Wouldn't want to interrupt the creative flow.'

'Thank you, for sharing that with me. And yes, that must have been it,' I conceded, letting him win. He wiggled into position in his chair, pleased with himself. And happily, for once, wearing the correct clothes. He reached up to the shelf above and flicked his Roberts radio on to the test match.

'Didn't think to do that when you were in here for ages?' I murmured. I mixed my paints. 'Not like you.'

He barked out a laugh. His eyes gleamed delightedly at me from beneath bushy eyebrows. 'You're shrewder than people think, Flora.'

'Only when it suits me,' I told him, turning to face him properly now, poised with my palette. 'Sometimes it suits me for people to think otherwise. Something I'm sure you can relate to, Roger.'

He regarded me appraisingly and not without a glint of admiration, I thought. I settled down to paint.

My brushstrokes started carefully and speculatively as usual, my eyes darting from Roger to my canvas, back to Roger, back to the canvas. Presently, though, they became faster and more feverish. Yet in equal measure more precise and efficient. As always when I was upset, worried, alarmed, my work absorbed me completely; it took on the energy of my emotions. The transubstantiation – and I don't use the metaphor lightly, for when I came down to earth later, it always seemed to me I'd been possessed – was complete and utter. Today the metamorphosis from anxiety to creativity was total. Roger's face, which thus far had eluded me, so I'd sketched it in only roughly, concentrating instead on his hands, his shoulders, his chest, became so obvious all of a sudden. The way his eyes clouded, then cleared dramatically. The way that muscle in his cheek affected his mouth. The occasional tension, but abrupt joy, too. Roger's was a face that could turn on a sixpence, and suddenly I got it all, in what seemed like minutes, but was probably hours. That precious, elusive stretch of creativity which was such a mixed blessing, occurring as it did for me, at its most fruitful, when I was most upset. It once more took control.

Finally, a little voice said: 'Can I move?' Roger was looking pathetic. Wretched even. He gazed at me beseechingly.

'Of course.' I smiled. Lowered my brush.

'God, Flora. You're scary when you're like that,' he grumbled. He rolled his stiff shoulders around. 'I daren't breathe.'

I grinned. 'Sorry. Got carried away.' I glanced at the portrait, then at him. Was pleased. But the moment had passed. Blood, rather than passion, flowed through my veins now, and as it did, all my worry flooded back with it. I rinsed my brush in turps, considering. Wiped it on a rag. Then I took a deep breath.

'Roger, is Hugo OK?'

He frowned. 'What d'you mean?'

'I mean, work-wise?'

Roger's face made a lunge for opacity and inscrutability, then reverted to its habitual transparency. 'Well, let's hope so,' he growled. 'Tommy's on the case, at any rate. He'll sort it out.'

'He's clever, Tommy, isn't he?'

'Very. And Hugo's not.'

'Of course he is – he went to Oxford.'

'Because I got him in. My old college.' He regarded me fiercely. 'I knew the master. Oh, he's not stupid and he works hard, but he's weak.'

'You mean kind.'

'I mean weak.'

I stared. 'Well, what's that got to do with anything anyway? I mean—'

'We're talking about stopping sewage leaks, pollution, and that is reliant upon solid infrastructure, something Hugo knows nothing about. At least I did engineering. He did fucking theology.'

I swallowed. 'Yes, OK. But Hugo has very good directors. Engineers, even, who know—'

'Lining their own pockets. Like all shareholders do. Wouldn't have happened in my day.' I could see he was angry suddenly. 'Living in London – why isn't he down here? Where it all began? In Cornwall?'

'But Bellingdon contracts all over the country now. Even in the Home Counties. So London makes sense.'

'Makes no sense. You need to be by the coast, hands on. Near the filtration pumps, the underground tanks, the pipelines. Not in some ivory tower in Hampstead.'

'But he's expanding the company, surely?'

'There's no sense in overexpansion. Not when you can't see what's happening. Yes, he's got sewage filtration contracts with Buckinghamshire, with Thames Water even, and there's no doubt he's enlarged it, but he's lost sight of it. He'll filter the crap out of anyone's water. Wrong. Misguided. You know what his philosophy is?' His fists were clenched and his face grew red.

'What?'

Roger got to his feet. 'We take shit from anyone.'

I gazed at him. 'That's not true.'

'It is true. And since we're dealing in myths and untruths, the reason he left Cornwall was not to be near the London and Home Counties contractors, and you know it, Flora.' He burned me with his bright blue eyes.

'He's never loved it here,' I murmured. 'Not like you and me. Not like Babs, Iris, Mum—'

'No, he prefers the London life. Drinks parties in Chelsea. Hobnobbing with wealthy shareholders.'

'Sharing ideas,' I countered. 'New methods of technology, innovative projects.'

'All of that can happen anywhere in the country,' he told me angrily, parroting someone I'd heard very recently. 'That's just Hugo's party line for running an essentially Cornish company from London. But the main reason he left Cornwall, as you and I know, Flora, was not that.' His eyes blazed. 'It was to get away from his mother.'

A silence prevailed as our eyes communed. It was broken by the sound of a car coming up the front drive. Tyres, crunching up the gravel slope. As it swept around the fountain under the gunroom window, we turned as one. Belinda's blue BMW passed sleekly by, containing the two fair heads of Belinda and Hugo. Car doors opened then slammed. Footsteps went round to the front, where Belinda insisted, unaware that real country folk used the back. There were so many pitfalls for Belinda, lurking in the class system, and she fell into many of them: to be snobbish from such a disadvantaged position must surely be exhausting. But there was one hole Belinda never fell down, and that was the one that kept her grip on her son.

I wanted to tell Roger that. Tell him that geography and a distance of three hundred miles made no difference. Belinda had never loosened her hold, not when I was married to him – he phoned her at seven every night, and if he didn't, she called him, and he always spoke from another room. And every month she made a trip to London. Every month. A pilgrimage. She'd arrive at Paddington and get a taxi to the City where she'd have lunch with him at Wheelers. Not with me, she never saw me, unless it was to tell me to move flats or, on one famous occasion, to deliver all the family recipes, the ones Hugo liked. No, just her son. And I had no reason to suspect, I thought, as Christina hove into view, returning slowly from the beach, her children in her wake arguing over a bucket, that things were any different now. I washed my other brushes as Roger gazed out too, lost in his own thoughts. I'd like to tell him that. That Hugo hadn't got away. Had never escaped. But I suspect he already knew.

20

I went from the room, leaving Roger to his thoughts. He was still staring out to sea when I departed, hands thrust in his pockets. Very uncharacteristically for me, I then risked a spot of confrontation. Down the passageway I went, and into the kitchen. Belinda and Hugo were perched at the island together, about to have a cup of coffee. There was no sign of Yvonne. Hugo was facing me and Belinda had her back to me, pressing down the percolator. She turned.

'Oh, hello,' she said, in a surprised tone. Her smile didn't quite reach her eyes. 'You still here?'

'Yes, we had a bit of a session this morning. Took a bit longer than usual. I just popped in to say goodbye,' I said, by way of an excuse.

'Oh, no need to do that! You can breeze in and out as you please, you know that.' She got up and went to the fridge for the milk. *Don't come in the rest of the house*, she meant. Hugo was already on his feet and coming round the island to greet me. He kissed my cheek.

'Flora! Haven't seen you for ages,' he said with a wan smile, sweeping back his soft fair hair. His face was pale, but not like Tommy's from lack of sleep. More than that.

'You saw her a couple of days ago!' trilled Belinda. She filled a little milk jug.

'You look tired,' I told him, ignoring her.

'Nonsense, we've had a lovely day at the arboretum, haven't we, darling? The Friends of the Earth are sponsoring some new trees from Madagascar. I wanted to show Hugo.'

'It was great, Mum.'

'Then we had lunch at that Raymond Blanc bistro on the front, you know, Flora? No, actually, before your time.'

'Or after,' I said bravely. 'I've just been chatting to Tommy,' I told Hugo with a smile. 'I hear he's giving you a hand.' Belinda's face went rigid with shock. Even Hugo looked surprised. He recovered.

'Yes, he's been brilliant, actually.'

'A hand!' Belinda finally found her voice. 'Hugo doesn't need a *hand*, he works incredibly hard. I thought you of all people would know that, Flora.'

'I do,' I told her evenly. 'But a fresh pair of eyes is always useful, isn't it? To get a different perspective?'

'Exactly,' Hugo said as his mother opened and shut her mouth. 'Speaking of which,' he went on quickly, 'Flora – I'd love to see your painting. Is it too early? I wouldn't ask, except I know you never usually mind.'

'Of course I don't mind!' I told him as we both took advantage of his mother's temporary incapacity to breathe. 'I'd love to show you.' We made to leave and Belinda made to follow. 'But weirdly –' I turned to her – 'and this is going to sound ridiculously precious, I only like an audience of one at this stage.' Partly true. 'I find the chatter rather off-putting.'

'I get that,' said Hugo quickly. 'And you've always said that. Come on, let's take a look.'

And off we went, like naughty children. Leaving Belinda holding her silly little milk jug, outraged and impotent, in the middle of her kitchen.

As we walked down the passageway, we exchanged a secret smile which took me right back to our illicit courting days. Hugo pushed on through into the tall, sunlit gunroom and I followed. I'd swung my easel round to face the wall, not that I cared, but I always felt it was too in-your-face left on display to all comers. Belinda, principally, who was no doubt always creeping in, having a peek. There was no space to view the painting from the wall, however, and since I knew we were going to go through the Picture Viewing motions first before we talked – oh, we knew each other very well – I walked across and swung it round to face us. Hugo gazed, considering. Presently, a small, delighted smile spread to his lips.

'You've got him,' he whispered.

'I have, haven't I?' I agreed. No point dissembling. I had no truck with false modesty. 'But only literally today. The face, I mean. Up until yesterday, no, only the body. But I had a bit of a breakthrough.'

Hugo was properly smiling now, like a little boy. I loved that look: totally candid and open. 'You've got everything,' he said delightedly. 'The naughtiness, the shrewdness, the showman, the quizzical gleam – integrity, too. Not too twinkly. It's brilliant, Flora.' He threw his head back and laughed, looked back down at it again, tears of mirth in his eyes. He shook his head in wonder. 'I love it.'

'Not quite there,' I admitted, but I was quietly thrilled.

'That shoulder . . .' I peered critically. 'Looks a bit broken . . .'

'Well, it is,' he told me, moving closer and peering too. 'He broke his collarbone playing rugby at Oxford. But I know what you mean.' He always told me the truth. 'He's old, but not quite that slumped.'

'Exactly. But that's fine, at least I haven't made him too square, that's harder to fix.' My fingers were already itching for my brush. Now that I had the face there was so much I could improve on, but I knew from experience I needed the man there, too. Hugo helpfully turned it back for me, taking care not to touch the wet paint. He'd had some practice.

'Are you OK?' I asked him, when he'd set it straight.

'Yeah, I'm fine. Just tired.'

'I know.'

'And Mum's right. I'm on the right track, I know it. Dad thinks I've overexpanded but there are so many more opportunities these days that simply weren't there for him. There's room for business creativity, which, as you know, is my passion. What I wanted to do postgrad at Harvard.'

But hadn't got in. Unlike Tommy.

'Whereas your dad's skill was on the engineering side?'

'Exactly. But, as Mum says, he doesn't move with the times. And he certainly doesn't understand the City. Dad's fundamentally parochial – not that there's anything wrong with that.'

'No.' I paused. 'Was it your dad who asked Tommy to help?'

He hesitated. 'Sort of. I mean, he suggested it, and I said I'd think about it. And before I knew it – well, you know Dad.' I laughed. I did. 'And as you said earlier, a fresh pair of eyes. Two heads are better than one.'

At what, I wondered.

'I sometimes get bogged down with all the figures,' he admitted.

'Ah! Well in that case Tommy will be brilliant.'

'Exactly. He loves all the forensic stuff.' He was opening the door for me now, holding it for me to pass under his arm. As I came out I caught a glimpse of Belinda in the kitchen: waiting, watching. She turned quickly to the sink. 'And he can't stay long, anyway – he's got to get back to running his own company.'

'Well, quite.'

Polite chat now, not that we'd gone deep in there. But particularly since Christina was coming down the staircase behind us with the children, both looking washed and brushed after the beach.

'Darling!' He turned. 'I've just been looking at Flora's painting. It's terrific!'

'Is it?' Her face broke into a wide, genuine smile. 'Oh *good*. I'm dying to see it, but I won't intrude.'

'Oh, I never mind,' I told her. 'But I might just get his shoulder under control. He's a bit Richard the Third at the moment. I'll show you tomorrow.'

'I'd love that, thanks.'

'Daddy!' The children jumped the last few steps and threw themselves against Hugo's legs, imploring him to look at their buckets of shells.

'And crabs! Live ones, Daddy – outside!'

Out on to the front step they dragged him, one on each hand. We all went, actually, to look. Crouching down we

271

peered into sandy buckets, at urchins and tiny starfish. Tiger shells with spots were lined up carefully on the steps by Ibby and much admired. 'To sell,' she told me, looking up at me gravely. 'Like in a shop.' I listened to their chatter for a bit. I heard Hugo being sweet with them, promising he'd come tomorrow to look for more. Suggesting a rock pool round at Dragmar Bay where he'd always had success, as a child.

At length I took my leave of that little family, leaving them to admire the fish skeleton Ibby retrieved right from the bottom of the bucket, covered in seaweed. Theo insisted he'd seen it first.

'Did not!'

'Did!'

As I went, it occurred to me that it hadn't been as hard to leave them to their happiness as it might have been in the past.

Down the wide clay track to the cottage I strolled, my hands in my skirt pockets, deep in thought. The sea was glistening before me in the bay. A few small boats bobbed around but there wasn't much wind. It wasn't really a sailing day. It was very much a beach day, though, and having made a quick detour to the shop in the village for some fish for tonight's supper, I took a circuitous route home, and walked back along the cliff path. As I went, my eyes tracked down. In the spot she favoured, halfway down the cliff, perched precariously but privately with her easel, was Celia, who, unlike me, still tended to paint all day, a packet of sandwiches in her bag.

I wondered where Edward was. Apart from a few rather

tense, whispered words last night in her bedroom, during which I entirely and cravenly blamed Babs for upsetting Edward, I hadn't seen much of my friend. They'd gone out for a walk on the beach later, and I'd been in bed when they returned. At least, I'd assumed the pair of them returned, but when I'd gone down this morning, I'd seen only Celia through the kitchen window in the garden, chomping on her muesli in a desultory fashion. Perhaps he was still in bed? Or had he gone back to the B&B he'd apparently booked? Home, even? I didn't ask because her face did not invite it. In fact, I didn't even venture outside. Instead, grabbing a couple of bananas from the fruit bowl, I'd called a cheery good morning from the kitchen, yelled something about getting an early start, and legged it up to the house.

I paused above her now on the cliff path. She was dabbing away minutely at her canvas, eyes flitting every second back to the sea, totally engrossed in her work and oblivious to me. I walked on.

The next cove was almost entirely empty, but there was a reason for that. An even more hazardous climb down than Celia's, it was not for the faint-hearted. You had to be pretty agile to attempt it, plus it took ages to achieve, and then, of course, you had to get back up again. Two people who had achieved it were Tommy and Janey. I felt a ridiculous wave of relief at seeing them together. Janey was paddling with her back to me in a yellow bikini, tanned, lithe and gorgeous. She was daring herself to go further into the freezing water, arms held aloft. Tommy, flat on his back behind her in shorts and a T-shirt, was fast asleep, by the looks of things. His skin was fair and I found myself wondering if he had cream on, something I couldn't see him bothering with. Catching up on some shut-eye after last night, no doubt.

Janey gave a shriek as a wave threatened to engulf her and instinctively turned her back on it. As she did, she saw me, up on the cliff top. She waved madly. Then she put her finger to her lips, tilted her head to one side and put her hands under it, like a pillow, pointing at Tommy. I nodded and smiled broadly and gave her a thumbs up in recognition. Then I pantomimed taking a hat off my head and putting it over his face. She got it immediately. She nipped out of the water, up the shore, and very gently, and rather tenderly, I thought, put his faded blue country club cap which was lying beside him over his face. He didn't stir. Then she gave an elaborate, despairing shrug as she regarded his bare arms and legs. We'd become a pair of mime artists. Suddenly she imitated having a brainwave, finger raised in the air. Very gently, she draped a towel over his bare legs and then her own T-shirt and shorts over his arms. She stood back and admired her handi-work. I gave her a silent clap and she swept an elaborate curtsy back. I laughed softly and walked on.

Back at the cottage, the front door was ajar, which was odd, but not unheard of. We certainly never locked it, having nothing to steal but our phones which were on us, so I went in thinking it was probably Babs. The little sitting room was cool and dark at this time of day. As I shut the door behind me, my phone beeped with a text. I retrieved it from my pocket.

Are you about?

It was Peter. But as I turned from the door I simultaneously saw him through the French windows in the garden, feet up on the table, texting away.

'I'm right here!' I called through the house with a laugh, delighted. I'd been wondering when I might steal a moment with my son, and this was perfect. Celia out, just Peter and me in the garden.

'Oh good!' he called back, flashing me a quick grin but not actually pausing from texting. Clearly he had people to talk to other than me. 'I was just about to give up.'

I came out and planted a kiss on the top of his distracted head and ruffled his hair. He submitted docilely enough. 'Haven't seen you for ages!' I told him in a scolding voice. I had, but properly was what I meant.

'I know, I was just thinking the same.' He glanced up from his text. 'Got any food, Mum?'

I laughed. '*Always* hungry. And yes, actually. I missed lunch so I bought some crab on the way back. Sandwich?'

'Please. And more than one. I'm starving.'

'Excellent.' I sailed back inside, leaving him to his phone. I was thrilled to see Celia had got fresh bread this morning – she must have been up early. Notice how I was *thrilled*. I sliced and buttered away. Not just *pleased*, as most mothers would be. Oh yes, I caught myself out regularly. I found a lemon – which we always had for the gin, no surprise there – and loaded a tray with a pile of sandwiches, a bottle of rosé, a couple of glasses, and then, with joy, I have to tell you, in my heart, swept back outside. This was turning into a very good day. And with Ted coming for supper tonight – well. Who knows? Perhaps Shelley von Strunckel had been right after all when she'd said the sun in Uranus was going to spark a spectacular chain of events for Virgos: perhaps the wheel of fortune, which for so long had been hanging limply by its axle, would be spinning merrily before long.

Peter had the grace to swing his legs round off the table and pocket his phone. He even took the tray from me as I sat down. He looked greedily at the pile of sandwiches.

'Oh great. Thanks, Mum. Been surfing with the boys all morning.'

I smiled indulgently as he took one and slipped a plate his way. I took one for myself and poured us both a glass of wine, by which time he was reaching for his next sandwich.

'From Annie's?' he asked through a mouthful.

'Where else?'

He made a circle with forefinger and thumb. 'Best crab in Cornwall. Do they still know you in there?'

'Certainly they do. Well, at least Bob and Annie do. Kelly gives me a funny look as if she almost recognizes me but can't quite place me, but then I struggle, too. She's so changed. It's always the same when you've been at school with someone then see them hundreds of years later.'

'Tell me about it. I saw a boy the other day who was my head of house when I arrived and he was like – a man!'

I laughed. 'Well, he'd be twenty-three or so by now, which *is* a man.'

'I suppose.' He looked thoughtful. 'Although not really, these days, d'you think?'

'No. I read in the paper the other day that childhood goes on until twenty-four, would you believe it, now that we're all living till we're a hundred. So you've got bags of time yet.'

'Exactly.' Somehow that seemed to suit both of us. 'Which is sort of why I popped in.'

'Oh? Not just desperate to see your mother?'

'Well, yeah . . .'

I laughed. 'Go on.'

'Well . . . the thing is, Mum, I think I might delay Oxford.'

I frowned. 'What d'you mean?'

'Just by a year.'

I stared at him. 'But, Peter, you wrote and asked if you could have a gap year. They said no.'

'I know, but I could reapply.'

'Oh, don't be ridiculous! What – turn down a place at Christ Church? Have another go and risk being turned down?'

He shrugged. 'I'd back myself, obviously. But if not, there are other universities.'

I couldn't speak for a moment. Finally, I found my voice. 'Peter, if you remember rightly, they said come now or don't come at all!' My voice was shrill.

'That particular college, yes.'

'*Christ* Church, Peter, *Christ* Church. Not any old college.'

He looked at me calmly.

'No,' I said firmly. 'No. It is absolutely not all right, it is out of the question. I forbid it.' I was sweating. Trembling.

'You can't. Don't be silly.'

I stared at him impotently. Felt sick. I also knew I was hyperventilating. I got up. Walked around the garden, arms tightly clenched, my heart pumping. I came back but couldn't sit.

'Look, Mum, I knew you'd be upset—'

'After all we've worked for,' I whispered, close to tears. 'To chuck it in.'

'All *I've* worked for.' But he knew what I meant. Years of hoping I'd got it right: hoping I was keeping this clever boy on track, away from too many festivals, away from drugs. Every exam he took, pacing the kitchen, looking at the clock, thinking . . . he'll be going into Maths. Now lunch. Now Spanish. And it *had* just been me, because Hugo had been much more relaxed, hadn't got involved. If you asked Hugo, he'd have to think what A levels Peter had taken. Four: Spanish, Biology, Physics, History. But I'd pretend not to remember one of them, as many hovering, helicopter mothers disingenuously did.

'Golly, what's the last one?' Brow furrowed. Indelibly planted in my brain, I'd finally retrieve it. 'Gosh, what a mixture!' mothers would then respond. 'Is it?' I'd reply innocently, as if I didn't know. Didn't know he was a polymath, could dip into the Sciences just as easily as the Arts. Could indeed do anything. No tutoring, thank God, because he hadn't needed it, so I hadn't had to lie about that as some did. 'Just a bit of help with a local girl on a Thursday.' The truth being every day in the Easter holidays, with a History professor. Or, at a ruinously expensive crammer, where Sandy's eldest had gone, Peter told me. Sandy didn't. They had no money. But somehow she'd managed it. Quietly.

Most didn't want to be seen to push, to be sniggered at, although one friend cheerfully told everyone she gave her son mock Oxbridge interviews every night for a week before his own interview. Having been there herself and read the same subject, she knew the form. People laughed at such a professional mother, but he got in. It was all such a race. A struggle. And with so many highly educated, highly trained circus animals performing, it was something of a lottery. Peter may well back himself but there was every chance he wouldn't get in next year. I forced myself to be calm. To sit down again. I took a large slug of wine.

'What does your father think?'

'He's pretty cool.'

'He would be.'

'Mum, that's not fair.'

'No, but he doesn't take the same interest.'

'Which is good. Takes the pressure off.'

I acknowledged this. Had always thought we made a good team in this respect. So he'd told him first.

'I saw him up at the house, literally just now,' he told me, reading my thoughts. 'Had a quick chat. He told me to think about it first. And to come down here. I told him I'd been on my way anyway when I met him.'

'Right.' I was calming down a bit. Not a lot, but a bit. Still felt sick. 'Well, he's right, you should think about it. I mean – last week you were going, am I right?'

'Yes.'

'And suddenly, just to partake in some Sloaney rite of passage, some jaunt to South East Asia to get off your head at half-moon parties—'

'Full.'

'To be able to say you've drunk buckets of vodka on the Ganges and vomited as much as you consumed, which no doubt all your surfing mates you met at the pub are doing, Adam, Sam, whoever.'

'I'm not going to Asia.'

'Well, Columbia, then.'

'I'm going to America.'

'America.' I stared. 'Why?'

'I'm going to get a job. I want to work in New York.'

My mouth fell open. I stared at him. Suddenly the dawn came up. The chats. The walks. The discussions. 'Janey,' I hissed.

'Yes, OK, I've been talking to Janey. But I had the germ of the idea anyway.'

'*Liar!*' I roared.

'Mum! Get a grip.'

'She's influenced you,' I snapped. 'Whispered in your young, vulnerable ear about the Big Apple, the buzz, the excitement, the glamour – oh, you *stupid* boy, Peter.'

Peter widened his eyes. 'This is going well.'

'Well, what did you expect? Oh yes, fab idea, darling! Any old eighteen-year-old, with no experience and no connections, and no *work permit*, incidentally, can get a job on Wall Street, no problem at all. How *naive*, Peter. Did you expect me to say go for it, darling?'

'No, but I expected some considered thought and talk.' His eyes were steady. Mine were wild, I knew. And my pulse was up again. I was out of control and I knew it. Peter also knew, and he knew why.

'Mum, I know this is hard. I know the single-mum stuff. You feel you've worked for this, too, but I'm not throwing anything away. And Janey will get me an internship, she says, that will look good on my CV. Not just a year bumming about, but a year working properly.'

'Whereabouts?'

'Well, publishing, obviously. And, to start with, where she is, but she doesn't know empirically. Needs to make some enquiries.'

Janey. Bloody Janey. Who I'd liked so much. How *could* she?

'I saw you both leaving the beach party the other night.'

'I know, you said.'

'Where did you go?'

'Into town. To a club.'

'What – just the two of you?'

'Yes, just the two of us, Mum.'

'What – a dancing-type club?'

'No, a pottery-type club.'

I stared. 'Peter, she's in her thirties!'

'I know. Thirty-six.'

'And you're seventeen!'

'So? Emmanuel Macron was fifteen. Brigitte was forty.'

I regarded him in horror. 'Are you and Janey having an affair?'

'Why would it be an affair? Neither of us is married.'

'You know what I mean!' My temperature was rising. 'Are you having sex?'

'That really is none of your business.'

'Peter!'

He drained his glass. Got to his feet. 'Well, this has been interesting.' His face was pale. He looked angry. Peter and I had never rowed like this. Not even in the so-called troublesome early teenage years, not ever. My brain was spiralling but I nevertheless caught it into halt. For a moment. I tried a different tack.

'Peter, I can see how this all looks very rosy and

romantic, a seminal moment in your life. But trust me, in a few years' time you'll look back at it as a summer romance – albeit a highly inappropriate one – and—'

'Fuck off, Mum.' He glared at me fiercely. I stared, horrified. That had never been said. 'I love her, all right? Is that what you want to hear? I love her. Satisfied?' His eyes blazed into mine. Then he strode out, through the French windows, straight through the house, and slammed the front door hard behind him.

21

I sat, dumb and dazed. Stared blankly down the garden to the dunes beyond. A seagull, taking advantage of my inertia, hopped on to the other side of the table. He put his head on one side and looked speculatively at the crab sandwiches, then at me. At length, he waddled across and pecked at one. I didn't stir. Didn't shoo him away, this rodent of the skies; just watched as another joined him, then another. Snatching, flying away, coming back for more, bringing their friends with them. Not even bothering to fly away now, just eating at the table. One was on my plate. Beady black eyes still darted my way, but they clearly thought I was dead. I felt dead.

My darling boy. My easy, only child. Who was destined to sail off to Oxford in two months' time, then on to a brilliant career, hopefully with a lovely, clever, beautiful girl who he'd met at university – not too blue stocking, of course, I'd always hoped: not too terrifying. Not one who used words like 'empirically', like Peter, but could talk handbags and shoes and who maybe read, um, History of Art, or something accessible, not Chinese or Greats. Whatever they were. But instead – instead, fucking *Janey*. What did she think she was *doing*, taking advantage of a young boy like this, and I'd liked her so, but then . . . I didn't really know her, did I? And she was from New York. *Sex and the City*. Cougar Woman territory. They were probably all at it. This was nothing to her. Small beer. A roll in the hay with a lithe young lad, the only high point in an otherwise stiflingly dull, middle-aged house party. And she was unattached, so why not?

I tried to make myself breathe from my diaphragm as Celia had taught me, but it was all up in my chest, making me feel a bit light-headed. Why not? *Why not?* Oh, she'd soon see why not. I'd tell her. Anger – fury, actually – replaced the numbness and rushed into my heart. I was so enraged I could hardly see straight. I flew back into the house, swapped my espadrilles for some trainers; tied the laces with trembling fingers. Then I ran out of the back and down the garden without bothering to close the French windows. On I raced, not towards the dunes and the beach, but to the cliff path beyond.

As I jogged along, I rehearsed the dialogue in my head, which would be delivered, not shrilly or hysterically, but calmly and reasonably. Without inflammatory and exaggerated language – or swearing – but with a rational, albeit censorious lexicon. It would include words like 'inappropriate'. And . . . yes, inappropriate. I'd think of more later. Right now, I had to get down to the beach and that involved getting down this sodding steep cliff. I paused at the top, panting. I'd jogged quite a long way. Celia, a dot in the distance, was still painting in the next bay, much further along. Hers was the easier climb down, the one most people took, but I chose this one: the vertical, more direct route, knowing from childhood experience it was doable. It looked sheer and hazardous, but it actually had good hand and footholds and – if I didn't break my neck – it was certainly the quickest way down.

Tommy was still on the beach, flat out, with Janey's clothes over him. So she was still there, even though from this vantage point I couldn't see her. She was most probably on the rocks where people lay and sunbathed – particularly minus a towel as she was now – directly below me. Beneath the overhang of the cliff.

Unfit I might be, but it helped that I was small and agile. The climb came back to me in moments. The trainers helped. I almost remembered each foothold, each step down, which tussock to trust and hold on to. I eased myself down slowly, facing the cliff. Oh yes, a proper climb. The others would have come around the other way. When I got to the bottom I dusted off my hands, pleased with myself. I turned and trotted towards Tommy, still comatose, glancing about for Janey as I ran. Damn, no sign of her. Where was she? Coming to a running kneel in the sand like a footballer after scoring a goal, I tapped Tommy's T-shirt-draped arm.

'Tommy. Tommy, wake up.'

'Huh? Whaa?'

I removed the cap so he could see. He squinted and tried to focus, his eyes cloudy. I gave him a moment. He blinked. Presently he found his voice.

'Jesus. You? Again? Who are you, Macbeth? You don't half like murdering sleep.'

'Sorry. Really sorry, Tommy, but this is urgent. Where's Janey?'

'Urgent?' He blinked. 'I'll tell you what's urgent. I try

and catch a few Zs in the study, but no, you have to have me awake. Then I come down here to get away from you, but no, you have to have me again. Are you stalking me, woman?'

'Tommy, please be serious, this is really urgent. Where's Janey?'

He sat up. Rubbed his eyes blearily. Gazed around. 'Damned if I know.'

'But she left her clothes to cover you up. She must be here somewhere.' I stood up and stared at the rocks. Had she seen me arrive and was *hiding*?

'That's what women do, hon. They see me, they take their clothes off, they throw them all over me. Happens all the time.' He shook the T-shirt and shorts off his arms. 'Often I get panties, too, but I guess—'

'Tommy, *please*. Don't joke about this. I must find Janey.'

He yawned widely and implacably in my face. Smacked his lips languidly. Then he frowned. 'Why so?'

I told him: being as considered and reasonable as I could. Not just detailing the affair, but Oxford as well. The whole story. And using words like 'inappropriate' a lot – albeit putting 'fucking' in front of it. I also used words like 'tragedy' and 'scheming bitch', and unfortunately, I did not have complete control of my voice, or as much as I would have liked, at all times.

He regarded me in wonder as I ranted on. He waited until I'd finished and then stared some more, in disbelief. Suddenly he started to laugh. It started as a chuckle at the back of his throat, but then it got louder. His mirth became more and more riotous, until he was howling. He was roaring, now, in my face, mouth wide. Finally, he flopped theatrically over on to his side in the sand, gasping for air. At length he sat up. Wiped his eyes, which were streaming.

I watched in horror. '*What* is so funny?'

'You are. Oh God, you are, lady.'

I gaped at him. He shrugged despairingly. Spread the palms of his hands wide. 'Dear God, where's the harm?' he yelped. 'A boy of seventeen gets his rocks off with a fit, savvy, beautiful woman of thirty-six – who's a real piece of work in the sack, incidentally – and who's gonna show him all the moves and more, and you call it a *tragedy*? The real tragedy is it never happened to me. Jeez, I could have done with a girl like Janey before I went to college. Reckon my daddy might even have *paid* some broad to do it.'

'Your daddy would have done nothing of the kind and you know it. He was a decent, respectable man and this is a seedy, tacky, indecent act of impropriety, that's what it is.'

'Act of improp— Oh God.' He was off again, flopping sideways into the sand, holding himself, convulsed with mirth. I fumed silently beside him.

Finally he sat up. Composed himself. 'Flora, honey, this is no big story. This is no breaking news. And frankly, if it was good enough for the President of the Republic of—'

'*If* you mention Emmanuel Macron I *will* slap you.'

He gave a rather Gallic shrug. 'I'm just illustrating that as career moves go, it's not the worst.'

'Well, a fat lot of help you've been,' I stormed. 'As usual. Thank you for that, Tommy. Thank you very much for your help.' I got to my feet, fuming. 'I'll go and find her myself.'

I made to go, wondering where on earth a girl in a yellow bikini and absolutely nothing else could have disappeared to, when he flicked out a hand and grabbed my ankle.

'Sit down. At the risk of getting sand in my eyes, sit down. I'll be serious with you just as soon as I've recovered my breath. It's just . . . boy, you English girls. You crack me up.'

'And I'm sure you know many, Tommy. And no doubt we have different standards and it takes some getting used to. But it's not all *Sex and the City* over here, you know.'

He looked about to dissolve again, but contained himself, with difficulty. His mouth twitched. 'Sit.'

I hesitated. Then obeyed. I swallowed hard as I waited for him to speak.

'OK. First off, the sex isn't a problem and you know it. And I know he says he's in love with her, but you and I know he's not really. Agreed? And Janey's a nice girl, and she won't have encouraged that. Agreed?'

My pulse came down a bit. 'I would have thought so, but it helps to have you say it.'

'OK, well take it from me, she wouldn't. So relax on that front. And now I'll help some more. You say Peter originally wanted a year out, but they said no, right?'

'Right, but—'

'So perhaps he still wants one?'

'Yes, but you don't understand—'

'I do understand. I went there, hon. But Harvard or Yale would have been just as hot.'

Harvard or Yale. In America.

He shrugged. 'I don't know. I'm just thinking outside the box. Or Edinburgh or Bristol or wherever. I'm just saying, even if he doesn't get in, he's clearly a super bright boy so it's not the end of the world. And frankly, Flora, he's a lovely boy, but he is quite young. I think he needs a year.'

'What d'you mean?' I bristled as I always did when anyone even vaguely criticized my perfect child.

'He's a delight, don't get me wrong, but as far as I recall he's a summer birthday?'

'August,' I admitted.

'So he's not even eighteen. And not just that, he's polite and a bit shy. And so like Hugo at that age, and not a bit like me.'

'No.' I remembered Tommy. Swearing at his friends out hunting, his face red and heated. A very angry young man. 'What's wrong with him being like Hugo?'

'Well, he was kind of wet behind the ears. A bit mothered.' He caught my eye. 'Peter is a bit, too.'

'No. I won't have that. I've tried so hard not to—'

'And you've done a remarkable job,' he interrupted. 'But take it from me, he could do with a year in New York. It'll make a man of him.'

I wanted to say I didn't want a man. I wanted a boy. My Peter.

Tommy's eyes were serious now. 'If he was my son, and I knew he pretty much had the world at his feet anyway, I'd be advocating this. What did Hugo say?'

'Hugo would let him do whatever he liked.'

We loyally tried not to exchange a look, but we did, nonetheless. Tommy shrugged.

'Well, that's Hugo. And I'm not saying he's right, because personally I think a degree of direction helps at this age, and I'm not saying you're totally wrong, Flora. I do know not many kids would, or should, turn a place like this down. But in Peter's case, it might be right.'

I took a very deep breath. Let it out shakily. Knew I was scared. 'It's such a lottery. Places there . . .' I said in a small voice.

'Life is a lottery. And life isn't fair, either.'

I blinked at him. 'My dad used to say that.'

'So did mine.' We paused. He took a minute. 'So, what would your dad say if he was here now?'

I opened my mouth to state categorically that Dad would tell him not to be a bloody fool. To take his place, and go to Oxford in October, but suddenly . . . I couldn't. Because it struck me that he might not. He might say quite a lot of what Tommy had just said. Tommy's eyes were blue and intense as he looked at me. He'd set his cap on his head at a jaunty angle. 'The Hamptons Country Club', it read. His arms were linked around his knees which flopped loosely to either side in front of him. I held his gaze for a bit then looked away. Out at sea. Tried to breathe. Tried to think. A small white boat was zipping across the horizon, against the blue sky and the turquoise sea. A speedboat. Behind it, a girl with flowing blonde hair was waterskiing. A girl in a yellow bikini. Tommy saw it, too, I guess, because I heard him give a low chuckle.

'That's my girl.'

I wondered if he wished she *was* his girl. I mean, she had been once, but I found myself wondering if he wished this funny, headstrong, likeable girl, who clearly picked up captains of strange speedboats on the beach and cajoled them into letting her have a ski – except I don't imagine there was much cajoling – was still his.

'We fought like cat and dog,' he told me, as if reading my thoughts. His eyes were still on the boat. 'She's too tricky for me. Got a bit of baggage.'

'Who hasn't,' I said softly. We watched the boat slow down, the engine cut, and saw her sink gracefully down into the water. The boat circled to pick her up.

'Oh sure. But some people make an effort to unpack it and put it tidily away in the closet. At least, that's what I was taught. And some people don't.'

I turned to look at him. It struck me that this was rather a wise thing to say, and I told him so.

'Really?' His eyes widened in amusement. 'I heard it on *Family Guy*. Must use it some more.'

I felt my mouth twitch involuntarily. I turned away so he didn't see me smile. Janey was being helped into the boat now by at least three eager young men. One of them then resumed his place at the engine to bring her back to shore.

'Now you get back up this cliff, Flora, honey, and leave this to me. I'll talk to Janey. But not necessarily now,' he said, holding the palm of his hand up as my mouth opened. 'Not right this instant, like you ladies like to have things done. All your ducks in a row. All tidy and lickety-split. When I find a good moment. Maybe today, maybe tomorrow, maybe next week. OK? And I'll talk to Peter, too. I'll make sure he at least thinks about this.'

'Will you? Will you really, Tommy?' I spotted a glimmer of hope. 'I mean, you are his godfather, so—'

'I said I would, didn't I? But not in a dictatorial fash- ion. Just making sure he's considered all his options, OK?'

I badly wanted that conversation to be now. This minute. Today. Ducks in a row. A quick fix. But I made myself nod.

'OK. And you don't think I should talk to Janey, woman to woman?'

'No, I do not. Because, trust me, if you kick off like you did with me, with all that righteous indignation, she may not roll in the sand laughing. I told you. Janey's not straightforward.'

'OK.' I breathed. I got to my feet. Swallowed. 'And, um, Tommy . . .' It took me a moment but I did get there. 'Thank you.'

His mouth twitched. 'Twice in one morning. Bet that hurt.'

I didn't respond. But he gave me an American-style army salute, and, as Janey swam ashore, and assorted men watched admiringly, I made my way back up the beach. On to the cliff I went, in my ancient trainers, my five-year-old summer dress, the bulldog clip in my hair I wore for painting, whilst Janey, as I glanced back, strolled up the beach like Ursula Andress coming out of the sea. She was only really missing the dagger in her bikini bottoms.

22

I'd considered cancelling my dinner with Ted that evening. As I walked back to the cottage, I'd told myself I was too upset, too distracted and emotional to have a romantic tête-à-tête, which, however much I reminded myself it was just supper at my place, I knew it would be. I'd also bitten all around both thumbnails, taken my phone from my pocket and even composed the text to him, but then I thought – no. I'll do it later, if I have to. If I decide I really want to be on my own to think. However, the rational side of my brain, which has always been very, very small, told me that actually, if I didn't see Ted, I was indulging my much larger, overdramatic, unrealistic side. And that I needed to be doing something, in order not to be doing something else. Not to be drinking a bottle of wine on my own, reigniting the fire of indignation and injustice, and striding up to the house in high dudgeon to have it out with Janey, thus ruining any clever, patient damage limitation Tommy was to perform.

It wasn't going to happen, this U-turn of Peter's, of that I was absolutely certain. Tommy hadn't convinced me otherwise – and neither had he intended to. What he had done was persuade me that there were other ways of getting what I wanted. Well . . . obviously what Peter wanted. And that going about it in my own sweet, loose-cannon way was a guaranteed suicide mission. I could see that. I could see that getting Peter to really think about it was smarter.

I took my phone from my pocket. Put it back again. Because I was also torn about ringing the one person I really wanted to talk to about this: Mum. I feared what she'd say. My mother resembled Hugo in that she thought people should be left to do what they wanted, but, whereas Hugo took the less confrontational path, the path of least resistance to keep the peace, Mum didn't. It wasn't about an easy ride. It was more of a philosophy. She felt people should be allowed to make mistakes because that was how they learned. Especially the young. She felt it was good if children failed exams, if it made them want to do better the next time. And she felt today's young generation was too goal-oriented. She also thought things happened for a reason, the reason being all about learning who you are, gaining insight into your own character, which let's face it, takes years, and if you're shielded from doing it in your formative ones, it doesn't help you later. So she disagreed with having the immediate path too tidy and swept by others.

Her tutoring job both depressed and distressed her, and, but for the excellent money, she'd give it up in a heartbeat: go back to proper teaching. This obviously distressed me because I knew why she was in London, but she never complained. Never spoke of it. I just knew. Knew that she found spoon-feeding an uber-rich child to do something they weren't intellectually capable of continuing later borderline immoral. It sat more than uncomfortably with her. Of course, this was completely different. But I knew which way she'd lean, if I actually asked for her advice. Mum didn't watch like my father had, but that didn't mean she didn't have an eye. A view.

I walked on, deep in my thoughts, neither texting Ted nor ringing my mother.

Once at the cottage I lay down on my bed for a bit. I stared up at the ceiling, feeling, if I'm honest, slightly traumatized by the day's events. But then, I am prone to exaggerate. Notwithstanding the hyperbole, however, as I've got older, I've noticed that I'm less able to surf the hummocks; to withstand those emotional shockwaves through my body; less able to shrug off the bumps and pitfalls of life. These days, I need to recuperate quietly, lick my wounds. But perhaps that's just me.

After a bit, I heard Celia clattering away downstairs, back from the beach. At length she came up. She put her head around the door. Saw my face.

'What's up?'

'Nothing. Just having a little lie-down.'

She regarded me a moment. Knew this famous face of mine. And I knew she thought – *Hugo*.

'OK. Well, I'm here if you need me. Edward and I are going out for supper later.'

I made myself smile. 'Have fun.'

'Thanks.' She smiled back and shut the door.

After a while I got up. I had a bath and changed and tried to make myself look pretty. I wished, not that Ted wasn't coming, but that he'd come yesterday. Before I'd taken this body blow. When I was still in the mood for fresh starts and new relationships and a bit of scent behind the ears and painting my toenails. Wished that I already had this evening under my belt. Perhaps was even vaguely going out with him. Instead of which, I had it all to come. Not the best way to approach a hot date.

Funnily enough, though, once the make-up was on, plus a clean dress, I felt better. I squared my shoulders in the mirror. Tucked my straight dark hair behind my ears. Come on, Flora. Candles on the table. Plump those cushions. A snog on the sofa. You can do this. Down I went.

Celia had gone by now and the place was clean and tidy, which was nice of her. No cushion-plumping necessary. All the lunch debris in the garden had been cleared away, too, which was a relief. I didn't want to look at it. *Fuck off, Mum.*

Instead I set about making the fish pie, the only thing I'm good at, but, as Celia and I agree, you only need one. More than one, and guess who's doing the cooking? It involved smoked haddock, salmon, scallops, eggs and two different kinds of cheese and breadcrumbs, not to mention cream and lemon juice, and I flicked on some music and opened a bottle of wine as I went about it. Then I laid the table with a cloth in the garden, found some candles and even began to enjoy myself – the wine helped. So that by the time Ted rang the doorbell I was approaching the mood.

'You don't need to ring,' I told him as I answered the door. He was standing there with a bunch of flowers.

'I dithered,' he admitted. 'But somehow these made it too formal to barge in.'

I grinned as he handed them to me. 'Thanks. I love white roses.'

'Except they're refusing to open. They're all tight and clenched and they've resisted all my advances. I even put them in the airing cupboard.'

'Perhaps they're nervous.'

'Or playing it cool.'

Over supper, which Ted was suitably enamoured with, and which he helped make a salad for, or at least tossed some leaves in a bowl, and opened some more wine, he asked me how Roger's portrait was coming along.

'It's good. I might not have said that three days ago, but today it's good.' I popped a scallop in my mouth. Chewed on in silence.

He blinked, amused. 'That's it?'

I sighed. Put my fork down. This again. 'Thing is, Ted, it's so sort of . . . internal.' I tried to explain. Never could. 'I can't really talk about it. It's not that I'm precious about it, it's just – I don't know. It would be like talking to myself. Having a conversation with myself, and what's the point of that? To be honest, I'm always amazed when people have an opinion on it. I mean, good or bad. I do it for me.'

He nodded. 'I get that.'

'I do it for me, and it's about me, and I have a friend who's a poet who says the same. Says when people say they've enjoyed his latest volume, he thinks, what on earth are you doing reading that? What do you mean, you bought it in Waterstones? It's weirdly private, but of course, it's not. Disconcertingly, by definition, it's also incredibly public.'

'Do you hate exhibiting?'

'Oh God, I'd loathe it. But I don't have to, mine are private commissions. But ask Celia about opening nights, she almost cuts her throat. One time, a couple of years ago, she didn't even show up. It was a joint exhibition, so the other guy did, happily, but it wasn't nerves or stage fright; it was just – what are you all doing here? Looking into my heart?'

I paused. Ted was regarding me intently. He came to and nodded down at his plate, which was almost empty. Mine was almost full and I hadn't taken much. Couldn't really eat. I drank, though. No problem there. He was looking very Fisherman's Friend tonight, I decided, in his navy-blue cable-knit jersey and jeans. His tousled hair was quite grey, I realized, and whose wasn't? His huge frame leaned back rather precariously in one of our tiny wrought-iron garden chairs and I hoped it wouldn't collapse.

He smiled. 'What are you thinking?'

'Captain Birdseye.'

He laughed. 'Thanks!'

This was better and I endeavoured to keep it light. The mood I was in could have me being far more revealing about myself than I'd like. All that stuff about painting. I could feel myself coming over all confessional.

'Minus the beard, of course.'

'Oh, I did that once, but d'you know what?'

'It came through white?'

'How did you know?'

I shrugged. 'It's a young man's craze at the moment, so all the older guys think, *hey, yeah, I can do that* – and look like Father Christmas. They think they're so cool and they get edgy new clothes to go with it and . . .' I tailed off. I didn't like the way I was sounding. Mean. Cavilling. And I knew why.

'Something wrong?'

'No, just ignore me.' I gave a wan smile. 'I'm not entirely myself tonight. I'm sure you looked totally hot.'

'I'm sure I didn't, and you're right, I did buy some new clothes. Bright red. Even got a sack of toys as well.'

I smiled down at my plate.

'Want to tell me about it?'

I sighed. Put my fork down. 'Not really.' But after a pause, I did anyway, knowing I couldn't think about anything else, and knowing it would be rude not to.

He nodded thoughtfully when I'd finished. Frowned.

'Not sure the affair is entirely appropriate.'

I sat up, delighted. 'It's not, is it?'

'Not really. I mean, some would say it's fine, but it's slightly taking advantage, isn't it? I've met your Peter. He's a bit of an innocent.'

'He's a baby!'

'And I think he's wrong about Oxford.'

'Yes. I know!'

'I don't think he realizes quite what he's turning down.'

'Exactly!'

'Quite what an opportunity it is.'

'I love you.'

He shouted that laugh up to the sky, and again, I enjoyed hearing it. Suddenly it came to me.

'Will you talk to him?'

'Me?'

'Yes, he likes you, I could see that yesterday. And you're

an academic, he'll respect you. Oh, please talk to him, Ted, promise me you'll do it!'

He laughed. 'Sure. If you think it'll do any good.'

'I do, I do!' I was forking fish pie into my mouth, suddenly hungry, ravenous, and then weirdly – not. I put my fork down.

'He'll listen to you,' I said decisively, feeling better than I had for – ooh, two hours. Sorted. Fixed. I liked that.

'Well, he may not. And I'm not sure I can interfere on the female front . . .'

'No – no, he wouldn't like that. Doesn't know you. And also, he'd smell a rat. Because – how would you know?'

'Well, how would I know about anything?'

'Because obviously I've told you, and that's fine. But not – you know. Janey. Excuse me.'

I was rapidly clearing the plates. Ted rose to help but I shooed him down. 'No, no, you stay here. Honestly, I prefer to – to stack the dishwasher on my own. Bit anal, about where it all goes, plates touching, that type of thing.'

'Oh, OK.' He lowered back down.

'Back in a mo.'

He stayed put and I hurried inside. Threw the plates in the sink any old how and got my phone out. The number had to be found first and I panicked briefly about not having it, but – oh, thank God. There it was. When Peter had gone sailing with him in Cowes a couple of years ago, invited to race with him in the regatta, Tommy had sent it to me. My thumbs flew about.

'Do not, under any circumstances, talk to Peter. I have a new plan.'
I paused. Deleted *new plan*. I swallowed, my mouth dry, trying to think. How not to sound cunning. Calculating.

'I have a feeling I should try again myself.' I left it at that. No explanation. Did it look a bit weak? 'Mother to son' I added. More emphasis was needed. 'So please do not, OK?'

The shortest of missives, but the composing of it had taken longer than I thought. When I turned, Ted was behind me, bearing the salad bowl.

'Hi!' I leaped a mile in the sky. Pocketed my phone.

He blinked. 'Hi . . .'

I knew he'd seen it. I patted my pocket. 'My mum,' I told him. 'I'd um . . . told her earlier. About Peter. She was just asking how it was going.'

'Ah. And what does she think?'

'She, er – she – agrees with you.' I flew to the fridge, my face hot. 'Cheesecake? Not mine, I'm afraid, but it's from the bakery.'

'Sure, why not.'

I handed it to him. 'I'll get the plates and cream.'

I waited. I hadn't managed to send the message. He needed to go. He looked a bit disconcerted, but then he went out with the cheesecake. I furtively retrieved my phone and pressed send. Then I joined him outside in the garden.

Equilibrium had been more than restored, in fact I was verging on euphoria. I suddenly found myself laughing again, eating all my cheesecake, and having another piece. The banter flowed easily, and we chatted and laughed and drank away in the dusky evening light. The dark came upon us quite quickly, crept up on us without our noticing, and the chill, too. I popped inside for a sweater. We agreed it was nicer to stay outside, although we did relocate to the creaking swing seat on the lawn. The one with

301

the old-fashioned floral hood, positioned to watch the sun sink over the horizon, or, in this case, the moon to rise and send its milky glow across the water. At length Ted put his arm around my shoulders in an easy motion, laughing at something I'd said. He gently pulled me close. I snuggled happily. The chair rocked slightly with our shifting positions.

'Only fair to tell you I can get motion sickness even on this,' I told him as it swayed.

'That's seductive. Do we need a bucket?'

'I'll give you fair warning if we do.'

'Excellent news.' When I looked up to smile at him, his eyes were shining down into mine. He took my chin in his hand and lightly kissed my lips. Drew back a moment to gauge my reaction, which was not a bad one at all. Indeed, I believe he must have seen that it was good. He kissed me again, more thoroughly this time, and I found something unclenching and uncoiling within me. It was as if the white roses inside in a vase on the breakfast bar had taken this moment to relax: to unfurl their petals, hold their heads up to the sun and submit to nature's warmth, or perhaps, to a Cornish summer.

As we regrouped and he held me, it felt so good. I could feel his heart beating through his vast blue jumper and I'm sure he could feel mine. But then we heard something else. The front door was opening then closing.

'Flora?' called Celia.

We glanced at each other warily.

'Out here,' I called back.

We instinctively shifted positions a bit, although Ted didn't take his arm away from my shoulders, and I was glad. I waited for Celia to come out into the garden. The candles were still burning on the table, French doors open, occupation obvious. I heard hurried footsteps, and then she popped her head round the covered swing seat. Her eyes found me in the dark. She looked a bit hectic.

'Flora, can I have a word?'

She hadn't greeted Ted and was definitely distracted. She'd gone again. Casting Ted an apologetic look, I shrugged, and followed her inside. She was looking more than hectic; she was looking positively manic. Her hair was weirdly greasy and standing on end, her face was a bit puffy and shiny, and she had a strange look in her eyes, pupils hugely dilated. She seized my arm and pulled me into the sitting room, so Ted couldn't hear.

'Edward and I,' she breathed, really close up in my face, 'have been to a spa. In a hotel. You have a meal first, very fancy, and then you go up to the spa bit and they give you a massage, OK?'

'OK.'

'Full works. Side by side, tiny towels. Dim lights, music, candles, couple of Thai girls.'

'Right.'

'And Edward, right, is about to pop.'

'Sorry?'

'He's about to pop. He's got like this massive . . .' She looked at me imploringly. '*You* know, Flora.'

'Oh!' I did. Suddenly.

'So obviously we need to hustle it upstairs. He's just parking the car.'

'Right.' I blinked. 'Well, yes. Obviously.'

'So I need you to go,' she hissed urgently.

I frowned. 'But . . . Ted and I are in the garden. We won't see him come in, we won't see you go up . . .'

'Yes, but the point is you're here! And you know how Edward has to have complete privacy. At all times.'

'What . . . no one in the house at all?'

'Remember how we always had to wait until his flat-mate was out?' She glanced nervously at the door.

'You said that was because the walls were so thin.'

'Flora, please don't be awkward. He'll be back any minute, and *you owe me this.*' Her dark, crazy eyes bored into mine, very close. She looked slightly unhinged.

'Yes.' I swallowed. 'I do. I see. Quite right.'

'Why don't you go to Ted's?' she hissed.

'Celia, we're not there yet.'

'Well, just – hurry it along a bit. At his place.'

'No!' I glanced gardenwards, alarmed. 'No,' I whispered. I licked my lips. 'Can *I* sleep here?'

She hesitated. 'Could you . . . you know . . . sneak up later? Maybe read for a bit? In the garden? For about an hour?'

'What the hell's wrong with his B and B?'

'The owner lives there. It's her flat, she's about.'

'Right.' I remembered now. Not just impotent Edward, but tight Edward. What was wrong with that fancy hotel? She was looking a bit tortured, though. 'OK, I'll sit outside.'

'And tell Ted to go out through the garden. Not round the front. Are these his?' She picked up his keys and wallet from the breakfast bar. Thrust them at me. 'And blow out the candles. I'll lock the French doors behind you.'

'Do not!' I yelped. 'How will I get back in?'

'True, good point. Now go.' She thrust a handy guide book at me. 'Here. To read.'

I went. She watched me blow out the candles then she ran across and shut the French doors. Drew the curtain in a huge swish. Great. At precisely that moment, I heard the front door open. Edward doubtless eased in, greased from head to toe in baby oil, pupils horribly dilated, monstrously priapic. I shuddered.

Ted regarded me quizzically in the darkness as I tiptoed back across the lawn to him, my finger to my lips. I sat down beside him quietly.

'Problem?' he murmured.

I mimed that complete silence was crucial. He complied, but his eyes and ears were pricked, like a horse out hunting. I kept my finger to my lips. Muffled voices came from inside. Celia seemed to be entreating, insisting, pleading now. Imploring for them to head upstairs. But Edward had worked up a head of steam and I had severe misgivings about Celia being able to hustle this particular masterpiece upstairs. Clearly Edward was all for exhibiting downstairs, on the sofa, before the wood-burning stove, perhaps.

'*Darling, here, now!*'

Ted thrust his fist in his mouth. His eyes were wide and enquiring at me.

'*No – no, darling – upstairs!!*'

'*I can't!*'

'*Yes!*'

Celia's voice lowered suddenly, but there was no doubt she was prevailing. There were more urgent murmured entreaties from her, something about a soft bed, pillows, and finally, the stairs creaked. Their feet echoed upstairs, and then thankfully, mercifully, a door slammed. I sighed with relief. Flopped back theatrically on the seat. Then I remembered Celia's bedroom was above us and the window was ajar and I sat bolt upright again. Ted was already looking up expectantly. He knew exactly what was going on. And he was enjoying this far too much. I got to my feet, hauling him up with me, which was not easy, a finger to my lips again. He looked mock horrified, but I ignored him. I hastened him around the side of the house, leading him to the track, and shoved his keys and wallet in his unwilling hands.

'What's going on?' he wailed, just a touch too loudly. I hustled him right down the track, frowning in horror. We reached his car, which was out of earshot, but I still kept my voice low.

'Edward, right, has to have complete privacy, in order to – you know . . .'

'Perform?'

'Exactly.'

He chuckled. 'Blimey. That's a bit of a handicap.'

'Tell me about it.'

'So – what, I'm off?'

'It rather looks that way. Sorry, Ted.'

'Oh. I was enjoying that.'

'Yeah, me too.'

He scratched his woolly head. 'Really enjoying it, actually. God. Bugger Edward.'

'I know.' I waited for him to be difficult. He wasn't.

'But no, I get it.' He shrugged. Then he lightly rested his hands on my hips. Smiled. 'Some other time, then. My place, maybe?'

'I'd like that.'

'But not tonight?'

I hesitated. 'I think . . .'

'The moment has passed?'

'It has rather.'

He nodded. Grinned down at me from his great height. Then he moved his arms right around my waist and pulled me in close. Kissed me properly again. I felt about fifteen standing by the car in the dark. I cursed Celia and Edward, my surrogate parents, in the house.

'It will return, though,' he told me, getting in his car and buzzing down the window. 'The moment. Edward's not the only man in South Cornwall on a mission.'

I laughed. Ted let out the handbrake and, giving me a wave, drove away. I realized I was still standing there, smiling broadly, as his car bumped along down the track, and turned out of sight.

23

The following day, as I was painting in the gunroom, I got a text from Peter.

Sorry Mum. I was a bit harsh.

I couldn't reply quickly enough. I was all fingers and thumbs. Luckily, Roger was asleep.

No no – I'M sorry, darling.
I totally over-reacted.
Let's forget it.

Cool.

I pocketed my phone. Perfect. My heart lifted and soared away, like a bird, one of the gulls, in fact, outside the window, cruising up into the now-cleared air. Not only was the air clear, but the stage set and ready for Ted to perform on later, down at the Mariners, where most people gathered before they went out. Peter would certainly be there, I'd told Ted, and with the reins dropped by me he'd be much more receptive. I picked up my brush and painted on happily, regarding my sleeping beauty.

Roger's face was finished now and I'd wanted his body

very relaxed, so I'd said he could snooze. To this end we'd rescheduled our session to after lunch.

'Probably help if I drink heavily, eh, Flora?' he'd said hopefully. 'Put me right out.'

'It's not crucial, Roger, I just don't want you too stiff and upright.'

To be on the safe side he'd had a riotous picnic with Babs on board his motor boat, after a morning puttering around the estuary. In the old days the discreet little creek he favoured would have found his boat deserted later: anchor down, a darkened cabin, rocking hull. I've no idea if those days were gone, but when he'd crept into the house through a side door later and found me ready and waiting with my palette, he had a very wicked smile on his face. He scuttled to his chair. His bottom hit the seat just moments before the door opened again. It was Belinda.

'Ah. There you are.'

'Flora wants me asleep, darling. Must comply. Probably be here all afternoon.' He shut his eyes.

'You smell terrible.'

'Do I? Can't think why.'

'I can. Have you seen Hugo?'

'No, darling.'

'He's missing.'

'Ah.'

She shut the door.

His eyes snapped open again. 'Missing,' he said grimly. 'He's a grown man. Bah.'

I didn't comment. Painted on in silence. My phone beeped a few times but I was in the zone now so I ignored it, important missive received, everything else irrelevant.

310

I'd always been capable of shutting the world out; was delighted to, in fact, with the exception of Peter. But even then, when he was small, I'd been known, like many working mothers, to plant him like a bomb at school with a minor bug and then feign surprise when a teacher called to say he'd been sick, but they'd keep him in the san until the end of the day. Needs must.

Roger's shoulder was fully restored now, unbroken and mended. But I didn't like that arm. As my sitter really did nod off, his hand relaxed its grip on the chair. Ah. Good. Now. My brush moved feverishly about the canvas. Killing it, as Peter would say.

A few hours later I sighed and put my brush down. Unlike Celia I peaked after about four hours. When I was younger I could go back and paint all evening and most of the night, too, but these days I was spent. Also, Roger was awake and had been for some time. He was looking mutinous.

'Flor-aaa!' he roared.

'Yes, yes, we're done. Sorry, Roger, you've been brilliant by the way.'

His face transformed. 'I have, haven't I?' He perked up instantly, like a child. Roger was terribly easily flattered. It was actually what I was hoping to capture; that transient, childlike quality. I regarded my picture speculatively.

'Can I see?'

'Of course.'

He came around eagerly. He stared at it for a while. I could tell he didn't hate it. Eventually, he beamed.

'I look as if I might steal the last jelly.'

'I don't think there's any "might" about it, Roger. I'd say you're in the larder with the trifle.'

He stepped closer and peered more forensically. 'Could look a bit younger?'

'Absolutely not. I've taken years off you as it is.'

Not years, but one or two. It always helped. Not every single wrinkle. Not every single shred of sadness or disappointment. And these things mounted up, over the years. Less so with Roger, which was why it had been a joy to paint him. His joie de vivre, his enthusiasm, were still intact. It was the depressives who were so hard. Most people having their portraits painted at this age and stage of their lives were successful, sometimes quite grand: I'd done one or two captains of industry. But, often, when they'd sat for you for hours, for days, their faces betrayed the projected pomp and ostentation, and that was hard. I could only speak the truth and they liked happier results. 'I look like I'm going to shoot myself!' one brigadier had roared furiously. Six months later, he did.

'Day off tomorrow,' Roger told me gleefully. He gathered up his things from the table: a book, reading glasses, coffee cup.

'Absolutely. The regatta.'

'Can't miss that! Organizing the beach sports as usual. *And* on the captain's boat. What fun. Toodle-pip, Flora.'

And out he hastened. He paused in the doorway, though, and I saw him glance furtively left and right. Then he tracked left, to the back stairs, no doubt in order to avoid his wife in some other remote corner of this huge house. Rumour had it Roger had a TV in his dressing room and liked to watch reruns of *The Simpsons*, roaring with laughter at Homer's antics, a packet of digestives on his lap,

Truffle, not allowed upstairs under any circumstances, on the bed beside him, sharing. One for you, one for me.

As I went along the corridor to the front hall, I fished my phone out and turned it on. A text on my screen read:

Too late.

I stopped dead. Stared at it. Tommy Rochester. Heart pounding, I walked on quickly. Shit. Bugger. I mean *really* shit bugger, actually. I pushed through the front door and went outside, casting about. Where was he? I went around the side of the house to the terrace.

It was late afternoon now and the sun was casting long, extravagant shadows across the lawn. The huge cedar with its wide horizontal skirts sank a pool of darkness right up to the wide York stone terrace where I'd sometimes seen Tommy reading. I'd glanced at his abandoned book once: philosophy, which had startled me. I'd read the title upside down. *Fear and Trembling* by Kierkegaard. Lots of torn bits of newspapers sticking out of the top, marking places of interest. But not today. The terrace was deserted. No book, no Tommy. Perhaps everyone was still on the beach? Or actually . . . I turned and nipped back inside.

The green baize door was a godsend, shielding the kitchen, and if Belinda did appear, I could always say I'd left something in the gunroom. I didn't go there, though. Instead, I pushed through another door, without knocking. Just as I thought. Tommy was in situ. Not asleep on the sofa, and not wading through piles of papers, but with his back to me, sitting at the computer. His voice, when it came, made me jump.

'What?' he barked, swinging round in his chair. His

face was ashen. It took my breath away. For a moment, I even forgot why I was there.

'Oh. Um . . . I – I just got your text,' I faltered.

He stared at me as if unable to place me: certainly not remembering any text. Then it came to him.

'Oh. Yeah.' He rubbed his face vigorously with both his hands, which I'd seen him do several times of late. A regrouping gesture. 'Sorry, Flora. Got your text too late. I already talked to him. He's thinking about it. And I talked to Janey, too, but listen, this is kind of important. Can I catch you later?'

He was faintly scary. Very serious. Withdrawn. Pre-occupied. Similar, perhaps, to how I was when I painted. Certainly it was a side to Tommy I'd never seen. All at once, I caught a glimpse of him at work in Manhattan. In a high-rise office overlooking the city, on the phone, making powerful executive decisions: chairing meetings, giving instructions involving probably millions of dollars. Suddenly a seventeen-year-old boy's love life and university choices seemed rather irrelevant. A bit ridiculous.

'Of course,' I said humbly. But he'd already swung round in his chair and gone back to the screen.

I shut the door softly. Walked quietly back down the corridor, problems somewhat in perspective. And anyway, I couldn't complain, could I? I'd gleaned a tiny morsel. Peter had apparently said he was thinking about it. Not as good as I was sure Ted could do, but better than nothing. Should I leave Ted in place? In the Mariners? Or would Peter feel besieged? Regard it as a pincer movement and smell a rat? Yes. Definitely. I sent a text to Ted to stand him down and he replied immediately: no problem, he wouldn't mention it. I thanked him and walked on back to the cottage, wondering, as I went, why on earth more mothers didn't go into politics, when lobbying for support, doing secret deals, and watching carefully for that special moment when they can negotiate from a position of strength, was all part of the remit.

As I neared home I realized I was dog tired, but then I hadn't had the best of nights. Tossing aside the local guide book Celia had thrust at me and which I could have written myself, I'd stretched out on the swing seat in the garden. Eventually, covered in cushions of the slippery, solid, uncongenial outdoor variety, I must have nodded off. I'd awoken, cold and uncomfortable, and looked at my watch. One in the morning. Since all was quiet upstairs, I'd decided it really was fine for me to go to bed, in my own room, in my own cottage. In fact, I'd jolly nearly banged my bedroom door shut in irritation, but had just managed to catch it.

When I'd come down this morning, Celia and Edward had been having breakfast on the terrace, bathed in a rosy glow. They were holding hands over a pile of pancakes Celia had made and gazing radiantly into each other's eyes, mission clearly accomplished. They'd barely seen me approach, but then Celia was all unctuous accommodation. She'd leaped up and pulled out a chair. Then she'd insisted on getting me a plate from inside.

'We didn't hear you come in last night,' she'd trilled, avoiding my eye as she came back out with the plate. 'Were you late?'

'About two o'clock,' I told her, adding an hour for good measure.

'Gosh, you must have been having a good time.' She flashed me a guilty look.

'I was having the time of my life,' I told her as she shov-elled pancakes and bacon hastily on to my plate. 'Had a very instructive tour of Tintagel Castle. Did you have a nice evening, Edward?' I asked innocently.

'The best.' He beamed, blinking rapidly behind his spectacles. 'Celia and I had supper at this wonderful hotel. It's got all the toys – you know, swimming pool, sauna, gym.'

'Oh, splendid.'

'And we thought we'd go again tonight, didn't we, dar-ling? To use the – you know – facilities.'

'The gym?'

'Amongst other things.'

'Work up a bit of a sweat before bed?'

'Exactly.'

Celia shot me a warning look.

'You should join one in London,' I told her. 'You always say it's not your thing and you can't bear all those narcissistic pumped-up gym bunnies, but I really think it might be.'

'Edward's already surfed the best ones,' she told me, ignoring my sarcasm. 'We're going to join one in Putney, aren't we, darling?'

'We are indeed, my sweetest.'

They'd locked fingers again over the bacon and were exchanging fond smiles. I'd squirted golden syrup on my pancake, folded it in half and headed inside.

Now, as I arrived back after work, some hours later, and pushed open the cottage door, I blessed the hotel spa as I realized it was yet again responsible for the empty house – and a quiet night in. It seemed quite a palaver to me. Ages ago, in London, when I'd first heard of Edward's predicament, I'd suggested to Celia that modern medicine might solve it, but she'd told me he never took a pill.

'Not ever?'

'Not even for a headache,' she'd said firmly.

'What – my body is a temple, type thing?'

'If you like.'

It was clearly going to become even more sanctified with all the attention it was receiving from the Thai girls, but mine was not to reason why. Instead, I had a long bath, flopped horizontally on the sofa in my dressing gown with a bowl of pasta, and let the cathode rays wash over me.

Later, as I went to bed, I texted Peter.

> Just wondered – is Dad OK?

> Yes why?

> Granny was looking for him earlier.

> He went for a walk with Truffle and Flurry. Granny fusses.

Didn't she just. But I was relieved. Belinda and I didn't have much in common, but our love for Hugo was a given. Then, on an impulse, but actually not that much of an impulse because I drafted the message three times, I texted Tommy.

> You looked pretty stressed today, sorry I interrupted. Hope all OK?

You wouldn't think there were three ways of saying that, would you? But I didn't want to look too nosy, or too obviously concerned for our mutual friend. I think I hit the right note. The UN would be proud of me. The response was surprisingly quick.

> Yes all fine. I got to the
> bottom of it. All good. Sorry if
> I was short with you.

There, see? No drama. Everything was fine. All was peachy. Indeed, for two entire minutes, my life was perfectly balanced. Naturally it was pivotal, but I'd learned to make the most of any brief beatific moment, any minuscule ray of sunshine. The sun came out completely when my phone beeped again. It was Ted.

> Hope you found a bed last
> night. Mine was rather lonely.

I smiled. 'Are you suggesting it's going to get crowded?'

> Are you sexting?

I almost dropped the phone. 'Ha! No. God no. Night.'

> Night night.

I smiled – blushed too, massively. But a particularly warm and delicious feeling came over me as I snuggled down under the duvet. One might almost call it a rosy glow.

24

The day of the regatta dawned bright and clear: the heat-wave looked set to continue, but this particular morning was without the heaviness and mist of the last few days, less still and steamy, infinitely fresher. A stiff breeze swept off the sea to the estuary. In response, a myriad of colour-ful sails at sea and on the shore fluttered violently, so that a positive cacophony of marine noises filled the air, complete with what seemed like an above average quota of seagulls circling and calling, as if they'd rounded up a few more recruits from further down the coast for the occasion.

To call it a regatta was pushing it, frankly. Indeed, the elderly in the village still called it The Fête, but Belinda had seen fit to expand it over the years and renamed it into the bargain. It was very much her show and, although the villagers joined in, there was a fair amount of feet-dragging and sniggering behind hands about self-designated Queen B's misplaced aggrandisement. Unlike Falmouth, which was a week-long event with carnivals and floats, this was a tiny one-day affair, with beach sports in the morning for the children and sailing races in the afternoon. At some point during the day, the local brass band would take up position on the quay to embark on the musical programme and could happily be relied upon to provide chaotic light relief. They rarely practised, or at least not together, comprising as they did of retired businessmen and local schoolchildren, and were officiated over by a very pompous female conductor who became more and more irritated with her tuneless assembly and banged her baton furiously on her music stand as the audience dissolved. To everyone's amusement she usually fell out with Belinda, and on one famous occasion a stand-up-knock-down had ensued over whether 'God Save the Queen' should have one or two verses; it was said Belinda's ample bosom had been poked with the baton, but that may be wishful and apocryphal. Time and again a local rock band, or even a folk band, had been suggested, but Belinda wouldn't budge: this was how it had been done in Roger's father's day and grandfather's day and by golly she was not breaking with tradition now.

This, however, and more, was all still to come. As I walked down a winding path with the least treacherous of climbs to the sandy Banfield Bay, deemed the most suitable for beach sports, I could see that the children's races were already in progress. Roger, in empire-builder shorts, pink, delighted, and hopping up and down with childish excitement, was behind the foghorn, bellowing instructions, oblivious to the fact that his voice was already amplified and there was no need to shout. Belinda, along with some parents and teachers, scurried around the mass of children from the local school, all over-excited and pleased to see each other during the long school holiday and not concentrating terribly hard. Visiting children, those who dared, or whose parents pushed them – certainly the second-home owners liked to consider themselves part of the community – looked nervous and wary as the host children stared and whispered about them. This obviously included Theo and Ibby who, Christina had told me quietly, hated it, but there really was no way out for them. I saw them sitting glumly by and slightly apart, Christina beside them for moral support. She caught my eye and rolled hers. I grinned back sympathetically. I liked Christina, it occurred to me with some surprise, despite her having stolen my husband.

'Line up for the egg and spoon! The egg and spoon! Anyone in Year Four – straight line, please!' Roger boomed.

'It's Year Five, you fool!' Belinda beetled across and told him in a loud hiss, which everyone heard because she was too close to the loudhailer, and as Year Four children obediently lined up.

'Apologies, apologies! As you were, Year Four! Hold hard, stand by your beds! Year Five – quick march! Tight formation!'

So anachronistic was Roger's mix of hunting and military commands that bewildered small children wandered around, looking for beds to stand by and hold hard and no one knew what was going on. Belinda got more and more irritated, rushing back and forth in a frock of such voluminous proportions one felt she really might take off and sail magnificently out to sea, contradicting his every pronouncement.

'Number seven wins!' Roger roared. 'A very well-deserved victory for little Ryan Trelawney if I'm not mistaken! Knew his great-grandfather! Took me on my first fishing trawler!'

'Number *four* wins!' Belinda rushed up to him. 'Number seven is disqualified for holding on to his egg, are you blind, Roger?'

'Nonsense, shows initiative. I always held mine. Just don't get caught, that's all. Well done, Ryan!'

'But he *did* get caught,' she seethed, as number four promptly burst into noisy tears on being handed second place. Ryan, a beefy, confident lad, beamed smugly.

'I think we're going to declare a dead heat for this race!' announced Roger jovially, whereupon Ryan, miffed at being robbed of solo status, augmented number four's tears by giving him a hefty shove to the sand.

'Easy, boys! Decorum, decorum!' Roger boomed as Belinda ran across and grabbed her son by the arm.

'Hugo. Come and take over at once. Your father's hopeless, as usual.'

Hugo shrugged and wandered up.

'But I was doing so well!' Roger protested as he surrendered the foghorn to his son. In reality, though, there was an element of complicity about the abdication, and possibly, one or two tactical forced errors. He'd already officiated over the running race, the sack race and the three-legged race for all age groups. Enormous fun though it was to see the little imps scurrying about, if truth be told, he was keen to join his cronies on the balcony of the Sailing Club, the sun being close to the yard arm, and even if it was a mite short, somewhere in the world it would be over, and a sharpener therefore called for.

I watched from the rocks with some of the parents as Hugo took the foghorn, flushing slightly at the responsibility. He was prompted all the time by Belinda, standing right beside him, telling him exactly when to announce each race, when to start it, and who the runners were. The constant corrections and bad jokes had departed with Roger, and now Hugo's lovely calm tones ensured the races went smoothly again. Everyone visibly relaxed. He had that effect on people, I thought as I watched. Reliable, reassuring, kind. Bothering to bend down and congratulate each child on their achievements as they came through the finish line, shake their hands, and encourage those who were not necessarily destined for sporting prowess: the bespectacled, the overweight, and the downright dreamy in the case of one boy who, during the obstacle race, sat down on the fishing net he was supposed to crawl under, to inspect a crab he'd found caught in it.

'A David Attenborough in the making?' said a familiar voice in my ear. Iris materialized, still in jodhpurs, with Babs beside her, gorgeous in pink jeans and a stripy Breton top.

'Not that that sort of star potential will stop Lady Bountiful,' commented Babs, as Belinda hurried to chivvy the child down to the finish line, causing him to drop his crab and wail miserably. She took him firmly by the wrist and ran the rest of the race with him, beaming, as if he was enjoying every second of it, holding his wrist aloft as he crossed the line as though he were an Olympic athlete. Hugo, meanwhile, walked down the course and retrieved the precious sea creature, searching the sand to find it. He handed it to the boy, who gulped and pushed his glasses up his nose, sniffing loudly, equilibrium restored.

'Bully,' muttered Babs. 'Can't think how she managed to have such a lovely son. Must be the Bellingdon genes, Iris.'

'Oh, she means well,' said Iris, never one to be drawn.

'Just gets it entirely wrong. Oh look.' Babs puffed glee-fully on her cigarette. 'It's her big moment.'

A trestle table was being carried across the sand from the rocks by a couple of fathers. An efficient off-duty games teacher in a tracksuit and with a whistle round her neck carried her precious cargo to it: ribbons and medals and a few silver cups in a large plastic crate. Belinda scurried into position behind the table. She busied her-self arranging all the medals in a row, whilst Hugo asked the children to very kindly come and sit before it – he and his mother really were Sergeant Wilson and Captain Mainwaring – which they dutifully did. They lined up in their school classes, cross-legged and chattering excit-edly. Babs pottered across in her wedged espadrilles and had a word in the ear of one of the fathers she knew. He nodded and looked rather pleased. Then he went across to the table of goodies to relay the information. There was a moment's excited discussion between the games teacher and Belinda, and then the latter scurried across to her son. She took the foghorn from Hugo.

'Ladies and gentlemen and children,' she announced in her best cut-glass accent with exaggerated vowels. 'I've jarst been informed that the local BBC news crew are here to film the prize-giving. So I *hope* you'll all understand if we delay for a few minutes, until they arrive vair shortly.'

An excited buzz went round the crowd. Belinda seemed to glow and expand in her regal magnificence. She beamed benevolently at the assembled throng. Babs sauntered back to us, smiling.

'What are you up to, you witch?' Iris asked dryly.

Babs widened her eyes innocently. 'Shona's here, didn't you know? She's covering the prize-giving for *Look South*.'

'She's here?' I asked, astonished. 'Where?'

'Round by the Sailing Club, apparently. With a film crew.'

'And which prize-giving, pray, is she covering?' asked Iris sarcastically. Belinda, having retrieved her handbag from behind a rock, was busy powdering her nose in her compact mirror. She teased her hair into even loftier waves, applying lipstick now, glancing about expectantly. The children, bored by this time, rolled around in the sand and played, or pinched one another, the games teacher struggling to keep order.

'Oh, I couldn't possibly say,' grinned Babs. She sashayed off, bottom wiggling, towards the path up the cliff.

'The sailing, obviously,' said Iris grimly. 'I'll go and tell Hugo.'

Hugo was likewise involved in keeping the children quiet as his mother primped and preened. On listening to the quiet, assured tones of his aunt, in a rare show of command, and instead of informing Belinda, he took the foghorn. He explained that there'd been a slight misunderstanding, he apologized for the confusion, and confirmed that the prize-giving would now go ahead. Handing over to the gym teacher, who was more than capable of naming each winning child, he went to have a quiet word with his mother who was gaping, astonished. Albeit furious, she had no choice but to congratulate each child and award them a ribbon and a medal, her big moment of the year, the eyes of the village upon her, somewhat diminished. Her smile definitively did not reach her eyes as she shook each child by the hand. I had no time to sympathize with my ex-mother-in-law, however, and increasingly less inclination to these days. Instead I hurried off to find my friend, experiencing only a twinge of jealousy that I hadn't been the first to know. Although – hang on. I whipped my phone from my pocket. I hadn't checked it this morning.

> If the trawler race doesn't go
> ahead in St Mawes we may be
> reduced to covering the
> sailing races at Trewarren. It's
> the silly season. Are you
> about??

Ah. See? Never doubted her for a moment. I texted back. 'Yes!!' And pocketed my mobile with a smile. Then I headed back up the sandy, winding path to the cliff top, and thence to the centre of the village.

The Sailing Club was almost as crowded as the Mariners next door. Indeed, at this time of year, the narrow street outside which hosted the overflow was a rather pleasing eclectic mix of each respective clientele, the young from one merging with the pillars of the community from the other. Ted had said he'd be around at some point and I had a quick glance about, but couldn't see him. Roger was unmissable, though. Holding court with his cronies up on the balcony, he was florid and booming, large glass in hand. He saw me and gave a cheery wave, indicating with a huge sweep of his arm and a point at his glass that I should come up immediately for a drink. I nodded and mouthed: 'Will later!'

Tommy and Peter were racing the Wayfarer together,

which Peter would enjoy enormously. They were no doubt getting the boat ready further down the estuary. I thought about going to chat to them and decided I was the last person they needed before a race. Instead I joined the crush for a drink at the Mariners, which I could then take out to the wall, where I could see Celia and Edward. They were sitting with their backs to me, kicking their heels and watching the dinghy racing. I could perch with them and wait for Shona to arrive.

As I muscled into the scrum, making it to the bar reasonably quickly, a girl beside me placing her order looked familiar. She likewise glanced at me in recognition and I realized where I'd seen her.

I smiled. 'I think I saw you on the beach, at the party.'

'Yeah, you did. How is Professor Fleming?'

Her formality threw me a bit. 'Ted?'

'Yeah, well. I did call him Ted. Did call him a lot of things. But I guess I'm a student again now.' She flashed me a deliberately ironic smile. Then she paid the barman, collected her drinks and moved away from the bar, turning her back on me.

I gazed after her for a moment. I'd like to say I was confused, but there was no confusion, actually. No disguising what she'd meant. I remembered her leaping up with a friend to dash across and drag him to sit with her group by the fire when we'd arrived: remembered her coming up after we'd kissed by the rocks, when the boys were complaining we'd drunk their wine. She'd said something cutting to him, which I'd missed, but could tell by her tone she was not amused. One of the boys had calmed her down. She'd been more than a student. Clearly.

Heart pounding, I paid for my drink. As I went out I saw her again with some friends in a group by the window, her profile to me now. I wondered if she was aware I was watching her. Certainly her gestures were self-conscious as she threw back her head and laughed, then ran a tanned hand through a mane of silky blonde hair. She was very beautiful, with fine features and almond-shaped eyes. And very young. Swallowing hard, I quickly walked away. I went, not towards Celia and Edward, but right to the very end of the wall, at the fringe of the crowd. I could pretend I was waiting for someone. Take a moment. Compose myself.

I sipped my drink. Perhaps she was postgrad, I reasoned. Twenty-three or four. But she didn't look it. It was so hard to tell these days. And obviously, whatever had happened, had happened before I met him, I reminded myself. So what business was it of mine anyway? And actually, it might just have been a flirtation on her part, a crush. But somehow I knew that wasn't true. My glass of white wine tasted sour, unpleasant almost, in my mouth. I abandoned it on the wall, my mood plummeting.

Below me, on the slipway to the beach, an excited commotion was unfolding. I guessed it was Shona arriving. Rightly regarded as a bit of a local hero, she pretty much knew everyone and was greeted warmly wherever she went. Everyone secretly wondered if she might just choose to interview them, about the state of the restraining sea wall which crumbled frequently in the winter as the waves lashed against it. Or perhaps the marauding dog, that killed sheep by the dozen and which no one could catch let alone see, leading to a story about it actually being a black panther. Shona had dutifully followed this up, since a few years earlier a similar story had unfolded on Exmoor, but Peter had shown me a hilarious outtake on YouTube, which had Shona rolling her eyes after she'd done her piece to camera in a windy field, wondering aloud where on earth this panther might have sprung from. St Mawes Cattery? Should she go there next? Eventually a huge Doberman belonging to the Porthmarron caravan-site-owner was caught in the act and shot by a farmer. Shona had to politely decline to show the dead dog on TV, despite the farmer's insistence.

I hung over the wall now and watched her. She was springing from the passenger seat of a BBC van with her crew: a cameraman with a beard and a young chap with a furry boom. I was close enough to give her a shout, when I realized she was very much in work mode. She was on her mobile, nipping round to the back of the van in a hurry, wearing white jeans and a navy silk shirt, looking fab. Shrugging on a jacket, she collected her crew, who were still getting their equipment from the back. With a jerk of her head, she led them towards a group of people on the beach. Smiling broadly and shaking hands with them all, she then efficiently sectioned off an important-looking chap in a blazer, who I recognized as a friend of Roger's, and the captain of the Sailing Club.

She had a few friendly words before the camera rolled and they looked out to sea at the dinghies. When it was clear they were on air and she was posing a question, it seemed he might dry up. He began opening and shutting his mouth and growing a bit pink, and then with her easy manner she prompted him gently. He grew more verbose, even rocking back on his heels, expanding on his theme: the growing importance of the regatta, the sense of community it engendered, the bonding between tourists and locals. A little group had gathered to watch. Overhead, the throng on the Sailing Club balcony had moved to the railings to listen, amongst them Roger and Belinda, beach duties accomplished. When the interview was over, a small cheer rang out from the crowd. Shona looked up at the balcony and laughed. Seeing so many people she knew, she executed a mock bow. Suddenly she spotted me. She hurried up the beach to the sea wall. I leaned over.

'I've literally got one more person to interview round in Kylatter Cove and then I'm free. Shall we meet back here? In an hour? Have some lunch?'

'Yes! Or – so crowded here, Shona – shall I come round to Kylatter? There's that beach café there.'

'Good idea. I'll see you there.' She gave me a huge grin and a thumbs up. She was about to speed back to her crew when she turned. Sped back.

'Oh, by the way, I'm meeting that friend of yours there, Ted Fleming? He came and saw me in Truro. Wants to do a piece on the clean-up operations on the beaches.'

I stared. 'Oh . . . right. Gosh . . . I didn't—' But she'd gone, leaving me gaping.

She hurried back to her crew who threw their equipment in the back of the van and then leaped in themselves. Job done, dinghy racing in the can, it was a bit of local colour which might be useful on the six o'clock news, but if truth be told, could well end up on the cutting room floor if something better came up in the meantime. The cameraman started the engine, and, with the three of them in a row in the front, they roared back up the slip-way to the road.

I decided to walk round to Kylatter. It would take about an hour, which would give Shona time to do what she had to do, and meanwhile, give me a chance to get the wind in my hair and some endorphins pumping in my body. It would also give me time to consider that absolutely no one of my age was ever going to be perfect. That they would always have a past littered with ex-girlfriends and ex-wives. But that it was all history, and I needed to stop being so exacting and jolly well grow up. If only she wasn't so young, I thought, my tummy churning as I moved away from the crowds towards the cliff path. And if only he hadn't said that thing about Peter and Janey. About it being inappropriate, because of the age gap. I didn't mind the fact that he'd had a young girlfriend – although I did mind that she was quite so young. But what I did mind, what I really minded more than anything, was the hypocrisy.

25

Kylatter was shallow and long and not the most popular of bays. It was on the shady side of the estuary, unsheltered from the wind, and the small amount of sand it possessed near the shore soon turned to shingle or pebble further back. Amongst the drift of seaweed, wood and stones there was also a fair amount of washed up detritus. Because of its length, it was more of a dog-walking beach than a sandcastle or paddling one, and it was also a fair old leg stretch from the main resort. This, as we know, had been the point of me making the effort, but when I achieved it an hour or so later, suitably windswept and endorphin-pumped, other objectives had not necessarily been achieved. Indeed, I'd only added to my angst. I'd decided, for instance, that a certain amount of secrecy and deception had been involved on Ted's part in not mentioning to me that he'd been to see my best friend at her office in Truro: that was certainly up there in lights as a Have It Out conversation. As the cliff path plummeted abruptly and the whole bay swept suddenly into view, it was to see the man himself, climbing the last few steps up from the beach. He was approaching the car park.

'Ted!' I shouted.

He turned. Saw me and smiled, his hand shooting up to wave. He walked across, quickening his pace; pleased, it would appear, to see me.

'Flora! Excellent, that saves me the trouble of coming to find you in town.' He grinned and gave me a kiss from his great height, the wind in his hair.

'Where's Shona?' I asked, glancing about.

'Oh, she's gone,' he said in surprise.

'Really? I was meeting her in the café.' I glanced around at it, perched by the car park. It looked pretty empty. In fact, the whole place was deserted, apart from a man walking a black Labrador in the distance and a couple sitting on the rocks. Everyone was at the regatta.

He shrugged. 'She said she had to head off back to the studio. An emergency.'

I whipped out my phone. Sure enough, another message.

> Sorry sorry sorry!! Change of
> plan – there's someone I have
> to see, I'm on a story. Will
> ring I promise! HUGE
> apologies NEVER be a
> journalist. xx

I nodded. Pocketed my phone. Gazed at him a long moment. 'How come you met up with Shona?'

'You mentioned you knew her, so I popped in to see her.'

'What about?'

'I wanted to ask her if she'd do a piece about the beach clear-ups. Yet another plastic-and-pollution story, obviously, but more positive this time. About what people can do, even when they're on holiday. How they can help. A rallying cry, if you like.'

'Right. Why didn't you mention it?'

'What, that I was seeing her?' He laughed. 'Didn't know I had to!'

'Well, you made the connection through me. Might have been polite.'

He considered this. 'Yes, you're right, I'm sorry. I should have done. I just didn't think.'

'Or think to say, the other night, that you'd been to see her?'

'I only saw her yesterday. But yes, you're right, I should have texted you or something.' He put his hands together Japanese-style and executed a formal little bow. 'Mea culpa.' Then he dropped his hands. Shrugged. 'On the other hand, she could have mentioned it to you.'

'She did, just now, in town.'

'Right. Well, yes, I'm sorry I didn't clear it first and of course I'd have told you about it afterwards. I was coming to find you in town, actually, to tell you all about it. It went really well.'

'You did a piece to camera?'

'Yes.' He scratched his head sheepishly. 'Which is far more nerve-wracking than you'd think. Went OK, though, I think. Hopefully we'll get more support, maybe even local government funds if we can get them involved. It's just constant bombardment that's needed. Every radio station, too. I'm trying Radio Cornwall tomorrow and Radio Devon on Wednesday. Plus all the papers.'

'Right.' I felt a bit foolish suddenly. Ted and Shona were busy people. Professional people. They fired off emails all day long. Shona once told me she got four hundred a day.

I nodded. 'Well, I'm sure Shona will give you as much coverage as she can. She's pretty ecological herself.'

'I know, veered off her Geography degree to do Environmental Science, we talked about that.' He glanced at his watch. 'I must get on, but d'you want a quick coffee?' He inclined his head to the café. 'Less of a scrum here than round the coast.'

'Yes, there is a scrum there,' I said, ignoring the coffee. 'In fact, the Mariners was packed. I met a friend of yours in there, funnily enough. While you were meeting one of mine. Blonde? Very pretty? Quite young. We saw her at the beach party and she recognized me. Asked how you were. Or, actually, she asked how Professor Fleming was, now that she'd reverted to student status.'

I watched it drop; the penny. Saw it slowly dawn in his eyes. 'Ah. Chloe.'

I shrugged. 'Yes, perhaps. Chloe.'

He sighed. 'OK, so what d'you want to know? That I had a thing with her? I did, last term. But nothing of any consequence.'

I made a face. 'Seemed of consequence to her.'

He frowned. Regarded me searchingly. 'Not sure I like this, Flora. Am I being questioned about a past girlfriend? Before I met you?'

'She's very young.'

He considered this. 'Yes, she's young.'

'How old?'

He hesitated. 'Twenty-three.'

I raised my eyebrows.

'Yeah, OK. Twenty-one. But God, she's an adult, not a schoolgirl. It's not a criminal offence.'

'No. But you were quite coruscating about Peter and Janey.'

'Peter's seventeen.'

'Which is over sixteen. Therefore an adult.'

'True. And you're right, I did have an opinion. Perhaps a bit of a guilty, knee-jerk reaction, if I'm honest. But don't you find people often do that? When a nerve has been touched by something they're guilty of? People who manipulate will always let you know when others do it, for instance. Because they recognize it in themselves.'

I gave this some thought. 'That's true.' It had a whiff of honesty about it.

'And you're right. Ripping into Janey was definitely wrong of me. But, again, not treasonable.' He met my eyes steadily.

'No, of course not. Not crime of the century.'

It left a bit of a nasty taste in the mouth, nonetheless, quite so early on, if I'm honest. But he was right. I was overreacting. A bit of a forte of mine. The trouble was I'd got so picky these days. So . . . unable to settle for anything less than perfect. And I had to admit, it was big of him to admit his faults. I certainly couldn't call him defensive.

He shrugged. 'I'm sorry, I guess.' He smiled disarmingly. 'As you'll discover, if you decide to stick around, Flora, I am far from perfect. But then who is?'

I sighed. 'Yes, well, no – I'm certainly not. Where to begin with my litany of flaws?'

He jerked his head to the beach shack. 'We could make

337

a list over a drink rather than coffee? I think they have a licence.'

I grinned. 'Why not. I could do with one.'

Later, when we'd actually laughed about what annoyed us about ourselves, taking it in turns to fess up, he drove me back into town. He dropped me off at the quay, going on himself to the university. We kissed in the car before I got out.

'Supper tonight?' he asked, before I shut the door. He leaned across and held it open, smiling enquiringly.

'Good plan,' I agreed.

I walked away, smiling myself now.

By now, all the sailing races had finished. As I approached the Sailing Club, I realized the prize-giving was in full swing upstairs on the first floor. Up on the balcony, a sea of backs faced inwards, into the famous Stewards' Room, where it was taking place. Obviously the Bellingdons were in their element, and I saw Belinda and Hugo's backs amongst the very select, members-only audience who were allowed up there, all quite pickled and merry by now, no doubt. Hugo suddenly turned towards the street. He saw me and gave me a huge smile, indicating I should come up.

'Really?' I mouthed.

'Yes!' He nodded vigorously as Belinda turned as well, but too late to interfere. Her smile froze as she realized. I grinned to myself. *Sorry. I'm on my way.*

I went through the plate-glass doors and pushed my way through the crowd in the room below, still known locally, and, if I wanted to play a trump card, which I rarely did, still Peter Bellingdon's mother. As I mounted the stairs, which were crowded with people standing, listening to what was going on above, Bobby Sadler, the harbour master, made them stand aside for me. He gave me a helping hand.

'Up you go, love,' he said. 'Your lad's won a prize!'

'Really? Peter has? Oh, great!'

Making more haste, I bustled past people, who kindly made way. The stairs emerged at the front of the oak-panelled room, lined with wooden shields and trophy cabinets, heaving with the great and the good. I immediately spotted Babs' blonde head, right at the back. She was obviously not down the front where Belinda and Hugo had made their way with the rest of the family, but still rather naughtily in attendance, which wouldn't have escaped Belinda, whose social smile was now firmly in place for me as I appeared. Hugo waved me over, but I pointed to Iris – rather than Babs – at the back, indicating I'd stand with them. He nodded enthusiastically and turned back to his mother. I couldn't see Christina, but no doubt she was with the children somewhere. Ah yes, over there, in the corner. How odd, she was already watching me. She gave me a rather weary smile, still in the same old jeans and shirt, I noticed.

Then all eyes turned to Roger, as, behind the trophy table, and totally in his element like his wife in the morning, he began doling out the prizes. Roger no longer sailed competitively, but his pre-eminence in this field was undisputed if anyone fancied looking closely at the names engraved on the cups and trophies arrayed before him. Trewarren was a small pond, but he was still undoubtedly the biggest fish. I muscled to the back with the naughty girls. Babs was even having a cheeky fag.

'You'll get struck off,' I hissed.

'Not sure I was ever struck on, darling. And rather like Groucho Marx, not sure I'd want to belong to a club that would have me as a member. Anyway, I'm practically outside.' She puffed away merrily.

As we clapped hard for Matt Featherstone, who'd come third in the Wayfarer class, together with Cindy Hawkins, another of my old hunting buddies, Iris shouted in my ear above the din: 'Peter's done well in this class.'

'I know,' I yelled back. 'Any idea where he came?'

'Second, I think.'

'Oh, *good*.' Suddenly my eye caught something. I tugged Iris's arm to alert her. 'Is this being filmed? I thought they weren't coming?' Tucked away in the corner behind me, I'd spotted the bearded cameraman with a tripod. The soundman was beside him with headphones and a boom.

Iris looked, then turned back. 'Yes, they're putting a voiceover on later, apparently. Shona had to dash off on a story. Shame, I'd have liked to have seen her.'

'Not as much as your sister-in-law would,' Babs commented. We followed her twinkling eyes to Belinda, who, every time she handed Roger a cup, a role she'd totally invented for herself as Roger was quite capable of picking up the cups himself, would flash a little smile at the cameraman. She was handing her husband the cups rather slowly, too, clearly wanting her moment. Babs found my ear.

'Rumour has it – via Yvonne, our spy in the camp – that Belinda has taken to emailing Shona her movements. Wednesday: Church Roof Committee. Thursday: Ancient

Building Trust. Wants to be her NBF. Who would have thought?'

'Yvonne reads her emails?'

'Only when she's cleaning the computer screen. Or polishing her phone, when it's left on the island.'

Iris's mouth twitched involuntarily. She wasn't immune to finding Babs amusing, but she declined to comment, never joining in the bitchery.

Babs was now choking with mirth because Belinda had got Hugo to consult a list, pick up a trophy, then pass it to her, and Babs wondered if perhaps *Peter* could hold the list, read the name to Hugo, who'd pass the trophy to his mother, who'd pass it to her husband, and then the whole Bellingdon relay would be complete?

'Shut up, Babs,' Iris told her, trying not to laugh. 'Ah. Here is my great-nephew.'

A cheer rang out, not least mine, as Peter went up to get his second-place trophy. Tommy, no doubt, would follow in his wake. Except it wasn't Tommy's name which was announced as crew, it was Janey's, and she was going up beside my son to collect her prize.

'I thought Tommy was crewing for him?' I turned to Iris.

'He had to work. Janey stepped in instead.'

My tummy clenched a bit. I watched as Peter, clearly embarrassed by the fuss but nonetheless delighted by the enthusiastic response he was getting, was fawned over by his grandmother. She insisted on shaking his hand with both of hers. He looked on in adoration as Janey collected her ribbon and trophy, and then as they both turned and grinned at the cheering crowd, he glanced again at Janey, eyes shining.

'Popular win?' asked the soundman, leaning in towards us. He pushed one of his headphones up.

'It's the chairman's grandson,' Babs told him. 'Peter Bellingdon. You might want to write that down. And his girlfriend, Janey Karachin,' she added, shooting me a wicked glance.

I blazed hotly back at her. Babs threw her head back and roared with delight above the applause that was still ringing out. As the winner was announced for first prize, more applause rang for yet another local hero, rather than a second-home owner. The latter were tolerated for the money they brought to the resort but slightly despised for the cottages they bought, which traditionally locals would buy but could no longer afford. I, meanwhile, was making my way to the side of the room, where Janey and Peter were congratulating each other. They were comparing medals, thrilled to bits.

'Well done, darling,' I breathed, my face hot. I gave him a hug.

'Oh, Mum! Didn't see you. Yeah, we had a good race. Janey was brilliant.'

'Good. And well done you, Janey,' I managed for form's sake. 'Peter, Adam's over there.'

'Adam?'

'Yes, your friend, with his father. He was asking after you,' I lied, although Adam, who I'd spotted at the top of the stairs, did indeed look across, and come over to congratulate Peter. He had no choice but to go and greet his friend.

'Shall we?' I asked Janey, jerking my head towards the balcony and fresher air. Away from the throng.

She rolled her eyes dramatically. 'Did you just say *shall we?*' she murmured as she followed me. 'Isn't that what the Dowager Duchess in *Downton* says when she's about to lay into one of the under-stairs maids? Jeez, I feel about six!'

I ignored her and muscled my way through, well away from Babs and Iris and the film crew. I led her to the opposite side of the balcony, where there was space in the corner.

'God, if I was Babs I'd be lighting a ciggie for sure for this one,' Janey told me. Her eyes were shining almost as much as Babs', who'd spotted us. 'Tommy tells me I'm hereafter to be known as Cougar Woman.'

'Well, no, obviously not,' I said nervously, and as reasonably as I could, but with a very real feeling I was about to make a fool of myself here. 'But the thing is, Janey, he *is* only seventeen and—'

'A pretty hot seventeen,' commented Babs, who was on her way out and heading for the stairs.

'Only seventeen,' I repeated, ignoring Babs, 'and not terribly sophisticated in the – you know. The ways of the world.'

Janey frowned. 'Oh no, I disagree. He's a terrific kisser.'

I gaped at her like a goldfish.

She grinned back at me. 'Don't gawp at me like that, he is. But that's all he is, as far as I know. God, Flora, we went to a beach party, then on into town. I'm so up to here with seventy-year-old civilized chit-chat around the table and the uptight British reserve. We found a club, for God's sake. Yeah, your son's got a crush, and yeah, we had a dance, and a kiss, but no, I did not shag him.'

I breathed heavily into her amused, dancing eyes. I was ridiculously relieved. 'Right. Well. I mean, obviously I wasn't asking that—'

'Obviously you were. And you even got Tommy to quiz me. And obviously So What If I Had springs to mind. Jeez, you've gotta lay off, Flora, if you don't mind me saying so. Cut those apron strings.' She made a snip in the air with her fingers. Her eyes still danced at me as Babs' would have. Another similarity between them occurred.

'You're not a mother,' I told her. 'You can't possibly understand.'

'No, but I'm a person. And that makes me a much better objective critic. And trust me, Flora, you're a great mom, but you're too on it. Too watchful. Even at supper, wherever, your eyes are on him. Just let go.'

I stared at her, ready to deny it, but then I hung my head. It had been on my list. At the café. With Ted. Stop pretending to be a relaxed mother. *Be* one. I looked up. Wanted very much to tell her it was hard, almost impossible in my situation, as a single mother, with an only child, but I found I couldn't speak.

'And don't beat yourself up about it, either,' she added, more kindly. 'I told you, you're a great mom, and he's a great kid because of it. And despite the rest of his totally weird, fucked-up family. You've done a good job, but just let go from here on in. Let him think about America.' She sipped her drink. 'It's not such a bad place, you know.' She grinned. 'And we're not such a bad lot.'

A loud throat-clearing noise could be heard from the front of the room. We glanced up. Belinda had caught us chatting, which wasn't in the script at all. She wanted total

344

silence for the final prize of the day, the Admiral's Cup. We turned our backs on the whole show and leaned over the balcony out to sea.

'You think they're weird and fucked up?' I whispered.

'Totally bonkers, don't you? I mean – where's the daughter? Etta? Why is she never mentioned? And why is that guy,' she jerked her head back at Hugo, 'your ex-husband, totally welded to his mom's side? What's with the silent Iris? Who refuses to join in, and is like some Greek chorus, some all-seeing, all-knowing sage, and who I rate, incidentally, but who baffles the hell out of me. And the adorable Roger, who's escaped, but only so far, and only into Babs' arms, not her life. He still has to exist in this madhouse. And the sad, inscrutable and fading-into-the-background-by-the-day Christina, also baffling, because I ask myself, what's in it for her? And then at the top of the tree, at the top of this crazy, bulb-busting Christmas tree, the weirdest, maddest, loony woman herself, Belinda fucking Bellingdon. Fat controller extraordinaire, puppeteer woman, pulling every string, who is now telling her son she misses London – where I gather she's never lived – and is thinking of buying a little place up there.'

I glanced at her, horrified. Janey nodded. 'Swear to God. She said it as plain as anything at lunch the other day. And no one says, *fuck off, Belinda, give the boy some space*, everyone just goes a bit quieter. And a bit greyer. Toys limply with their Caesar salad. I mean, what the fuck?' She knocked back the remains of her whisky, eyes wide.

I nodded. Licked my lips. 'You're right. They are a bit . . . strange.'

'And despite you thinking Pete's swerved away from

345

the family business, dear God, is she doing her best to swerve him back again.'

'Belinda?'

'Oh, every opportunity. Family name, family reputation, all that shit. We had a chat that night, though, in the club. He's not doing it.'

'No, I know.' I did. Nonetheless, I was thinking about what she'd said earlier. About Peter really getting away. How it wasn't a bad idea.

She read my thoughts. 'He's his own person, Flora. Not saying he needs to get away to America – this isn't some *Brideshead*, Catholic, bullshit dilemma – just saying, let him look at the options.'

I regarded her gratefully. 'You're right. Of course you're right. And thank you.'

She grinned. She raised her glass and waggled her eyebrows. 'You wanna thank me for not shagging him, too?'

I smiled. Looked sheepishly at my feet. 'God, I'm an idiot.'

'No, you're not, you're great. In fact, I almost think you're as great as Tommy does.'

'Tommy? Oh no, Tommy and I have never got over our hate at first sight.'

She blinked. 'Oh, OK, guess I read that wrong. He certainly goes out of his way for the rest of this dopey family, though. He one hundred percent goes out of his way for Hugo.'

I remembered Tommy's face as he'd swung round from the computer in the study. I'd thought he was angry at being interrupted. And worried about what he'd seen, obviously. But now I realized. Worry was putting it mildly.

'Where is Tommy? Still up at the house?'

'I guess. Holed up in that godforsaken little office again. Said he had a heap of things to do, that's why I stepped in to crew with Pete. Oh, talk of the devil!' My son appeared. 'Hey, listen, young Pete, if you ever need someone to yell instructions at in a beautiful pea-green in the States, I'm your girl. Or is this the new shipmate?'

Peter had come across with Adam and was proudly introducing Janey, flushing with pride as he said her name and where she was from. I saw that Janey was right: he had indeed got a major crush, and she would indeed gently tease him out of it. Starting by calling him young Pete. So that, in time, he'd look back very fondly on that kiss, in a night club with an older woman. Maybe even wonder wistfully what might have been, had Janey not had more integrity than to lead him on. And more class, I thought, looking at her joking around with the boys. She was instantly putting them at their ease, letting them feel like men for a moment, and not boys just out of their last term at school. And why ever not, for heaven's sake. But for once, my mind was not on my son. It was elsewhere.

I made my way over to the cameraman who was folding his tripod away in the corner. Carefully slotting the lens cap on his huge camera. I introduced myself and told him I was a friend of Shona's, and that I'd actually been supposed to meet her today.

'Oh yeah, she said.' It was the soundman who turned and answered. He looked apologetic on her behalf. 'Said she was hoping to have lunch with an old mate, but she got wind of a story. And you know what she's like.' He sniffed the air theatrically. 'Like a bloody bloodhound.'

He grinned. 'We're picking her up in about an hour, which will give *us* time to eat, finally.' He shrugged. 'Her loss.'

'Oh, right. Where are you picking her up from?'

'Some bar in Newlyn? The Shipwright's Arms. She said she was meeting an American guy there.'

26

The Shipwright's Arms was tucked away up a back street in Newlyn. It was an ancient pub, awash with history, right at the top of one of the steepest streets of tiny terraced houses that led up and away from the bustling fishing harbour. By rights it should have attracted every tourist in town, being seventeenth-century with low beamed ceilings and ringing with fiercely Cornish authenticity. Due to the fiercely Cornish authenticity of its owner, Gordon Pascoe, however, it didn't. Absolutely no concessions to the twenty-first century were made in here. No mobile phones were allowed, and Gordon had eyes like a hawk. He'd turf out anyone he saw even receiving a text on one. The food was filthy. Really filthy. It was cooked by his wife, Linda, who'd been serving up the same chilli con carne or shepherd's pie – it alternated daily – since I was a teenager. Both dishes looked like Labrador sick and tasted accordingly. Other than that it was a Ploughman's, which should have been safe, but the butter was margarine, the bread Mother's Pride, and the cheese cheap and processed.

And yet. Up on the walls, yellow with tobacco stains, were banks of framed photographs, mostly of local heroes:

lifeboat men, generations of fishermen who'd trawled these seas for hundreds of years, the most salty dogs imaginable. But also, weirdly, Michael Caine, Dirk Bogarde, even David Niven. Some were posing with Gordon or Linda, some just perched at the bar in the little room below. Not the front bar, no one ever sat there. Hence, if a brave tourist ever did glance in curiously, to be glared at fiercely by Gordon as he kept watch, pretending to polish glasses, but actually, indulging in his favourite pastime of scaring customers away, they wouldn't know anyone was in there at all. Gordon only survived because he owned the pub outright and didn't pay rent. It was what you might call a niche destination, and an extremely private place, which only someone like Shona, or me, not even the Bellingdons, I'd hazard, would know about.

I parked easily enough, right at the bottom of the hill. Then I walked to the top of the precipitous, narrow – so narrow only one car could pass – cobbled street. Crampons were virtually required to navigate it, another effective deterrent. Obviously there was no parking outside, or indeed for a good quarter of a mile, and no pub sign hung gaily, either. Instead, painted green letters, just below the upstairs window sill, bore the legend: 'Pascoe's'. Gordon was Cornish but referred to himself as Celtic, and in many respects his establishment resembled an Irish pub. I could have been pushing open someone's front door now, leading into a front parlour in a private house, albeit that of a run-down terraced cottage.

Gordon was indeed behind the bar. His famous, fiery red hair and beard were faded almost white now: only a few traces of pale orange remained. The furious, pale blue eyes were still alert, though. He polished a glass all the quicker as he fixed me with them. It took him a moment, but then his face relaxed. That was as good as it got. He never actually smiled, it was part of the charm. He nodded in recognition as if he'd only seen me yesterday and not twenty-five years ago, and jerked his head to the little room below.

'Down there.'

'Thanks, Gordon.'

'What'll you have?'

'Orange juice, please.'

He looked furious.

'With vodka,' I added hastily. If people were to come into his effing pub they could effing well spend some money. And I could sip it, I reasoned. Since I was driving.

'How's your mum?' he asked as he turned away towards the optics, which was beyond charming for this publican, so I told him she was well and would be pleased to hear of him. He swung back and glared at me. Too much conversation, clearly. I pocketed my change, collected my drink and went down to the gloomy little room below.

I think Shona, who has the sharpest eyes and ears known to man, had already heard me above, because all I can say is that when I went down the few steps into the dark little parlour, neither she nor Tommy looked surprised to see me. Wary, yes, and tense, but not that surprised. Tommy got up and found me a chair from another table. Shona stood to hug me briefly and move her chair around to accommodate mine, but only murmured 'Flora' in my ear, before sitting down. She didn't apologize for standing me up earlier, and suddenly, having bowled over here at quite some speed, mind whirling like a dervish and in something of a high dudgeon, I didn't know what to say. I looked at her nervously.

'How was the regatta?' she asked politely, as if it were perfectly normal for me to have driven twenty miles and walked in on her and Tommy Rochester having a private drink together in this out-of-the-way place. I rallied and played along, not quite knowing what else to do.

'Oh, you know, same old. Peter and Janey came second in the Wayfarers.' I glanced brightly at Tommy, hopefully conveying that, no, I didn't mind that they'd sailed together, and that I'd grown up a bit, but tricky in the space of one glance. He rose to the occasion enough to say 'good' and gave a polite smile and contrived to look interested. Then I babbled on about Belinda, who, as usual, had queened it over everyone, and how she referred to 'dear Shona' these days, when she hadn't been so *dear* when she was young! I laughed nervously.

'Oh, I don't care,' Shona replied. 'I'm as much of an opportunist as Belinda. Goes with the territory, I'm afraid.' She fell silent and looked at Tommy. Tommy didn't say anything. An awkward silence ensued. After a moment, I broke it.

'Sorry,' I said instinctively, glancing from one to the other. 'I shouldn't have come. This is clearly private. But I couldn't help thinking . . .' I tailed off hopelessly. What couldn't I help thinking?

'That it concerns you,' finished Shona. 'And you're right, it does. At least – indirectly.'

I glanced at Tommy but his eyes were averted. He looked wretched. Seemed intent on the wood grain of the table. Eventually his eyes came up to meet mine.

'Hugo,' he said quietly.

'Right.' My heart stilled a moment: then pumped frantically. 'Oh God, what?'

They exchanged a glance. Shona raised her eyebrows for a green light from Tommy and he nodded curtly, looking sleep deprived again, I noticed, his handsome face grey and drawn, not an ironic joke or snide remark in sight. He took a sip of what looked like bourbon. Shona took a deep breath. Looked at me squarely.

'I met Ted Fleming today, as you know.'

'Yes, you told me,' I said. 'And I saw him earlier. You interviewed him about a beach clear-up he was doing?'

'Yes, well, ostensibly that was the ruse to get me out there. And we did do that interview. But what he really wanted to talk to me about was Bellingdon Water.'

'Again?' I was appalled. 'I thought Hugo had talked to him about all that. Had a meeting up at the house, assured him they were cleaning up their act – I thought Ted was happy? Well. Satisfied, anyway.'

'Up to a point. And Bellingdon *are* cleaning up on the Bio-Bead front, as all these independent subcontracting companies are having to, even though it doesn't always suit them financially. But Fleming is on to something else. Bellingdon Water, and more specifically the infrastructure it provides – the pipelines, the pumps – are apparently responsible for the most sewage leaks and the most water pollution, the most fish-and-marine-life poisoning, in the entire country. Far worse than any other subcontractor providing to all the major water boards in the UK.'

I stared at her. 'Bollocks.'

She shook her head. 'True.'

'It can't be. They've always been so rigorous about that sort of thing, so big on the environment. Bloody hell, Roger's got an award in his study – he's got that wrong.'

'He hasn't got it wrong.'

'But . . . no, rubbish, I would know. I *would* know, Shona.' I clenched my fists.

'No one knows. Because somebody has seen fit to cover tracks and massage the figures and lose a lot of the records.'

My mouth dried. 'Hugo.'

Shona looked at Tommy. He hesitated. Cleared his throat. 'It looks very much that way. Anecdotally there's evidence of other senior managers in similar positions destroying evidence and the Environmental Audit Committee is on the case, and I'm afraid I can see why. There are huge gaps, Flora, huge.'

'Is that why he asked you to come across?' I looked at Tommy. 'I mean – no, actually, why would he? If he knew there were gaping holes, surely he wouldn't want you to see? Surely he knew you'd discover them?' I felt sick.

Tommy massaged his forehead with his fingertips. 'They've actually been really cleverly covered up. Explanations given. Lengthy and investigative reports written. I've read them. Very plausible. Frost, hard winters, then sudden thaw. Natural causes, leading to pipeline leaks in Penzance, or explosions actually into the sea in Falmouth, on to beaches. But, in one case, left for eight months, Flora. In Newquay. *Eight months.* Well into spring and summer. Broken, badly made pipes, pumping raw sewage, straight into the harbour. Fishermen, taking their trawlers out, bringing back their catch. Ready to eat. Local kids diving off the quay, coming up with shit in their mouths.'

'Perhaps he didn't know. I mean – didn't know until it was too late. Then tried to fix it?'

'Except there's evidence of it being reported and of him ducking it as far back as February, and it continues until October.'

'But why? Why not fix it in February?'

'Because he was scared of the shareholders. Scared of the millions it would take to do it, what it would wipe off the shares. Not just one pipe, but endemically, systemically, across the whole of this coastline. All Bellingdon pipes. And scared, too, of the fine from the Environment Agency, which used to be piffling, so much so that frankly companies took fines on the chin, accepted them as the price of doing business. But they're getting much bigger. So he covered his tracks, did minor repairs and held off on colossal overhaul. At first when I looked it seemed fine, and I think that's why he asked me to come across. To check his records, his accounts – his whitewash, if you like – and it all looked in order to me. I told him so, that it looked fine. In fact, I wondered why he'd asked me to come. I mean, he'd paid me. Or the company had. He said it was just an excuse to get me over here really, slapped me on the back, and we went sailing. Had a great day. But his mood was so changed. So . . . buoyant, compared to his earlier, anxious one, that it made me think. I guess it made me suspicious.' He looked sad. 'Not a nice thing to say about a friend. That night, I went back into the study and dug deeper. I was horrified. He had been very clever – Hugo's no fool – but not clever enough.'

'I found you on the sofa, that morning.'

'Exactly.'

'You looked dreadful. Like you'd seen a ghost.'

'Honey, I felt like shit.' Tommy's blue eyes, so unhappy, were trained on mine.

'Did you tell him?'

'No. Still haven't. But, as I say, he's no fool and I think he can tell that my mood's changed.'

'We all can.'

'Yeah, quite. Mr Transparent. Belinda can tell, too.'

'You think she knows?'

'I do. In fact, I think he may have confided in her. Confessed. He'd never go to Roger. And she may have encouraged him. Or even –' he hesitated – 'persuaded him to do the cover-up. Maybe they both panicked.' He shrugged. 'Look, I'm just surmising. I don't know.'

'It's a good surmise, though.' I thought about it. About how Hugo would go to her. Always.

'She keeps taking me aside and reminding me what a very old friend I am of Hugo's, and how she knows I'll always be there for him. Her fingers pressed into my arm, pussycat smile in place.'

I licked my lips, which were dry. 'What will you do?' I breathed.

'Well, I won't cover it up, if that's what you mean. And which I have a feeling is what Belinda wants me to do, i.e. make a better job of it than Hugo, which frankly, I could. But I obviously won't report him, either. I'll ask him to do that. Report himself. I'll have that conversation. Tell him he has to fess up to the authorities.'

'Before someone else goes to the Environment Agency,' said Shona grimly.

I looked at her. 'You mean . . .'

'Fleming.'

'But—'

'He is so on it,' she interrupted, leaning across the table urgently towards me. 'He doesn't know exactly the scale of the underground pipe corrosion or the cover-up, but he can tell there's something dodgy going on. Repairs are very detailed but not that expensive. Why? I know he's trying to gain access to Bellingdon Company records, some of which are public, some clearly not. He wants to get to the bottom of it.'

'And destroy the Bellingdons.'

'Well, indirectly, maybe. But it's all in the name of the environment. And whilst what Fleming is doing seems underhand to you, to most people it would seem totally justifiable.'

It occurred to me to wonder if he'd embarked on a relationship with me to glean information, but I dismissed the thought as soon as it arrived. No. Absolutely not. It nevertheless struck me as unforgivable that he hadn't mentioned any of this when we met earlier. Just the beach clear-up. Lying by omission. My heart began to beat fast. 'What will happen to him? To Hugo? To the company?'

'If he puts his hands up?' asked Tommy.

'Yes.'

'Up to the sentencing council at the Environmental Audit Committee.'

'*Sentencing* council? You mean—'

'No, unlikely. If you mean prison. Certainly that's unprecedented. But a whopping great fine, for sure. The scale of which is new. In East Anglia, two months ago, a manager who destroyed data and coerced colleagues to falsify records incurred a massive fine. It caused a horrendous fish kill. And he lost his job, obviously.'

My mind was spiralling. Prison. Unlikely. But not out of the question. 'Hugo can't lose his job, he runs it, owns it,' I whispered, forcing myself not to go there.

'He will if Bellingdon goes under.'

'Is that possible?'

Tommy shrugged unhappily. 'It's big, Flora. Big. And with Fleming on the case . . . and obviously Shona has responsibilities.'

I turned to her, aghast. 'You wouldn't!'

'What, report a huge whitewash story pertaining to the most sensitive coastal issue of the day? As a Cornish journalist?' She widened her eyes at me.

I seemed to have no saliva left in my mouth at all. I managed to steady myself before I spoke. 'So – you met Ted today, and then texted Tommy, and then met here, in the most secluded spot in South Cornwall. What had you both decided to do? Before I came in?'

'Talk to Hugo, obviously,' said Tommy. 'But the problem is, Shona's now compromised. Because she asked me, and I told her what I know. What I've just told you.' He looked beseechingly at me. 'Don't ask me to be any other way, Flora.'

I stared at him. Looked down at my hands. 'No. I know. You had to. But . . . you told her in confidence? As an old friend?'

'How could I demand conditions? Guilt-trip her in any way? I have asked her to hold her fire, though, and she's agreed. But she's in a hole, now, Flora, because of me. Because I couldn't lie to her.'

They both looked at me, horribly worried: Shona about what it would do to me, and by extension Peter, and Tommy about what he was doing to his friend. But there was certainty there, too. And an element of – not defiance – but steadfastness. They would do this, eventually. And no amount of argument or pleading from me would make things any different. These were decent people, loyal to their friends, but loyal to their own integrity and morals, too. More so. They had to be. And when I examined my own conscience, I knew, despite my initial panic, that I couldn't ask them, and indeed wouldn't want them, to be any other way.

'I'm giving you the worst-case scenario, Flora,' said Tommy, leaning forward, his elbows on the table. His earnest face was close to mine. 'Because I want you to go there in your mind. Yes, Bellingdon could collapse, but I give you my word, if Hugo fesses up, I'll do everything in my power to make the collateral damage as limited as possible. I'll be with him all the way.'

His blue eyes were steady and true. Eyes, I realized, I'd come to respect and very much like to see around these days. They made me feel safe.

'Thank you,' I breathed. I took a great gulp of my drink to steady myself.

As I set my glass down, a bearded chap stuck his head around the corner. He blinked in bewilderment.

'Blimey. It's like something out of *Poldark* in here. Planning a shipwreck?' Shona's soundman stared round in wonder.

Shona drained her glass. 'Mike. Right. Gotta go. Stay in touch, Tommy.'

She got up and wriggled into her jacket. Before she went, though, she reached out and grabbed something from the table, which I realized was a tape recorder. She looked at me.

'Tommy asked me not to turn it on and I didn't. It's all off the record. But Flora . . .' She looked searchingly at me. Pleadingly even.

'I know,' I said quickly. 'I know.'

She nodded. 'Good.' I swallowed hard. She gave Tommy a steady look. 'Tell her the rest,' she told him firmly.

27

'What did she mean?' I asked him. 'Tell her the rest?'

Tommy looked at me. He sat back in his chair. He seemed about to speak, then, abruptly, he reached for his glass, drained it and stood up. 'Let's get out of here. This place is driving me nuts. I feel like the Spanish Inquisition is going to appear at any moment, brandishing sabres. Anyway, I'm driving and one bourbon is enough. I need to walk it off.'

He plucked his linen jacket from the back of his chair and shrugged into it in an easy motion. I finished my drink and followed suit.

He was quiet and pensive as we left and I felt somewhat intimidated by his air of preoccupation and seriousness, so that, despite all my natural inclinations to seize his arm and cry, 'What? *What?*', I followed him silently outside. We fell into step beside one another down the precipitous cobbled street, which took a degree of concentration in itself. Gordon had simply nodded curtly as we departed, but I'd noticed, as I shut the door behind us, that he'd watched us go through the front window with more than his usual interest, curious, perhaps, at people even more taciturn than himself. We headed on down to the harbour, watching our steps on the cobbles. The silence was dreadful and I was full of fear for what it held, but just when I could bear it no longer, I realized I had to be the grown-up here. Help him along a bit. Give him some time. And not just wait in anticipatory silence, but fill the gaps, conversationally.

'Busy little place, isn't it?' I ventured, keeping my voice steady. I nodded towards the buzzing port as we approached, clanking with fishing boats and machinery and men bringing in their catches, shouting to one another as they hauled up brimming nets. Seagulls screamed overhead, poised to plunder. Tommy glanced up gratefully from his shoes, pleased, I could see, that I was going to give him a certain amount of time to collect his thoughts.

'It certainly is. Your man at the bar told me it's the largest fishing port in England.'

'Gordon did? That's uncommonly garrulous of him. He's a silent soul.'

'Only when I told him I was waiting for Shona. She's something of a local celebrity, clearly. Let's walk round to the end of the quay.'

As we followed the jetty, the seagulls seemed to increase their screeching and the mainsails slapped and jangled all the louder, as if someone had hit the special-effects button in a Radio 4 play. Appropriate, I decided, under the circumstances, since I felt I was taking part in a drama of someone else's creation and direction. Certainly not mine. That fear of the unknown and lack of control suddenly made me unable to tell Tommy that, despite the new restaurants, it was still fishing that kept this port afloat, or even about the colony of artists who'd settled here in the thirties for the light and made it famous. Instead, I just let the cacophony of seaside noises be the soundtrack to his contemplation. We walked down the long quay around the harbour in silence, skirting the mooring lines tied to huge bollards, heading out to sea. Finally we found a bench, right at the end, looking towards the horizon. I'm sorry to say that the moment my bottom hit the salty wooden slats, I reverted to type.

'What did she mean, Tommy?' I asked nervously. 'Tell her the rest?'

Tommy leaned forward to rest his elbows on his knees. He narrowed his eyes into the watery blue distance. After a moment, he spoke.

'Did you ever wonder why I was so against you marrying Hugo?'

I blinked in surprise at his profile, but he kept his eyes on the small blue fishing boat chugging slowly towards us.

'Yes, of course. You didn't think I was right for him. Not good enough.' I hesitated. 'No, OK. That's harsh. That's what I told myself then.' I struggled to verbalize the truth, which had taken years to admit, even to myself. 'You knew he wasn't in love with me. Knew he was in love with Christina.'

'Correct. But still only halfway there. He loved you, Flora, but he wasn't in love with you. He loved Christina, sure, but he wasn't in love with her either.'

I frowned. 'What d'you mean?'

'Hugo's gay, Flora.'

I stared at him. Went very cold. It seemed to me I turned to stone on the bench. It was as if Prospero, or Merlin, or some higher celestial being, even, had lightly touched my shoulder and petrified me. I couldn't speak. Tommy let me attempt to absorb it. He waited in silence.

'No, he's not,' I quavered eventually.

'Yes, he is,' he said with quiet certainty.

It obviously couldn't be true. But nonetheless, I was aware of something of great magnitude rolling in, as if from the sea before us: huge, dark and inexorable, not the sunny horizon I stared at. Something forceful and tremendous and indisputable. Nevertheless, I doggedly disputed it.

'But . . . he married me. Christina . . . Married twice.'

'Yes.'

'But how . . .' Even as I tried to form some sort of question, I knew it was rolling in fast, this force of nature, and to stop it was like trying to hold back the tide. I also knew that this was the huge piece from the jigsaw puzzle of my life that I'd never found. It had been hiding under the lid of the box, or under the table, for years. And somehow, it had finally slid into view.

'But – hang on – no!' Suddenly my mind wouldn't have it. It was too old, this brain of mine: too set in its ways. It could be a strong force, too. I rounded on him furiously. 'What d'you mean, he's *gay*? You can't just say that, how do you know?'

'I found him in bed with a guy at Oxford. I was in college with him, remember. Same staircase. Opposite room. I know.'

I was shocked by the sudden visual freeze-frame, but – at university. Years ago. I scrabbled around in my brain.

'But – but that could just have been a one-off! An experimental thing – you know – an undergraduate fling, or even—'

'No, he's gay. Or at least was *fluid*, back then. More so now, I think. More craving a man. Or indeed men. Exclusively.'

A hole opened up inside me. Gaped wide. It all made terrible sense. The love for me, indisputably, but the lack of *real* love. And the paucity of sex, of intimacy.

'But why marry Christina?' I said incredulously.

'Because she's sexually ambivalent, too. Can't you see that?'

I stared. 'What d'you mean?'

'Look at her, Flora. Think about her.'

I caught her in my mind's eye: in her jeans, same few unisex-style shirts rotated every other day. Blue, green, yellow. I thought back to when I first met her, flying over that stream on a rope, short hair, trainers, huge smile.

'Just because she looks – you know – boyish. That doesn't mean she's gay, for Christ's sake!'

'No, of course not. And many very beautiful, very feminine women are gay. But she's kinda androgynous, don't you think?'

She was. She really was.

'But . . . do you *know*?'

'Oh, I know she has girlfriends, if that's what you mean.'

I got up off the bench. Then I sat down again abruptly. '*How* do you know that, Tommy? Have you walked in on *them*, too?'

'No, but Peter has.'

'*Shit!*' I got up again. Swung round and stared down at him. 'What? *What?*'

'Sit down, Flora.' He reached up and took my arm, gently. I sat, tremulously. I felt numb. Horrified.

'Peter sailed with me two years ago at Cowes, remember? Crewed my Laser. He told me he'd come home unexpectedly and found Christina curled up on the sofa with another girl, watching TV. Arms around each other. Nothing graphic, fully clothed. But he knew at once what it was. Also, a friend of his – Adam? Who's here?'

'Yes,' I whispered.

'Who's gay, had asked Peter about his father. Once, when he was pissed.'

'God. He knew.'

'Apparently. And Peter asked me, when we were sailing, what I thought about his father. Whether he was. I had to tell him the truth.'

'You did?'

'Yes, I did.'

'So Peter knows,' I whispered.

'Has done for two years.'

'And was he . . .' I stalled. Couldn't speak.

'Confused. Upset, obviously. But not as much as you'd imagine. Because he'd left it a year before he spoke to me. So he'd got his head round it, to an extent. More so, now. We email. I ask him how he's doing.'

I stared at him, stupefied. Then out to sea. I swung back again.

'So why the *fuck* didn't anyone tell me?'

Tommy was silent. 'Why, Tommy? Why didn't I know?'

'Peter didn't want you to. He thought you'd be too hurt by it.'

'What, like . . . like I'd *turned* Hugo, or something?'

He shrugged.

I went cold. '*Did* I?'

366

'Don't be ridiculous, Flora.'

'No, but – shit. I *did*.'

'I said *don't* be ridiculous. Human beings don't work like that. You know that. But that may be why he didn't tell you, because he knew you'd think that. You, with your guilt. And he didn't see any reason for you to know.'

I felt as if all breath had been sucked from my body. Felt limp. Lifeless. There I'd been, carrying on as normal. Life, my life, had been going on, as usual. Peter at school, me at home, painting, seeing Mum, chatting to Celia. Yet all the time, it was different, the picture, to the one I thought I was seeing. The treachery struck me as colossal. Unforgivable. Such deception. And yet, all in the name of protection. Protecting me. My brain scrambled to keep up.

'And – and why didn't *you* tell me, all those years ago? Why, Tommy?'

Tommy leaned forward on his elbows again. He massaged his forehead with his fingertips. 'Ah, shit, that's the million-dollar question. But it was so hard back then. And so much more complicated. We were all so young, and as you say, *was* it just an undergraduate thing? I know now it wasn't, but didn't know for sure back then. And was Christina gay? I *thought* so, at least guessed so, and, as you know, I even had a go at talking to Hugo, just before your wedding. You walked right in on us. I questioned whether he was really in love with you, and doing the right thing, but even *I* couldn't say – shit, buddy, aren't you gay? Using Flora as a beard? Conveniently acquiring a wife – and let's not forget – a child? All of which is fine, don't get me wrong, if it's out in the open, but don't you need to tell her?'

I licked my lips. Swallowed hard. 'No, not then. Not

at that precise moment. But maybe before? When we got engaged? Presumably he knew you knew – you'd walked in on him?'

'He hadn't seen me. Neither of them did. There was a lot of noise, and they – they both had their—'

'Yes, OK,' I interrupted quickly. Backs to me. I got up again. Walked to the edge of the quay. I folded my arms and held myself tightly, as if I'd crack. Then I bent my head and stared down into the dark water. Swirls of coloured oil from the boat's engines on the surface made it impenetrable.

'So . . .' I came back and sat down again. He kept his profile to me. I plucked a salty strand of hair from my mouth. 'I mean . . . why? Why all of it? Why didn't he come out?'

'Why do you think?'

Tommy turned his head to look at me properly. Gave me a penetrating gaze. It took me a moment but then we communed silently.

'Belinda.'

He shrugged. 'Don't you think? Hugo's always been such a mummy's boy. So in thrall to that powerful mother of his. And Hugo is not . . . a strong man.'

'He's weak,' I agreed. I swallowed. 'Lovely, but weak.' It had taken me a long time to finally admit it to myself. 'And even had he been strong, that conversation would have been terrifying.'

'Exactly. And hence why he's always lived in London. Miles away from sharp eyes, from Trewarren. Where he can have something of a secret life. And Christina can, too.'

I looked out to sea, computing it all. Digesting. Suddenly I sank my head down into my hands and tugged hard at my hair. I gave a low moan. 'Oh shit, Tommy, if only I'd known!'

'Really?'

I jerked upright, furious. 'Yes! *Yes*, really! Fucking hell, my whole life – or a lot of it.' I stared wide-eyed across the sea. A lie. Longing for a man who wasn't there. Didn't exist. I struggled to explain. 'I wouldn't have found it so impossible to get over him. Wouldn't have always yearned, put my life on hold. Which I did. Ask Celia, I did.'

'But I didn't know that, Flora. I lived in the States. Or, if I did know, or at least guessed, from what I gleaned from Peter – I . . . yeah, OK, I dodged it. I'm a man, for Chrissake. It's what we do. I mean – OK, maybe I should have come across when he left you and married Christina, told you then. But I had all these strange loyalties to Hugo, too. He didn't know I knew – how could I tell you without his say-so? *He* should have fucking told you. Told you then. Should have set you free. He should have damn well told *every*one. I mean, shit, no one knows.'

'No one?'

'Least, not so far as I can tell. I mean, sure, his gay friends will, obviously, but it seems to me, for Hugo, it's like something out of the nineteen fifties. Still is, for some poor people. Young folks, though, mostly, with soccer-mad brothers, fathers, in tough neighbourhoods, secretly liking guys. And yet Hugo, who is all grown up, is still one of them. And, Flora, I guess I also thought – darn it. She was married to him for two years. She must have had an inkling, surely?'

He looked at me imploringly. I met his incredulous bright blue eyes in his sculpted, narrow face.

'Not a clue,' I told him, equally incredulously, as I considered this. 'Not one single iota.' I looked away and stared blankly back down at the water. 'And I agree, you would think, wouldn't you . . . ?'

I recalled our early days together: at schools miles apart, then universities at either ends of the country. Talking a lot, meeting occasionally. Later in London, in the flat; happy if tense times. The bedroom. Hugo turning the light out, saying sorry, he was tired.

'I mean – he wasn't highly sexed, sure, but I was pregnant for a lot of our marriage. Then after a baby . . .' I swallowed. 'I just thought he'd stopped fancying me. After Peter. I'd read about it. And it had been . . . a difficult birth. Peter didn't exactly slip out. I wasn't gagging for it myself, for a while. Later I was. Then he left.'

I tried to imagine what I'd have felt like if I'd known he was gay. *Fluid*, as Tommy put it. I turned to him. 'Do you think they had an arrangement? Hugo and Christina? D'you think they discussed it?'

He shrugged. 'No idea.'

A flurry of possible scenarios hurtled into my head and flew around up there, chasing each other like a kaleidoscope. All the potential discussions they'd had – or maybe not had. Just an unspoken, tacit knowledge of the possible, perhaps. The possibility of living a double life, with a home, children, all the trappings. An affluent, normal family in Hampstead. Hugo Bellingdon, father of three, chairman of his family's water company. Why couldn't he still be all of that, with a boyfriend? Why? I thought of Belinda and Roger. No. Unthinkable. Not Roger. But Belinda.

'I *so* wish you'd told me, Tommy!' I said vehemently, balling my fists and thumping them on my knees. 'I would have got over it. I'm not that wet, not that guilt-ridden. I would!'

'Back then? When you were about to get married? Pregnant?' He shook his head. 'You'd never have forgiven me.'

'Maybe not, but so fucking what? So what!'

He paused. Some colour drained from his face. 'So everything. So everything.'

I frowned at this, confused. I shook my head. 'What?'

He was staring down at his knees. He looked up. Regrouped. 'Yes, I should have done. I know I should have done. Even then, I knew it. But I had my own reasons.'

I made an incredulous face. 'What – that I'd have hated you? Sure, I would have done. But no more than I probably did alrea—'

'Yes, but you see I minded that.' He rounded on me fiercely, interrupting me in mid-flow. 'I minded very much that you would never forgive me. That you would always hold it against me.'

His eyes were blazing with a strange intensity. They burned into me.

I blanched. Then I shrugged. 'OK, you minded . . .' I said, confused.

'In fact, if I'm honest, if I'm totally, unutterably honest, it was my prime, overriding motivating factor for not telling you. Nothing to do with loyalty to Hugo. I could have got over that. Reasoned it out with him. Toughed it out. But I didn't want your hate. I couldn't entertain it.' It was his turn to get up off the bench. He thrust his hands deep in his trouser pockets and walked to the edge of the quay.

He stood with his back to me, staring into the water. At length, he spoke gruffly, but I could hear every word he said. 'Contrary to popular opinion, Flora, I've always been very fond of you. Strange, but true.'

I stared at his back. Brushed some hair from my eyes. 'Define fond.'

There was a silence. 'Loved you. I've always loved you. I was the one who should have married you. The one who really wanted you. Properly wanted you. Not Hugo.'

28

The seagulls cawed in the sky and circled in the wind, filling the silence with their sound. Their swooping and diving made the stillness of his back all the more apparent. I stared at it.

'Tommy – I . . .' The wind whipped my hair into my face; more strands stuck to my mouth, which was open in wonder. I pulled them away. But I had no breath or words to draw on. He continued his contemplation of the blue trawler, which was quayside now. The fishermen, having unloaded their morning catch, were hauling their empty lobster pots back into the boat, preparing to turn around and sink them again for tomorrow. I watched absently. For a moment I wondered if I'd dreamed it.

'But you hated me,' I breathed suddenly, with feeling. I remembered those same blue eyes, younger and much fiercer; much more defiant, glaring at me from under his hat out hunting; shooting me a loathing look just after he'd apologized to Shona, in the kitchen, at home. Much nicer to her than to me. Always. And keeping in touch with her. Never me.

He turned, his face pale. 'Jesus Christ, I was seventeen

when I first met you! And of course I hated you, it was my coping strategy. Don't you know anything about men, Flora? I could see Hugo had got there first, could see he was impressed with you flying over fences. I had no idea about his sexuality then, was just quietly furious about being pipped to the post *and* making a fool of myself into the bargain. Business as usual, Tommy Rochester. Except, getting the girl, which even in those days usually happened. Oh, I followed up smartly with a series of "I'll show you" girlfriends. I played fast and loose, but none of them matched up. I still saw you flying over four-foot hedges. Even back in the States.'

'*Tommy*,' I was flabbergasted. 'You cannot be serious.'

'Deadly.' He looked deadly, too. He gave a twisted smile. 'Not so Mr Transparent, huh?'

'But you were so—'

'Mean?'

I remembered his mocking eyes at Oxford, as I'd arrive from the train station and Glasgow; walking to Hugo's room across a grassy quad where Tommy and his friends would lie reading; how he'd ignore me. Later, in London, in smart restaurants, as I dithered over the cutlery, failed to get to grips with an artichoke. Latched on to other insecure girls. Always a snide look from Tommy.

'I told you: a defence mechanism. I loved you back then and goddammit this trip over here was a mistake and I knew it would be because I still love you now. I'm gutted to realize it but, shit, it's a relief to say it. Maybe I'm purged? Maybe that's all that was needed, to spew it all out? Who knows. Anyway, that's me done making a fool of myself again. Twice in two decades. Give my regards to Professor

374

Fleming, Flora. He's making a nuisance of himself in so many ways.'

And with that he turned on his heel and walked away. I watched him go. My eyes followed his back in amazement, his pale-biscuit linen jacket. I thought of running after him, of taking his arm, swinging him round and saying his name – 'Tommy!' But then what? What was there to say? I was as staggered by this revelation as by the one about Hugo, and actually . . . I couldn't believe it. Oh, Hugo being gay I believed, all too clearly – that dawn came storming up – but Tommy Rochester in love with me? Man about town, lothario, a girl in every port, joker extraordinaire, Peter's naughty godfather, Hugo's fast friend – he was *so* unlike me. The introspective, reclusive painter who'd wasted her best years pining and hiding in a garret with her excuses for not living, whilst he – he'd *lived*. Sailed, hunted, skied – shagged, for sure – but he'd packed his life with successful work and friends and travel. No. He was having me on.

Or was I the one girl he *couldn't* have, who hadn't responded to his charms? The one that got away? Ergo he wanted me? Maybe that was it. Testosterone-fuelled, competitive spirit surging to the fore. I remembered girls at Oxford, hanging on his every amusing word in the college bar as he held court, still in his rowing kit, always surrounded. Not by me. Was I simply a challenge? Was this something male and macho, some unfinished business? Whatever it was, it was a myth he'd nourished and kept alive, as people do. As I'd nourished the myth of Hugo. Tommy might think he loved me – *loved* me, for Christ's sake, crackers! But he didn't. Of course he didn't. And now it was spoken, he'd feel as much of a fool – he'd even said it, *maybe I'm purged* – as he had done all those years ago.

I got up slowly. The sun had gone behind a cloud and it was getting cooler. My knees were stiff and I realized I'd been sitting there for some time. Something about those eyes, though. Fierce and true beneath a mop of still-fiery, still-russet hair. If only I hadn't seen those. If only he hadn't turned round; had carried on looking out to sea. I walked down the quay towards town.

I sat in the car for a while before I started the engine. I felt frozen in my seat, staring out, deep in thought. Then, abruptly, I reached for the ignition, and drove home. Determinedly putting Tommy to the back of my mind, I thought about Hugo. About how, actually, he'd probably managed to have a relatively happy life. With Christina. Who was a lovely, kind, generous person, as he was. And who'd given him the cloak of respectability he craved, to pass under the radar, to pass muster with his family. As no doubt he'd given her. Had they recognized each other's sexual ambiguity when they first met, that time in Wales? Had that been part of the attraction? Even though he'd been with me and Christina had been with Sam? Had a light bulb gone on in their heads? Subliminally, perhaps. And maybe it had crept up on them later, as a more conscious thought, after Hugo had married me. Overwhelmed them with possibilities.

I realized now I couldn't have done it. Couldn't have lived with a gay man. I loved Hugo so much, but I could not have done that. Oh my God – why hadn't anyone recognized that? Known that I'd find it impossible? Except . . . nobody knew. Apart from Tommy, who lived in America, and who apparently had his own reasons, and Christina. No one close to me, anyway. And Peter would want to deal with the situation himself, on his own, I knew that. Without his mother adding her cloying, maternal worries about his welfare. He'd want to contain it, too. Wouldn't want me asking how he felt about it every five minutes, worrying he had even more baggage. In time, with maturity, who knows, he might have told me; might have realized it was a way of setting me free, but right now he was a teenage boy dealing with his own problems. Yes, possibly with time. Because although I always resisted seeing his father and purported to hate any contact, Peter had the emotional intelligence to know the truth, the relationship between love and hate, and how they could be the same thing. Not unlike another boy of about Peter's age, who, years ago, had figured that one out, too, on a cold winter's morning, just a few miles from here, over rolling green hills and steep valleys. Or so he'd told me.

I was glad of the journey. Glad it took nearly an hour to get back to Trewarren; it gave me some time to absorb the shock, but also, to welcome it gladly. Hugo's culpability in the water pollution and its ramifications still loomed, but my mind flew selfishly to my own life. My new emotional life, which I would so welcome. I could be friends with Hugo and Christina; could even envisage suppers together, barbecues in their garden, all the things I never could before. And I'd have lunch with Hugo, tell him that: tell him if only I'd *known*. Watch his eyes, still dear, beloved eyes, widen with recognition, with relief, over his Dover sole at Wheelers where we'd meet in the City. Realize that, if only he'd *told* me! But Hugo was one of the few people who had no idea I had still been in love with him. Just that I was bitter and avoided his family. Although it wouldn't take a genius to work it out.

But there were other repercussions to full disclosure on his part. He might not want Peter to know. Or, he might have wanted to tell him himself, when he was eighteen, or twenty-one, perhaps. Or not at all. This last struck me as entirely possible. Hugo was not a brave man. Plus it's a huge thing for a child to absorb. Would still be, it occurred to me, for his other children, Theo and Ibby. It suddenly struck me as a profoundly selfish thing to do, but that was another story. My mind was on my own story. Because, actually, how could I have known, I who had my heart plastered permanently to my sleeve, and not told Peter? My mother, Celia? How could I have walked around with something that huge? Hugo would have known that I couldn't.

The car windows were down and I took great gulps of salty sea air as I came off the main road and followed the familiar country lanes. The high banks and towering hedges precluded any glimpses of the fields: the stunning, rolling green vista was only teasingly revealed in quick glances through a five-bar gate, or from a particularly high hill, before a vertiginous drop down into a hollow. Very occasionally, as I climbed a hill, a sliver of silver blue, a tiny glistening triangle, would flash in the distance. When I was young, and we'd been away, I'd shout from the back seat that I'd seen it, and Dad would pretend he hadn't, but I knew he'd seen it first. Glimpse by glimpse, it would become a stretch rather than a sliver, the centrepiece, framed by the hills, beckoning me on as it did now.

Eventually I reached the bend in the road with a run of white bungalows, the garage, and Rod Cooper's store. I swung sharply round into the estuary itself, following it down from the mouth. It was immediately apparent from the crowded water that the finale of the regatta was in full swing. After the serious sailing races and the prize-giving came the novelty races: the swimming, the rowing, the windsurfing, culminating in what was now underway, the fishing-boat race. Crabbers, with throbbing engines, all billowing dark smoke, with whole families aboard, often third and fourth generations of fishing folk, were manoeuvring as close to each other as possible, to lob flour bombs into each other's boats or faces. It was a riotous, hilarious debacle, but as fiercely competitive as the sailing races – in some cases more so.

This last race of the day would be followed by the final toot of the harbour master's horn, and then the huge barbecue on the beach, organized by so many families, and to which everyone, locals and tourists alike, was welcome. The whole community took part, with the Bellingdons taking centre stage. The thought of setting eyes on Hugo and seeing him in a new light was something I very much looked forward to. Despite the colossal problems brewing for him, for an entirely selfish moment I just welcomed seeing him in a way that didn't make my heart race and my tummy turn over. It would be so liberating. This was a different kind of love.

I drove up a car-lined lane and left my car in a little-known spot in the driveway of a deserted house. Local knowledge. Then I walked down to the front. Inevitably, Bellingdons were all I saw, in their green Bellingdon

379

Water aprons, and not the person I was actually looking for, who was not Hugo, but Ted. Lovely though it would be to see Hugo, Ted was the reason I'd hotfooted it down here. I badly needed a word with him. I'd messaged him en route, asking him to meet me quickly, but had got no response. Unsurprising, given there was no reception in this particular neck of the estuary, so I'd seek him out.

I walked along the crowded front, looking in the most likely places. Outside the Mariners I saw Peter, drinking with Adam and a few others. He gave me a wave. Just along from them were Janey, Celia, Edward and Babs, rocking back on their heels and roaring with laughter, everyone well oiled now, before the barbecue. It was cooler since the sun had gone in, and Celia and Edward were in matching blue Sunnyvale Spa sweatshirts, which made me smile. Celia saw me and waved me across urgently.

'Where the hell have you *been*?' she yelled. I cupped my hands around my mouth and yelled back through the crowd: 'Five minutes! I'll be back!'

She nodded and went to help Janey, who'd had an unfortunate stumble, doubled up with mirth as she was at her new English girlfriends' humour, and needing an arm. Lord, they were pissed. I went down the slipway to the beach, looking about. Lots of students had spilled over from the pub, but ... I strained my eyes into the distance – no Ted. Back up the slipway I went. Further along the beach, perhaps, near the dunes, and the cottage, which I'd just driven past. I walked on.

As I rounded the corner, the wide, sandy stretch opened up before me, full of bustling activity. Preparations were in full swing here, awaiting the crowds to wander round, at their leisure, from the Mariners. I saw Belinda and Christina beetling about with bowls of salad; Ibby and Theo were helping, too. I stopped a moment. So strange to see people in a new light. I watched Christina, whipping cling film from a plate of bread rolls on a long trestle table; regarded her with real affection, for the love she'd given Hugo, and for what must have been a confused and anxious time of her own, too. Everyone in their own little worlds. No one sensitive enough to recognize the worlds of others.

Roger was holding court near the shore with his best buddies: a retired general and the lord lieutenant of the county. All three were great golfing and sailing pals and had glasses of something brown and sticky-looking in their hands. They were collectively off their trolleys, brick-red in the face, pickled with alcohol, fun, and the sheer exhilaration of there being every excuse – duty done in the morning and wives too busy to notice now – to stay here and drink until they literally toppled over. I ducked, but he'd seen me.

'*Flora!*' he bellowed.

There was no escape. I pottered across and said hello. I was greeted warmly – a little too warmly, sweaty cheeks and huge stomachs – with kisses from his friends. Roger told them about our little project.

'It's a masterpiece!' he roared. 'Going to submit it to the BP Portrait Awards. The National Gallery will be clamouring for it, eh, Flora? See it up in lights!'

'Oh, heavens, no, I don't think so, Roger, but I'm glad you like it. Um, actually I must get on, I'm looking for—'

'Like it? I love it! Hundred times better than all those

ghastly oils in the hall. All those bogus dismal fools Belinda found in some auction, Pa and Grandpa excluded, of course.' Bogus. I didn't know that. Buy an ancestor, eh? He *was* pissed. 'And what's more,' he went on, his face in mine, prodding his chest, 'it's of *me!*' His eyes popped with pleasure. '*Me!*'

I laughed. 'It certainly is, Roger. Although it's not quite finished yet.'

'Argggh! No more!' He staggered about theatrically, clutching his heart like King Lear on the heath. 'No more sittings!'

'No, we're done with that, actually. I'll just have a few days in the cottage with it, work on the background, that type of thing. I don't need you. Oh! There he is.' I'd spotted Ted in the distance, heading up towards the dunes. Possibly in the direction of the car park.

'Scientist chappie?' Roger followed my eyes. 'Nice man. Got integrity. Spoke to him earlier. Need more like that on the board. Marine biologist, that sort of thing. Frightfully knowledgeable, could talk to him for hours. Hey!' His eyes came back to me and lit up. 'Might be just the ticket for you!'

'Oh, er – I must go, I—'

'Got to find you a man, Flora. Too pretty a filly to be on your own. Hey – wassisname – Ed? Hey, Fleming – oh, look out, she's off anyway! At a trot! Chase him! Run!'

I was legging it, followed by a roar of laughter and a bellow of 'Run! Run – you'll catch him!' from the naughty boys.

Ted turned at their voices, which wasn't ideal – I was bright red with embarrassment – but it did at least stop him. As they continued to dissolve with glee into their drinks, he waited for me, grinning.

'Hi.'

'Ignore them,' I told him, panting. The sand was deep here and hard to run on. 'They're pissed.'

'You don't say.' He grinned. 'By the way, I've just got your text.' He produced his phone. 'Only works when you're off the beach.'

'I know. Ted, I need to ask you something.'

He glanced at his watch. 'Can it wait? Aren't we having supper tonight? I've stayed for longer than I should have done, had no idea it was such a jamboree. I'll shoot back for supper later, though.'

'No, no, it – it can't wait.'

He blinked. Saw the seriousness in my face. 'OK.' He shrugged. 'Fire away.'

I walked on a few steps towards the dunes. Sat down in front of one. He looked surprised then followed suit and sat beside me. I'd thought about this in the car. No recriminations. No *how dare you go behind my back to my friend Shona*. I felt it, but I wouldn't say it. I was growing up, you see. And I wanted something from him. Making him my enemy was not going to help.

I licked my lips. Gave myself a moment. 'Ted, I know everything you know about Bellingdon Water. About the infrastructure. How badly maintained it is.'

He instantly looked defensive. 'Shona.'

'Yes.'

'Who was not supposed to tell you that.'

'But she did.'

'Do you mind?'

'That you spoke to Shona?' *Yes. Bloody hell, yes.* 'No, of course not.'

He relaxed. 'I had to, Flora. It's too big not to. I know I went behind your back but – you know.'

'Sure.' *No. I don't know. I don't behave like that.* 'The thing is, Ted, I know they've got a lot wrong.'

'Oh, you have no idea,' he said bitterly.

'Yes, I have.'

'We're talking a criminal investigation here.'

My heart pounded. 'I know.'

We regarded one another: his strong features were framed by salty greying curls, whipped around in the breeze. His weathered face showed his years of research and academic study, his time by the coast, by the sea. His life.

'Ted, I know you're horrified,' I said quietly. 'And I understand that. It *is* horrific.'

'*Years* of neglect, *years!*' His face tightened with anger. 'And if I'm right – covered up, in a frantic, cowardly fashion. Known about, there's the rub, Flora. *Aware* that pipes were leaking raw sewage, that fish poisoning was endemic, protracted – and *not stopped!* It's one thing to be unaware of corroded pipes under the sea, the ground, but to know and cover it up! To submit fictitious reports, fairy-tale stories about detailed repairs and maintenance that never happened – it grips my shit!'

'I know, I know. And I feel it, too. I lived here, I grew up here. I'm a native, Ted. I love these beaches, these waters.'

I watched him take this on board. He couldn't speak, but he nodded curtly in acknowledgement.

'All I'm asking—' I said as levelly as I possibly could, knowing he was on the brink.

'What are you asking?'

'All I'm asking for is some time. Just, please, give Bellingdon some time.'

'To what?'

'To fess up. To go to the Environment Agency, to let *them* do it. Tell the truth.'

'They won't,' he sneered. 'Or if they do, they'll fudge it. Make excuses, cite environmental problems – the weather, frost – as they did before. No, Flora, I'm blowing the whistle. I want them and I want them badly. I want them all over the front pages of the papers. I want them dead in the water they poison.'

My breathing was very irregular but I kept it together. 'I understand that, Ted. I understand, after all your years of research, clean-up operations, and – and the fact that someone is deliberately doing this, I understand you want your pound of flesh. But I'm asking you to do this for me.'

'While you talk to Hugo.'

'Yes.'

'Who you're still in love with, I know that, Flora.'

'At our age we've had a lot of loves in our lives. Still have some. You know that, too.'

He looked away and narrowed his eyes out to sea. His arms linked around his bare knees in his shorts. The sky was grey and lowering now. After a while he spoke. 'Are you threatening me, Flora? Do this for me or we won't have a relationship? I won't have supper, I won't be your girlfriend – is that it?'

'Of course not.' *Yes. Definitely.* But that particular die

was already cast, in any event. And I also knew what he was going to say. He shook his head.

'I can't do it, Flora. You can tell me you're a Bellingdon, that your son's a Bellingdon, you can plead with me, but I still can't do it. I know too much. And it's too fucking enormous. They're shits. Not the father – it would never have happened in his day, in fact he was one of the first subcontractors to encourage stricter maintenance measures, to sign up to scrutiny, one of the first to recognize the environment. But that disaster of a son of his, the one you love so much . . .' He regarded me with a mixture of dismay and horror.

Still I kept control.

'Hugo was under pressure. So much. You'll never know how much. His mother, the shareholders—'

'His *mother*! Jesus fucking Christ, he's a *man*, for Christ's sake!'

'Ted, sometimes personal issues, problems, can seem bigger than – than—' I grappled for the word, 'than world problems. Don't you know that?'

He stared. 'Of course.'

'And sometimes – sometimes sacrificing personal life for the greater good – is impossible. For some people. Not for you, I get that. The cause was bigger than your marriage, for instance.'

He looked at me sharply.

'That's why she left you, Jilly. Isn't it? Because you loved the environment more than you loved her. She realized that. She couldn't play second fiddle.'

He stared out to sea. 'Is that so wrong?'

'No, plenty of other people, plenty of righteous, famous

people – the Pankhursts – God, I don't know, Martin Luther King, off the top of my head – have done the same. But some people *can't*, Ted. They're not strong enough.'

'Weak. It's what sorts the men from the boys.'

I let that go. 'Everyone's different,' I said evenly. 'You sacrificed your family. Hugo can't do that.'

'You mean his mother,' he said bitterly. 'And, yes, I sacrificed my wife. Having kids. Much bigger.'

'And me. On a smaller scale.'

He nodded. 'And you. If that's how you see it. Or want to see it. And on a . . . different scale. No longevity between us, no past, but lots of feeling. I like you, Flora. Don't know you, haven't known you long enough to say I love you, but I like you a lot. Think we could have had something together. A future, maybe.'

'And I like you. But Ted, I lied when I said earlier I didn't mind you seeing Shona.' I closed my fist and put it on my heart. 'I do. I *am* one of those "personal" people, not a "greater good" person. I mind. About personal relationships, loyalty. It *does* matter that you went behind my back and told tales about my son's family. I'm not like you.'

He was quiet a moment. We both watched the crabbers coming in, laughing and tooting their horns now, whole families on board. The race was over, they were on their way to the shore. Ted's mouth twitched ironically.

'I suppose supper's out of the question, then?'

I smiled down at the sand. I think we both knew the answer to that. Sad, but not devastating. Not by a long chalk. And I'd have walked, eventually, as Jilly had done, I knew that, too. Better now. Ted needed a very particular kind of woman: one burning with the same fire, perhaps.

Or perhaps no woman at all. No kids at all, to get in the way of his real passion. His driving force. The blood in his veins.

He cleared his throat. 'And, incidentally, just as it's a "no" to supper, it's a "no" to what you've just asked me, too. I'm blowing the whistle. Loud and clear. In fact, you might be too late.'

I gazed at him, uncomprehending. 'What d'you mean?'

'No, not too late. I haven't done anything formal yet. But I saw Hugo, earlier. Down here on the beach, cooking sausages. Like he was the nicest man alive. Cooking supper in his pinny for all the poor local kiddies. The ones who swim in his polluted waters. My arse,' he snarled. 'I couldn't resist letting him know I knew.'

'What did you say?' I breathed.

'Oh, not much. Just let him know his dirty little secret wasn't safe with me. That's all I said. "You're not safe, Hugo."'

I stared at Ted. He looked impassively back. Then I looked down the beach, to where the Bellingdon clan were doing their usual annual thing. Running around with plates of food, putting burgers on racks, even Roger, barbecue tongs in hand, a green Bellingdon Water apron on. But I couldn't see Hugo. And then I realized, he was the only one I hadn't seen since I arrived on the beach.

29

I stood up. Scanned the beach. 'He's not there.'

'He is. They're all there. Publicly exhibiting their magnanimous, charitable, philanthropic sides. But it's all show. Unlike the grandfather who donated the beach to the village, sadly all the real compassion has filtered away. Got contaminated. Like the murky water they produce. Goodbye, Flora. I hope we can still be friends. I've offended you, I know, but I can't help myself. And I think we both know about not being able to help ourselves.'

I turned to him, but I wasn't really listening. 'Yes, yes, I do,' I muttered, half realizing he was talking about me not being able to help loving Hugo, and even submitting willingly to the hug he gave me. A fierce one from his vantage point, holding me tight, but my eyes were still roving the beach, over his shoulder. He gave me another squeeze, and, as I broke away his hand went to clasp mine, but I was off.

I ran down the dunes, which is impossible with shoes on, so I paused and whipped them off. Then I raced across to the large gathering on the beach, which had swollen to a couple of hundred people. Luckily the green Bellingdon Water aprons helped. Ted was right; Belinda was very much emphasizing her family's noblesse oblige status today, giving everyone the same broad smile as she served them but never doing more than move her mouth. I saw her bustle across to Roger at the long row of barbecues which every family had brought down, the Bellingdons' obviously the biggest, and I realized I had to keep this casual, offhand, no panic. I therefore avoided them both and Peter, too, with Ibby and Theo as he showed them how to turn sausages over without them sticking to the racks. I headed instead for the salad bar, where Christina and Iris were helping people pile their plates.

'Christina, you haven't seen Hugo, have you?' I asked, as nonchalantly as possible.

'He went up to the house to get more burgers. Why? Problem?'

'No, not at all. I met an old friend who was asking after him, that's all. But I'll tell him he'll be back in a mo.'

'Hope so, we haven't got nearly enough food. Plus I think we need to feed them quickly as I reckon it's going to rain.' She glanced up at the heavy, leaden sky: the air was thickening and contracting as if thunder was imminent. Perhaps signalling the end of the heatwave. She leaned across the table. 'And I wouldn't get involved, if I were you, Flora,' she added in a low voice. 'Belinda is on the warpath and at her very worst today, probably because she's under-catered. Anything you do will be wrong. She's already told me my potato salad is dismal and hasn't got nearly enough seasoning.'

'Thanks, I stand warned.' I smiled and left her to it, but already, I was somewhere else in my head.

I had a vague idea both she and Iris watched me

curiously as I left the beach at speed and fled up the dunes, taking them as if I were out hunting and they were Irish banks, but I was too concerned to care. Not panicked, note, because he'd simply gone back to the house to get burgers, but I badly wanted to find him, set eyes on him and reassure him . . . reassure him of what? That all would be well? It wouldn't. But – yes, with Tommy's help, it would. And I'd help him back with the food, my excuse for going to find him.

Car or walk? I dithered. The lanes were choked with cars, everyone having to pull over and wait in hedgerows while others passed in the opposite direction, so although driving should be quicker, I put my shoes back on and ran instead. Or jogged. I wasn't that fit. I must have cut an unusual figure puffing up the sandy track past our cottage, which was also a public footpath, and I was aware of families with picnic baskets making their way down for the beach supper giving me strange looks as I went against the traffic.

As I soldiered on, I recalled Christina's chumminess over Belinda: I liked it. I'd never heard her criticize her before, but then I'd never talked to Christina much at all. She'd tried but I'd been difficult. Frosty. And to her credit, she'd nonetheless never stopping trying. As I jogged on, feeling the strain in my thighs now, breathless and hot, it occurred to me that our relationship could be very different and my heart soared as I realized how happy Peter would be about that: Hugo, too, as we had lunch, or shopped together. What a difference it would make to everyone. As long as there wasn't a family scandal, of course, with the Bellingdons on the front page of every paper, as Ted had threatened. Headlining the six o'clock news. Feeling slightly sick, I quickened my pace.

Around the next bend the track finally became gravel, the prelude to the Bellingdon estate proper. A cattle grid heralded the entrance, no formal gates. Roger had put his foot down even though Belinda had wanted them. 'A cattle grid was good enough for my father and his father before him, so it's good enough for me!' he'd roared. One of the few battles his wife hadn't won. I hopped over it now and then jogged on up to the gravel sweep, complete with stone fountain in the middle, very definitely a Belinda addition, installed when Roger was in India for a month. With Babs, as it happened. Even Belinda had realized she had to distress it, so pristine and nouveau did the stone appear, so she threw yoghurt and cow dung at it, and perhaps imagined Babs' face, as she did.

Exhausted, I held my sides and staggered on, too tired to run now. No cars in the drive. So either Hugo planned to carry the food back, or take the Land Rover, perhaps? Yes, that's what he'd do. Walk up, and take the Land Rover back. I found second wind to jump up the steps and push the front door, which was on the latch. Truffle padded down from the kitchen, old tail wagging slowly, but, other than that, the house was still and quiet, just the familiar ticking of the long-case clock. I flew down the passage and through the green baize door to the kitchen. Sure enough, signs of fridge and freezer raiding were evident. Large white polystyrene trays from the butchers had been discarded, with torn bits of cellophane, as Hugo no doubt decanted the whole lot into – I crouched to the cupboard below – ah yes. The large Aga pans had gone. OK, so was he still toing and froing, back and forth to a car in the yard? I glanced out of the kitchen window which looked on to the stable yard but couldn't see any sign of him.

On an impulse, I decided to search the rest of the house. I raced around downstairs, throwing one door open after another and spinning about. Empty. Empty empty empty. Finally, the drawing room, whose huge double doors I threw wide. No one there. I fled upstairs. Taking the stairs two at a time, past the – we now know – bogus ancestral portraits, I tried all the rooms off the landing, four or five, and mostly spare. Nothing. Then down the corridor to Hugo and Christina's bedroom, which ratcheted up my anxiety levels, but thankfully, was empty, and very tidy, as was their bathroom. Roger and Belinda's room, right at the end, vast and with windows on three sides, was equally immaculate. Obviously it was Belinda's room really, since Roger slept in his dressing room, and it was a long time since I'd been in here; in her inner sanctum. It gave me a jolt to see all the photos and paintings of Hugo on the walls.

I remembered that first Christmas morning, when we'd been bidden to assemble in here and open our stockings with Roger and Belinda – *in our pyjamas on the bed*. Peter too, of course, a tiny baby. I'd perched on the very end of the bed, where Belinda had indicated. Belinda had sat in regal splendour, propped up on lacy pillows; Roger, in his paisley dressing gown, dapper and groomed, was in a chair; but Hugo *got in beside her*. I'd found it breathtaking. In bed with his mummy. And all those portraits, looking back at him, on the walls. I'd left in a state of shock, and even Mum, who tried to think the best of every Bellingdon foible, and would reassure me they were perfectly normal, had listened with eyes like dinner plates. But hadn't said a word.

I shut the door firmly. Then I raced up to the nursery floor in the attic, the old servants' quarters, but all was quiet and empty up there, too, so I went back downstairs. Feeling mightily relieved and, actually, faintly ridiculous, I went outside. I walked round to the stable yard where the Land Rover was usually parked, at the far end, ready to tow the horse box. Still there. OK, so one of the other cars, then? These would be parked at the back. Belinda's, Hugo's and Roger's were indeed on the hard standing. I shrugged. OK, so he'd walked. Or maybe taken the new quad bike, bought for the grandchildren, that would be sensible.

I went back to the yard and opened the stable door where it was kept: there it was. As I shut the door pensively, two of Iris's beautiful horses, who'd sensibly been keeping away from the flies, came from the back of their stables where it was cool and dark to poke their elegant noses over the doors and prick their ears curiously. I stroked their velvety noses thoughtfully and let them blow into my hand. One old hunter licked the salt. The thing was, if he'd walked, I'd have passed him, surely? I frowned. And all those pans of food. So heavy. Suddenly I had a thought. A rather mad one, because why on earth would anyone of any sense take one of those much flashier forms of transport? Nevertheless, I set off down the back drive to the agricultural barn some few hundred yards away, with its three or four loose boxes beneath the hay loft.

At one time the barn had been Iris's overflow block, but she no longer kept horses there as she'd done when Shona and I were young. They all were stabled at the house, so it was where Roger, and to a lesser extent Hugo, kept their classic cars. I say classic, and in the plural, but in Hugo's case it was actually just one, and a modern one at that. A Ferrari, which, to his credit, he was embarrassed about and rarely used. It had been a present from Belinda on his thirtieth birthday, one which Peter, upon discovering its existence a few years ago, was obviously fascinated by. Hugo had even let him . . . Oh dear God.

I was halfway to the barn when I stopped. Stared. Listened. Then I broke into a run. The open side of the Dutch barn was facing me. Both the floor and the loft were stacked solid with hay bales, ready for the winter, neatly piled and crammed in. But from the other side, where the loose boxes were, came an almighty commotion. A banging and a crashing. I raced along the track. Round the other side of the barn I darted. Tommy, red in the face and wracked with exertion, was wrestling with a lock on a stable, which I knew could be locked from the inside. He stood back and smashed it with what looked like an iron scaffolding bar. The heavy bar broke the wood but not the lock. There was a terrible smell. Noxious. Gas, and it was seeping from inside.

'Nooo!' I shrieked in horror, as I raced towards him.

He turned. 'Get an axe!' he bellowed. 'From the woodshed – quick!'

I froze for a moment. Then tore back down to the stables. I remembered nothing later of the journey to and from the yard, except that I've never run so fast in my life. There were two axes lying on the top of the woodpile. I reached up and grabbed them both. Then, as I turned to go, I remember glimpsing the old Mule bike, which Hugo and I had roared around on as teenagers. It was kept in the corner, and it was covered with sausages and pans. I choked back a sob and fled. Back at the barn, I thrust the larger axe at Tommy, who'd almost broken in but not quite. The huge axe was the thing.

'Hurry, Tommy – hurry!' I pleaded, standing back, tears streaming down my face.

'Stand clear!' he shouted.

He swung the axe back in a great arc behind his head, and then, with tremendous force, brought it crashing down on the lock and the wood around it. It shattered the entire area, so that with one yank, the door was open. Fumes came billowing out and I had to cover my face as nausea and panic overcame me.

'Get back!' Tommy yelled, advancing on the car, his forearm over his mouth. He bent and seized a tube on the exhaust pipe and pulled it off easily. I ignored him and followed, and saw the other end, feeding through a tiny gap in the front window. Hugo was in the driving seat, visible through the fog within, slumped back, acres of neck exposed, eyes shut, his mouth open.

I shrieked again as Tommy wrestled with the car door, then I ran back for the smaller axe. I thrust it at him and he ran round to the other side of the car, to the passenger seat, where there was no risk of hitting Hugo. With a horrible smashing of glass and metal which spattered everywhere, he reached in, but still he couldn't open the door. In desperation he smashed the front windscreen, blow after blow, glass going everywhere, over Hugo too, but it couldn't be helped. Tommy climbed up on the bonnet, and reached in. It took two of us, though, to dig him out from that angle, and I was up on the bonnet, right beside him. It took all our collective strength to haul him clear as somehow, limp, lifeless and heavy, like an enormous rag doll and with shards of glass sticking to him, we dragged him head first down the pristine, shiny red bonnet, and then half carried, half dragged him outside.

'Is he dead? *Is he dead?*' I shrieked hysterically when we finally dropped him.

Tommy didn't answer. He flipped Hugo over so he lay face down, sprawled on the gravel. He held his shoulders, put his knee into the small of his back and pressed hard. Nothing happened. Neither of us spoke. I made myself not scream. He put his knee in again and pressed with more force so Hugo's shoulders came right back. Suddenly, a thin stream of vomit flew out of his mouth. Tommy was pumping Hugo's arms backwards and forwards now.

'He's not dead,' he panted. His voice came in bursts. 'The pipe wasn't fully attached to the car. It had slipped. Half went in the garage. Ring for an ambulance.'

My hands were trembling so violently I could barely press the numbers. I managed it, though, relief flooding my heart. Not dead. Not dead. Message conveyed to the ambulance services, I pocketed my phone and raced to help Tommy, who was moving Hugo off the gravel, and further from the vomit and fumes, on to the grass. The smell of gas and sick was revolting. More shattering, though, was Hugo's face, as Tommy turned him over. Blood was trickling from dozens of cuts on his head where we hadn't been able to shield him from the glass, and he was deathly white. *Was* he breathing?

'See if you can stop the car,' Tommy told me.

I ran and did as I was told, wondering if he didn't want me to see Hugo like this. It was a ridiculously hi-tech vehicle, but there was at least a key and, leaning in from the passenger side, I yanked it out. The ominous, expensive purr of the engine, which had been rumbling quietly away like a horror movie soundtrack, came to a sudden halt, which was a relief. Quiet descended. It was punctuated suddenly by a great rustle of trees, as a high wind whipped around. A flock of crows flew away in a great surge from the top of one of the tall chestnuts in the avenue. Tommy had Hugo propped like a child between his legs now, sitting up, head lolling forward, and making no sound. No heavy breathing, no vomit.

I seized his wrist. Couldn't feel a pulse. I looked at Tommy in horror.

'It's there,' he assured me, his eyes on mine, steady and unwavering. 'It's just faint. Look at his chest.'

I put both hands on his chest and did feel some slight movement.

'Oh, please God, be quick,' I breathed to the paramedics men of Truro. 'Please God, hurry.' As I said it, Tommy and I looked knowingly at each other, realizing it couldn't be so. The hospital was miles away and the lanes were choked today.

'Should we take him?' I urged. 'Shall I get a car?'

'No, we'll never get through without a siren, and he'll need the oxygen in the ambulance. We'll wait.' He was wiping vomit from Hugo's face and neck with his sleeve. 'Trust me, Flora, he's alive, he's breathing, we just need him checked.'

He was very limp, though, very full of poison. Suddenly I had a thought. 'There'll be one on the beach,' I said, as it struck me. 'For the regatta. D'you think they'll even know they've got one close by? Should I ring and say?'

Even as I said it, the wail of a siren could be heard in the background. We looked at each other with relief. Blood trickled freely from cuts on Tommy's hands and face and I wanted to wipe them. Closer and closer it wailed, the siren, and up above, a noisy rumble, too, in the low, threatening, thickening clouds which had been a feature of the afternoon, but which now let fall huge plops of rain. They were intermittent to begin with, one landing on Hugo's forehead, then on me, then Tommy. Then, with a sudden vengeful hiss, down it came. It poured on to the parched clay ground, the dry yellow grass, bouncing off the gravel, and before long was running in rivulets and paths. Another tremendous rattle of thunder erupted above as rain steamed down on our heads. If nothing else, it covered the nauseous smell of fumes and sick and I was glad of it.

The sound of the ambulance got louder and came into view from the lane, having gone to the back drive. It came careering down through the avenue, yellow and green with flashing lights, towards us. I stood up, soaked, and went to the middle of the path to wave my arms above my head. In no time at all it had stopped. A man and a woman leaped out.

'Gas,' Tommy told them.

They nodded, mutely, then ran to open the back door and pulled out the stretcher. They lifted Hugo on to it, then, crouching low, fixed him up to some oxygen. They were just manoeuvring him into the van when the girl turned and looked at us enquiringly.

'Anyone?'

'You go,' said Tommy quickly. He knew I couldn't have done otherwise. 'Someone has to tell the others.'

I looked at him gratefully, knowing he'd got the worse option.

'Keep in touch, Flora. Let me know,' he said quietly.

'Of course.' I realized then that he was more worried than he was letting on, but didn't want to alarm me.

I clambered in behind the stretcher. As I sat down, I turned. Before the doors closed, Tommy and I looked at one another: a long, searching look. His blue eyes were very bright, very steady. Nothing was said, but it was a look that reached back across the years, across the oceans between continents, across generations even. It was full of pain for a friend, but also, something I'd never seen before, and couldn't quite place. It rocked me. Tenderness. That was it. Then the driver came around to slam the door, and in moments, we were away.

Later, as I sat in a corridor outside a room in A&E, my head resting back on the wall, a polystyrene cup of coffee cooling in my hand, having watched a team of nurses race Hugo in on a trolley, a mask to his face, then more doors close, I thought about that look. It was a look I liked to think I'd seen on my husband's face, years ago, when we first were married. Engaged, perhaps. But I knew in my heart it was different. Hugo's face, when he looked at me with tenderness, which he did, was always tinged with remorse. With guilt, I suppose. I hadn't recognized it for what it was back then, principally because I hadn't known any other regard, from any other man. But I now under-stood how stark the difference had been. Hugo loved me, but he loved me not. Could not. In Tommy's eyes there'd been a fire, a passion, that I realized I'd never seen before. I'd got to this great age, and never seen it before in my life.

30

An hour or so later, when Christina came flying down
the corridor in her trainers, I got to my feet. She fell into
my arms.

'Oh God oh God oh God—' she sobbed into my shoulder. I held her tight. She was trembling and she could
barely speak.

'He's fine,' I told her quickly. 'He's going to be absolutely
fine, is *already* fine,' I assured her. I took her shoulders and
made her look at me: forced her white, pain-wracked face
to believe me. 'I swear to God, Christina, they came and
told me ten minutes ago. Tommy got there just in time,
there'll be no long-term effects. Plus, Hugo bogged it to
a certain extent. A lot of the fumes went in the garage.'

'Oh, thank God,' she whispered, clutching her mouth
with both hands. 'But why!' she wailed suddenly, sinking
down abruptly in a chair. She raked a hand through her hair
in despair. 'I mean – I *know* why, the business obviously,
such a worry. Such a mess – he was so concerned, and Tommy's just told me it's got much worse. But why do *that*, out
of the blue?' She turned her incredulous face up to mine,
full of horror at the magnitude of the act, the ramifications
for her and her children. 'Why?' she repeated imploringly.

I did know the answer. But equally, I didn't think it was Ted's fault. He wasn't to know the entire scenario. Wasn't to know the pressure on Hugo, from all quarters; that he might just have delivered the final blow. Luckily Christina meant it more rhetorically and her mind was already racing ahead.

'Have you seen him?' she pleaded. I wanted her to have been the first to see him, but I couldn't lie about this.

'Yes. I have. Briefly. But he's asleep now.'

'Oh, thank God. I mean – that he saw someone he loved first, and who loved him.'

My eyes filled with tears at her generosity. But it occurred to me that Christina's love for Hugo was like mine. Whole-hearted, but different to physical, jealous, sexual love. What we shared was the love of two sisters for a most beloved brother.

'Did he speak?'

I sat down beside her and told her about how he'd kept saying sorry. *Sorry-sorry-sorry*. And how tears had poured down his cheeks. They'd poured down mine, too, and Christina's now, as I told her. I told her how he'd said he was so ashamed, but how – in that split second, as he'd opened the door to the woodshed, about to get the Mule bike, trays of meat in his hands – suddenly he couldn't see any other way. He'd been overwhelmed by panic. How he'd thrown the pans in the air in despair and raced up to the top barn, far away, where no one went, although, as Hugo had said as I sat there, holding his hand, look-ing at his yellow, almost jaundiced face, he hadn't at that moment honestly been thinking of anyone else. Not Peter, not Christina, not Ibby and Theo. Just himself.

'Not even your mother?' I was running on pain and adrenalin, which is my only excuse, but the moment it left my mouth, I wished I hadn't said it. More tears streamed down his face, so that I was really sorry. I stuttered to tell him so, to take it back, but he suddenly controlled himself and motioned for me to stop apologizing.

'No. No, you're right. And it had to be said. I need to face it. Face how much influence she's had on my life, but mustn't any more.'

I paused and let him gather himself. Let him breathe. 'But why, Hugo?' I said gently, at length. 'What sort of a hold did she have on you?'

Although I knew this might not be the moment, even more compelling was the realization that it might be the *only* moment. I had a strange feeling this was the time to ask. He turned his face away to the wall. Became silent for a long while. It was at that point, as I told Christina in the corridor, as I'd sat with Hugo by his bed, that I told him I knew he was gay. I told him the truth, but I varnished it slightly. About Tommy suspecting since university days. It was up to Tommy, I thought, if one day he told him he'd walked in on him: somehow I didn't think he would. I told him I knew he could never have loved me properly and had done his very best, and I told him I knew about him and Christina. About what they'd no doubt recognized in each other all those years ago, and why they'd married. Why he'd left me. So that he didn't have to feel guilt and remorse any more, could be himself. As she could be herself. I saw Christina visibly relax as I did.

'I always said you should know. You and Peter. My parents and my sisters know about me, have done for some time, about my happy but unusual marriage, and they're pleased for me. Why not Hugo's family?'

I told Christina that Hugo had relaxed, too. That his face had come back from the wall, from the past, initially full of sorrow and shame, but how I'd silenced it in one look. In one squeeze of the hand. Hadn't said, '*I wish you'd told me.*' Hadn't added to his pain, but had just asked him why he hadn't ever been more open about it.

'I was.' He looked at me squarely. 'Once. When I was young. About fourteen. I was at boarding school and I was very confused. All my friends were talking about girls but I didn't feel it. I tried to kid myself I was a late developer, but I knew I was different. At home that summer, in the holidays, I was half-heartedly Blu-Tacking posters of models, the Spice Girls, like my friends had, to the wall by my bed, when I suddenly just broke down and sobbed. Mum came in. She'd been tidying the airing cupboard down the corridor and she heard. She was so sweet. She sat on the bed and hugged me and persuaded me to tell her what was wrong. She listened. When I'd finished, she sat back and, when I looked up, I saw her face was horrified. But she gathered herself. She said, very calmly, that it was natural for adolescent boys to be confused about their sexuality. But that was all it was. An adolescent phase. She said it was entirely possible to choose, to make a decision, one way or the other. And she knew that I knew where my duty lay, to choose the right way. Because if I was to choose the wrong way, that was just a weakness. A giving in, and the only way I'd be truly happy was to avoid that at all costs. She said that if I went the wrong way, if I was to be a homosexual, it would break her heart. She said it would break my father's heart and it would break my grandparents' hearts. The only boy in the family. And it would destroy the family. Not only that, but its reputation. She was very calm, very measured. And then she got up off the bed and left the room. She didn't hug me, or take my hand, or anything. Twenty minutes later, I was downstairs having tea with my parents and Etta on the terrace, and that was it.'

Christina's hand went to her mouth in shock as mine had done when Hugo told me.

'So cruel,' she whispered.

'*So* cruel.'

'And Hugo was such an obedient boy.'

'Exactly. So biddable. And he told me that from that moment on she maintained that distance, withdrew all maternal love. She was cool towards him. Until he went out on dates, with girls. Then she was warm to him again.' I remembered Hugo's cracked voice:

'And I missed that, Flora. Sounds wet, I know. But I loved her so much. I was young. She was my mum.'

As I repeated this to Christina, she had to breathe to steady her anger, her emotion. Tears choked her throat. 'He would have done anything to get her love and approval back, Flora.'

'Quite. Not like Etta.'

'I've only met Etta once, at our wedding.'

'She's more forthright. Bolshie. Hugo never said, he was too loyal to Belinda, but I suspect she wouldn't play her mother's game. Wouldn't be controlled. She always wanted to get away, far away. I mentioned her just now, in there, asked him if Etta knew. He said he didn't know, but that before she went to Australia, they'd had lunch together. When she left the restaurant she looked at him very hard and told him to be true to himself. Always. At whatever cost.'

Christina nodded. 'Hugo wants to visit her in Sydney. Soon. After all this time. But . . . why didn't he tell *me*? About Belinda. I mean – I knew all about him being gay from a young age, we'd both talked about that, obviously, about realizing at school, the trauma that came with it – but why didn't he tell me about his mother? That conversation?'

'I don't know. Perhaps he was ashamed of what he didn't do. Didn't defy her. Didn't man up. But I think it's more complicated than that. I think he didn't want to cast her in a terrible light. To anyone. Didn't want us thinking badly of her. It's about that loyalty he has to her and that hold she has over him. That love that she offers . . . then withdraws. To the extent that his whole life has to be a lie – at least, when he's with the Bellingdons.'

'Yes. Not in London. I mean – we're not blatant, we're so discreet, we have children. It's not an open secret, for their sake. Although it might be one day.'

I was quiet. I had nothing to say on this subject. Because I couldn't imagine it. Couldn't imagine the confusion. Was glad the muddle wasn't mine. I sat up a bit. A regrouping gesture.

'Peter knows what's happened,' I told her. 'I texted Tommy when I knew Hugo was going to be OK, and he said he'd go and find him on the beach and tell him. I worried that it should be me, but Tommy said he wanted to be sure he didn't hear through gossip.'

'He's right.'

'I know.'

'How did he take it?'

'Shocked, obviously. And rang me immediately, but Tommy had done a good job. Had persuaded him Hugo would hate Peter to see him like this, and not to come here.'

'Yes, Hugo would hate that.'

'Exactly. Does Belinda know?' I asked.

'Yes, and Roger. Tommy scooped us all up off the beach in his car and took us back to the house. He told me first, upstairs in the bedroom. Said it was to do with the business. And a possible scandal. He'd let Hugo tell me. Then he told the parents in the drawing room, so I wasn't there to witness it. But I saw Roger afterwards, as I was leaving to come here, in the kitchen. He looked grey and old and shattered. He was sitting limply at the table, staring into space. Belinda was in her room. I didn't pause to ask Tommy how she'd taken it, I don't care, frankly. She's always been foul to me. Oh, sweet as pie on the outside but wears you down eventually with her sly, horrid remarks. Well, I don't have to tell you. I never want to set foot in that house again,' she said vehemently. She glanced down at her hands. Blinked miserably. 'Of course, I will. For Roger. For the children. You do, don't you?' She looked at me beseechingly.

'Yes,' I agreed. 'You do all sorts of things for love. You have to.' I swallowed. 'Have you told the children?'

'No. And I may not. Probably won't. Iris has taken them to put the horses back in the fields, then they'll be shattered and go straight to bed. Iris . . .'

'What?'

'She looked so strange. Like she knew more. I've always wondered if Iris knew about me and Hugo.'

I nodded. 'Although . . . this – what Hugo's done – has nothing to do with that. This is about the company, the water.'

'Yes, but it's all connected, don't you think?' She shifted round in her seat to look at me properly. 'It's about Belinda's influence on him. She's constantly on the phone to him, in London. I hear him talking to her in the study, he always takes the call in another room, always. And she came up to see him recently, at the house, and I listened.' She glanced fearfully at me. 'At the door.'

'Good for you,' I encouraged her. 'And?'

'It didn't make sense to me. But she kept saying it was all above board, and that she'd had something checked by a lawyer, and by an independent team of accountants. That it was all fine. That all Hugo had to do was write some reports to fill in the gaps. I have no idea what she meant.'

I nodded, my eyes widening in horror at the scale of her involvement: at the magnitude of her influence and the overplaying of her hand. I didn't want to heap any more grief on Christina right now, didn't want to tell her what Tommy and I knew. Hugo would tell her, of that I was sure; Tommy had laid the groundwork. It felt disloyal to tell tales. Clearly Tommy had felt the same. Fortuitously, at that moment, a nurse popped her head out of Hugo's room.

'Mrs Bellingdon?'

Christina stood up smartly. 'Yes?'

'You can come in now. He's awake, and he's feeling a bit better.'

Christina's face cleared as if the sun had come out. She disappeared inside.

Later, when I got back, having left Christina with Hugo and got a taxi, I texted Peter.

> I'm back. Just me down at the cottage. Celia's out. Meet me here?

He was down in minutes, roaring into the garden on the quad bike. He looked pale and worried as he leaped off. I went out to greet him.

'How is he?'

'He's fine.'

We hugged hard. And then I'm ashamed to say I lied a bit.

'Totally recovered and obviously can't imagine why he did it, but—'

'Mum, Tommy told me everything,' he interrupted, standing back. He looked so grown up suddenly. 'Literally everything. About the company, about what Dad did, or maybe didn't do. He didn't want me to hear on the grapevine. I know Ted was on to him.'

'Right. Yes.'

'He said he was going to let Dad tell Christina.'

I nodded. 'It's happening now.'

We went inside. We perched side by side on the sofa together, neither wanting to be even remotely disloyal to his father. Not at this moment. Not when he was lying ill, in a hospital bed. Fessing up to his wife. We stared at the slate floor.

'He got in a muddle,' I said carefully.

Peter was no fool. 'I think it's more like, once he'd set a tiny stone in motion, a tiny, negligent stone, it was really hard to pick it up and stop it getting faster. To stop it rolling on and getting huge and horrific and just too bloody impossible to stop.'

I nodded. Imagining Hugo's fear; his panic. 'Yes, that's more like it. Not a muddle. More of a runaway train.'

'That he was responsible for,' he said quietly.

'Yes,' I concurred, after only a moment's hesitation, knowing only the truth would do. 'But one that Granny,' I turned to look at him, 'knew about. Possibly persuaded him into. To destroy records, massage figures . . .' I looked at him to see how he'd take this.

Peter returned my gaze. He didn't say, 'Granny? What would she know?' As if she was some sweet, snowy-haired old lady. He knew. And if we were going for veracity, as quite rightly Tommy was, for full disclosure, then for heaven's sake, Peter *should* know this.

'It doesn't excuse Dad,' I said firmly. 'But if you're going to know everything – I want you to know this, too. Have all the facts.'

'Mum,' he said wearily, 'she's my grandmother. I know her. Of course I know her. I've spent weeks down here, every summer. Seen her with Dad. The fact that she's a scheming, manipulative old cow who tells him what to do is not breaking news. She's a bitch.'

'Right.' I was rather shocked. It had taken me years to finally get my head round that. Christina, too. 'Right.

Good. Well, good for you. As long as you know. As long as you're – you know – informed.' I got up and made us both a very large gin.

Later that night, in bed, I lay there thinking about Belinda. About her colossal confidence, her chutzpah. She'd been ghastly to me, just as she was foul to Christina, and *I'd been a girl*. Christina was a girl. Belinda hadn't even come to my wedding. Surely she should have been delighted? Welcomed me, particularly at that age and stage of Hugo's life, with open arms? But I knew about Belinda: knew about her hubris, about her ambition. I knew that she felt she'd comprehensively cracked that nut; that fourteen-year-old one, in the bedroom, with her bare hands. She'd moved on. I believe she honestly thought that particular crisis was over. That's what I mean by hubris. And that now she'd straightened her son out, whilst I might be fine for an initial bunk-up in the hay barn – she might even encourage it to get all that nonsense out of his head – as a wife for her son, I didn't match up. Christina, I knew, she was happier about because Christina's father was a surgeon and the family lived in Holland Park. But she wasn't glamorous enough for Belinda. Didn't dress up. Did too much sport. Had taken up rowing. Spent a lot of time in a three-woman scull down on the river, in Putney. Belinda didn't like that. She wanted her daughter-in-law on the committee of Save the Children, floral and fragrant. Dressed up to the nines at the Chelsea Flower Show, having ladies' lunches. Christina had ladies' lunches. Dinners, too. I turned over and shut my eyes. Just not the sort Belinda had in mind.

31

The following morning, when I woke, I instinctively reached for my phone on the bedside table. There were three messages from Ted.

> I am so sorry. Obviously feel dreadful and will of course put on hold my plans for exposure. I had no idea he'd do a thing like that.

I sat up. My thumbs tapped back:

> It's a long and complicated story, Ted. And not entirely your fault, you were just the catalyst. But thank you for holding off. I have an idea you won't need to expose. Have a feeling he'll do it himself.

He came straight back. 'OK. I haven't spoken to Shona.'

I frowned down at my screen. This was open to misinterpretation. I rang him. He answered immediately.

'You mean, you haven't told Shona in case she publishes it? I don't think she will.'

'I don't think she will either, but there's kind of a professional integrity, Flora. If she knows stuff, she's duty bound to report. Otherwise her boss will say, "What, a local bigwig attempts suicide because his cover-up of his corrupt water business goes tits up? And he's still leaking sewage and pollution over the Cornish coast? Why the fuck didn't you report?"'

'I need to speak to her. Because suppose she hears through someone else?'

'Well, quite. The Bellingdons' cleaner was on the scene soon after apparently, following a trail of sausages. The news leaked out on to the beach last night.'

'Shit. I'll ring her.'

I did. Shona listened. She was quiet for a long moment. 'No, I didn't know. God, poor Hugo. He must have been desperate. And yes, Ted's right, I should do a story, but I can sit on it for a bit. Pretend I don't know. But Flora, it's only a matter of time before someone on my team does know, and they won't have the same qualms. It won't be their godson's father. There's nothing I can do about that.'

'No.'

'But don't worry, we're not complete sharks. Suicide attempts are not generally reported. A previous prime minister's daughter had a go and, believe it or not, even the London mob left them in peace. The water's a different matter, though. That's in the public interest.'

'I know.'

'But I promise I won't let anything go on air without letting you know, how's that?'

'Thank you, Shona.'

'And you look after yourself, my love. This is his tragedy, not yours. Thank God.'

We said goodbye. I sank back on my pillows. Through my open window I could hear Celia and Edward having breakfast in the garden below. The air had cooled slightly after the storm, but it was still warm and soft, the sky blue, the earth steamy after rain. In the distance I could see the arching spires of the orange *crocosmia* by the back gate, flattened by the rain, but already perking up and staging a comeback. The voices below were ostentatiously hushed as if aware of my open window, keen not to be heard. I strained my ears for a bit but eventually decided I could lurk up here no longer. Throwing on some clothes I went downstairs. They stopped talking immediately when they saw me and adopted bright smiles. Then Edward diplomatically withdrew, saying he'd make some fresh coffee. I thanked him and sat down opposite Celia.

She squeezed my hand across the table. 'Poor Hugo.'

'I know.'

'But Flora, it's not your—'

'Tragedy. No, I know.'

She nodded, surprised at my sensible tone. No sobbing, no hysterics. I'd tell her the reason for that later, I determined. In London, in our studio, not here.

'How's Peter?'

'He's OK. More than OK, actually. Remarkably calm and phlegmatic.'

'Good.'

'Celia, I thought I might go back home today. I don't

need Roger any more for the portrait, so I can take it back to London. Work on it there with my photos.'

She looked at me carefully. 'Yes, OK. I get that. Leave the Bellingdon clan to it. And Peter will probably follow suit.'

'Exactly.'

'But . . . Ted? I thought . . .'

'Ah. No.' I gave a wan smile. 'Not to be. Too principled for me, I'm afraid. Not frayed enough at the edges.'

She nodded thoughtfully. Sipped her coffee. 'Well, you are quite tatty.'

'Aren't I just.'

She put her cup down carefully. Gazed into it. 'Well, we might stay on. Ed and I. I know this probably isn't the moment to say it, but this is the best my life has ever been.'

She was trying hard not to show her shiny eyes above her coffee cup: to reveal that not only was her painting going well but that her love affair with Edward had rekindled beyond belief under the Cornish sun and in this coastal cottage.

I smiled. 'I'm glad.'

'In fact, Ed and I,' she went on, emboldened now, and I knew she was unable to stop herself, sort of bursting, 'are thinking of maybe relocating down here. You know, for good. We love it so much.'

'Oh, *Cele*.' My turn to reach out and squeeze her hand.

'Would you be jealous?' She looked anxious; stricken, even.

'Why?' I said in surprise.

'Well, it's your home. Where you were brought up and I've found lasting happiness here, love, too and – oh. No.'

418

She stopped suddenly. Saw my astonished face. 'I forgot. You're not like me.'

I smiled. Reached for her coffee cup and took a sip while Edward brewed me some more. 'No. Not like you. I wouldn't be jealous. I'd come and stay with you, lots, that would be fun. I'll miss you in London, though.' I looked wistfully over her shoulder.

'I was thinking Mimi Hargreaves, or Jack Bolton,' she said quickly, clearly having given it some thought. 'They're both desperate for studio space.'

I smiled and nodded, trying not to show that actually, she would be a huge loss. Celia was beside me all day. She was sort of part of me. Half of me, even. At least, the working me. We were a double act, in a strange way. Morecambe and Wise, Tess and Claudia, Celia and Flora. I narrowed my eyes quizzically as if genuinely giving it some thought, not wanting to upset her.

'Mimi, I think, don't you? Last time I saw Jack he was suffering from the most spectacular narcissism. No less than twenty-two self-portraits.'

'And he smashes his canvases if they upset him.'

'Puts his head through them, so I've heard.'

'Could get annoying?'

'Mimi it is.'

After breakfast, I drove up to Trewarren. I was quaking slightly at what I might find, my espadrilles unsteady on the pedals. It was already late morning because Celia had chatted on, with Edward, about their plans. Edward told me that since he worked from home anyway, freelance copywriting being his bread and butter, he could work anywhere, but he felt his playwriting would flourish down here, without the competitive stress of London. And of course there was the Minack Theatre, he'd love to get involved in that. He said they rather fancied Kynance Cove, or the hills beyond, and did I know the villages around there? I did. Maps were instantly produced; pored over. Then, just as I was leaving, Peter came by. He leaped out of a car as I went down the front path and said he was going sailing with friends for a few days, staying at their house along the coast, which I thought was a good idea: getting away.

'Really? I mean, Dad . . .'

'Will be fine, as you know. Now go.'

It occurred to me now as I drove up to the house that I'd forgotten to ask exactly where he was going, and with whom, which was most unlike me. But I could text him later. He'd disappeared looking pleased and relieved: hopped back into a crowded car with music blaring. Away they'd sped.

Now, as I walked up to the front door, coming round from the stable yard where I'd parked the car, leaving the boot open to accommodate the portrait, and avoiding the back in case I ran into Belinda in the kitchen, I thought how changed and different everything was. Already, it seemed to me, the house seemed to exude sadness. Mourning, even. Perhaps it was the silence. No Truffle, opening the front door with her nose and wagging down the front steps. No Ibby and Theo playing Snap on those steps, Truffle scattering their cards as they yelped at her. No Belinda, bustling in from flower arranging at the church and letting everyone know how busy she was. No Tommy and Janey, playing backgammon on the terrace, heads bent competitively, teasing each other, Janey accusing Tommy of cheating because he won so often. And no Roger, bearing down on them, rubbing his hands as he offered them a sharpener, and what did they mean eleven-thirty was a bit early even for them: and then, as they relented, Janey and Roger knocking it back with gusto, Tommy, I knew, sipping it.

Tommy. I didn't want to think about him. I was glad he wasn't on the terrace reading. He'd been so tremendously kind, so brave. He'd shown such strength of character yesterday, always taking the difficult option; it was dizzying to contemplate what I owed him. And then there'd been that extraordinary declaration on the jetty at Newlyn which I was sure he'd rather forget and which hadn't been mentioned since, but then when, exactly, would have been the moment for that to have resurfaced? When he was axing in the lock on a fume-filled stable door? When he was breaking the sad news to your son that his father had decided he had nothing worth living for, including him? A little loving text to yours truly, perhaps? Or maybe, maybe – I stopped suddenly in my tracks, mid-thought, realizing he was right in front of me.

He was sitting on the ancient swing rocker in the garden with Roger. The backs of both heads were visible over the swing seat, one russet, one white. Tommy was no doubt gently bolstering Roger; reassuring him that he would do everything in his power to limit the damage. Look after Hugo. I stayed still a moment. How strange. I could only see the back of Tommy's head, and yet it rocked me. Moved me. I had to take a breath to steady myself, but then I'm like that. Easily knocked. Or was that insincere, too? An excuse? Was the truth, actually, that I hadn't been brave enough to address my own feelings, protected myself, in case of being hurt, because he was, after all, Tommy Rochester? Just shoved it to the back of my mind? I crept into the house, ashamed.

The front hall was empty and, beyond the green baize door, the kitchen seemed quiet, too, but I already knew Hugo was back. I'd met Iris in the stable yard when I parked my car. She'd been mucking out one of the loose boxes. She pretended she hadn't seen or heard me, but I walked across and put my head over the stable door.

'How is he? Do you know? Hugo?'

She turned. Rested on her pitchfork. 'He's back,' she told me, nodding up to his window which was above the back door. 'Belinda went to fetch him at six o'clock this morning.'

'*Belinda* did?'

'Beat Christina to it. And she knew they'd release him early, they always like the empty bed.'

'Typical.' I seethed.

'But Christina's made of sterner stuff.' Iris lowered her voice and came to the door. 'Once Hugo was upstairs in bed, she came down and asked if I'd take the children riding. I got one of my girls to do it. When they'd gone, Christina tracked Belinda down in her sitting room, where she pretends to sew, entry to mere mortals forbidden, and had a stand-up-knock-down with her. It all came out. For the whole house to hear.' She eyed me carefully. 'And I mean, everything. Including his sexuality. I wouldn't mind betting it had been sanctioned by Hugo.'

'Good for her.'

'They're going back to London. She's packing now.'

I nodded. 'Was Roger devastated?' I asked softly. 'When he heard about the business?'

'I don't know. Tommy's gone to find him, I think, to have a chat. But Christina was crystal clear on the water front. She said that yes, he was a grown man, and yes, he should be responsible for any bad decisions, but Belinda's influence had been insidious and devastating. Roger would have heard that.'

I nodded. 'Good. Do you think he knew all along about Hugo being gay?'

'No. Not that he'd have minded. I mean, eventually.'

'Did you know?'

'Of course,' she said in her sphinx-like tones.

Of course. And for the first time, I thought there was something wrong about Christina, Iris, and Etta's loyalty to Hugo: their conspiracy of silence. When, after all, has being an ostrich ever been much of a success? Yes, it was Hugo's secret, but look how much damage keeping it quiet had done. I was pretty sure if I'd known, or Roger, it would have come out. At least, we'd have persuaded Hugo to *let* it come out. Roger wouldn't have even have bothered to do that, he'd have just foghorned out the news over lunch onc day.

'So you're gay, boy. Well, fine, each to his own. But for God's sake own it. Be yourself!'

It would be a bit crass, a bit awkward, as Peter would say, sure. But as I often pointed out to my son, there were worse things in life than *awkward*. And it would have put out Belinda's nasty little fire in one great sloshing bucket. Broken her horrid little threatening, tugging, umbilical cord, alternately cloying, then withdrawing. Yes, there was a lot to be said for Roger's approach to life. And there was surely a lot of danger in well-meaning, non-confrontational silence. Iris would no more have shared that news than reveal her own true self, which only meant a life less lived, as far as I was concerned. I loved Iris: at many times had wished I was more like her, but the fact remained I was firmly in Roger's camp.

I went down the hall away from the kitchen and into the empty gunroom. Turning the easel around, I unclipped the portrait. I paused, regarding it in my hands: smiled fondly at my ex-father-in-law. Then I went back down the corridor and took it out to the car, stashing it carefully. Next I went back for the easel, and finally my paints. I hesitated as I closed the boot on it all. Really? Just sneak away? Not tell anyone you're leaving, not say goodbye, just leave without a word? Of course I couldn't. But I quaked at the thought of Belinda. And Roger was out of the question right now, so shattered, so sad – probably crying, which he did a lot. I remember witnessing it, years ago, when we'd watched a documentary about the Somme. Roger was a very emotional man. I decided to go upstairs and track down Christina, packing. Knock on her bedroom door.

I went back in, but bypassed the main staircase. Instead I crept softly to the far end of the house where the back stairs were. Unobserved, I nipped up the narrow flight, but unfortunately, someone else was nipping down. Tommy. He and I came face to face, and since he was descending at speed, we very nearly cannoned into each other. The stairs gave him more than his usual height over me, and when we'd both recovered from our surprise, he looked down at me. His face was suddenly impenetrable, his blue eyes unusually guarded. He glanced at the car keys in my hand.

'Off somewhere?'

'Oh, yes. I – I just came to say goodbye.'

'To who?'

'To – well, to everyone, really.' I floundered. 'Well, no, Christina, I thought.'

His eyes widened in mock surprise. 'Did you? Is that what you thought? Just Christina. Ask her to pass it on. And then – what, disappear? Just like that?'

'Well, no, not *just* like that.' I could feel myself reddening.

'It's a good moment to run, I'll give you that. A good day to get away. No one will notice.'

'I wasn't running, Tommy. I just feel . . . I don't know. Maybe I'm in the way.'

'How very English.'

'After all, I'm not really family.'

'Lord, no. Not involved at all.'

I didn't like his tone, but at that moment we heard Belinda clear her throat from below, and then her quick footsteps down the hall towards us. I froze. He jerked his head. Fear kicking in, I instinctively nipped upstairs after him, then down the passage and into one of the spare rooms off the landing, clearly his.

We listened from behind the closed door. There was no sound of Belinda following and he motioned for me to sit beside him on the end of the bed. I felt rather ashamed suddenly, rather foolish, and decided to speak first.

'You're right,' I agreed. 'It was shabby of me not to come and find you. But firstly you were with Roger, and secondly . . .'

'Secondly?'

'I . . . I thought you might be embarrassed.'

He blinked. 'Me? Really?'

'Yes. You know – by your, sort of – you know. Declaration.' I could feel my face burning up.

'Declaration?'

'You know.' He wasn't going to help me out at all. 'In Newlyn.'

His eyes widened in pseudo astonishment. 'Oh, *that* declaration. That little outburst of frivolity and nonsense. Lord, no, I stand by every word of that.'

I stared at him in surprise. His smile was ironic, though.

'You do?' I said uncertainly, knowing at any moment he could wrong-foot me.

'Jeepers, yes. You make a declaration, by God you stand by it. Where would America be if Jefferson hadn't stood by his?'

'Well . . .'

'Or your own excellent little island, even. If William the Conqueror hadn't nailed his colours to the mast, then stuck to them?'

I narrowed my eyes suspiciously. 'Are you laughing at me?'

'God, yes. Absolutely yes. You see, the thing is, Flora, I think you're the one who's embarrassed. I think you're the one who hasn't allowed herself to think through what I've said, and work out what your feelings are. So you decided you'd just grab your portrait and scuttle off home. Dodge the whole issue. Hide away in your garret. But I've caught you, so you kind of *have* to give it some thought, otherwise – jeez, where does that leave me? Squashed? Rejected? Spurned?'

'You've never been any of those things, Tommy Rochester.'

His mocking eyes changed abruptly. For the first time ever, I saw real hurt there. His chin went up. 'Don't make me do it again. That would be harsh.'

He did mean it. And he'd meant it at the time in Newlyn. I'd known that, too, and he was right, I'd shielded myself. It hadn't been hard, a great deal had happened since then, but now I allowed myself to believe it. To believe that this funny, handsome, confident, clever, wise-cracking, kind – incredibly kind – man, who could surely have any woman he wanted, could actually be in love with me. *Had* been in love with me, for a long time.

As I finally allowed myself to absorb the truth, it was as if a sluice gate burst within me. A torrent of emotion poured through. All the pent-up feelings of so many years released, because the thing was, I'd known this man for a long time, but vicariously, through other people. I'd never allowed myself to know him personally. I'd kept him at a distance. And perhaps deliberately misinterpreted him. Yet why would Hugo, the sweetest of men, not have a best friend who was thoroughly decent? Why would Peter turn to his adored godfather for advice over the years as I knew he did, rather than his own father? Yet whenever he was mentioned, I'd make a joke. 'Oh Tommy,' I'd say. 'That old roué. What would he know?' I'd spin him into someone different. Why? A defence mechanism? Mirroring Tommy's self-confessed defence strategy, his snide mocking of me? Perhaps. Maybe we were both at it. When Shona had recently revealed a friendship, I'd questioned it immediately, had never allowed myself to know the real man, the one they all saw. And allowed was the right word. In case that way madness lay. More grief. More pain. Because recently,

I'd learned how dangerous Tommy Rochester really was. He made me feel safe.

He must have seen some sort of awakening in my eyes, some sort of realization. A yielding and an acceptance. I didn't know – couldn't know – if I loved him yet, but that light was enough for Tommy. I'm sure he'd seen it a lot over the years, and it had surely never taken so long, but recognize it he did and Tommy wasn't slow. He took me in his arms and kissed me and I didn't resist. Not for one moment. In fact it was lovely. I had been kissed, quite recently, by Ted, but not like this. And never like this by Hugo, Tim, or Rupert – this was in a different league. I felt myself joining in with such enthusiasm that when Janey opened the door, we were both oblivious. Obviously we sprang apart a moment later – or, rather, I sprang away from Tommy.

Janey stared in surprise. Then a slow smile spread over her face. It became a huge grin.

'Oh my,' she drawled. 'Now isn't that what this house needed? And there was I thinking it was *all* doom and gloom. All gothic novel and *Fall of the House of Usher*. This is much more like it.'

'Butt out, Janey,' Tommy told her.

'Oh, I'm *well* on my way. And frankly, I couldn't be more pleased. *Santé!*' She swept an elaborate low curtsy with lots of hand-wafting and left the room backwards. 'Carry on!' she told us before she shut the door. And, after Tommy had nipped up to lock it, I'm ashamed to say . . . we did.

32

A few hours later I was driving back to London with the window open, Dire Straits blaring, and a banging heart. I also had a huge smile on my face. Tommy had agreed we'd take it slowly, take it gently, this courtship, but with a huge smile on *his* face, too, and somehow, I knew he wouldn't.

'The thing is,' I'd whispered earnestly, my head on his chest, wondering what on earth I was doing having sex in Belinda Bellingdon's best spare room at this particularly tragic moment in time, 'the thing is, Tommy, it's obviously early days. Yes, we've known each other for years, but we haven't *seen* each other. I don't really know you.'

'God, no, you're right.' He contrived to look terrified. Inched away from me. 'How chilling. I could be anyone. Who the hell are you?'

'Seriously, though, Tommy, let's not rush into anything, just because – you know.'

'You've slept with me? Seduced me? While the whole house is in mourning?'

I covered my face in shame, moaned low, and slid under the duvet. He roared.

'Stop *shouting*,' I hissed, popping my head up.

He composed himself with difficulty. 'Tell you what,' he said in a stage whisper, 'I'll leave my calling card whenever I'm in town, which is about twice a year, and then we can perambulate around Regent's Park together taking the air. How's that?'

'Oh, for heaven's—'

'Too slow? OK, OK. So why don't we skip the formalities and ship you and your easel over to New York for a bit? You can paint a few pictures and have the whole Village at your feet, and then in no time at all we can move to Connecticut and have loads of children?'

'Well no, obviously *that's* out of the question—'

'So somewhere in between?'

'Ye-ess,' I said, confused. 'Somewhere in between.'

'OK, I'm all ears. You run me through that little scenario.' He locked his hands behind his head on the pillows and grinned cheerfully at me. 'I leave on Tuesday, by the way.'

'You do? Oh.' I propped myself up a bit and frowned down at him. 'And you're back?'

'In the fall. After Thanksgiving. Actually, maybe nearer Christmas.'

'Oh.' My face fell.

He rolled over on top of me and regarded me in delight. 'You already know you're going to do it.' He chortled. 'You already know that for once, Flora Bellingdon, you're going to say damn it, this isn't a rehearsal. I *will* follow this devastatingly handsome man with his spectacular sexual magnetism across the pond. I *will* walk across Central Park every day to the studio he's found me in SoHo. I *will* succumb to his irresistible charm.'

'Oh, don't be ridiculous.'

'You already know!' he said happily. 'You will, you're in love with me.'

I knew nothing of the sort, I thought, palms rather sweaty on the wheel but still unable to stop smiling as I roared up the slip road to the M5. I was nothing short of outraged, frankly, at the magnitude of his arrogance and gall.

In the event, of course, I did it. I went. In an embarrassingly short space of time. Well, three months. Just before Christmas, there I was, stepping off a plane at JFK Airport. Just for a visit, I'd told him on the phone. But as I flew into his arms at Arrivals I knew it was forever.

'You ran,' he said huskily in my ear, when we'd kissed.

'Did not.'

'You did, dragging your bag. Look – it nearly lost its wheel.'

The notion of forever was confirmed, ridiculously, in my mind, as we sailed over Robert F. Kennedy Bridge minutes later in his sensationally smart something-or-other. I'm rather afraid it might have been an Aston Martin. Tommy was casually spinning the wheel with one hand and looking extremely handsome, and I was sneaking glances and wondering if I could really be so shallow as to be incredibly impressed. Another glance at his knowing, grinning profile told me he knew I was impressed and that the whole thing was hopeless. I broke into a grin and felt my heart soar.

To be fair, prior to all this frivolity, the preceding three months had been of a much more sobering variety. Infinitely grimmer. A great deal had happened. Tommy had delayed his departure on the Tuesday and stayed another week in London. During that time, he and Hugo had gone, with Roger, to a meeting of the Environmental Audit Committee at the House of Commons. There, in hallowed chambers, they'd confessed that the strict maintenance guidelines imposed by the Environment Agency had, indeed, been breached. They cited pressure from the shareholders to maintain profits, but realized that was no excuse. The devastation, and the raw sewage spills, which, when Shona was given the go-ahead to investigate, with the help of Ted, who was like a rat up a drainpipe – were colossal.

According to Babs, Shona's report made the national as well as the local news. I didn't watch it. Neither did Peter. Apparently, Hugo even allowed himself to be interviewed. He admitted that many mistakes had been made. He held himself entirely accountable, fell cleanly on his sword, and resigned forthwith. Babs said it was rather moving and dignified. She said that Shona had said very little. Had let him do the talking. She said the footage of the cracked and broken water pipes, unearthed from the ground and leaking into rivers with dead fish floating in them, was not pretty. Mum saw it, too, in London. The fine levied on the company by the sentencing council was the largest ever imposed on a private company; they were made an example of. Bellingdon Water lost its account with South West Water. That accounted for seventy percent of its business and the company collapsed and went into liquidation.

Having said he was going back to America, Tommy, in fact, flew back to London fortnightly. I saw him as much as possible, but mostly he was in oak-panelled rooms in the City with Hugo and Roger and the receivers – and a lot of angry workers. He was doing what he did best: helping people and trying his best to salvage something.

A few investments Roger had made were what remained, once the terms for redundancy pay had been scrupulously adhered to. Trewarren House and the estate were to be sold. Roger, Tommy said, after his initial shock, was measured and patient. If he became scandalized by or angry at the trail of Hugo's woefully bad decision-making, which now became glaringly apparent, he simply left the room. Had a walk around Liverpool Street and then came back. And anyway, they didn't dwell on the mistakes, but the absolute commitment to do the very best for the workers Roger had known for years. To make sure they were all right. He and Tommy did most of the talking with the receivers, I gather, but Hugo was in full agreement.

Hugo, Tommy told me, when yet again he'd returned to my flat well after ten at night, exhausted, slumped on the sofa with the supper I'd cooked hours ago on our knees, was strangely calm. In fact, he'd almost go so far as to say Hugo was relieved by the turn of events.

'It's weird. It's almost like he's been waiting for this day.'

'I can imagine that,' I said slowly. 'It's probably worse living with such tremendous pressure, a guilty secret. A knowledge that you've done wrong. Once it's out and the axe has fallen – well, you can't go any further down.'

'Particularly when you've attempted suicide already.'

'You don't think he'll do that again?' I asked anxiously.

'No, I really don't. I think that moment has passed. You know they're going to Australia? Him and Christina?'

'Peter said. To see Etta.'

'Yes, but I think it's with a view to staying permanently. Taking the children. Hugo wants to teach.'

'Oh, he'd be *so* good at that!'

'Exactly, and Christina, too – PE, sports. They thought they'd retrain together out there. Etta's going to help them with visas and things; apparently teaching is a good way in. She's on the case.'

'They'll have a totally different life.'

'Quite. And obviously thousands of miles from Belinda.'

I was thoughtful. 'So she's lost both her children.'

'Well, one she doesn't appear to care much about, and the other has got to go.'

'The house hasn't sold yet, has it? How long is she staying there, d'you know?'

'I haven't heard. There's talk of her moving to Wade-bridge with her sister. Iris even told Roger she was looking forward to it.'

'No.'

Tommy shrugged. 'Why not? Might even be a colossal release for her, too, who knows? But no one really mentions Belinda. Roger's moved out, though.'

'Babs said that was about to happen. When?'

'Yesterday.'

'And they have some plan to keep her house, but actually spend most of their time on some extraordinary boat?'

Tommy smiled. 'He's sold all his smart dinghies and bought this thing at auction. It's huge and ancient and he's got it into his head they can sail it from Southampton to Barbados together. First thing he's shipping down to his cabin, by the way, is his portrait. Together with crates of booze, obviously.'

'Obviously. How *old* is Roger?'

'Well, quite. He's still in short pants. But he'll make it. *They'll* make it.'

434

'If they don't fall overboard intoxicated. But, actually, what heaven for him.' I sipped my wine. 'I'm sure he only stayed with Belinda out of a sense of duty. Losing the house must be a huge wrench, though.'

'He hasn't said a word, and actually, I'm not so sure. I personally think the house is what kept him there, loyalty to past generations of Bellingdons. But it was a tie. Now it's gone he doesn't have to stay. I actually think this whole affair will be pretty liberating for him.'

'Yes, you're right. God, once this is over he'll be like a pig in clover. It's actually the best thing to happen to that family.' I hesitated. 'Well. Except, maybe . . .'

'She brought it on herself, Flora,' he reminded me.

'I know, but still.'

'Hey. Don't start getting all angsty about that woman. Don't you dare even attempt to state her case or I'll put down this very strange dish of sausages wrapped in batter which is weirdly growing on me, and allow you to ravage me, *again*.'

'Oh, like the ravaging is always my idea?'

'Honey, I haven't been so thoroughly seduced since I spent six months in Rome with a divorcée who couldn't keep her knickers up.'

'Tommy, *why* would I want to know about that?'

'It's a good story. I'll tell Peter instead. When he's back from his outing with Janey.'

'*Do* shut up.'

'I don't see why, I'm very good for you, Flora. You take yourself far too seriously.'

It was true, I did. And my son. All that was to change. But not quite in the way I imagined. I'd resigned myself

435

to Peter loving New York, where he'd been for the past month doing an internship, but in fact, he found it rather sharp and frantic. A bit too full on, he'd told me on the phone. At least right now. A bit too *Wall Street*. Maybe later. In a few years' time. A taster had been a good idea. The best. He started at Oxford in October – thankfully he hadn't given up his place – so that by the time I flew out to see Tommy in December, he was almost at the end of his first term, and coming with Mum, for Christmas, in a couple of weeks' time, in fact. We were all going to Tommy's mother's house, or, actually, his sister's, on the Connecticut coast.

Tommy's mother, of course, I'd met before, and had adored. Neither of us could really believe our luck as she walked into Tommy's apartment in New York to visit us. We hugged, and then she stood back and took both my hands in hers. As we faced one another in Tommy's book and picture filled drawing room overlooking the Museum of Natural History on the Upper West Side, the years slid away: back to the two of us in my studio in London, where she'd shyly brought a few pictures to show me and admired mine.

'I'm *so* pleased, my dear,' she told me, blinking hard. 'It's the most wonderful Christmas present I could possibly imagine. I don't mind telling you you'll be so good for Tommy.'

'And him for me,' I assured her.

She glanced down at my hand. 'May I see?'

I proudly showed her my engagement ring. Which, naturally, had been another story.

'You don't think it's too soon? That we're being too

436

hasty?' I'd asked Tommy, after he'd presented me with it in Central Park, on our way back from the Museum of Modern Art. It was a sunny, frosty morning and we were huddled together on a park bench in a patch of winter sunshine, hugging each other close. I twirled it on my finger, mesmerized. 'I mean, obviously, yes, please, with all my heart. I'm completely thrilled. But—'

'You're right,' he agreed suddenly. 'We're far too young. Let's wait till at least one of us is in our bath chair.' He went to snatch it back but I was too quick. I held my hand high above my head as he reached for it.

'Not so fast, Mr Rochester. This ring is staying right where you put it, but I think you've forgotten something.'

'Which is?'

'I'm English. You haven't asked my mother.'

For a split second I had him. I saw it in his eyes. Then he narrowed them. 'Oh God. You're something else, you know that? And for that, I jolly well will, as you say in that funny little country of yours. I'll ask her.' He did. He rang her. Obviously I'd spoken to her first, but still, it was lovely of him. And then she came over for Christmas.

When she arrived at JFK Airport with Peter, whilst Tommy and I stood waiting for them, she looked tiny. Minute. Peter, to be fair, was huge, six foot three, but still, my eyes filled as she came towards us in her old black coat, at a trot. Suddenly I was ducking under the barrier and racing to meet her.

We held each other tight. '*So* pleased, darling. So pleased at your news,' she whispered in my ear.

'You *all* run at airports?' Tommy had mused a few minutes later, as he'd loaded a trolley with their baggage, Peter helping him. 'I must remember that. Some kind of family tradition?'

'It's that famous English reserve,' Peter told him, throwing his bag on top. 'The moment it's dropped, they're insane. Only the women, though. But it's a worry. Can be scary.'

'Oh God, thanks for telling me. Any more tips?'

'Hundreds. You're going to need all the help you can get. It's as well we've got a day at the ice hockey on Wednesday.'

'That bad, eh? Reckon we're going to need another? The New York Rangers are playing in Boston on the twenty-eighth.'

'I'd say it's pretty much mandatory.'

'Consider it done, Pete. And don't forget, it's all in the name of family harmony. All in the name of keeping the future Mr and Mrs Rochester firmly on the right tracks.'

And with Mum and me protesting and laughing, we all sailed out of the airport together, pushing a loaded trolley across a road filled with yellow taxis, into bright, horizontal, December sunshine. As the light momentarily dazzled my eyes, I knew I could live happily by that light, paint with it, love by it, and generally do wonders with it.

Also by
Catherine Alliott . . .

'Laugh-out-loud'

Press Association

Also by
Catherine Alliott . . .

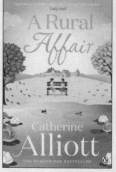  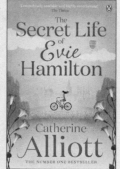

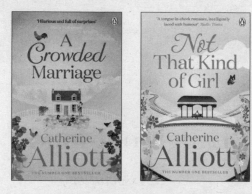

Also by
Catherine Alliott . . .

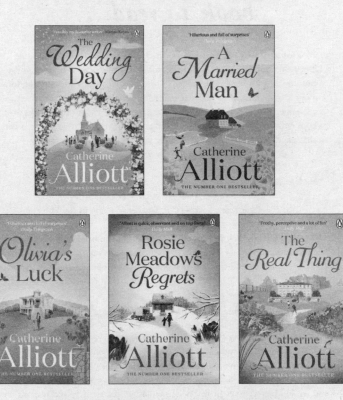

He just wanted a decent book to read ...

Not too much to ask, is it? It was in 1935 when Allen Lane, Managing Director of Bodley Head Publishers, stood on a platform at Exeter railway station looking for something good to read on his journey back to London. His choice was limited to popular magazines and poor-quality paperbacks – the same choice faced every day by the vast majority of readers, few of whom could afford hardbacks. Lane's disappointment and subsequent anger at the range of books generally available led him to found a company – and change the world.

'We believed in the existence in this country of a vast reading public for intelligent books at a low price, and staked everything on it'
Sir Allen Lane, 1902–1970, founder of Penguin Books

The quality paperback had arrived – and not just in bookshops. Lane was adamant that his Penguins should appear in chain stores and tobacconists, and should cost no more than a packet of cigarettes.

Reading habits (and cigarette prices) have changed since 1935, but Penguin still believes in publishing the best books for everybody to enjoy. We still believe that good design costs no more than bad design, and we still believe that quality books published passionately and responsibly make the world a better place.

So wherever you see the little bird – whether it's on a piece of prize-winning literary fiction or a celebrity autobiography, political tour de force or historical masterpiece, a serial-killer thriller, reference book, world classic or a piece of pure escapism – you can bet that it represents the very best that the genre has to offer.

Whatever you like to read – trust Penguin.